The Lady Who Loved Him
The Brethren Series

For more information about the author:
www.christicaldwellauthor.com
christicaldwellauthor@gmail.com
Twitter: @ChristiCaldwell
Or on Facebook at: Christi Caldwell Author

For first glimpse at covers, excerpts, and free bonus material, be sure to sign up for my monthly newsletter!
Printed in the USA.

Cover Design and Interior Format

The Lady Who Loved Him

THE BRETHREN
THE SERIES

USA TODAY BESTSELLER

CHRISTI CALDWELL

DEDICATION

All my heroes and heroines are special to me. But sometimes, you meet one character who seems even more so. For me, Chloe Edgerton has always been one of those heroines. I often call her my fictional 'daughter'. To every reader who has ever emailed, written, or messaged asking about Lady Chloe Edgerton…Chloe and Leo's story is for you.

CHAPTER 1

London
Spring 1821

SEATED AT HIS PRIVATE TABLE, with a half bottle of empty brandy within arm's reach and a whore on his lap, Leo Dunlop, the Marquess of Tennyson, was spending his night like he had so many others before.

Well, all but the whore part.

Leo ceased nuzzling the buxom beauty's neck and glanced about the raucous floors of Forbidden Pleasures… one of the most disreputable hells in London. From where she stood at a hazard table with Lord Robinson, a pretty brunette caught his gaze. With a slow, sultry smile, she sauntered over and, uninvited, perched herself upon his lap.

There, problem rectified. He reached around the delightful bundles in his arms to grab for his half-empty snifter.

His briefly neglected partner for that night, Emma, pouted. "You know I don't like to share."

Finishing off his drink, Leo set his glass down. Actually, he hadn't known that. Emma made to climb off his lap. Catching her about her lush waist, Leo urged her back into place, and she went unresistingly. Of course, her upset was all for show. A bid to wheedle more coin and secure the upper hand. Content to let her believe herself triumphant, even as he had no intention of giving her a pence more, he cajoled, "Come, sweet. You know I'm capable of pleasing two women on any given night." He cupped them by their buttocks and guided them each astride a thigh. "Oftentimes, three or four."

The other whore on his lap giggled and adjusted herself, grinding against his wool breeches until little panting moans spilled past her lips.

Emma gripped him by the lapels of his jacket and dragged his mouth close to hers. "It ain't your leg I'm wanting this evening, my lord. And even with your prowess, you still can't manage to spring another pole." She slipped a hand between his legs. His erection sprang all the harder. A triumphant grin wreathed her fleshy lips. "See, love. You don't need anyone else but me."

His was purely a physical reaction. One he'd had countless times, with countless women. "No. I do not need anyone else tonight," he drawled, and the whore beamed. No. He did not *need* anyone. Not in any way, either emotional, sexual, or some variation in between. "However, I want someone else tonight. Two someones." He worked her skirt higher around her waist, and she melted against him, her objections quelled under his attentions.

Sex was sex for Leo. It always had been and always would be. It was the safest, most uncomplicated act where a pair simply used each other as a vehicle to sate their lust. No different than an itch that needed scratching.

Then the other whore grinding herself against him grew greedy. She edged herself in front of Emma.

Fire sparked in her eyes as she shoved at the younger woman. "He called *me* over."

"Well, now he can send you away," Emma cheekily rejoined.

He was one sharp outburst away from two battling whores. And though he preferred that fire in his bedroom, he'd far better uses in mind for the two women than breaking up any fight.

"You can leave, you—"

Leo crushed his mouth to the pretty brunette's lips, swallowing the remainder of her words. Not breaking contact, he explored the generous bounty of Emma's enormous bosom. The faint scent of sweat doused in pungent rosewater was off-putting.

Just another night. Just another whore. Or in this case, two…

When had his life become… *this*?

Oh, he knew precisely the moment he'd started down the path of debauchery. After all, a gent tended to remember the day he was tapped by the king's men to serve the role of agent of the Crown. Somewhere along the way, however, the young pup who loved his books at Oxford had been inculcated on how so perfectly to shape himself into someone else—a hardened rake—that the world was content to see only that. Society didn't glance past the veneer, and Leo had ultimately crafted his until he'd become the reprobate from the surface down to his very soul.

Yes, he was getting old. Thrusting aside his maudlin sentiments, he shifted his attentions to the younger whore, plundering her mouth—still bored.

But then, he'd always been one to bore easily. Carrying on as he had for the past twelve years was surely enough to make any man grow tedious. It was why he'd become more inventive, descended into greater depths of impiety.

Emma bit the corner of his mouth and he winced.

"I thought you liked it violent," she breathed against his mouth, her breath stinking of cheap champagne.

Committing his efforts to dislodging the ennui, he devoted himself to the other whore's breasts.

From the corner of his eye, Leo caught a pair of legs pull into focus. A pair of spindly breeches-clad legs.

"Ahem." Oh, bloody hell. That disapproving utterance, the blasted mark of only one bothersome twat. Fucking Haskins. Mayhap the blighter would go away if properly embarrassed into it.

"Busy," Leo muttered, freeing Emma's flesh from her plunging décolletage. He dropped his head to worship at that skin.

"I said—*ahem*."

Leo broke the kiss and glowered up at the gray-haired gentleman who'd made it his life's mission to make *Leo's* life absolutely miserable, whenever and wherever he could… and that included his wicked clubs. "What?" he snapped impatiently before old Haskins could speak. There was only one of two reasons Haskins sought him out: Crown business… or displeased uncle, the Duke of Aubrey.

Haskins cleared his throat loudly over the din. "His Grace has requested—"

"The pleasure of my company," he snapped the familiar phrase. So, it was to be displeased uncle, then.

With a sigh, he pushed the two women off his lap. They landed on their feet, quick like cats. "Afraid we are done here."

They pouted, lingering.

Offering them a swat on their arses instead of the coin they really craved, Leo redirected his focus to the old bastard. With his face heavily wrinkled and his sunken features gleaming with disapproval, Haskins managed to kill Leo's remaining erection.

"This had better be important," he muttered, rising. With the disapproving servant looking on, Leo poured himself another brandy and downed it in a long, slow gulp. Grimacing, he abandoned the snifter. The crystal rocked back and forth, before settling in place.

Not bothering to wait for Haskins, Leo started through the club.

As he walked, he surveyed the lords present. Wastrels and reprobates, all of them. But occasionally, some of them more—men who'd sell secrets of the Crown or a vote in the House of Commons for the right amount of coin.

Stepping through the double doors, Leo did a sweep of the streets.

Haskins cleared his throat in the infuriating manner that always set Leo's teeth on edge. "His Grace's carriage awaits."

"I can ride my own damned horse," Leo gritted, starting in the direction of the street urchin who held his reins. He stopped abruptly. Or where the lad had held his reins. He swung back, favoring the bloody servant with a glower that would have set most men tearing in the opposite direction.

"His Grace asked that you arrive by his carriage. He instructed me to inform you that he'd not have you breaking your…" The old, loyal servant coughed into his hand, his cheeks going an uncharacteristic red. "*Goddamned* neck because you imbibed too much whiskey," he whispered, as though scandalized at his own use of that blasphemy.

"I am insulted by my uncle's lack of faith in my drinking capabilities. The duke knows I quite despise whiskey. Only drink it when I absolutely must."

And there had been a good many "absolute must" moments in the course of his twelve years working for the Brethren.

Starting quickly for the carriage in debate, Leo strode past the driver waiting with the door opened and pulled himself inside.

Haskins followed in behind.

A moment later, the driver closed the door hard. His perch dipped, the carriage lurched, and they were rolling onward.

"Well?" he asked in the privacy of the comfortable black conveyance as soon as they were on their way. Those back-and-forths between them for public consumption had only fed into Society's opinion of the manner of dissolute rake Leo, in fact, was. In truth, however, the line had become so blurred that the part was firmly enmeshed in who Leo was. *Nay, who I've always been.*

"I am unaware of the reason for your meeting, my lord," Haskins said with one of his usual laconic, wait-until-The-Order-shares replies. "I was merely instructed to remove you from your club."

His club. The wicked halls of Forbidden Pleasures were very much his, a world of depravity and sin that was more comfortable than any place he'd ever called home. And the best part was the availability of those denizens of every dangerous street of London.

Sprawling back in his seat, grateful for the silence, Leo consulted his watch fob. The gold piece stamped with the mark of the Brethren, a lion passant regardant with a blood-red ruby at the center. It had, long ago, been adopted in place of the too-obvious signet rings. He stuffed it back inside his jacket. Had the world looked a bit closer, they would have wondered long ago and marveled at why a rake who'd sell his soul for a pence should keep something of value still.

But they didn't question. And they didn't see.

And Leo was better for it.

A short while later, the duke's well-sprung carriage rolled to a stop outside the pale yellow townhouse. Slightly higher and set apart from the ones flanking its sides, it served as a perfect symbol of the man who dwelled within those Grosvenor Square walls.

His uncle's driver pulled the door open. Jumping out, Leo moved at a brisk clip toward the residence awash in candlelight. Despite his advancing years, Haskins easily caught up and, increasing his step, rushed to open the slight wrought-iron gate that served as a barrier between the world and the Duke of Aubrey's residence.

Haskins took the steps quickly.

Trailing at a slower pace, Leo climbed behind his uncle's servant.

The butler, Parsons, hurried to admit them. Parsons was dutiful, as all in the duke's employ were.

"He is waiting in his office," the man of middling years said by way of greeting.

"We will show ourselves in," Haskins assured, handing over his cloak and hat.

Parsons did a quick up and down of Leo's cloak-less frame. He offered a sardonic grin for the man's benefit. "One less garment to bother with when tupping a whore," he explained.

His gaunt face a set mask, Parsons looked over to Haskins, dismissing Leo outright. "He asked that I tell you he's waiting."

The duke was impatient. It was Crown business, then. There could be no other explanation. Nothing—not even his frequent lectures about Leo's vices—received that response, *ever.*

Setting a lazier pace, Leo followed his uncle's devoted servant. Spanish iron sconces better suited for a medieval dungeon than a Mayfair residence lined the wide corridors, lighting the way. The long, white, tapered candles played off the gold brocade satin wallpaper and gilded frames hung with portraits of the duke's late, great ancestors. A portrait of Leo's late mother, when she'd been a girl of sixteen or seventeen, alongside her brothers, the current Duke of Aubrey and Lord Edward Helling, and their long-deceased parents hung outside his uncle's office, marking the end of Leo's trek through the winding corridors. As Haskins opened the door, Leo made the mistake of looking at that large rendering... and froze.

Your mother was a whore and, by God, if she won't pay for her crimes, I'll take it out of your flesh...

And mayhap it was too much drink that night, but under his leather gloves, his palms moistened at the remembered horrors...

His childhood screams pealed around the chambers of his mind, holding him rooted to the floor, a prisoner of his past.

"My lord?" Haskins' hesitant prodding jerked Leo back from the fleeting moment of madness.

Adjusting his rumpled cravat, Leo brought his shoulders back. He'd not allowed himself to be weak in the years since he'd pledged his life and fealty to the Brethren.

Entering behind his uncle's head servant, Leo immediately came up short.

Three officious gentlemen, all clad in black and donning the same somber countenance, were in the room. Had there been any doubt at all that it wasn't official Brethren business, then that possibility died with their presence.

Had it been solely his uncle, there would have been some doubts. But this was Lord Higgins, the Delegator, second only to the Sovereign of the Brethren, and responsible for handing down assignments. To have Higgins present... *and* Viscount Rowley, the one Leo answered to during assignments, could only mean official Brethren business.

Haskins closed the door at Leo's back.

His uncle was the first to break the silence. "Leo, been waiting for you," he said, coming forward. He was broadly powerful, with the faintest dusting of silver at his temples, but his formidable strength, however, came from within. He came up short three paces away from Leo and sniffed the air. "You smell like you've been tupping a whore in a garden."

Leo quirked his lips at one corner. "No garden necessary," he drawled. "A bottle of cheap perfume is capable of the same *effects*."

The duke's face remained as stony as the statues outside the pillars of his townhouse. "Sit," he ordered, gesturing to the button-tufted Chesterfield sofa situated at the center of the room. "There are... matters we've to discuss." As if on cue, the hulking figures moved to take the leather library chairs flanking each side of that sofa.

"Matters," Leo repeated slowly.

His uncle nodded once.

Vague. Cryptic.

Unease immediately stirred, a primitive response that had saved his arse—both literally and figuratively—in the time he'd served as an agent to the Brethren. However, he'd been removed from his last case: investigating the Cato Street Conspiracy that had nearly seen all the prime minister's Cabinet killed by *commoners*. "Is this in reference to my last investigation?" he quizzed, refusing the indicated seat in favor of the French wine liquor cabinet. Yanking the doors open, he rummaged through and availed himself of a bottle of brandy and an engraved glass goblet. His bounty in hand, he at last joined the trio. "I've told you all that I believe I've stumbled upon something where the Cato Street Conspiracy is concerned."

That plot had shaken England to its core—particularly the lords who spent their days in Parliament. Society, polite and otherwise, was content with the assurances that the plan had been thwarted and the risks were gone.

The trio exchanged looks. It was Leo's uncle, however, who spoke. "This is about a plot of noblemen attempting to sow unrest to establish support for an oppressive agenda?"

At the heavy skepticism there, Leo set his jaw.

"What proof do you have, Tennyson?" Rowley diverted Leo's attention his way.

"Ah, Rowley, my ever-practical *mentor*. Driven by fact-based details only," he said with a jeering edge. Leo lifted his glass in mock salute. Most men and women relied so heavily on having proof in hand that they failed to trust their gut instincts.

"I am not your bloody mentor. I am your damned superior. And you answer to me, you insolent cur." Lord Rowley peered down his hawkish nose. "Either way, I take your reply to mean 'none.' You have no proof." Almost two decades older, proper, officious, and well respected by the peerage, Rowley could not be more different from Leo. The viscount looked over to the still-silent Delegator... always assessing. "It is as I told you. Rubbish. It is an overall waste of the agency's time to unearth a nebulous threat that has offered up not one single suspect to investigate."

That cold unfeelingness had driven the other man's wife to seek comfort in Leo's bed... many times. Refusing to rise to the pompous bastard's bait, Leo stretched his legs out and crossed his ankles. "Is that what this is? Tattling on me to my uncle?" Color suffused the viscount's cheeks, and Leo pressed him. "And for what? Because I'm attempting to ensure the safety of the people?"

"The *people*," Rowley sneered. "Let us not forget on whose behalf you work."

Leo sipped his drink. "Crown and country." He arched an eyebrow. "Though, at times, I appear the only one to remember my allegiance to anyone outside the nobility."

Rowley scoffed. "You do not remember anything beyond the contents of a bottle and whatever whore you're currently bedding."

With a cool grin, Leo again lifted his glass. "Oh, come. 'Tis hardly polite to refer to your wife in those crude terms."

The viscount's eyes bulged.

With a thunderous bellow, he surged forward.

Leo's uncle and Higgins immediately moved to restrain him, grabbing him by the shoulders.

"You bastard."

Leo smirked.

Rowley only renewed his struggles, fighting to get to him. "You are a wastrel, a lecher, unfit to do the work of the Brethren and unfit to move amongst Polite Society." The viscount spit, catching Leo squarely on the cheek.

He stiffened. It was an offense that would have seen most men meeting over pistols at dawn. Leo, however, had been the recipient of every vile—and oftentimes accurate—insult, where they'd simply ceased to matter.

A thick tension instantly blanketed the room.

Removing a white monogrammed kerchief from inside his jacket, he dabbed the folded cloth at Rowley's spittle.

"Are we done?" Uncle William snapped.

"We are." Leo lifted his head. "That is, unless Rowley cares to further discuss his wife?"

Instead of his earlier show of fury, his superior ripped free of the hold on him. He peeled his lip in a condescending sneer. "Make light all you want, but you are nothing, Tennyson. Nothing. The end of your work for the Brethren is nearly twelve years overdue, and the day you are tossed out on your worthless arse is near. The only reason you ever had a post was because of your un—"

"That is enough," the duke interrupted, injecting an edge of steel that drained the color from Lord Rowley's cheeks. "You presume much and know even less."

Instead of his uncle's defense, Leo fixed on one utterance made by Rowley. Leo's days were numbered with the Brethren. There had been the stir of warnings for years about his recklessness being a detriment to the organization. "The Brethren need me in my role."

"That *was* the case," Uncle William said quietly, with even more of his usual somberness.

"*Was* the case?" Abandoning his negligent pose, Leo straightened. "What is this?" he asked tightly, tiring of their games and the ominous partial statements. He downed his drink in one long swallow. "Whatever you have to say, be done with it."

At last, silent until now, Lord Higgins spoke. "Rowley is recommending you be cut from the Brethren."

Life without the Brethren? His stomach muscles clenched. It was all he'd been, and all he was. He searched for his usual flippant reply and came up empty.

"Rowley has doubts that you can change your ways."

Change? There was a greater likelihood of a leopard shedding its damned spots. With a sound of disgust, he surged to his feet. "My ways are what allow me to move freely about and perform the work I do. The Brethren demanded a cold, callous, ruthless bastard, and that is precisely what I have become." *Nay, it is what you've always been.*

Lord Higgins drew his gloves off with a meticulous precision. "Regardless of the role you fill, a code of honor must exist... among our members and the respectable members of Society." He paused, leveling a meaningful stare at Leo. "Otherwise, we are no different from the men and women whom we bring to justice."

Leo seethed. "You would place carousing, whoring, and wagering in the same category as you would treason?"

Lord Higgins' silence stood as a resounding answer.

His uncle settled a hand on his shoulder, giving a slight squeeze. "It has become too much, Leo. *Too much.*"

He gnashed his teeth, wanting to spit and snarl like the beast they took him for.

"We would be done with you if it were not for *your uncle.*" Rowley's slight emphasis left little doubt to his opinion on the reason Leo's position would be spared.

"How very typical of Polite Society to berate me for my wildness while so glibly accepting in their folds one who made a fortune off the backs of men, women, and children," he sneered in Rowley's direction. It was a secret to none that the viscount's dealings in the now-abolished slave trade had left him with a fortune to rival most small kingdoms.

"Pfft." Rowley flicked an imagined speck of lint from his sleeve. "It was business. And common citizens and do-gooders in Parliament need to stop interfering in honest business, especially when it comes to a trade accepted all over the world."

Higgins directed his next question to Leo. "You are of the opinion the Cato Street Conspiracy had different groundings?" Where Society had been content to believe it was solely unruly upstarts chafing at the restrictions placed upon them by the Tories, Leo had believed it was more. It was only a matter of puzzling through what the other reason, in fact, was. "You offered two names…"

"I personally know Ellsworth and Waterson," Rowley snapped. "They are not men to subvert the government."

Leo rolled his shoulders. "Their political leanings and influence in Parliament marked them suspect." As had their votes with the Six Acts.

"I'm not here to debate the names that Tennyson's produced," he said with an air of finality. "See what you turn up. You are not permitted another misstep. I don't want so much as a false rumor about you bedding a proper lady or member of the Brethren's kin."

"What of the *widowed* wives and sisters?" Leo stretched out that insolent question.

The Delegator went on as though he'd not spoken. "The Cato case is yours."

A familiar thrill gripped Leo. This was the reason for his existence… flushing out traitors and uncovering crimes against the Crown. He'd devoted his life to the Brethren with the hope that he would one day ascend the ranks that his uncle had.

"I'll remind you." Higgins held up one finger. "One more incident, and you are done. Your work for the organization will be through. Are we clear?"

"Abundantly, my lord."

Exchanging looks, Higgins and Rowley made their polite good-byes to the duke.

"Well, that went better than I expected," he said drolly, rescuing the bottle and glass from the floor. Settling back into his seat, he made to pour another drink.

His uncle plucked both from his grip. "That is enough, Leo." He spoke in his tutor's tones, as Leo had come to call them over the years.

He sighed. How very… cliché his uncle had always been. Every wicked scoundrel and unrepentant rake was in possession of a disapproving uncle who controlled the purse strings of a gent's future. It was the very formula for any Gothic novel and a staple of societal expectations and, as such, a perfect cover for Leo's dealings with his uncle, the Duke of Aubrey.

"You are out of hand."

"I am a rake," he said, bored by the increasingly familiar discussion even as annoyance lanced through him. When his uncle had plucked him from the schoolroom, a scholar hiding his love of books, the Brethren had, in turn, shaped him into... *this*. "It seems counterproductive to have me abandon my ways"—the very ways that had allowed him to ferret out invaluable details from enemies of the state—"when those ways have proven helpful to the Crown."

"You were not always like..." His uncle waved a hand at him. "*This.*" While the duke launched into one of his ever-familiar diatribes, Leo took the glass back and sipped at his drink.

Yes, there had been a time when he was scared and crying and sniveling. No longer... and never again. He owed the Brethren, and the organization had his fealty until he kicked up his heels and went on to spend eternity writhing in hell. When his uncle had finished, Leo touched an imagined brim at his forehead. "Thank you."

"It was not a compliment, Leo," his uncle said bluntly, claiming the seat opposite him. "If I had known recruiting you for the Brethren would have turned you into a coldhearted rake, without a beating heart in your body, then I would have—" Splotches of color filled his uncle's cheeks.

"What?" Leo waggled his eyebrows. "Left me as the whipping boy for my dear, departed *father*?"

Uncle William blanched. "Never," he said on an adamant whisper.

Worthless, pathetic bastard...

Leo blinked as that hated voice thumped his memory into remembrances he could do without. Needing to put to flight those demons, he climbed to his feet. "I trust we are done here." Leo forced the lazy steps the world had come to expect.

"Leo?" his uncle called out when he reached the door. "Do not forget... you have one more opportunity to redeem yourself. Do not squander it."

With that sharp rebuke following after him, Leo left.

CHAPTER 2

London

ᴇVERYONE IN THE WHOLE OF London was talking about swans.

Just as they had been for the better part of the year. The topic filled scandal sheets and gossip columns. It was spoken about and whispered of last Season… and with the newly minted one, the talk had remained.

Or not just any swan. More specifically, the *muted white swans.* Though the number invariably ranged from two to ten to twenty, it was all anyone had spoken of since the Duke of Hampstead had overtaken Mrs. Munroe's Finishing School and plucked the head-mistress, Mrs. Bryant, from the esteemed institution and made her his wife.

All young ladies sighed with wistful romanticism while the matrons and proper mamas spoke of the incident with nothing more than disdain and disapproval.

And though Lady Chloe Edgerton invariably and quite effort-lessly avoided all hints of gossip, this topic of discourse had been altogether different—for it had involved her family. Her sister-in-law's finishing school for young ladies of scandalous origins and impoverished families had gone from a respected, but still whispered about, establishment… to one that was spoken of in outraged tones.

At five and twenty years of age, Chloe had come to appreciate the dangerous power of gossip and scandal. Forces more dangerous than most acts of nature, they had the power to bring anyone or anything down.

Gossip and scandal resulted in impromptu marriages and hasty arrangements between unlikely couples. And they shattered reputations.

It would seem noble institutions were not exempt from that power. The problem was, in Polite Society, women weren't afforded a misstep. To the *ton*, it had been outrageous enough that a marchioness had established a school for illegitimate girls and other students of ignoble origins. For the headmistress of that respectable establishment to be embroiled in a scandal of her own—a gentleman storming the school with carriages full of swans—it was an act that had shaken the still-fledgling school.

Chloe stood outside her sister-in-law's office. Jane Edgerton, the Marchioness of Waverly, had started the school. Chloe pressed her palms together and quickly ran through the details of her upcoming meeting. Having been the fourth-born Edgerton, Lady Chloe Edgerton had learned early on the importance of timing.

As a child with a notoriously cruel—thankfully now dead—father, she'd found that fleeing an empty room was oftentimes the difference between a violent beating and a pain-free evening.

As a young woman, the only thing to stand between Chloe and a determined matchmaking mama and potential suitor was her skill of timing.

As such, this particular meeting she'd arranged with Jane was nothing short of meticulously planned and scheduled. And yet, here she stood, still searching for her most convincing argument.

"Jane," she silently mouthed. "I've come solely with the intention of solving the problems with your institution." She grimaced. Egads. No. She gave her head a shake. Having plotted and planned for the better part of two months—since their return for the London Season, to be precise—she'd time aplenty to prepare the opening statement of her argument.

Jane had been unable to find a suitable replacement for the former headmistress who'd quit her post for the role of duchess. A

woman who'd had all the freedom, security, and stability without the fears or worries of a husband had gone and thrown it all
away—on swans and a duke.

The fool.

Fueled by that determination, Chloe plastered a smile on her
lips, raised her hand, and rapped once.

"Enter," Jane called out.

Pressing the handle, Chloe admitted herself. "Ja—" Her smile
withered and briefly died as she settled her stare on the unexpected addition to this meeting.

Blast, damn, and double damn.

Her overprotective brother Gabriel, the Marquess of Waverly,
who'd done his best to see her married over the years, gave her a
droll smile. "No."

"I didn't say anything," she muttered, closing the door behind
her.

"You didn't need to," he drawled.

She lingered with her stare on the doorway, attempting to right
herself, and fought back the sense of betrayal that her sister-in-law
would include Gabriel in this exchange. Her mind raced. In the
orchestrated meeting, she'd not intended on having to deal with
Gabriel. Not yet, anyway.

She turned and faced him.

Alas, she could tell from the suspicious glint in Gabriel's eyes that
he knew her well too well.

Chloe smoothed her palms down the front of her lavender satin
skirts.

"Well?" Gabriel urged in a wholly un-Gabriel-like manner.

She frowned at that insolence. He'd always been high-handed.
Marriage had softened him, but that nobleman's veneer he'd perfected would always be part of him. *Gain control of yourself, Chloe.*
She wasn't supposed to be off-balance. *Gabriel* was. None of this
plan would work if he were the one in control. "It is a fortunate thing for you that Mother is visiting Alex and Imogen," she
chided. "She'd hardly tolerate such rudeness."

He had the good grace to flush, but he remained as obstinate
as always. "Nor do I believe your *precise* timing with Mother *just*
leaving for the country is any manner of coincidence," he returned
with such a direct wryness, she scrunched her mouth.

Well. In all her scheming, she'd not anticipated *this* forthrightness from her once-stodgy brother. Marriage to Jane had changed him. In only good ways, of course. What Chloe had not anticipated, however, was just how greatly he'd been affected by his falling in love. And how dratted inconvenient it was for her.

She sighed. Very well. When presented with an unanticipated parry, one thrust. "I would like to serve as headmistress at Mrs. Munroe's," she said calmly, directing that request at her sister-in-law.

Despite the heavy silence that descended over the room, Jane held her gaze. Her stoic countenance gave no hint that she'd either heard or disdained such a request, and Chloe took faith from—

"What?" Gabriel blurted.

Upended, just like that. The only way to be with one's opponent. Angling her shoulders so all her attention was reserved for Jane, Chloe reached inside the pocket sewn along the front of her gown and withdrew a small, folded page. "It is my understanding that Mrs. Munroe's once again has a vacancy for the post of headmistress." She slid the neatly clipped article across the small rose-inlaid table to the couple seated opposite her.

Both stared at it as though they'd never before seen a copy of *The Times*. Husband and wife exchanged a look. Gabriel carefully picked it up.

"According to the papers, your most recent headmistress has… uh… quit her post," she continued, while Gabriel skimmed that sheet. Since she'd made her Come Out, Chloe had been striving for more than the existence of dutiful wife expected of an English lady. Or rather, avoiding that fate altogether. She'd spent her efforts, instead, at playing matchmaker for each of her siblings and her friend. Those goals now achieved—with one brother being wed to said friend—there was nothing else for her here in London. "Of course, one can never truly trust the gossip columns," she conceded when Gabriel finally lifted his attention.

"It is true," Jane supplied, her evenly modulated tones still conveying nothing.

Chloe beamed. "Then I will gladly take on the responsibility."

Emitting a strangled cough, Gabriel slapped the sheet down.

"Do you require tea?" Chloe offered, looking over to the refreshments on a mahogany side table. She made to rise.

"Absolutely not," he barked.

"You needn't be so rude about it," she groused. "I daresay you could benefit from some time at Mrs. Munroe's."

Jane's lips tilted up at the corners, and she made no effort to conceal that smile.

Gabriel surged to his feet. "The Season has just begun and you've arrived—" She narrowed her eyes. "*We've* returned so you might…" *Make a match.* There was no need for him to finish that sentence. Red splotches suffused his cheeks.

Chloe schooled her features into a mask of confusion. "So I might *what* Gabriel?" The miserable bugger. He, Alex, her mother, all of Society saw that as her eventual… inevitable fate.

He shot a beseeching look at his wife, who shook her head. The meaning was clear. Gabriel yanked at his cravat. "You are not taking on the post of headmistress." Fire glinted in his eyes.

Their father's eyes. That fury familiar.

Hand me the rod, Chloe…

Reflexively, she curled her toes into the soles of her slippers. That slight tensing of her muscles provided a distraction from the fury. A mechanism she'd developed long ago and used in this very office. *This is Gabriel…* The brother who thought he'd been unable to stop their father's abuse had never lifted a hand in violence to her. The reminder that gave her the courage to continue. She tipped her chin up. "Jane requires a headmistress and—"

"No."

Hmph. "It is fortunate for me that you are not the one to make the decisions at Mrs. Munroe's."

At his growl, she smiled all the more. It was a wonder, with a sister and sister-in-law who were models of strength and resiliency, that Chloe had been relegated to the role of young miss in need of protecting and coddling.

Only, her siblings and mother failed to realize that the time of protecting and coddling had long since come and gone. The time for that had been when she'd, in fact, been a child, suffering a caning at the late marquess' hands.

Registering Jane's prolonged silence, Chloe delivered a retort for her sister-in-law's benefit. "As I said, Jane, I am not asking Gabriel," she said in deliberately even tones that sent his brow furrowing. "I am asking *you*." And there it was. The dream she'd allowed herself nearly two years since her sister-in-law had established her finishing school. Control of her own fate and future.

Her sister-in-law's smooth, even features revealed not a hint of what she thought of the request Chloe had put to her.

"Jane says no," Gabriel barked gruffly.

Gabriel, the Marquess of Waverly, was more progressive than most lords of London in allowing his wife the freedom and power to establish and run her own institution. But he was still the same commanding brother he'd always been.

Both women leveled matching glares at him that sent a deserved color rushing to his cheeks.

Chloe swallowed a stinging retort. After all, he'd expect a volatile reply, a response that would only feed into Society's expectations of how a lady behaved.

He tugged at his previously perfectly tied cravat. "Jane?" There was an imploring thread there.

Husband and wife exchanged a long look, and Gabriel let out a long sigh. "Very well," he said tersely. "I... we," he swiftly amended, "are listening."

Chloe concealed her surprise. She'd anticipated a far grander argument on her brother's part than... that. Then, since his marriage to Jane, he'd been a changed man. Never before would he have ever heard out her request. It fueled hope in her breast.

"As I was saying," she repeated in calm, modulated tones her mother had despaired of her exhibiting. "After six Seasons, I'm certainly no longer a debutante."

"No, you are not," Gabriel concurred. And rather quickly at that.

Chloe frowned. At twenty-five, she'd not considered herself a woman in her dotage. Yet the truth remained that she would not marry. Nor would she be content to be the eccentric, unwed aunt dependent on the mercy and kindness of her relatives. Oh, she'd no doubt that her siblings and their spouses would gladly take her in. Chloe, however, longed for some control of her existence. A desperately needed control that had been missing since she'd drawn her first breath and suffered through the late marquess' abuses.

"You were saying?" Jane's gentle prodding was the antithesis of the tension pouring off Gabriel's frame.

Chloe cleared her throat. "I have no intention of marrying." Surrendering that truth to Gabriel eased the tension in her frame.

"Chloe," her brother began in the same calming tones he'd adopted through the years. Those placating ones. Ones he'd not yet realized were futile where she was concerned. "I understand your," he began, then grimaced, "reservations in marrying." He knew how Polite Society was. They spoke of dark memories past in casual words, instead of drawing forth the explicit evil they'd both been victim to. "But there are good, honorable—"

She cut into Gabriel's protest. "I've no intention of marrying, Gabriel. No matter how much you or Mother might wish it." Or how much her dearest friend and now-sister-in-law, Imogen, or sister Philippa spoke of love and happily ever afters to Chloe. To Chloe, the only end that might bring her happiness was one free of a husband who'd have complete and total control of her life. Chloe turned her palms up, willing him to see. "You have taken it into your head that your responsibility for me can only be complete when I marry. But I do not want to be your responsibility." She looked to Jane. "Or yours. Or anyone else's." She hungered for control of her own existence.

Her brother sank back in his chair. "Is that what you believe?" he asked quietly. "That this is about a sense of obligation? That I see you as a responsibility I'd rather be free of?" Hurt marred her brother's features.

Guilt needled at her conscience. Drat him for flipping the tables once more. Before Jane, Chloe's reply to that accusation would have been very different. Then, he'd been driven by his sense of responsibility for the marquisate. "No," she said truthfully. "What I do believe is that you believe I cannot have a life outside of marriage."

He made a sound of protest. "Have I proven to be an oppressive husband to Jane?" he challenged.

No, he hadn't. "But I am your sister."

"And I would have you wed an honorable gentleman such as—"

"The Earl of Waterson." They spoke in unison.

The earl, a lifelong friend of Gabriel's, was proper and respectable, and inspired nothing but boredom.

She lifted her head. "I remain uninterested in marriage to Lord Waterson."

He frowned. "You need a gentleman who would be considerate of your head—"

Jane held a hand up, staying his words.

Chloe balled her hands, grateful for that interruption. Her bloody megrims. The debilitating weakness that reduced her to the same pathetic, weak girl she'd been long, long ago. God, how she hated the reminder of that… particularly at this time when she wrestled for her own freedom.

"Gabriel, I'd speak with Chloe," Jane said.

Bloody hell. Chloe didn't want to talk about her debilitating megrims. Ones that no doctor could make sense of and that her late father would have undoubtedly seen her imprisoned for, as he'd threatened countless times.

Gabriel leaned back in his chair. "Alone," his wife clarified.

Surprise sparked in his eyes, and through hooded lashes, Chloe braced for his displeasure. Instead, he hesitated and then came stiffly to his feet. Jane waited until he'd taken his leave and closed the door behind him before speaking. "Since the moment I met you, you've disavowed marriage."

Chloe eyed the other woman cautiously. "This is not about seeking the post to avoid the future my family hopes for me." Having arrived with false references to secure the post as Chloe's companion more than two years earlier, they'd struck up a friendship. But even with all the truths between them, and everything Jane no doubt knew about the Edgertons' pasts, there were parts Chloe hadn't shared. Couldn't and wouldn't with her… or anyone. No good came from giving those darkest secrets life again.

"No," Jane acknowledged. She came to her feet and strode over to the neat secretaire at the back center of the room. Perching her hip on the edge, she picked up a nearby stack of notes and letters. "You know who my students are."

"I do." Young women who were, by their birthright, bastards or children of merchants with scandalous pasts. It increased Chloe's overall desire to work with those very women.

"I have no doubt with your education, courage, and compassion that you would be the ideal headmistress for them."

Hope sprang to life, staggering in its intensity. In a world where a woman was remarkably without control and options, this post presented a future where Chloe would be mistress of her own fate.

Wordlessly, Jane grabbed a copy of *The Times* from her desk and held it out. "I take it, given your knowledge of the latest headmistress to leave, you also know what Society is saying about the school." And just like that, hope faltered.

Pushing to her feet, Chloe came over and accepted the recent article. She skimmed the page, already knowing the words printed there. Already knowing that Society had called into question Jane's school, time and time again.

Despite her reading—and already knowing for herself—Jane proceeded to enlighten her. "Regardless of my views of women and independence, the truth remains that Society has expectations. When I hired an unwed woman besieged by scandal, I had honorable intentions…" Worry flooded Jane's pretty eyes. "And yet, I did not think of the women who are taken in as students at my school." Women of already scandalous origins who'd been turned out of respectable institutions. "However, in hiring my last headmistress in a bid to help, I failed to truly consider how that decision could possibly jeopardize the security and stability of not only the women employed by Mrs. Munroe's, but also how it would impact the reputations of the girls who are students there."

Chloe waited for her to go on.

"Society has not only questioned the institution, but my instructors, as well as my ability to properly staff a respectable institution." Her sister-in-law's mouth tightened at the corners.

Having been born a bastard to the coldhearted Duke of Ravenscourt, Jane had been frequent fodder for gossip. Even the good work she did and the schooling she provided had not exalted her in Society's opinion.

"They can all go hang with their opinions," Chloe said passionately. Those same lords and ladies who'd so condescend to Jane had courted the late Marquess of Waverly's favor. She balled her hands. *May his black soul be burning even now.*

Jane smiled gently. "I do not disagree with you." Her smile dipped. "However, the fact remains that there are women who desperately need Mrs. Munroe's. Instructors and servants now rely on the establishment for their own security. If I were to offer you, an unmarried woman without any experience in educating girls in proper decorum, the position… what would Society say?"

Bitterness burned strong in her mouth and, with it, regret turned inside. For whether she liked it or not… her sister-in-law was, indeed, correct. And Chloe was not so selfish that she'd demand a post and endanger everything Jane had created, and all those who relied on the institution.

She studied the damned page. Hating Society. Hating the expectations and more… the lack of expectations. Where Jane had forged a life of her own and then, even after marrying, still continued to do so, Chloe remained… here. Dependent upon her family's goodwill and the funds in her name.

Her sister-in-law settled a hand on her shoulder. "I am sorry," she offered. It was a gentle pardon.

"Of course," she said stiffly. "It was not my place to presume you should offer me the post simply because of our relationship to one another."

Jane immediately straightened. "Never think that," she said vehemently. Gathering Chloe's hands, she gave a slight squeeze. "Never believe I don't see your worth and strength and capability. But the time for you to take this particular post is not now. Someday…" she promised, dangling that offer that was not truly an offer.

If she'd had experience like the previous headmistress, then there would be merits to Chloe's request. Jane released her hands. "And yet," Chloe began, and her sister-in-law went motionless. "It is a situation I can never win. I'll never come to you with the experience for the position and can never receive a post because of it." She detested the edge of bitterness to that pronouncement.

Jane smiled wryly. "Oh, I did not say I'd not ever have a post for you, Chloe." Just not now. An *unmarried* woman… and without experience. And still, when the offer did, in fact, come, it would come without any genuine work Chloe herself had done.

Footsteps sounded in the hall, and they looked up. Someone knocked once.

"Enter," Jane called out.

A young servant entered. "You asked me to call when Lady Gabriella awakened, my lady." The maid lingered.

A little glimmer lit the young mother's eyes. As much as Jane loved her work with the finishing school she'd established, mere mention of her young babe brought a smile to her mouth and color to her cheeks. That dream carried by so many women, so very far removed from Chloe's own hopes. Not because Chloe didn't love her family. She'd lay down her life for her siblings and her mother. However, she'd long ago vowed to sacrifice such a dream so as to never see her own children suffer the way she and her brothers and sister had.

"Go," Chloe said softly. There was nothing more to say. Certainly not now. Nothing short of begging or pleading for a post that Jane correctly pointed out Chloe had no right to. And Chloe was a good many things: a plotter, a matchmaker, resolute. She was not, however, one with hurt sensibilities over the truth.

Jane lifted her head. "I'll be along shortly," she called. After a respectful curtsy, the maid rushed off. When the servant was gone, Jane retrained her attention on Chloe's face. "I understand what you are feeling, Chloe, because I know what it was like to want control of my life." Ultimately, the other woman had found it, and love with Chloe's brother. "After there is some stability at the school. After—"

"It is fine," Chloe said quietly. She didn't want her sister-in-law's apology... and certainly not for being correct in her reservations. Indecision warred in Jane's blue eyes. "Go," she repeated. "Gabriella is waiting."

Still, Jane lingered, searching Chloe's face. "I'll speak to your brother. If you wish to be spared another London Season, I can speak to him of your visiting Imogen or Philippa."

Of course. Again, properly looked after and cared for. For even if her wishes to stay behind were accepted, this was still their home and Chloe was just a guest. A spinster aunt dependent upon the kindness of her family. That was what she was destined to become. "That will not be necessary." She would suffer through yet another London Season.

The other woman nodded and then rushed off.

Chloe stood rooted to the floor, counting the passing beats of the clock. When the trail of Jane's footsteps faded altogether, Chloe let out a frustrated sigh.

The irony was not lost on her. All her life, she'd disavowed the state of marriage because it presented as nothing but a prison... only to be proven wrong. Women such as her sister, Philippa, a proprietor of her own establishment for disabled souls, and Jane were afforded power and freedom Chloe would forever struggle to possess—all because she was unwed.

The broad, mahogany secretaire called her over. Sliding into the comfortable folds of the leather chair with a grace and aplomb even her miserable former headmistress, Mrs. Belden, would have lauded, she sat forward and layered her arms over the surface of the desk.

What must it be like to have such command of one's life?

She scrunched up her brow.

And how would she go about getting it?

CHAPTER 3

BLOODY, FUCKING SOIREES.

Leo didn't take exception to every ball. The naughty ones were quite all right, those orgies and masquerades where sinners with souls as black as his spent their night descending into further depravity.

As such, if there was ever a doubt as to his sacrifice for Crown and country, attending the Earl of Waterson's infernal affair was certainly testament enough to take to his grave. And as if it weren't chore *enough* suffering through any of Waterson's balls, he had discovered that the first one he attended turned out to be the one when the blighter had forgone spirits.

Any kind of spirits: champagne, brandy. By God, he'd settle for a bloody ratafia at this point.

"Tennyson, my boy." He stiffened at the aged, cultured tones of old Lord Carter. He was as bald as he'd always been. His cheeks were as florid and rounded as when he'd visited Leo's now, thankfully, departed father. The man smiled. "Unexpected seeing you here. Then, all young men, even the rakes and rogues, settle down and find brides, eh?" The man guffawed at his own jest.

Leo passed his hopelessly bored gaze over Waterson's guests. Putting to use his disdain, he masked his true interest in the guests circulating around him. As such, the dreadfully dull Earl of Waterson's ball would have been, at any other time, an event he'd have rather yanked his fingernails out than attend. And yet… the stodgy and boring earl's conservative political leanings and efforts to wed his unmarried sisters off to equally stodgy Tories had marked him as a suspect in Leo's investigation.

Leo lazily studied the guests. The crowd consisted of largely proper lords, most vocal members of Parliament… and their equally proper sisters and wives.

He grimaced. With the dearth of rakes, rogues, and scoundrels, he was wholly out of place. Hardly his normal crowd… or event. With his dire financial state, however, none would dare question why a man such as Leo was in attendance. They'd take him as any other rake in dun territory, in need of a fat-dowered, desperate-to-be-wed miss.

"Unfortunate about the lack-of-spirits business," Carter lamented, still standing at his side.

"Indeed," Leo drawled, wholly in agreement with the old earl.

Seeming to take that first reply as an invitation, Lord Carter continued on. "Some scandal or such when a fight broke out at Waterson's last affair. A soiree. Lord Bedford imbibed too many spirits and knocked over a candelabra and—"

And just like that, he'd been provided the means with which to quit the earl's ballroom and find himself… another place inside the earl's household. "He still keeps spirits, then?"

The earl scratched his paunch. "Certainly does. Some of the best French brandy, in fact." He lowered his voice and whispered the way one might about a delicious secret. "I've had the opportunity to sample it myself a number of times when we've met to discuss business." So Lord Carter also had business dealings with the Earl of Waterson… as well as like political leanings in his voting record at Parliament. "Not the inexpensive rubbish most of the younger gents your age are drinking these days."

The earl had two daughters and a son married, but Leo had forgotten the man's eldest, daughter. Suddenly interested by the earl's appearance and, more specifically, by each tidbit revealed, Leo shifted closer. "Tell me, then, old chap. If a scoundrel was so inclined to partake in a sampling of this treasure, where might one find such a bounty?"

A glimmer sparkled in the earl's eyes. "In his office."

Bloody lackwit. "Where?" he snapped.

At the brief lapse in conviviality, Lord Carter blinked.

"I'm in desperate need of a drink, old chap."

"Ahh," the earl replied, thumping Leo on the back. "I remember those days all too well."

Like an Oxford boy plotting mischief, Lord Carter turned over concise directions as to where Lord Waterson conducted business dealings. Leo neatly filed those details away.

This one's lips were far too loose to ever effectively engage in subterfuge. Oh, it didn't mean even lesser men than the one before him hadn't tried. They had. It was, however, easy enough to size a man up and determine whether he was engaged in anything sinister. "Waterson's also fat in the pockets," he put forward in bored tones. "Manner of gent I suspect you'd like to saddle your daughter with." A few years older than Leo's thirty years, Lord Carter's homely daughter had been destined for the shelf the moment she'd made her Come Out.

"Quite true. Quite true." Lord Carter stuck an elbow in Leo's side, pulling a grunt from him. "I've tried. Believe me, I've tried to orchestrate an arrangement between my Mary and the earl." He screwed his mouth up. "Alas, Waterson has already set his sights on another."

Leo followed the earl's stare over to their host... presently in discussion with the Marquess of Waverly.

Lord Carter elucidated, "The marquess' spinster sister, Lady Chloe."

Lady Chloe. Leo tried to recall the marquess' unwed sister. Alas, he'd put his days of dallying with innocents to rest long ago, and only after he'd cemented his place as one of London's most debauched rakes. His mind quickly worked. "There is talk of a match between them?"

"There has been, for several years now. Pretty filly. A fat dowry. Lovely bosoms. Not overly plump, but sufficient enough to earn notice."

Leo rubbed at his chin, assessing the two men engrossed in discussion.

Waverly had recently married a bastard-born woman who'd established a school for scandalous offspring. Both his selection in bride and his support of that institution for women outside the nobility had marked him an unlikely participant of the Cato Street Conspiracy.

Useful information from Lord Carter officially at an end, Leo touched his brow in thanks. "Carter." Abandoning his post at the back corner of the ballroom, he quit the nobleman's side. With the earl sputtering and stammering in his wake, Leo donned his usual rakish grin and wound his way through the crowd.

Proper mamas yanked their daughters, with dangerous curiosity in their eyes, swiftly closer.

Those daughters, each and every one of them, would ultimately be ruined.

Alas, there would have to be another rake to lift them of their innocence.

Leo took up position beside another pillar, where he was free to study the guests now performing the intricate steps of a country reel. Spirits temporarily forgotten, he surveyed the crowd, now wholly focused on his mission.

Of the two suspects, only Waterson was present. The other, Lord Ellsworth, had yet to arrive. Over the heads of the prancing lords and ladies, Leo's gaze collided with a hard, glowering one… inconveniently belonging to the very host who'd not issued Leo an invitation.

Lifting his head slightly in a mocking acknowledgment, Leo grinned.

Even with Waterson's palpable loathing and, no doubt, a desire to toss him out on his arse, the blighter was too polite. Waterson was the manner of man who adhered to the rules of propriety, regardless of how stodgy—as he had with the oppressive Six Acts. Still conversing with the Marquess of Waverly, that equally stodgy bore from Leo's Oxford days spared barely a passing glance for Leo.

From the corner of his eye, he spied the lady's approach before she even draped herself against his side.

"Of all the places I'd expect to find you, Tennyson," she purred. "In my bed, in an alcove, in a stable, I should think this dull affair would be the last place we'd again meet." She was tall, statuesque, and buxom, and had she been any other woman and had these not been Crown-related circumstances, he'd have offered to meet her in the room of her choosing. But she was not. She was one woman with whom a dalliance would end his tenure with the Brethren.

"Lady Rowley," he forced in his usual bored tones. "These are hardly *your* usual haunts."

She smiled slyly back, curling her lips up in an inviting grin better suited for a bedroom. "I can show you some of them if you wish," she enticed. Pressing her breasts against his arm, she leaned into him.

Silently cursing, Leo did a quick search. Both his uncle and Higgins' warnings echoed around his mind. He took a step away from the tenacious beauty.

"Oh, la, Tennyson." She fingered the plunging décolletage of her dampened silk net gown. "Never tell me you, of all rakes, are nervous of being seen with me?"

"Actually, I am, sweet. Your husband isn't pleased with me."

She giggled. "When have you ever cared about displeased husbands, mine or anyone else's, Tennyson?"

Never. This, however, was altogether different. Another indiscretion with this woman would see him deprived of the only thing he wanted or needed—his work with the Brethren. In desperate need of liquor for altogether different reasons, he searched the room, stiffening when Rowley's wife cupped him between his legs.

"Bloody hell," he bit out. He swiftly disentangled her hand from his person. "I said no."

The woman was unrelenting. "My husband is otherwise occupied at his club," she cajoled, walking her fingertips back up his thigh. Bloody, bloody hell. She leaned up and placed her lips close to his ear. "Where can I meet you?"

He glanced about and found a number of disapproving stares upon them.

Leo relaxed. With both his exchanges here this evening—first with Carter and now with Lady Rowley—one would never take him as anything other than an indolent rake here for his own pleasures.

"Waterson's gardens," he lied, eager to be rid of her.

Triumph lit the viscountess' eyes. With a sultry smile, she sashayed off.

Staring after her for the requisite prolonged moment, with a suitable degree of pretend interest, Leo then shifted his attention back to the crowd.

Another figure stepped into his path. This time, a servant. Something akin to horror churned in his gut as he stared at the neat arrangement of glasses upon the liveried footman's silver tray. "What in the blazes is *that?*"

Puzzling his brow, the servant glanced at his tray. "Lemonade, my lord."

The expected, rakish response was an instruction of just where Waterson's footman could take himself. Yet, for Society's whisperings and statements on his lack of control, Leo had greater restraint than most... when it served a purpose that needed serving.

Wordlessly, he grabbed one of the earl's ridiculously fragile cups. Glass in hand, he proceeded to take a turn about the floor. All the while, he scrutinized his host's every movement.

His dealings with Waterson were limited. Together at Oxford, they'd both enjoyed their books. But whereas Leo had always concealed his love of literature, the other man had freely embraced his academic pursuits.

Sniveling, pathetic excuse of a boy... poetry and books... as empty-headed as your mother was... useless... you're utterly useless...

He tightened his grip upon the cup. Damn that hated bastard for refusing to stay buried in the grave he rightly deserved. After all these years, he still had sway over Leo's damned thoughts.

How ironic to go through the first eighteen years of his life being thought of and derided as useless... only to have proven with his work for the Brethren that he'd far more value than his father ever had.

From across the ballroom, Rowley's wife caught his eye. Not even the length of the dance floor could conceal the lusty promise there. Flicking an artful curl over her shoulder, she presented him with her rounded buttocks and slipped out of the gathering.

Leo sprang into movement. Some gents avoided gazes to avoid discourse. There was and always had been little reason to do so where he was concerned. All the proper sorts tended to step out of his path. Never before had that ever been more convenient.

Slipping out the same doorway Lady Rowley had moments ago, Leo set off in the opposite direction.

He'd established a life for himself these past twelve years. And he'd be damned if he sacrificed it for anyone—particularly a woman.

CHAPTER 4

GOD, HOW SHE DESPISED BALLS.

All of them.

The soirees. The masquerades. The intimate, formal affairs thrown by her friends or family.

All of them.

Nor was it simply the six Seasons' worth of those affairs that accounted for her apathy, but rather her family's unrelenting efforts to see Chloe married off.

There was the fortunate end that after so many London Seasons, no one paid Chloe much attention. Seated on the edge of the Earl of Waterson's ballroom, she surveyed the crowd. Couples twirled past, ladies in their white skirts and manufactured smiles waltzed about by respectable gentlemen.

She stared blankly off.

"There you are!"

Chloe looked to the owner of that familiar voice and hopped up from her shellback chair. "Jane," she greeted with a smile that threatened to shatter her cheeks. This was the first exchange they'd had since earlier that morn when Jane had gently but firmly denied Chloe's request for employment. Chloe was... at a loss for how to be around her friend.

Fortunately, Jane had always been one to command situations.

"He is plotting," Jane explained in a whisper. Her sister-in-law motioned with her hand, and Chloe followed that subtle point.

Conversing with their host, the Earl of Waterson, her brother moved his less-than-subtle stare in Chloe's direction and back to the earl.

Lord Waterson looked in her direction, lifting his head in slight acknowledgment, a pained look on his face. One that surely matched her own.

She lifted her fingers in a small greeting. "Dead," she muttered under her breath. "I am going to kill him dead."

"Well, that would certainly eliminate the possibility of a match with him," Jane put in, her lips twitching.

It was easy enough to be amused and amusing when one was mistress of her own universe. "I meant my brother," she said sardonically.

Jane winked. "I know."

At least one of them could find amusement in Gabriel's tenacious efforts at matchmaking. Since she'd made her Come Out, Gabriel had done everything within his power to attempt to coordinate a match between Chloe and his best friend. "I have no intention of relinquishing control of my life." Her father had control enough until he'd, thankfully, turned up his evil heels and gone to meet the devil. "And I'll not cede that power to Gabriel." Their sister, Philippa, had meekly stepped into the respectable match that Gabriel had encouraged… and what had that gotten her? Nearly killed trying to produce a male heir for her honorable husband.

Jane sighed. "He *means* well."

Where in the past Chloe would have vehemently debated that point, now she remained silent, in concurrence. Gabriel, as he'd been before marriage, had made it his life's mission to see all of his siblings—Chloe, Philippa, and Alex—properly wed. Since he'd fallen in love, his motives had shifted—somewhat. "He wants to be free of his responsibility of me," she predicted, moving her gaze to her sister-in-law.

Jane made a sound of protest. "He wants you to be happy."

"And he expects it is a husband who will do that?" she asked dryly. Though she and Jane had never spoken about the abuse the Edgertons had suffered as children, she'd no doubt Gabriel had shared those darkest secrets with his wife.

Jane nibbled at her lower lip, carefully weighing her words. "He expects the right husband will."

"Do you believe a man who supported the suppression of people's voices, movements, and freedoms makes for a *safe* choice?" she shot back.

To Jane's credit, she shook her head instantly. "No. No, I do not."

The other woman only grew all the more in Chloe's esteem. Having introduced Chloe to the works of Mary Wollstonecraft, she had ultimately opened her eyes to injustices and the possibility of not only having a voice, but being heard. "I believe the earl is a good man." She grinned wryly. "Just with bad political leanings."

Frustration needled at her, and she put a question to Jane. "What makes a man the right husband?" It was a question she'd never asked because, for her, there had been no traits, qualities, or characteristics that could have persuaded her to relinquish what little independence she had.

"Love," Jane said simply. "A gentleman who loves you and appreciates your mind and encourages you to take on whichever causes you wish. Who sees you as a partner and not as a prisoner."

Warmth suffused Chloe's breast. She recalled all over again why she'd come to view Jane as close as a sister—mayhap closer than she'd ever been with Philippa. "Not all ladies are fortunate enough to find that manner of husband," she said softly. That was as elusive as a pot of gold at the proverbial end of the rainbow, and Chloe hadn't even wasted a girlhood hope on one.

Jane stole a furtive glance in her husband's direction. "I want you to find love," she said in hushed tones. "If you do not wish to marry, I'll not allow your brother to maneuver you into a match… or even a dance."

"A dance?" she repeated, horror creeping into her voice. To most, a dance simply represented the polite movements all lords and ladies invariably went through. With Gabriel, however, it always began with a carefully coordinated pairing at a formal ball.

Sure enough, Gabriel and the earl now wound their way through the ballroom—to where Chloe and Jane stood.

Catching the lace adorning the bottom of Chloe's gown with the tip of her slipper, Jane dragged it until it snagged, tearing.

Both ladies stared down at the dangling fabric.

A twinkle lit Jane's eyes. "Oh, dear. My apologies. Go, see to that." She bussed Chloe on the cheek in a show of affection that earned several side-eyed stares from the stodgy lot invited by the earl. "I will keep your brother and the earl distracted."

With a murmur of thanks, Chloe gathered her skirts and started in the opposite direction of her rapidly approaching brother. Although Lord Waterson had long been a friend of Gabriel, he would never do as a husband for the very reasons she'd given Jane. After all, as Mrs. Wollstonecraft had once written, every political good carried to the extreme must be productive of evil. A man who'd been one of the greatest supporters of the Six Acts, Waterson would never grant the freedoms Gabriel had Jane... and Miles had Philippa.

Chloe sneaked from the crowded ballroom and did not break her stride as she continued down familiar halls she'd visited many times before. With only a handful of sconces lit, there was an ominous feeling to the darkened corridors. *Do not look.* "You are not a helpless child scared of a shadow," she whispered, needing to hear some hint of sound in the growing silence.

Despite those reminders and assurances, she glanced at the blood-red satin wallpaper. Eerie shadows flickered and danced upon the walls. A cold sweat broke out on her skin, and she frantically glanced about. There were doors, and the halls were wide and... those silent, desperate reminders fell away. Her breath rasped loudly in her ears, blending with the distant pleas of the past. *No... please... I will be good... Do not lock me in here... please...*

Her slipper snagged the dangling lace. Crying out, Chloe crashed forward. She shot her hands out, landing hard on her knees.

She sat. The hum of silence buzzing in her ears melded with her rapidly drawn breaths. When *he*, the monster who'd sired her, slipped back in, in he remained. Chloe clamped her hands over her ears, moaning. "He is dead." She whispered the familiar reminder she so often needed. "He cannot hurt you." She squeezed her eyes shut and counted to five.

She opened them just as a tall figure exited the earl's offices.

Chloe made herself go absolutely motionless. It was a skill that had saved her many times, and one she'd been forced to perfect in order to spare herself a beating.

Something white flashed in his hand as he reached inside his jacket—

Which will it be, gel… the rod or my fist…?

A scream tore from her throat, and she struggled to stand. Her leg instantly crumpled. Pain throbbed from her ankle and radiated up her leg.

"Bloody hell, shut your damned mouth, or you'll have us caught—*together*."

The gentleman pulled Lord Waterson's office door quietly shut. That faint click yanked her from the fog of confusion.

What in the blazes? She'd always prided herself on being ready with a sharp retort. Her mother had long lamented that her quick tongue would be the death of her. Yet, in this instance, indecently sprawled upon the earl's floor, she couldn't think of a single reply. In the darkened space, she squinted, attempting to bring the owner of that unfamiliar baritone into focus, praying the man would leave. Praying the floor would open up and swallow her.

And then, it appeared the Lord was real, after all.

The gentleman moved at a brisk clip and continued past her.

Chloe briefly closed her eyes, giving thanks for small favors.

Then he stopped. With an inventive curse that sent color rushing to her cheeks, he turned back and swiftly returned to her side.

She inched her horrified eyes up, from a pair of immaculate, gleaming, black boots, to muscular legs encased in cream satin, gold-striped breeches. *Boots* with *formal wear*? Who in thunderation wore boots to a soiree?

Craning her neck back, she met the flinty gaze of the Marquess of Tennyson, one of the wickedest scoundrels in England. A lady could be ruined by nothing more than a look from him. Of course, *that* was who'd wear boots to a ball. With a crop of closely clipped, golden curls, he'd the look of a fallen Lucifer. Yet, there could be no doubt the gentleman before her was all seven of the deadliest sins rolled into one towering figure of a man. "You," she groaned.

Irritated eyes did a cursory search of her. "Have I tupped you?"

"Tripped me?" Chloe shook her head once. "You startled me, is all." Because she'd let the demons back in… her stomach twisted. Mayhap the vicious remembrances this night would not take root. Mayhap the headaches would stay back. It had been nearly two months since she'd suffered one. But they were always there and always would be. "I tripped on my hem," she explained, gesturing to the offending garment. She sighed. To think it had seemed like such a grand idea when Jane had shredded it.

The marquess dashed the back of his hand over his face. "Tupped," he said coolly. "Have I *tupped* you?"

She opened and closed her mouth several times and then gasped. "You are loathsome." She'd never been one to listen to the gossips, and yet, with a handful of sentences, he'd proven himself as vile as they said.

"Undoubtedly." He spoke in bored tones, glancing past her.

Good. She was glad to be rid of the bounder rumored to be a debaucher of innocents and one who drank too much, wagered often, and whored even more. She'd already encouraged far too much discourse. And yet... bloody hell, she'd not have him thinking she would ever dare give herself to one such as him. "You most certainly did not... did not..." Chloe cursed the pathetically weak quality to that incomplete rebuttal.

The marquess winged a golden eyebrow. "Tupped, miss. The word is tupped."

What man didn't recall the women he'd... he'd... *tupped*?

Annoyed at having been so unsettled, she tilted her chin up. "Nor am I a 'miss.'" Misses were innocent debutantes in white, who simpered and preened before wicked men such as him. She'd never simpered, and she was three years past wearing white. "I am a lady. Lady Chloe Edgerton." It was a good deal less impressive to deliver a setdown sprawled on one's buttocks as she was.

Interest briefly flickered in his apathetic gaze, but then was gone so quick she might as well have imagined it. "So, *you* are Waterson's future wife."

Society was talking, then. "I am certainly not..." Chloe promptly closed her mouth. By way of explanation, she owed this man nothing.

Like the wolf all girls were warned of in folklore, the marquess waggled his golden eyebrows. "Marrying a stuffy bore like Waterson? Ahh," he said with a dawning understanding.

"What?" she asked before she could call the question back.

He searched about. "I take it you were sneaking off to meet a different gentleman, then?"

He would take it that way. And a reprobate such as he would never believe, for all her protestations, that she'd actually been avoiding a gentleman. Furthermore...

"What manner of man does not recall whether or not he—"

"Are you all right?" he bit out, wincing as though the question had cost him a pound of flesh.

And yet, the unexpectedness of both his return and question brought her up short.

He jerked. Was he startled by his own concern? In one fluid movement, he bent and scooped her up.

Chloe squeaked at the familiarity of his bold touch. Perhaps all the rumors and writings about a rake's touch had merit, because the heavy weight of his hand singed her through her dress.

He promptly set her down.

She gasped as her leg gave out. Reflexively, she gathered the lapels of his sapphire jacket, catching herself. Despite his wiry frame, there was a surprising breadth to his chest that belied his image of indolent lord.

"An injured ankle?" he drawled. "Cliché, love. Very cliché."

Unnerved by her body's reaction, she released him.

"You needn't put either of us through this show. You are on… your seventh Season now?" He flashed a rakish smile, displaying two perfect rows of pearl-white teeth, and then lowered his lips close to her ear. The unexpected hint of lemons, a wholly innocent scent, filled her senses.

But then he spoke. "Certain freedoms are permitted more seasoned women."

She sputtered. The arrogance of him. "I assure you, I would not ever let a bounder such as you *tup*, let alone touch, me."

Brava.

Leo had neither bedded nor seduced an innocent in ten years. A peculiar ache tightened his chest, a reaction that would have been remorse and regret in another man.

The person Leo had been had died in that library with the woman he'd intended to make his bride. From that moment, he'd carefully cultivated his image as a worthless rake, and he'd dallied only with wicked widows and unhappy wives.

But if he'd been of an inclination to revisit his younger days as a debaucher, Lady Chloe Edgerton was certainly the manner of spitfire he'd have met in a darkened corridor.

He passed an experienced gaze over her. Flawless, golden curls, a nipped waist only enhanced by the generous curve of her hips… a woman such as she would be wasted on a bore like Waterson. Mayhap a traitorous one, at that.

No, the lady was fire and needed a like blaze in her bed.

Continuing his study, Leo lingered his stare on her modest décolletage. Smaller than he generally preferred, but—

"Did you have a good look?" she snapped.

He grinned. "I hadn't finished." He followed the cheeky retort with a wink.

Luminescent blue eyes formed round saucers, and he braced for a stinging rebuke.

And yet, this brief exchange alone should have proven that Lady Chloe neither said nor did what one might expect. With her lean arms stretched out, the lady hopped over to the wall. Then, borrowing support, she inched toward the nearest doorway.

He stared after her. *Let her go. She is hardly your concern.* In fact, he'd found what he'd come for—a list of meetings and appointments regarding controversial legislation was copied, dried, and tucked inside his flask. He was free to quit Waterson's dull affair and seek out his naughty clubs, as all Society expected. It didn't matter that he'd begun to tire of—

The lady stumbled. An inventive curse better suited to a sailor spilled past her lips. Language no lady of his acquaintance had ever uttered. Not even the rakes and scoundrels, for that matter.

And he, who'd believed himself incapable of any real expressions of mirth any longer, felt a smile pull. It instantly withered. Giving one last look of longing down the opposite hall, he sighed.

In three long strides, Leo closed the minimal distance she'd put between them.

Blue eyes filled with a proper wariness followed his every movement. "You again," she muttered, laying her back to the wall.

Leo fell to a knee beside her. "Me again."

She gasped. "What are you doing?" she demanded, indignation rich in her voice as he lifted her skirts.

Trim ankles. *Delicious ones.* Even with the left one's swelling.

With the lady's protestations ringing around the hall, Leo gently slid her slipper free. "I assure you," he said drolly, "I've seen flesh of far more interest than your ankles." It was the requisite rakish response, and yet, he'd sooner announce himself an agent for the Crown than confess to this inexplicable need to caress that innocent flash of skin.

Leo probed for a break.

A hiss exploded from Lady Chloe's teeth.

He quickly stopped, looking up.

The young lady slumped against the wall. "In addition to more interesting flesh, do you have very much experience with assessing an injured ankle?" Her breath came in little spurts, as though they'd engaged in an evening of naughty pursuits in his bed. The thought conjured all manner of wicked pleasures he'd like to explore with the lady.

He took in her tense mouth and strained eyes. "Enough to know yours is, in fact, sprained, my lady," he evaded, reassessing her left foot.

"It was a minor fall," she protested. "Hardly significant enough to do any real dam—ahh," she cried softly as he applied an assessing pressure.

Yes, badly sprained. "I've seen many a man shatter limbs from the slightest stumble." He directed that very point to her lower limb.

"Many?"

He paused.

Bloody hell.

"Where would you see men shatter their limbs?" Curiosity wreathed the lady's voice, and he slowly lifted his head.

What was it about the spitfire that made him careless? Or was it simply that the manner of women he kept company with didn't notice details contained within one's speech? He shuttered his expression. "On a dueling field," he finally supplied. "I've known countless fools who've shown up drunk to a duel and didn't have the wherewithal to keep steady on their feet." It was a lie anyone in Polite Society would believe, and yet...

For all the times he should have been dueled at dawn and left with a bullet between the eyes for his sins, he'd never faced an angry husband. The extent of his chasing had been of suspects, in the darkest streets of London.

Lady Chloe made a noncommittal grunt.

"May I?" Not awaiting permission, he refocused on the lady's ankle.

He'd learned back in his university days the manner of delights a man could know from a woman's perfectly arched, delicate foot. He'd be wise to leave, and yet, as the expected scoundrel, he was free to stay.

Leo trailed his fingertips up the sole of her silk stocking-clad foot.

She giggled. "I-I did not hurt my foot," she assured between her little gasping laughs. "Merely my ankle."

Ignoring that declaration, he continued his search higher, ever higher. Leo guided Lady Chloe's satin gown up about her knees, the noisy sound of ruffled satin as headily erotic as it had always been as he worked his exploring hand up her thigh.

The lady gasped. "My God, you are incorrigible," she snapped. Laying her palms against his chest, she gave a firm shove.

Leo toppled back on his buttocks.

"Ascertaining if there was a sprain, my arse," she muttered, dipping her tones into a pretend baritone that only husked her voice.

He briefly closed his eyes. The lady's low contralto personified the perfect bedroom tones, a lush whisper that encouraged a man onward with his wicked designs. *You bloody, pathetic fool. Lusting after a proper lady in the middle of a hallway where anyone might stumble upon you.* Disgusted with himself, with this night, he let her skirts flutter back into place. "There *is*... a sprain," he said tightly. And the tart-mouthed lady's problem was her own. Abandoning her for a second time, Leo stalked down the hall, ready to put this damned night and the insolent slip behind him. When had he ever been a man to query after an injured miss? His work was reserved for the Crown, and nothing more commanded his attentions. The work he did was also what had sharpened his senses over the years, heightening his ability to see that which was around him... and hear.

That was why, as he turned into the next corridor, that the lady's quick, rasping breaths reached him. *Keep walking... keep walking...*

Leo slowed his steps and then stopped. A battle raged in a conscience he'd erroneously believed had died long ago. He scrubbed his hands over his face. *This is not the time to discover the last shred of morality in your worthless soul.*

Bloody, bloody hell.

Wheeling around, he retraced his steps to the intersecting corridor.

Her shoulders slightly slumped and her fingers on the Earl of Waterson's door handle, the lady borrowed support from the oak panel.

"You are determined to enter that room," he called out, ringing a loud gasp from Lady Chloe.

The lady nibbled at her lower lip... her enticingly plump lower lip. "You again," she said, the resignation meeting with that in her expressive eyes.

"Yes, me. *Again*. And now it would seem... again." Because the world had gone insane. His returning not once, but now twice, was an incongruity that, at any other time, would have been easily explained as a product of too much alcohol and a hope to land a place in her bed. But with his last drink a single brandy that morn, there was no accounting for this madness. Leo stopped beside her. Reaching past her, he pressed the handle of the earl's office. "Who was he?" He infused as much dry boredom as he could into the query. At her furrowed brow, he added, "The gentleman you are so determined to meet." He glanced past her into the darkened room. "I didn't take Waterson as one who'd dally with innocents in his offices, in the middle of his own ball, no less," he said, more to himself.

Annoyance settled in his belly at the thought of that pairing. Only because it was an unlikely one. Because the vixen deserved a real man between her legs and not a nobleman who might or might not have been involved in a plot to overthrow the prime minister's Cabinet.

"I already told you before. No. One."

He snorted.

Lady Chloe angled her slightly too-pointy chin a notch. "Not every woman sneaking about is seeking an assignation." His ears would have to be stuffed with cotton for him to fail to hear the lady's stiff rebuke.

"That is precisely the *only* thing ladies," regardless of station or degree of innocence, "seek." That wasn't altogether true. There had been one lady... his first, last, and only virgin, who'd desired more from him. His stomach muscles tightened as an unwanted and unwelcome remorse filled him… for a second time that night. What was it about Lady Chloe Edgerton that dragged forth those long-buried memories? Memories that he'd kicked ash and dirt upon until they were as black as Leo's own soul?

As though the lady before him had followed the dark path his thoughts had traveled, she favored him with a frown. "If that is true—"

"It is," he mumbled.

"Then *you*, my lord, have simply been keeping company with the wrong sorts of ladies."

He looped an arm around her slender waist. "For the uses *I* have of them," he said smoothly as he scooped her up, "I've been keeping company with the very perfect ones."

The lady's body trembled against his, and he reflexively drew her closer. "Wh-what are you doing?" she demanded, faintly breathless as she struggled against him.

"Worry not," he drawled as he carried her inside Waterson's library. "For all my sins, forcing myself upon uninterested ladies has never been one of them." He'd enough black crimes to his name. Though the heart-shaped birthmark upon her neck, where her pulse raced, spoke of a lady more aware of him than fearful. "You need to stay off your foot, and I suspect… someone will eventually come for you." And he intended to be far away when that proverbial search party went out for the missing lady. Or rather, he needed to be. The only thing that could make this night any more of a bloody disaster was Leo being discovered sneaking about.

The taut, white lines at the corners of her mouth and the strain in Lady Chloe's eyes bespoke the pain she now silently suffered. That uncharacteristic quiet from one who'd chattered like a damned magpie earlier only stood as further proof of her misery.

Steadying his hold under her knees to keep from further jarring her injured ankle, Leo eased her into the folds of Waterson's leather button sofa.

The lady clenched her eyes tightly and drew in slow, jerky breaths.

Leo hovered over her, hesitating, immobile. *Why do I want to continue holding her close, dip my head, and explore the plump contours of her lips?* His stomach lurched as unease churned low in his gut.

Because you are a damned rake. It would go against every code of being a scoundrel he'd ascribed to if he didn't yearn for more from the warm, tempting beauty in his arms.

Lady Chloe's endlessly long golden lashes fluttered open, revealing cerulean blue irises. "You should go," she whispered, gathering his lapels. Was it a bid to push him back? Pull him closer? And why did he so very much want it to be the latter?

She remained motionless, her delicate palms upon him.

He swallowed hard. "Do you want that?" he asked, intending the rakish purr he'd perfected long ago. Instead, that question came guttural and pleading to his own ears. After all, what manner of rake would he be if he left without tasting her mouth? Why, word of his chivalry and chasteness would raise questions about his reputation... and...

With a groan, Leo lowered his head—

"My God, Tennyson, you damned scoundrel. Take your bloody hands off her."

He froze, brow touching Lady Chloe's. With a sickening dread slithering around his belly, Leo glanced from the corner of his eye to the doorway—to the crowd of four now gathered.

Oh, fuck.

CHAPTER 5

THIS WAS BAD.

This was very, *very* bad, indeed.

The only thing that made Chloe's public ruin before Gabriel, Lord Waterson, Lady Rowley, and Jane anything slightly less than disastrous was the absence of Chloe's mother.

And if not for Lady Rowley, with relish in her eyes as she took in the sight of Chloe and Lord Tennyson, Chloe might have weathered the scandal. But there could be no excusing or explaining how an unmarried lady came to be under the gentleman in a darkened room with no other guests about.

Her stomach pitched, and she reflexively clasped the marquess' jacket.

"Hardly the time for an embrace, love," he whispered with an infuriating casualness that jerked her from the haze of shock.

"Unhand me," she gritted out, giving the marquess' shoulders a shove.

That abrupt movement seemed to startle him into action. He straightened.

She'd known the gentleman but a handful of moments and well recognized that practiced, icy grin on his lips as a false one. A like panic reflected in his hardened gaze. "Waterson, Waverly," he acknowledged. Then, angling his body in a dismissive gesture, he turned that rakish smile on Jane. "My lady," he greeted with a sweeping bow.

Gabriel and Lord Waterson stood shoulder to shoulder, palpable rage dripping from both of their frames.

And Chloe, who'd stood boldly before her father as he'd come at her, fists raised, fell to cowardice. She gave thanks for the marquess' willingness to fill the silence, sparing her from words.

"Get away from my sister," Gabriel ordered with an icy calm that only her eldest, stoic brother could be capable of.

The marquess inclined his head and edged behind the sofa, putting several more steps between him and her family. "Ladies… gentlemen… this is simply a *misunderstanding*," he said with a practiced grin.

How many times had he been caught in a like manner? And how many women's reputations had lived to be repaired?

None. I am ruined…

Her heart sank to the soles of her slippers. There could be no possible hope of a position at Mrs. Munroe's, or employment anywhere aiding young women, after this.

Chloe gripped the edges of the seat as panic clawed at her chest, robbing her of breath. *Enough! Be rational. Be focused. You are Chloe Edgerton. Not some simpering debutante.* "We were not meeting," she blurted. All eyes, including Lord Tennyson's, swung to her. "He was meeting another and—"

Lady Rowley flicked a gaze up and down Chloe's person. When she spoke, disdain dripped from her words. "And it appears, in Tennyson's usual fashion, he made do with whatever woman was about."

Ever the finishing school instructor, Jane quietly chided the daringly dressed beauty. "That is hardly appropriate or kind, my lady."

This was the woman the marquess had been meeting, then. That explained her appearance and indignant fury. A jealous lover.

"If you will excuse us?" Gabriel commanded Lady Rowley in clipped tones.

Only, when this cold-eyed harpy walked out with the story of Chloe's ruin, it would spread about Polite Society like a cancer, destroying Chloe's reputation and ending the dreams she carried of Mrs. Munroe's. "I fell." No truer words had ever been spoken. Desperation made her voice pitch high. "I tore my hem and was going to tend it when I tripped on the fabric."

Jane stared back with stricken eyes.

Chloe gave her head a slight shake. Even through the horror that held her in its fold, she could not blame Jane for having intervened on her behalf in the ballroom.

"Tennyson?" the earl gruffly demanded.

Chloe craned her neck back to look at the marquess, demanding with her eyes. *Tell them, damn it. Tell them, the reason we are both here, together…*

Except, his face might as well have been carved of granite. He lifted one shoulder in a negligent shrug. And with that go-to-hell gesture, he sealed her fate.

Lady Rowley pounced. "Never tell me the ever-*chivalrous* Lord Tennyson was good enough to see to your injury?" A cackle better suited to a witch than a stunningly beautiful woman spilled from her lips.

Chloe tightened her mouth, and a new, distracting emotion took root—annoyance. Yes, Lord Tennyson was a rake in every sense of the word, but he *had* attempted to help her.

Swinging her legs over the side of the sofa, she struggled to stand.

The marquess took a quick step toward her.

"Move away from my sister, Tennyson," Gabriel snapped.

Jane shot Lord Waterson a pointed look. He sprang into movement. "I will see your carriage readied." He turned to the countess. "If you will accompany me, my lady?" he urged, offering the sharp-eyed countess an elbow.

With no choice but to accept, she reluctantly allowed him to usher her from the room.

Closing the door behind their unlikely gathering, the earl at last secured a modicum of privacy. And that quiet click ushered in something more. *Resignation.*

It is too late… The damage has been done…

Her throat thickened, making it impossible to properly swallow, and she struggled once more to stand. She dimly registered Lord Tennyson's determined approach. Collecting her hand, the marquess helped her up. How very strong and steady his grip was, and she found additional strength from that unlikeliest of places. Her palm instantly ceased trembling. Accepting help from the stranger at her side, she motioned to her foot. "I sprained my ankle, Gabriel."

Gabriel and Jane exchanged a look, and then her sister-in-law was the first to quit her place at the front of the room. She hurried over, claiming Chloe's other side. "You should not be standing," she gently scolded. With the marquess' help, Jane guided her back into her seat. Jane caught her gaze, and guilt fairly bled from its depths.

"Do not do that," she softly whispered. She'd chosen to wander Lord Waterson's halls. The blame rested squarely with Chloe. She'd not be one of those woe-is-me ladies who cast guilt upon other parties.

The marquess inclined his head. "If anyone would care to know how she knows it is sprained, it is because I inspected it."

Bloody hell. Leaning around her sister-in-law, Chloe leveled a glower on the indolent lord. "Are you *trying* to make the situation worse?" she demanded, glad to have a place to direct her frustration.

"Oh," Lord Tennyson drawled, "I trust that is an impossibility." He reached inside his jacket and removed a silver flask ornately etched with Bacchus upon the front. Lord Tennyson uncorked it.

The gentleman stopped with the drink halfway to his mouth and then held it out, lifting an eyebrow in silent offer.

Chloe puzzled her brow. Mad. He was utterly mad.

He shrugged and took a long swallow.

Dismissing him outright, she retrained her efforts on her disconcertingly silent brother. "Nothing happened," Chloe felt the need to point out again. "Nothing," she added, holding his flinty stare.

"Of all the bloody gentlemen to be discovered with, it should be this one?" Gabriel slashed his palm in Lord Tennyson's direction.

Propping his hip on the arm of the sofa, Lord Tennyson lifted his flask in salute.

Had he become so jaded to Society's ill opinion that he should be so unfazed by a room full of people throwing aspersions upon his character? Could a person ever truly be that hardened? Thrusting aside questions about what turned a man to the stony figure before her, she jutted her chin out. "Forgive me. But if I were to face public ruin, I should have at least had the good sense to lose my reputation to a proper, respectable lord you approve of." Because then he could see her married, free of his household, and properly looked after. The same frustration at the lot he'd always expected snapped her last frayed nerve.

Her brother glared at the marquess. "I'll not have this discussion with him present."

"We need to leave," Jane agreed with such uncharacteristic solemnity that disquiet stirred all the more inside Chloe.

The marquess jumped up. "I take it I am done here?"

That was it. Seven words, a question, indicated the gentleman, with his lack of a formal offer, was, in fact, no true gentleman. Instead of any deserved upset, an unlikely appreciation filled her at his unwillingness to bend to societal pressure. For to do so would only further ruin both of their lives. "There is to be no proposal, then?" she asked quietly.

Gabriel choked, sucking in great, gasping breaths. Color filled his cheeks. "Are y-you mad?" he managed to strangle out.

"It was merely an observation," she said between tense lips.

"I do not care *what* it is or was. Even if he offered, your answer is 'no,'" Gabriel barked.

Her sister-in-law glowered at her husband. "What your brother intended to say is that you needn't feel obligated to marry the gentleman simply because of the ensuing scandal. Isn't that correct?"

He shook his head. "No. What I was saying was precisely that. She is not marrying him." Gabriel jabbed a finger at an entirely too amused-looking Lord Tennyson. "Not to save her reputation. Not to fill his empty pockets. Not if God Himself demanded it." Her insufferable brother stalked across the room, towering over the still negligently seated marquess. "Have I made myself clear?" he seethed.

The marquess stifled a yawn with his spare hand. "Go to hell, Waverly. You are as tedious now as you were as a boy with your head in your books at Oxford." Gabriel's nostrils flared. "It is a wonder this one," Lord Tennyson tipped his head in Chloe's direction, "has the spirit she does."

"No offer was made," Chloe bit out, and the two men going toe-to-toe looked to her. "And nothing was accepted."

Not even in this, her public scandal, would she be permitted to speak with her partner in ruin. Every single aspect of her life—as a girl hiding from a daily beating, to this moment nearly five and twenty years later as a grown woman—had been controlled.

Lord Tennyson adjusted his expertly knotted silk cravat. "My lady, marriage to me would be even more ruinous to you than anything that could have taken place here." Gabriel took a swift step forward. "But nothing did," he hurried to add, holding his palms up. "As such, I trust our exchange is concluded. I shall leave your family to your discussion." With that, Lord Tennyson left.

The click of the door and the distant fall of his steps ushered in a thick silence.

Gabriel was the first to break it. "Bloody hell, Chloe," he barked, dragging a hand through his always immaculate hair. "What have you done?"

"Gabriel," Jane chided.

Husband and wife launched into a tense debate on where proper blame fell. And yet…

Chloe stared blankly at the earl's office door, through which Lord Tennyson had just taken his leave. Mayhap it was the shock of the evening, or that the realization of all that unfolded would come on the morrow with the gossip columns, for it was not worry over the impending scandal that held her frozen, but rather her brother's charge.

What have you done, you stupid chit? Present your back for a proper punishment…

A dutiful daughter. That was what the late, dastardly marquess had expected and had attempted to achieve by beating her into submission. And though her brother never had, nor ever would, lift a hand to her in violence, Gabriel, in his quest to have her be a biddable wife to a respectable lord, was not, in that regard, unlike their late sire.

"She is ruined, and by the blackest cad in London…" His lamentations slashed across her silent musings, a confirmation of sorts.

Yes, there could be no doubting that there wasn't a more sinister scoundrel in all of London.

Chloe released a beleaguered sigh. "It is done, Gabriel," she said tiredly. All of it. Her hopes. Her dreams. Because, although it did not matter that her ruin would kill all marital prospects, her reputation was firmly attached to any future aspiration she'd had… or might one day have.

She briefly closed her eyes, wanting to flee. To put this room and this night behind her. For the scandal with Lord Tennyson had destroyed every hope she'd carried, in ways that Jane's rational rejection never could have.

"Your sister is correct." Jane reached down for Chloe's hand and squeezed her fingers, and Chloe took some solace in that. "Nothing can be accomplished by sitting here, discussing… what transpired."

God love her sister-in-law for always having been practical—even in this.

Gabriel gave a jerky nod. The column of his throat moved in a tangible sign of his grief. That uncharacteristic crack in his composure sharpened the ache in her chest. "You are not marrying him."

And for the hell of the past handful of moments, Chloe's lips tipped up in a wry smile. "As Lord Tennyson didn't so much as ask, then I think that is not a worry for you."

Her brother took a step closer. "No," he said, shaking his head. "Even if he did, I want you to know I would never, ever let you marry a man such as him."

Never, ever let you marry.

When most other noblemen would force a sister into a match to salvage a shattered reputation, Gabriel sought to protect her.

Help me… please… help me…

Her cries of long ago filled her mind.

And there was surely a deficit in her character, for his brotherly showing left a bitter taste in her mouth. He was more than twenty years too late in protecting her. She'd needed him as a girl.

Now she'd have control of her own future where she could. Chloe lifted her chin. "Gabriel, I am a woman of five and twenty. I'll not be bullied into marriage or any other decision by Society…" She held his stare. "Or anyone."

Not that an unconscionable rake such as Lord Tennyson would ever seek marriage, as her brother feared.

And she was better off for it.

CHAPTER 6

LEO HAD BELIEVED HIMSELF LONG past feeling fear, and yet, hurrying down the pavement to his uncle's townhouse, his breath came in quick, frantic spurts.

I am ruined… ruined… ruined…

The irony of that litany rolled around his panicky mind. It was not lost on him that he, who'd despoiled an innocent and seduced countless other women, should find himself suffering an ignoble fate that would break him in ways other men had only tried.

Great, heaving gasps at odds with the impressive façade he'd put on display for his host, Lady Chloe Edgerton, and a room full of witnesses filtered past his lips.

Why in the blazes had he gone back to help her? Why? It hadn't mattered that she was struggling or on the floor or against a wall. It had only mattered that he'd secured the information he'd needed from Waterson's library and done so largely escaping notice. He'd not only jeopardized his career, but also the mission he'd undertaken.

It was the first slip in his character and in his role as an agent.

If it hadn't been for the golden-haired spitfire with lush lips and a fearlessness that had given him pause, he'd be returning home with the information that he had needed.

And now my career is forfeit.

A growl worked its way up his throat.

It had been a sincerely honest chivalrous act, not, as the gathering believed, meant to seduce or debauch.

His cloak snapping about his legs, Leo sprinted up the handful of steps and pounded on the black door.

Mayhap there was something that could be done. After all, it could have been a great deal worse. He could have been found with Rowley's wife. This was Lady Chloe Edgerton, simply a lady on the verge of spinsterhood, who'd turned her ankle.

Though, there wasn't a thing spinsterish about the golden-haired beauty.

With a groan, he knocked again. Yes, he was a rake. His life and career were in possible shambles, and here he stood recalling the feel of Lady Chloe in his arms.

Frantic, Leo rapped all the harder. Where in the blazes was—?

The door opened, and by the placidness of Parsons' expression, Leo might as well have been paying a social call in the fashionable hours and not pounding to knock down his uncle's damned door in the middle of the night.

Uninvited, he swept past the older man. "Where is he?" he demanded.

"His Grace is in his off—"

The servant's words trailing after him, Leo started at a brisk clip down the hall.

Never before had Leo put a favor to his uncle, but this night he would. If anyone could reason with the leadership of the Brethren, it was his uncle. Storming through the corridors, he reached the duke's office. Not bothering with the pleasantries of a knock, he grabbed the handle and let himself in. "I need help," he said without preamble. "I—"

The pair with their backs to him, heads bent over the desk, brought Leo's words to an immediate stop.

His aunt spun about. "Leo," she greeted warmly in her singsong voice.

Any other duchess would have balked at greeting anyone, rapscallion nephew or polite lord or lady, in her modest wrapper and night shift. Lady Aubrey sailed over, hands outstretched.

He forced a grin. "Your Grace, as beautiful as ever." Married when Leo had been just a boy, after the duke's first wife was tragically murdered by an enemy of the state, the second Duchess of Aubrey had the same vivaciousness of those years past.

The duchess snorted. "Your Grace?"

"Aunt Elsie," he amended.

Releasing his palms, she hurried to close the door. "I learned long ago that any visitor to arrive after midnight can only represent trouble. And when it is my rogue of a nephew... who hasn't even bothered to shed his cloak? Doubly so."

Leo followed her gaze to the layered wool cloak he still wore. With numb fingers, he fiddled with the clasp and shrugged out of the garment.

"Now," his aunt started. Taking the cloak from him, she folded it over her arm. "Why don't you tell us what's sent you here so frantic?" A slip of a woman at barely five feet, the duke's diminutive wife had all the markings of a great field commander.

His uncle lifted an ivory sheet of vellum. "I gather your late-night arrival is a product of this urgent note I received from Higgins."

Stalking across the room, he took the page from the duke's fingers.

Leo scraped his gaze over the words there.

> Your Grace,
>
> There is a matter of urgency that requires an immediate meeting. It is in reference to the most recent discussed business. Please send word as to when you have time to meet with Rowley and myself.
>
> ~Higgins

"Nothing good is ever behind late-night appointments," his uncle put in.

No, there wasn't. His stomach sank. Gossip moved faster than a conflagration through a dry field. Absent of his usual flippant reply, he stared blankly at the inked words that marked the beginning of the end of his work.

The duke looked past his shoulder. "Will you allow us a moment, my love?"

Setting Leo's cloak on the nearby sofa, the duchess swept over. Leaning up on her tiptoes, she brushed her mouth over her husband's. The happy-after-all-these-years couple's soft exchange carried over to Leo's ears. "Do go gentle on him," she whispered, tugging at his shirtfront. "You were once very much like him."

"And you loved me for it," his uncle murmured, dropping a kiss on her mouth.

"I loved you more when you were reformed," she said dryly.

Disquieted by the intimate display, Leo looked away while husband and wife continued their hushed discussion.

His own parents had hated each other with a vicious ferocity. Even having witnessed the closeness between his aunt and uncle, he'd never been comfortable with those tender exchanges. *Love* had destroyed his mother and, as such, he'd be a fool to ever trust himself to any weakening emotion. His work had given him strength and made him immune to those sentiments.

And now I've lost it all...

His fingers tightened reflexively about the page in his hand, wrinkling Higgins' note at the corner.

"Leo." He snapped his head up as his aunt came over to buss him on the cheek. "Listen to your uncle," she murmured with far more affection than he'd ever deserved. "His advice is *usually* sound." She shot a wink in her husband's direction.

"Aunt Elsie."

As soon as she had gone, the duke marched over to the sideboard. Grabbing a snifter, he poured two glasses. The clink of crystal touching crystal and the steady stream of liquid, usually calming, had no effect.

"Here," his uncle said gruffly, with one glass extended.

"I thought you did not approve of my drinking," he challenged, accepting the offering.

"I do not approve of your overindulging. But there are times that call for spirits. I suspect this is one?"

With shaking fingers, Leo set down his untouched brandy.

His uncle paused, giving him a cursory search. "That bad?"

Leo swiped his hands over his face. "Worse," he muttered. He swiftly dropped his arms back to his sides. "But only because of appearances," he began, going on the immediate defensive.

"And we both know from," the duke gave him a pointed look, "our experience that appearances are oftentimes all that matter."

It was the first lesson given to him when he'd been presented by his uncle to the then leader of the organization. They'd enlisted Leo's services on behalf of the Crown when he was a pup at university, tasking him with the role of dissolute rake. How effortlessly he'd filled it. But then, he'd always been black to the core.

A hoarse chuckle pulled from his throat. How miserably full circle his life had come.

The duke motioned to the leather sofa. "Is there something amusing in all of this? If so, I'd prefer we begin there."

Claiming the chair opposite his uncle, Leo leaned forward, his palms up. "I was caught in a compromising position this evening," he said without preamble. Hardly the first time.

It was a testament to Leo's rottenness that his admission earned not even a slight crack in his uncle's stony countenance. "A lady?" the duke put to him in guarded tones.

"An innocent one." With a silken expanse of thigh he'd have liked to continue exploring. Leo winced. "I was exiting Lord Waterson's office with the information on his upcoming meeting schedules and found her in the hall."

A vein pulsed at the corner of his uncle's eye. "You were caught," he said bluntly.

"I was *nearly* caught," he felt compelled to point out. "The lady injured herself." Leo proceeded through a quick account of the damning event. He took particular care to omit the fact that he'd very nearly had the lady's mouth under his... or that, with his world ratcheting down about him, he hungered for a taste of her, still.

When he'd finished, his uncle frowned. Saying nothing for a long while, he sipped at his drink. "You returned to help the lady, then?"

He nodded once. "Yes," he said tightly. He braced for a stream of questions about the out-of-character move on his part... that did not come.

His uncle finished his drink. "Who was the lady?"

"Lady Chloe Edgerton."

Whether the duke knew anything of or about the spirited minx, he gave no outward indication. Questions—irrelevant ones—hovered on Leo's lips about the lady's identity. How did a woman with her generous hips and luminescent blue eyes come to be unwed after six Seasons? But then, no one ever said members of the peerage had brains betwixt their ears.

With a resigned sigh that sent Leo's panic spiraling, his uncle set aside his glass. "Higgins was clear."

"It was not my fault," Leo barked, jumping up, hating the child-ishness of his rebuttal.

"You've ruined a young lady's reputation, Leo," the duke chided. "What do you *think* Higgins will say, given his warnings earlier today?"

He gnashed his teeth. "And this from the same men who tasked me with leading a life of debauchery?"

All the color leached from his uncle's cheeks.

Leo slammed a fist into his open palm. "You and Higgins and Rowley, you all lecture me for the life I've lived." Mindful that even as the duke's servants were mostly former members of the Brethren, privacy was sacrosanct, he dropped his voice to a furi-ous whisper. "The truth is, you encouraged my lifestyle, and now you'll play the roles of offended, proper gentlemen, disgusted with what I am?" It was what he'd always been. His father had seen the blackness in his soul.

His uncle climbed to his feet. "I'll not debate morality with you, Leo. I ceased trying long ago."

Leo had spent his life believing himself immune to the world's ill opinion. So why did his neck go hot at the resignation in his uncle's tone?

"There is the matter of the ruined lady." And with that pro-nouncement, the duke started for his desk.

Briefly motionless, Leo jumped into movement. He positioned himself in front of his uncle, halting him in his tracks. "Th-the ruined lady?" he sputtered. "What of my bloody career?"

Smiling sadly, his uncle caught his right shoulder. "Since you were trained in your role, I marveled at you, Leo. How could the book-minded boy I'd so loved, with an impish grin and infectious spirit, so artfully don the façade you did? How did the world not see it?" he pondered, more to himself. "As your uncle, I was proud. As a former agent, with a not dissimilar role, I was in awe. But somewhere along the way, Leo, you *became* that man." A paroxysm contorted the duke's rugged features, with the faintest wrinkles beginning to appear as a mark to his age. "Until I no longer recog-nized you." Giving his shoulder a light squeeze, his uncle released him. The duke stepped around Leo, moved behind his desk, and sat.

There was an air of finality, a resignation, that held Leo frozen to the floor, incapable of movement.

The duke drew open his desk drawer and, taking out a piece of paper, reached for his pen.

"What are you doing?" Leo whispered in awed disbelief.

The rhythmic tick of the pen striking the desk was inordinately loud. "Arranging the meeting with Higgins," his uncle directed at the page.

After all his service, after every brush with death and valuable piece of information gathered, they'd all—his uncle included—simply wash their proverbial hands of him. He shook his head to clear the buzzing in his ears. "That is all you'd say?"

His uncle paused, the tip of his pen poised above the inkwell. "What would you have me say, Leo?" he asked impatiently, again putting words to that damned page. "I've stuck my neck out countless times, when every commanding officer reported to me that they were worried that you'd gone too far with your persona. They were right."

They were right.

His uncle finished writing and then set his pen down.

Jerking into movement, Leo lunged several steps. "I have never asked you to help me." Not once when he'd lain bleeding with bruised ribs from a well-placed kick by his father. Not when he'd been locked away without food or water. The offer of work with the Crown had come at his uncle's request. "Now I am. Help me." A worthless bounder without any good in his soul, he was not too proud to plead for this… only this.

"I cannot, Leo," his uncle said matter-of-factly, sprinkling pounce upon the ink. He blew lightly at that page. "You are my nephew… my godson, but I still have respect for the organization. Higgins was clear."

Leo's throat closed tightly as he struggled to breathe. *What am I without the Brethren?* He was nothing. He was every last useless rake who'd die one day from too much drink, or with a bullet in his head from some irate husband.

The duke folded the sheet, and as he reached for his lion seal, the mark of the Brethren, another desperate entreaty pulled from Leo's lips. "There must be something. I cannot lose this," he said hoarsely as the older man stamped the page. "*Please.*"

It was that single utterance that gave his uncle pause. He set aside the seal, saying nothing.

His legs giving out under him, Leo sank onto the edge of the leather chair.

Steepling his fingertips, the duke drummed them together, staring over their tops at Leo. "I don't know, Leo…"

"Please," he repeated. "I am close to solving the Cato Street Conspiracy. There is still much work for me to do. I do not want to be done with the organization." Where other members married and retired, Leo had been wedded only to the organization. It had earned a fealty and loyalty Leo was incapable of giving to any woman as his uncle had.

His uncle ceased that silent tapping. "What you're asking me… is out of my hands."

"Fine." Leo scrambled forward and gripped the edge of the mahogany desk. "Then tell me how I can fix this."

A long wisp of air sailed past his uncle's lips. "I do not know that you can, Leo." He went silent, his high, noble brow wrinkling as he thought.

"What?" Leo demanded, searching his eyes over his uncle's face.

"It is possible that it would change nothing—"

"What?" he cut in. He'd sold every corner of his soul over the past twelve years. There was certainly nothing he was not immune to trying if it would benefit him or the Crown.

"You can marry the lady."

Except *that*.

He was immune to trying *that*.

Leo sank back in his chair. "You are mad," he breathed.

"Am I?" His uncle arched a single brow. Then, lifting one finger at a time, he ticked off his points. "You were ordered to maintain some degree of respectability. A wife, a proper lady," he amended, "will afford you that. Marriage will preserve her reputation."

Marriage to Lady Chloe Edgerton. He let his mind wander to thoughts of the delectable minx, in his bed, under him. Desire surged through him.

And then the implications of the only arrangement that would see her in his bed.

"Is this some joke?" he snapped. "I'm fighting for my damned career and—"

"This is no jest, Leo. You were ordered to be respectable. And in less than twelve hours of receiving that command, you failed. Now, the way I see it," his uncle went on, "you're left with one of two decisions: accept being turned out of the Brethren, or…" Leo's palms went moist, and his throat tightened in preparation for that dangling thought. "You convince the world that you're madly in love with this now-ruined young woman and make yourself finally respectable."

Convince the world? He'd have to begin by persuading the lady that there was an ounce of respectability in him and that he'd been wholly transformed by their stolen exchange. As soon as the thought slid in, he discarded it. "Society," his superiors included, "will believe it was for her dowry."

His uncle grinned. "Then you must make them believe it is not."

Leo had a greater likelihood of sprouting wings and flying himself across the Thames. Prior to this moment, he'd expressed public interest in not one lady's dowry… but two. It didn't matter his reasons for either… it mattered what the world thought they knew.

"What is it?" his uncle encouraged.

"The lady would never believe it." Where most innocent debutantes and ladies on the verge of spinsterhood would leap at the prospect, built even on a lie of instant love, Lady Chloe Edgerton could never be that woman. "She is far too clever to believe *that* lie," he finally said, resigned.

His uncle's broad shoulders shook with the force of his mirth.

"I am so very happy that you find some amusement in all of this," Leo snapped.

"Oh, Leo. I wasn't suggesting you *deceive* the lady."

Leo frowned. "Then what in hell were you suggesting?" What *was* he still suggesting?

"You require something from the lady. Respectability. And she needs…" The duke nodded his head expectantly.

Leo shook his in reply. "I've no bloody idea." The only things he could speak to with a certainty where women were concerned was how to make them scream their release to the heavens. How to understand them? Their wants… their desires outside of bed? "It'd be simpler to bring down a plot to overthrow the king than sort out what she," or any lady, "*desires*."

Releasing another sigh, his uncle dropped his elbows on the

desk, framing that hated note between his arms. "You've wheedled secrets and confessions out of some of the most ruthless black-guards the world's seen. I trust that you can convince a ruined woman that there are some benefits to marriage to you."

"None," he said bluntly. "There is nothing she can gain being married to me."

The lady's bore of a brother had seen it. And the lady herself had, too.

His uncle snorted. "Then I suggest you find something… before my meeting tomorrow with Higgins." He shoved back in his seat, his earlier mask of seriousness restored. "At best, I can buy you a day before you're summoned."

"Summoned and then sacked," Leo muttered. That was the fate awaiting him and hung unfinished but clear in his uncle's promise.

"Not necessarily," Uncle William interjected.

His ears pricked up. "What?" he asked, unable to keep the hope from his voice.

"If I can make a case of your shifting to respectable lord, you can infiltrate unreachable, until now, circles of Society." Uncle William paused, and his meaning sank slowly into Leo's head.

"Waterson," he said with quiet understanding.

The older man nodded. "Precisely."

Leo's mind raced. Of course. Why had he not considered it? The same way he'd been tasked with pursuing the respectable Miss Justina Barrett to ferret out any possible connections between her family and the Cato plot was the same way ties to Chloe Edgerton and her family could link him to Waterson—and other Whig members who'd fanatically supported the Six Acts.

His uncle grinned. "All you need do is…"

"Make a bid at respectability," he finished for the other man. Leo glanced past the duke's shoulder to the enamel bronze clock. One o'clock.

He had, at best, seven hours before Higgins and Rowley arrived to meet with his uncle. That requested meeting had been given solely as a courtesy for the Duke of Aubrey's years of service, and his relationship to Leo.

"What will it be, Leo?" his uncle pressured.

Christ in hell.

Exploding to his feet, he stomped over and grabbed his cloak.

"I'll marry the damned chit," he snapped. Dragging the garment around his shoulders, he fastened it at the throat.

"Ahh." Uncle William waggled his eyebrows. "There is still the matter of convincing her. Something tells me you are going to be needing her assent before you secure yourself a bride. Come and see me after your… meeting."

With the duke's laughter trailing after him, Leo stormed from the room.

CHAPTER 7

ANY OTHER LADY WOULD BE softly weeping at the state Chloe found herself in following Lord Waterson's ball.

All of Society was talking. The front page of every gossip column she'd demanded sent to her rooms contained her name splashed across the center.

According to the Gothic tales her sister and mother had so loved over the years and that Chloe had frequently stolen, Chloe should no doubt be self-pitying and bemoaning the uncertain future that awaited her.

Instead, the following afternoon, with her leg propped above her heart, and staring up at the ceiling, she could fix on only one staggering realization—the headaches had not come.

Every time her late father's cruelty haunted her thoughts, she would suffer from megrims. But when the thoughts arose last night and sent her fleeing through Lord Waterson's home, the inevitable result, a debilitating headache, did not happen.

A giddiness filled her. For all the ways she'd craved control of her life, she'd been singularly lacking in this most simple way—over her megrims. They had the power to cripple her, silencing her so that nothing but darkness and quiet brought an uneasy solace.

Staring at the cherubs frolicking in the mural overhead, Chloe chewed contemplatively at her lower lip.

How to account for the demons this time remaining at bay?

She grinned wryly. "Because you were ruined, and that is distraction enough for any lady."

Yet, as she'd long been truthful, especially to herself, she recognized the lie there.

The Marquess of Tennyson had singlehandedly diverted her thoughts since the moment he'd come upon her sprawled in Lord Waterson's corridor. He was a nasty man. Uncouth, improper. A lecher that any lady, proper or improper, would be well advised to steer clear of.

There had been, however, a raw sincerity to him. It was as though he'd proudly shed the respectable, honorable replies and expectations of the *ton* and lived without regard for anyone's opinion but his own.

And if he weren't such a lascivious bastard with dishonorable intentions, it was a way to go through the world…

Worry crowded out any further thought of the marquess.

How was she to go through the world? Oh, she had never given a jot about Society's opinions or gossip. But as Jane had accurately pointed out, the options that existed for a lady outside of marriage were few and far between.

Those options were even less when a lady was found as Chloe had been, in a compromising position with Society's most notorious rake.

Polite Society wouldn't care that Lord Tennyson had been carrying her simply because of her injured ankle. In their judgmental world, appearances mattered more than reality. And with a room full of witnesses, the sight of Chloe with the marquess bent over her was all they'd needed to see to form an opinion on just what had been occurring in Lord Waterson's office.

Nothing untoward *had* happened.

Unbidden, her gaze went to her injured ankle. She moved her stare slowly over her leg, recalling Lord Tennyson's forbidden touch, the hard weight of his long fingers as he'd moved them from her stockinged foot up her thigh.

Her breath caught even as her skin burned in remembrance of that stolen caress. In that instance, there had been no cloying fear or panic, just a wild thrill unlike any she'd ever known… unlike any she would ever know again.

A sound of disgust escaped her, and she tossed her arms wide. And that was why rakes were to be avoided. At all costs. For she well knew that men could not be trusted when it came to desire or lust or any other sentiment in between. They were volatile, ruthless bastards who could shake a gentleman's hand with one palm and beat one's daughters with the other.

Yes, Chloe could separate the thrilling feel of Lord Tennyson's expert touch from the man he truly was. One who'd freely use the word *tup* with a stranger, all the while unable to recall the women he'd bedded. "Shameful," she muttered.

"With such a statement, should I ask, 'What?' Or, 'Who?'"

Chloe gasped at the unexpectedness of her sister-in-law's droll query. Standing in the open doorway, a small silver tray in hand, Jane offered a gentle smile. "Forgive me. I should have knocked." Entering the room, in more command than the queen, Jane shoved the door closed with the heel of her slipper and started over. Resting the pot of tea and pastries on the nightstand by Chloe's bed, she perched on the edge. "Well?" she drawled.

So she had no intention of abandoning her earlier question that hadn't really been a question.

"Jane," she greeted, struggling up onto her elbows. "I... I..." Oh, God in heaven. *I was... woolgathering.* Choking on her swallow, she studiously avoided Jane's eyes. Her stare snagged on the mound of papers next to her. "The gossip," she finally settled for, lamely. "I was referring to... the gossip."

Because, in fairness, it truly was shameful the words being written about her and the marquess... and the two of them together.

Color fired in her cheeks.

"Here," Jane murmured, pouring Chloe a cup of tea.

Accepting that proffered drink, she sipped at the lukewarm brew. "How is he?" she forced herself to ask after she'd swallowed.

Her sister-in-law managed a strained smile. "How do you believe he is?" Jane countered, not pretending to misunderstand.

"Angry," Chloe said automatically. Knowing her brother as she did, and his devotion to respectability and their family's name, she knew he'd no doubt still be riddled with rage the morning after. Where her brother Alex had been a rogue who'd flouted societal conventions, Gabriel had adhered to them. He'd not lost that, even in his marriage to Jane.

Jane prepared herself a cup of tea. "Yes. He is furious." She paused midpour and held Chloe's gaze. "But not with you."

Chloe shot her sister-in-law an incredulous look. "He did not say a word the entire carriage ride home." That thirty-minute ride might as well have been thirty years, as interminable as it had been. The journey they'd made from Lord Waterson's home to their own had been exhausting in its silence. "Nor did he say a word upon our return, or this morning."

The other woman wrinkled her nose. "Oh, very well. He is slightly displeased that you were sneaking off because of... of... the circumstances." Jane's teacup shook, and the always indomitable woman stared with agonized eyes down at the contents. "It is my fault," she whispered. "I shredded your hem—"

"Do not do that," Chloe demanded, setting down her glass. "Do not take on blame for my actions last evening. I wanted nothing to do with Gabriel's machinations, and you spared me. I made the mistake of being caught in..." *Lord Tennyson's arms.*

Powerful ones, with corded biceps and not at all the soft ones she'd expected of an indolent lord.

She blinked slowly. Where in the blazes had that come from?

"He is outraged with Lord Tennyson," Jane went on, thankfully yanking Chloe from the confusion of those musings.

Outraged. She sat up slowly. "He is not thinking of dueling him." Her fingers curled tight into the white satin coverlet.

Jane's silence served as her answer.

"By God, I'll retrieve his own damned pistol and properly place a ball in him before I let him put on that display for Society. Nothing happened, Jane," she said for surely the hundredth time since the discovery. "How many more times must I tell people that?"

Her sister-in-law eyed her thoughtfully for a moment. "There was an intimacy to your positioning."

"Because he carried me into the room," Chloe exploded in exasperation.

"His lips were very near your own," her sister-in-law said gently, her words stripped of judgment.

Jane had seen that, then. Which meant her brother and Lord Waterson and that harpy who'd gleefully spread the scandal around the earl's ballroom had also seen.

"You have gone quiet," Jane somberly observed.

"Lord Tennyson is a rake. But even as his reputation is black, he did not kiss me." Had the room not been crowded by witnesses of her ruin, he would have. Having never known a man's embrace, or so much as a stolen kiss from a bold stable hand or village boy, even Chloe knew that. A little fluttering unfurled in her belly. She rubbed her hands over her face. "What has Gabriel said?" she forced herself to ask.

"He would never urge you to marry a man because of a scandal," Jane needlessly assured. "He is…" She promptly closed her lips.

Narrowing her eyes, Chloe sat all the straighter. "He is *what*?" she demanded as her sister-in-law avoided her questioning stare.

"Gabriel invited Lord Waterson to speak later this afternoon."

Warning bells went off. "To speak?" Then the air left her on a whispery exhale. "My God, he is attempting to coordinate a match between me and the earl." Again. Only this time, of a different sort of desperation.

Jane's silence served as confirmation.

"No," she said, swinging her legs over the side of the bed. She winced at the sharp throb of pain from that sudden movement.

Ignoring her sister-in-law's protestations, Chloe grabbed the cane propped alongside her nightstand and propelled herself into an upright position.

Panting from the exertions, Chloe started for the pink upholstered window seat.

"His lordship offered for you."

Chloe stumbled, quickly catching herself with her cane.

"Chloe?" Her sister-in-law rushed over.

"I am fine." She stared forward at the pink and white tasseled curtains, lost in her thoughts.

As exceedingly proud and unforgivably proper as she was— just as her late father had been—her life would be as tedious as the current Dowager Countess of Waverly if she wed the Earl of Waterson. She'd vowed long ago never to become her mother, and she'd not compromise to appease her brother's sensibilities. Chloe set her jaw. "I am not marrying the Earl of Waterson," she announced, resuming her slow path forward.

Jane fell into step beside her, hands clasped before her, all the blood drained from her knuckles. "Lord Waterson spoke to Gabriel and offered to marry you to save your reputation."

It was a generous offer from a man who, despite his friendship with her brother, had never truly seen her. And yet, she had
seen *him* through the years. Lord Waterson, not unlike Gabriel, had
visions and views and expectations for the woman who'd one day
be his wife. Registering Jane's silence, she looked to her sister-in-
law. "You think I should marry him?"

Color flooded the other woman's cheeks. "I did not say that."

"You did not need to," she softly rejoined. "Your thoughts are
all there in your eyes." That swift kick of betrayal knocked the
air from Chloe's lungs. Jane, who'd opened Chloe's eyes to Mary
Wollstonecraft and the possibility of independence, would now
waver where Chloe's future was concerned.

Her sister-in-law studied her palms a moment. "I do not know
what the answer is. I was certain I knew what I needed and wanted,
and that was a finishing school. And it certainly was not a husband.
But I was ruined, too... and Gabriel and I... we were thrown
together. I've more happiness now than I ever knew was possible."

Chloe would not point out that Jane had not been ruined by
a stranger as Chloe had. Jane had been ruined by her employer,
with whom she'd lived for a number of weeks before their scandal. She tipped her chin up. "I'll ask you this, and this only...
Do you believe Lord Waterson is a man who would ever support
my opening an establishment as you have done? Is he someone
who'd allow me my dreams?" Or was he someone who wanted a
biddable wife and hostess? "I did not think so," she added when
her sister-in-law still did not speak. "Please tell Gabriel to express
my gratitude, but I'll not marry anyone simply because I've been
ruined." He'd still not accepted that Chloe wanted mastery of her
future and certainly wouldn't entrust herself in body, name, and
soul to a man who'd crafted and then voted on legislation to strip
people of their voices.

Marriage to Lord Waterson would earn her nothing but a
respectable match and an empty future. Chloe had always wanted,
and would always want, more.

Limping the remaining way to the window seat, Chloe balanced
herself on the silver-knobbed cane and struggled to open the curtains.

Jane was instantly at her side. "Here," she murmured, drawing the
ornate, white lace through the quartet tieback. Sunlight streamed

through the glass panels and bathed Chloe's face in a soft, calming warmth. Her sister-in-law helped her into the seat. Then, rushing across the room, she fetched the two pillows at the foot of Chloe's bed. Returning, she knelt and gently adjusted them under Chloe's injured ankle in a loving display that most proper ladies would cede to a maid or nurse.

"Thank you, Jane," she said softly. Jane truly loved Chloe like a sister. And with her talk of Lord Waterson, she sought only to look after Gabriel's sister. Chloe had gone through the earliest years of her life without even a sibling to stand up to their father for her, so that showing sent warmth to her heart.

Tears welled behind Jane's lashes in a rare display of emotion, and she angrily swiped at them. "I just want you to be happy." The words came as though ripped from her. "I wanted... hoped that you would find love, as I did, and as your siblings have." She lifted pained eyes to Chloe's. "I should have given you that post as you wished."

Chloe started to protest, but her sister-in-law shoved to her feet. "I should have. Because n-now..." Jane's voice broke.

"Because now no one would accept an unwed lady mired in scandal as a headmistress," Chloe gently finished.

Grief contorted the other woman's features.

Chloe was not, nor would ever be, the type of woman who placed blame for her failings or mistakes on another. *She* had rushed away from the ballroom. *She* had allowed the Marquess of Tennyson to help her into Lord Waterson's office. The mistakes of that night lay solely with Chloe. "The day you arrived as my companion, Jane," she quietly began, "I was so determined to turn you out. The last thing I desired was a stern companion sent to me by the headmistress of my former finishing school. But then you opened my eyes to the world in a whole new way. You made me question and dream for more." Jane looked up. "That is because of you."

Someone knocked.

A moment later, a maid ducked her head inside. "His lordship asked to speak with you, my lady."

So Gabriel would press Jane. Her sister-in-law rose. "Please tell him I'll be along shortly."

The young woman rushed off, leaving Chloe and Jane alone

once more. "I will speak to your brother."

Chloe offered her a reassuring smile. "Jane," she called after her sister-in-law, staying her when she'd reached the door. "Thank you."

Gabriel's wife gave a dismissive wave. "Do not thank me." She lingered. "I would be remiss if I did not point out that there will be no offer from the gentleman who ruined you. Your only offer is from the earl."

She inclined her head in concurrence. "It would, however, be unfair to both Lord Waterson and me to marry under these," or any, "circumstances."

A twinkle lit Jane's pretty eyes. "I agree. But your brother pleaded with me to make that point."

After her sister-in-law had taken her leave, Chloe's smile fell. The implications settled around her mind in a way that made them real, when before they'd been only nebulous.

I am ruined.

Her name destroyed and, with it, her respectability. There could be no post of governess or finishing school headmistress or instructor. She would simply find herself a woman who'd long be remembered for what transpired that night—and live off the generous dowry bestowed upon her by her late aunt. She could travel and devote her time to charitable causes and...

She knocked the back of her head against the wall.

And none of it was what she'd wished for. She'd longed to educate young ladies to use their minds and speak freely. Whether she liked it or not, Society dictated that marriage meant respectability. Though, as her sister-in-law had aptly reminded, there would be no offer of marriage from the Marquess of Tennyson.

Chloe stared down at the streets below and froze.

A tall, familiar, and wholly unexpected figure handed off the reins of his mount to a nearby street lad.

She was merely imagining him. Chloe scrubbed at her eyes. Yes, it was fatigue, or mayhap all the talk of him that day. For there could be no other accounting for the Marquess of Tennyson's presence on the pavement below. She dropped her hand, again looking down, just as Lord Tennyson bounded up the steps of her family's townhouse.

Chloe cocked her head.

Her sister-in-law had pointed out, at Gabriel's request, that there would be no formal offer made by the Marquess of Tennyson.

Yet… if that were the case… why was the gentleman bounding up the steps with a bouquet of hothouse flowers in his hand?

CHAPTER 8

IN TWELVE YEARS, LEO HAD never failed on a mission.

For all his failings as a man, he was skilled in the ways that mattered most—in the work he did for the Brethren.

Until now. Despite his uncle's confidence in Leo's abilities, Leo was not so proud that he didn't recognize his many failings and his likelihood of failing… in this.

With passersby stopping to blatantly stare, Leo sprinted up the Marquess of Waverly's steps and knocked several times.

And waited.

The way Leo saw it, after assessing the situation, the end result might play out one of two ways. Either the proper, stodgy bore of a marquess knew the precariousness of his sister's fate and encouraged the suit, or he tossed Leo out on his arse without so much as a meeting.

Which was all fine and well. It wasn't an appointment with the marquess that Leo sought, but rather the spitfire who'd single-handedly compromised his reputation.

He gave his head a wry shake at the irony of that.

No, she was the one person whose assistance he needed to enlist, and whose opinion he had to sway.

Sighing, he tapped the hothouse flowers against his leg. Perhaps the Edgertons had retreated to the country to brave the scandal there. That would certainly complicate matters, but it still would not account for a servant not opening the door, at the very least.

Frustration running through him, he knocked again, harder and sharper.

And when nothing but silence served as his greeting, the truth hit him.

Why… why… Waverly had no intention of granting an audience.

He glanced up.

Lady Chloe Edgerton sat framed in the window. Where a lady ruined not even twelve hours ago would have curtains drawn and remain out of Society's sight, she sat, staring boldly down at him. Even with the thirty feet between them, he could see suspicion better suited to an aged matron shining in the lady's revealing blue eyes.

Yes, clever lady indeed.

Raising his forearm over his brow to shield the bright morn sunlight, he lifted his other in salute, waving with the hothouse offering.

Lady Chloe narrowed her gaze.

Several rose petals rained down, and he swatted them from his face, sputtering as one landed on his lips.

As he looked up at the lady this time, a small smile tugged at her lips. Not the coy, tempting ones he'd come to expect from the ladies he bedded or seduced, but an innocent expression of unapologetic mirth. One that served as a stark reminder of just how very different she was. Whereas he? He'd never been pure or innocent in any way.

And if he successfully carried out the plan his uncle had given him, Leo would find himself married to the innocent lady. Forever. Until death did part them. With the enemies he'd acquired through his role for the Crown and the irate husbands he'd left in his wake, it would likely be sooner rather than later.

Sweat beaded his brow.

You do not have to do this…

Marriage… and to a lady, no less.

Leo shot a glance back to the boy holding the reins of his mount, his feet twitching with the urge to flee.

And then you will never work another mission… You'll never reach the leadership level your uncle did...

Society believed him worthless, and yet, if Leo did not have the Brethren, there'd be no point to his rotted existence...

Battling back the unfamiliar fear cloying at him, he faced the marquess' door once more.

He looked up to where Lady Chloe raptly studied him.

Leo turned his palms up and nudged his chin at the door. "Well?" he mouthed.

Matching his movements, she shook her head.

So the lady herself hadn't ordered he be turned away. Marking that as an encouraging sign, he flashed a crooked grin.

With a pointed look for the rapidly wilting flowers, she arched an eyebrow.

Following her stare, Leo swept his arms wide and offered a flourishing bow.

Lady Chloe rolled her eyes and, with a final wry grin, drew the lace curtains closed.

Well, that is hardly promising.

He beat the flowers against his opposite palm, sending more petals raining to the marquess' stone stoop. There had been only one woman he'd wooed. That had been a lifetime ago, back when he'd been on the road to blackening his soul even more. Now, his skill at charming a woman was relegated to acts of seduction, which he'd proven a master of. Frowning, Leo glanced up...

Lady Chloe's gaze collided with his.

That interest was certainly promising. He grinned.

She snapped the curtains closed once more.

Leo contemplated the glass panels from where the young woman had intermittently studied him. Mayhap she would prove more amenable to a match, after all. And yet, the ramifications of that hit him like a bullet he'd once taken through the shoulder. Leo's palms went moist, and he forced himself to return to the door. What other options did he have? He resumed his rapping.

Marriage. *Knock-knock-knock.*

To a proper lady. *Knock-knock-knock-knock.*

Mayhap there was another way. *Knock-knock-knock-knock.*

That his uncle hadn't thought of. *Knock-knock-knock-knock.*

And Higgins could be reasoned with, and Leo spared and—

The door was yanked open.

Hand suspended midrap, Leo stared back at the sullen butler. "His lordship isn't receiving," the older man snapped.

Having had many a door slammed in his face, Leo swiftly inserted his shoulder, preventing that panel from being shut. "I only require a few moments of the gentleman's time."

With a surprising strength, the servant shoved back. "His lordship does not *have* a few moments."

"Very well." At that capitulation, the butler relinquished his powerful hold. Pouncing, Leo pushed his way inside. "I require just a single moment, then," he corrected with a mocking grin.

A ruddy flush splotched the butler's cheeks, and he clapped his hands once.

Bloody hell.

Leo swiveled his head toward the pair of burly footmen fast approaching. Carefully keeping an eye on the three surly servants, Leo brandished a card. "Forgive me. It occurs you are unaware of who you are turning away."

The liveried footmen abruptly stopped. They glanced askance to the head of the household staff.

"I am the gentleman who ruined Lady Chloe Edgerton and request an—"

The pair of brutes surged forward.

Taking advantage of their carelessness, Leo rushed around them. With three bellowing servants racing after him, he sprinted down the closest corridor. "Waverly," he shouted as he went.

A lone maid dusting a gold-framed portrait took one look at the party charging toward her. With a screech, she ducked into the nearest room. The door slammed with a solid bang.

"Waverly," he boomed.

"My God, what is the meaning of this?"

The thunderous demand brought Leo to a staggering halt. He spun about.

The three servants, breathless from their exertions and chests heaving, came up quickly. Nostrils flared, his cheeks florid, Lord Waverly stalked forward.

His butler and footmen fell back, parting to allow him a direct path to Leo.

He dropped a bow. "Waverly," he called out jovially before the marquess could speak. "You've a rude-servant problem," he said drolly. The key to attaining the upper hand of a situation with anyone was to keep one's opponent unsettled.

Waverly scowled.

"I requested a meeting, and this one," he flicked his bouquet at the red-faced butler, "sought to deny my entrance."

"And so you invaded my home?"

Given that was precisely what Leo had done, he let his silence serve as his answer.

"I came to speak about the uh... *situation* with Lady Chloe. I would rather we speak in private." He shot a pointed glance past the marquess' shoulder. "But should you prefer we speak here?"

"I'd rather not speak at all." Lord Waverly turned toward his footmen.

The hulking figures resumed their forward trek to Leo. "We *are* speaking about the lady," he informed Waverly as he retreated. Careful to assess there were no servants coming from the opposite hall, he backed away. "Now, we might do it here or in your office. I prefer your office, given the gossip already circulating..." he dangled.

"Five minutes," the marquess snapped. Not bothering to see if Leo followed, Lord Waverly marched off.

With a smug grin for the snarling servants, Leo smoothed his lapels with one hand. Hothouse flowers in the other, he hurried to join Lady Chloe's brother.

As soon as they entered the marquess' office, Waverly shut the door firmly behind him. "Three minutes," he said, starting for his desk.

"I am here to present a formal offer of—"

The other man stumbled.

"—marriage to your sister," Leo finished anyway.

"No." Whipping back, nostrils again flaring, Lady Chloe's brother barked that one-word denial.

Tossing the hothouse arrangement down, Leo helped himself to one of the chairs in front of Waverly's desk. "The lady is ruined—ruined by me. As such—"

"No."

"It is the honorable thing to do, to spare the lady."

The marquess sneered. "*The lady* does not need an offer of marriage from *you*."

Leo would give credit where it was rightfully due. Waverly hurled that slightly emphasized word with an impressive modicum of viciousness. Leo stretched his legs out, looping them at the ankles in a feigned display of nonchalance. "Come, you are one who values Society's rules. You see there's no recourse to spare her reputation except marriage."

Waverly dropped his palms to the table and leaned forward. "You are a vile reprobate. A loathsome lecher, whose drinking, whoring, and wagering are the least of the crimes I expect you are guilty of."

"Well, *that* is an impressive read on your part," he drawled. "Mayhap I misjudged the depth of your keenness, after all."

The marquess stood. "Get the hell out of my office. We are done here." He scraped a hateful stare up and down Leo's person. "We were done before you even arrived."

Shifting in a seat he had no intention of abandoning, Leo settled in for the discussion. "Forgive me, I have not made myself clear. I merely sought to appeal to your gentlemanlike sensibilities. I am not making that formal offer to you."

Some of the tension left the other man's frame. "I did not think a rake would care whether he'd ruined—"

"I am presenting it to Chloe," he interrupted. The lady, a spitfire who'd challenged him boldly and hadn't dissolved into a puddle of piteous weeping, was not a woman who'd allow a bore like Waverly to decide any aspect of her life. He'd known that clearly even going into his meeting with the marquess.

Waverly went motionless, saying nothing for a long while. And then, "*Lady* Chloe."

"I know the lady. Spirited. Blonde hair. Trim waist. Large—"

Roaring, the marquess pounded his desk. One of those gossip pages jumped under the force of that thump and fell, fluttering in a whispery heap to the floor.

"Eyes," Leo said with a mocking half-grin. "I was going to say eyes. And here I'd believed you were a gentleman."

The marquess collapsed back in his chair. "My sister's reputation was left in tatters—*in tatters*," he repeated on a furious hiss. "And you come here with droll retorts. Nothing is sacred to you."

Leo kept his grin firmly fixed on his lips. Yes, Waverly would believe that. He would expect that Leo cared for nothing and no one. He wouldn't know that the reason he was able to sleep in

comfort without the worry of insurrection or conflict shattering
that calm was because of Leo's efforts for the country. Waverly
couldn't know that. No one could. And so Leo said nothing of it.
"I would like to request a meeting with your sister," he said quietly,
abandoning his previously blithe tones.

"I know your type," Waverly shot back, ice coating that insult.

"Do you?"

"Quite well." And here he'd taken the priggish Marquess of
Waverly as one who kept company only with equally tedious
lords. "You are heartless, incapable of feeling. Deadened inside... if
you ever had a heart that beat."

All true. That had been the gift his uncle and the Brethren had
bestowed—erasing the tears, fears, and feelings, so that only a shell
of a man remained. How much easier that emptiness was than the
misery he'd once endured.

"Nothing to say?" the marquess taunted.

The lady's brother was spoiling for a fight. Having had a lifetime of experience with that precursor to a good pummeling, Leo
saw Waverly's hunger to beat him senseless. Mocking him further
would serve only to impede his hopes for the gentleman's sister. Focused on his goals, Leo forced his shoulders up in a shrug.
"What is there to say?"

"Then I'll continue." The glee in the usually stoic lord's words
was a reminder of the ruthlessness they were all capable of—even
straitlaced noblemen such as Waverly, who'd never stick a toe over
the other edge of proper. "You are worthless. A fortune hunter
who'd whore himself for a pence to support your wagering. And it
will not be on the back of my sister's dowry. You have my promise
on that..." The marquess' biting diatribe grew muffled in Leo's
ears.

"You are worthless... a sorry, pathetic excuse of a boy..."

"Please. Please, God. No. No. Not the rod..."

"Sniveling coward..."

Those jeers of long ago merged in a confusing blend with the
present.

Leo focused on the marquess' mouth as it moved, fighting back
the demons, fighting back every last reminder of his fallibility.
He'd not be reduced to that. Not again. Not by this man. Not by
any man.

"Get out."

When Leo made no move to abandon his chair, Waverly took a lurching step in his direction. "Unlike you, I am a man of my word, and I promise I will, this time, have my servants haul you off and toss you out like the swine you are—"

"Oh, very well." Leo sighed. Grabbing the arms of the seat, he propelled himself upright. "No need to be testy or dramatic." With brisk, even strides, he marched over to the rose-inlaid table and swiped his flowers. Turning back, he pointed the sloppy bouquet in the other man's direction. "Before I do leave, however, I'd have you know. This," he motioned between them, "was merely a formality. I'll put my offer to your sister."

Whether Waverly liked it or not...

He let that vow dangle, unspoken, and with the marquess' thunderous shouts trailing after him, Leo let himself out.

CHAPTER 9

TWELVE HOURS AFTER LORD LEO had taken his leave and night having since descended, one thing became abundantly clear—her brother had no intention of speaking with her.

Chloe growled. She crushed the note she'd written, which had been delivered back to her. "What do you mean he is unavailable to speak with me? He just returned." From whatever pressing affairs had called him away earlier that afternoon. Chloe, however, didn't mistake his conspicuous absence as anything other than what it was—a bid to avoid her. Well, if he believed he could avoid her by disappearing, only to return when the rest of the house was abed, he knew her less than even she believed. She'd been stationed at her window seat since Lord Leo had come and gone.

Her maid shifted back and forth on her feet. "Uh…" The girl shot a desperate look over her shoulder. When she again faced Chloe, discomfort contorted her features. "His lordship instructed that he was otherwise busy," she repeated in a rote manner that indicated the words had been served directly from the lord of the household.

"Should I summon her ladyship again?" she tentatively ventured.

Call Jane? For what end? She'd no sufficient answers on Gabriel's thoughts and had proven largely unforthcoming on the details surrounding Lord Leo's visit. "No, thank you," she murmured distractedly. All the while, her frustration mounted.

He'd been invisible when she was a girl, absent while she'd confronted their father's abuse and cruelty. And now, when she was a woman, he'd interfere and exert control over her life. It didn't matter that he did so out of a fraternal love of her and a desire to protect her. The time for that had come and gone long ago. She wanted to be treated as one whose opinion he, at the very least, heard. Alas, he would never grant her that courtesy. He was incapable of it. Crushing the page in her hand, Chloe hurled it across the floor. That small, childlike display of outrage didn't do anything to quell the fury roiling in her chest.

Her maid winced and took a step forward. The maid's fingers were outstretched to rescue the scrap. She stopped abruptly, and indecision over which move to make filled her eyes.

Chloe tamped down a sigh. It was hardly the young woman's fault that Gabriel was a pompous bastard who'd even now ignore her note. Nor would she keep the tired-eyed servant up any longer than she had. "That will be all, Kay," she said, gentling her tones.

The freckle-faced girl's shoulders sagged. "Thank you, my lady." She expelled her gratitude on a whisper.

"I don't require anything further this night." Chloe should have learned long ago that if she wished for or wanted something, she had to see to matters herself.

"Thank you," Kay repeated, sinking into a hasty curtsy. And as if she feared Chloe would change her mind and force her into the uncomfortable role of go-between for Chloe and her brother, the younger woman bolted.

As soon as the door closed, Chloe sank back into the down pillows behind her. How dare Gabriel? How dare he so effortlessly cut her out of any decision or discussion over her fate and last evening's scandal? In his mind, he'd resolved himself to the only solution—Chloe's marriage to his best friend, the Earl of Waterson—a match he'd been in favor of and pushing since she'd made her Come Out. And one that he'd not relinquished. Instead, in a bid to maneuver her into a safe marriage that would see her cared for and her reputation salvaged, his efforts would be renewed with an even greater intensity. Chloe grabbed her cane. Propelling herself to her feet, she gritted through the pain, welcoming the distraction that sharp ache brought.

With fury fueling her movements, Chloe limped to the door. Balancing her weight over her cane, she pressed the handle and let herself out. She hobbled from her rooms, through hall after hall, until she reached the sweeping stairway.

Sweat beading on her brow from her exertions, Chloe made the slow, arduous journey belowstairs. She paused midway down and borrowed support from her cane. One-two-three-four-five-six steps. There were just six of them. How many times had she taken those same stairs two at a time, sprinting up to her rooms, either escaping her mother or avoiding her father? And yet, now, with her ankle injured, she appreciated what a gift each previously effortless step had been.

Exhaling slowly through her compressed lips, she forced herself to continue.

Think of your brother exerting control over your life. She completed another step.

Think of him once more determining what is best for you. Chloe descended the next.

Imagine a lifetime being under your family's thumb and Mother's influence. Yet another and another step completed. Each tortured step represented her reasserting a say in her future and circumstances. Her brother believed she was undeserving of answers, or so much as a discussion, and used her seeming inability to seek him out as a way to avoid her.

Chloe reached the bottom of the stairway and, through the agony each step had cost her, smiled through the pain.

She'd done it. Forcing herself onward, she made the trek through the corridors. It was an odd thing, pain. It made one appreciate something previously taken for granted—level land, a plush carpeted floor. With the aid of her cane, she finally found her way to her brother's office.

From outside his doorway, muffled voices reached her ears.

"See this delivered posthaste. Instruct him…"

Leaning over the head of her cane, she pressed her ear against the wood panel. A faint hum further muted the discussion taking place, and she strained to hear the intermittent revelations.

"Your mount has been readied, my lord…"

Frustration turned over in her belly. She stood here, listening at the keyhole as though she were a child. Straightening her shoulders, Chloe grabbed the handle with her spare hand and pressed it.

"I trust he'll not come 'round," her brother said, shrugging into his jacket. "But in the event he does…" His words trailed off.

Brother and loyal servant stared back at Chloe.

Joseph cleared his throat and tucked the ivory vellum inside the front of his jacket. Most other servants would have averted their gaze. They would have dipped a perfunctory bow and scurried off. Joseph smiled, a kindly smile that met his rheumy eyes. One that belied the tension spilling from her brother's taut frame. "Lady Chloe."

"Joseph." She acknowledged his greeting with a smile.

That seemed to spring her brother into action. He started across the room. "You should not be out of your bed," he bit out.

Chloe made a show of pressing both palms to the head of her cane. "And why is that?" she returned with an equal terseness. "Because it is far easier to make decisions and discuss my future when I'm conveniently abed?"

Her brother jerked to an abrupt stop. Color suffused his cheeks. How very predictable her brother was, and had always been. Even with the great changes brought by his marriage to Jane, he still would be the proper lord, mindful of appearances and decorum. He smoothed his palms along immaculate lapels. "Thank you, Joseph. That will be all."

After another bow, Joseph slipped from the room, but not before offering her a commiserative wink. That slight, teasing response, in light of her family's—and the entire household's—grimness, righted what had become an uncertain world, restoring Chloe to her usual self.

"Well?" she demanded as soon as the faint click of the door signified that she and Gabriel were alone.

"You should not be down here," Gabriel repeated, joining her at the front of the room.

She leveled an arch look at him. "If you had seen to answering my missives, I would not have found my way to your office."

"Touché," he muttered, scraping a hand through his hair in a wholly un-Gabriel-like way. That break in his composure provided a glimpse into the effects last evening had left. "Let me help you to a seat."

"I am fine," she said impatiently, limping over to the new, dark leather button sofa. She lowered herself slowly into the crisp folds. And waited.

And continued waiting.

Her brother was always contemplative, and never given to filling voids of silence, but even this quiet did not fit with his usual composure.

Chloe searched her gaze over his face.

The grim set to Gabriel's mouth, the dark circles under his eyes all bespoke the direness that had followed them from Lord Waterson's affair.

Unease knocked around her breast. For there was something more real, more sobering in being here with her shaken eldest brother than the isolation she'd known in her rooms.

Determined once more to gain her footing over her scandal, she folded her arms. "What did he want?"

Her brother opened his mouth. He closed it. He tried a second time.

"And do not think to fob me off by pretending to not know of whom I'm speaking," she warned. Eventually, she'd pull the truth from him.

A muscle twitched at the right corner of his mouth. "How did you..." Guilty color immediately splotched his cheeks.

Chloe arched an eyebrow. "How did I know Lord Tennyson had come to call?" With a bouquet of wilted flowers and trailing those petals in his wake. "I've been confined to my rooms," she drawled. "Not a tower, Gabriel."

Stalking over to his sideboard, Gabriel poured himself a snifter of brandy. "It doesn't matter what he wanted," he said. The steady stream of liquid grated on her frayed nerves. His conceit infuriated her. Again, he'd made a decision for her, and there was to be no discussion of it. He set aside his bottle and faced her. "I assured him, once more, that I have no expectations of him." He carried his drink over, joining her at the hearth. For all intents and purposes, they might as well have been any sibling pair chatting over mundane familial matters.

Chloe narrowed her eyes on him. Once more, everything came to Gabriel's role as head of the family. It was a wonder he'd not only allowed, but fully supported, Jane's establishment of Mrs. Munroe's. But then, no one and nothing could prevent her sister-in-law from conquering the whole of Great Britain if she so desired it. Striving for calm, Chloe flicked a speck of dust from the sleeve of her dress. "And what about my expectations for him?" she asked when she trusted herself to speak through her annoyance.

"For..." Gabriel gave his head a befuddled shake.

"Lord Tennyson," she said simply as he sipped his brandy.

Her brother choked on his swallow, dissolving into a sputtering fit, until tears streamed down his face. Leaning across her seat, she slapped him hard between the shoulder blades.

"You have none of him or for h-him," he finally said when his paroxysm had faded to an intermittent cough. "You'd be wise to have no expectations for one such as Tennyson."

Yes, there was certainly some truth there. "Given Philippa's first husband was one of the most proper peers in London and nearly killed her in his hopes for an heir, I think I have good reason to have limited expectations of most gentlemen," she pointed out.

Gabriel was already shaking his head. "Tennyson is different even from Winston."

"Why?" she pressed, settling back in her seat, wholly warmed to her argument. "Because he presents himself precisely as he is to the world?" She smiled drolly. "I would venture there's something at least honest in it." The scandalous Marquess of Tennyson didn't make himself out to be anything more or anything less than what he was—the wicked image he presented was precisely what he was. "It is the ones who don a façade who are to be feared," she murmured softly, a reminder to herself.

As though you require any reminders.

She shivered as the unwanted memories that would forever be with her whispered to the surface.

I'll find you now, chit. If you come out now, it will go easier for you...

Gabriel set his drink down hard on the rose-inlaid table beside them, jerking her back to the moment. "You cannot even begin to fathom the depth of Tennyson's depravity."

You needn't put either of us through this show. You are on... your seventh Season now? Certain freedoms are permitted more seasoned women.

She cursed the blush she felt burning up her cheeks, giving thanks for the cover of darkness that concealed that telling reaction. "On what do you base your opinion of Lord Tennyson?" she interjected, infusing curiosity into the query. "Rumors? Gossip?" She smiled wryly and continued on before her brother could speak. "Or have you yourself kept company with the gentleman?"

"Do not be silly," he sputtered, surging to the edge of his chair. "Kept company with him?" he muttered, giving his head a shake. He grabbed his brandy.

"Ah." Chloe inclined her head. "Then rumors."

Gabriel paused with his snifter halfway to his mouth. "Do not."

She held her hands up, settling her features into her most innocent expression. "I couldn't even begin to gather what you're speaking about."

Her brother jabbed a finger in her direction. "Do not make me to be the dishonorable one." His nostrils flared. "I would never dare sully the reputation of an innocent lady as Tennyson did you. The way he has countless other women."

That was the manner of the world they lived in. Where, as far as ladies were concerned, appearances mattered most, and the world saw nothing more than the surface. Where one's insistence that nothing untoward had taken place couldn't be believed by one's brother because of the reputation of the perceived offender.

Her patience snapped. "Sully a lady's reputation? He carried me injured to a nearby sofa." *That was not all it had been.* His touch had been electric, hot and dangerously tempting, the kind of forbidden caress for which virtuous ladies traded their reputations. "It was not as though we'd snuck inside a theater alcove and toppled out after stealing an embrace." As her always staid brother had been discovered with his now wife—then Chloe's former companion.

Gabriel's color heightened. "That was different."

"Why?" She arched a brow. "Because it was *your* scandal? Or because you are a man."

"Because you are my sister," he gritted out.

"It is *always* different when it is someone else." She pursed her lips. "Nay. It is always different when it is a woman involved."

He jumped up. "My only intention is to protect you."

How could he not see that he exercised the same control he had with Jane following their scandal? "Just like you attempted to protect Jane after you were caught in flagrante delicto?" she asked gently.

He recoiled like one who'd taken a blow to the belly. "We are happy—"

She lifted a finger, staying his defense, needing him to see. "Just because the end result was your loving union does not make your masterminding aspects of her life acceptable."

Gabriel dragged a hand over his face.

Grabbing her cane, she shoved herself to her feet. With her spare hand, she took one of his in her own. "I love you, Gabriel, and I know you love me. But loving me in return and protecting me is not making determinations on information I should be in possession of."

They stood there, locked in a battle.

Gabriel was the first to look away. "I should not have ignored your summons today," he conceded.

She grinned wryly. "No. You shouldn't have." Her smile withered at his next words.

"But neither do I regret denying Tennyson access to you," he said flatly. "He's a scoundrel, in dire financial straits, and his coming here today is testament to the fact that he is a fortune hunter."

"He offered to marry me?" It made sense. How else to account for his earlier visit and the hothouse flowers he'd arrived with? And yet... the wickedest rake in England had been willing to cede his bachelor state and take a bride. She chewed at her lower lip. The marquess couldn't know what her dowry was—or was not. Nor had the man who'd backed out of Lord Waterson's office with horror in his eyes been one who'd so easily consign himself to the parson's mousetrap. "It doesn't make sense," she said quietly.

"It does if he's financially bankrupt," he said. She started, unaware she'd spoken aloud. "His wagering and whor—" Gabriel coughed into his hand. "*Other* activities have destroyed a once-great fortune of a once-respectable family." Her brother spoke with an air of finality, as one who would not—nay, could not—be reasoned with.

And standing, the dull throb of her ankle a muted pain, she saw her life stretched out before her: the sister of a domineering brother who meant well, but whose decision ultimately prevailed. "I see," she said softly, seeing too much, all too well.

Gabriel adjusted his cravat. "I am journeying to Leeds."

She was already shaking her head. Her dearest friend and brother now awaited the birth of their first child, and Gabriel would impose on even that. "Imogen—"

"Mother cannot receive word from the scandal sheets that make their way to the country about... about... this."

It was decided. That much was clear in the hard set of his jaw. A sound of disgust slipped from her lips as she spun with all the grace she could muster and shuffled slowly to the door.

"Chloe," he called after her. "Let me help you abovestairs."

"I am fine," she bit out.

The floorboards groaned, indicating he'd moved.

"I said I am fine," she said sharply, letting herself out.

Her brother wisely fell back.

And even as every step proved excruciating and moisture beaded on her brow, outrage kept her moving forward. Resentment at a woman's lot sent frustration knocking around her chest. There were no freedoms permitted her. There never had been. This home had represented a prison when she'd been a child, one where she'd suffered through tortures better suited to Newgate, and now, it was a different prison. One imposed in a bid to keep her safe, but stealing control and power.

As if in a mocking echo of that very thought, heavy footfalls depressed nearby floorboards.

She paused, shooting a quick glance over her shoulder.

Gabriel lifted a sheepish palm. "I'm merely making certain you don't require any assistance."

Where were you ten, fifteen years ago? That unfair scream reverberated silently around the chambers of her mind. Mayhap it was guilt that drove him now. Mayhap it was regret for not having been there when he should have been. "I do not require any assistance." Not sparing another look back, she resumed her trek.

Minutes? Hours? Later, she'd managed the slow climb of the stairs and found her way to her rooms. The same thrill of accomplishment that had met her earlier efforts now felt hollow, an empty victory that merely reiterated her absolute powerlessness.

Her chest heaving from her exertions, she pressed her door handle. The door hinges squeaked, blaringly loud, as she let herself inside.

As soon as she'd closed the door behind her, she squeezed her eyes shut and collapsed against the panel. Her breath came in quick little spurts. Damning her brother. Damning her circumstances. Damning herself and... Lord Tennyson. Chloe grimaced. "It is hardly his fault," she muttered, opening her eyes. "It is—" Her words came to a jarring halt. The cane slipped from her fingers.

The Marquess of Tennyson flashed a wolfish smile. "In my experience, it is invariably a gentleman's fault," he whispered and followed the droll observation with a wink.

As the cane fell to the floor, Chloe shrieked.

Lord Tennyson slapped his gloved fingers over her lips, swallowing the sound. The lingering clatter of her walking stick upon the hardwood floor sounded like a shot at night.

"Chloe." The voice boomed from the hallway, and Chloe and the marquess looked to the door. He sprang into action. With his spare hand, Lord Tennyson reached past her and turned the lock.

Oh, bloody hell. Gabriel had been following her. Of course he would have made sure she'd gotten to her rooms. Her heart nearly beat a rhythm outside her chest. She cast a frantic look up at the blighter who threatened her reputation—for a second time.

"Quiet," the marquess warned, nearly soundless against her ear.

"Chloe?" Her brother jiggled the door handle. If he learned the marquess was in here, there would be no help for it—he'd call the man out. Nor could there be any doubt that Gabriel, who'd never so much as sparred at Gentleman Jackson's, would be destroyed at dawn by the blackguard. A man who'd built a reputation as a dastard had surely scores of duels to his name and experience. "The brother calls," Lord Tennyson whispered against her ear, his breath a cool sough upon her heated skin. "Respond." It was a shockingly strong command from a man who seemed too indolent to muster anything more than boredom in his speech. Lord Tennyson removed his hand slowly.

"Chloe." Gabriel pounded at the door.

"I am fine," she called out. "I…"

"You hurt your ankle," the marquess supplied quietly.

"I hurt my ankle," she repeated.

The rattling stopped. "May I come in?"

Panic mounting, she glanced up at her captor.

He arched a golden eyebrow.

"N-no," she managed to force out. "I don't want to speak any more. I've said all there is to say for now." Silence met her pronouncement. That would deter him. He'd believe she'd gone off to nurse her frustrations and annoyances.

Unknowing all the while that she entertained the wickedest rake in England.

As if to punctuate that very thought, Lord Tennyson stroked his hand down the curve of her hip. She pinched his thigh. The efforts proved ineffectual against the heavily muscled contour under his black breeches. "Stop it," she gritted out.

"My apologies," Gabriel said tersely, incorrectly, but fortunately taking the directive as one meant for him. "It was never my intention to do anything but help this day. I will allow you your rest now."

The quiet tread of his footfalls faded into silence.

And the ramifications of that hit her like a lightning bolt.

I am alone with the Marquess of Tennyson.

Chloe opened her mouth to blister his ears, but he touched a fingertip to her lips. "You are rot at subterfuge, love. Have a care unless you want me facing your brother at dawn."

She clamped her lips closed.

"That is better," he murmured.

Capturing her about the waist, he drew her back against his chest. Panic cloyed at her breast. The agony of her ankle forgotten, she shoved against him.

He pressed his lips close to her temple, the blend of vanilla and chocolate on his breath an innocent contradiction to the threat that poured off him in waves. "If your stuffy brother were scandalized by the sight of us in Lord Waterson's office, whatever would he say if he were to see us now?"

Her stomach churned violently.

For… no one would see. She'd allowed her maid to retire for the night and ordered Gabriel gone. The whole house—including the servants—slept, meaning she was well and truly alone with the Marquess of Tennyson.

What have I done?

CHAPTER 10

THE EVENING HADN'T GONE AS planned.

Lady Chloe Edgerton was to have been sleeping peacefully in her bed and… well, the whole shock and terror of waking up to find Leo there had certainly been inevitable. But Leo at least anticipated there would have been the delayed effects of her heavy slumber.

Said lady squirmed in his arms, and he adjusted his hold on her. With every thrash and twist of her body, she risked further injury to her ankle.

No, the evening hadn't gone as Leo had expected. It had, however, proven vastly more interesting.

"Why in the blazes are you even on your ankle?" he whispered.

She stilled in his arms. The question startled him as much as the quieted miss. And then her fire roared to life once more. "My ankle, Tennyson?" she hissed. "You enter my home… my rooms uninvited—"

"I am *delighted* to know I only needed to wait for an invite," he purred.

The lady went silent and then a barrage of black, inventive curses exploded from her lips.

Immediately shifting his palm over her mouth, he glanced to the door. "Hush, or you'll have Waverly upon us again." And next time, the protective, but deplorable at it, brother wouldn't be content until he'd verified with his eyes that his sister was well.

Lady Chloe sank her teeth into the thick leather of his gloves, the fine Italian material making her efforts futile. Appreciation snaked unexpectedly through him. "The kitten bites," he marveled.

In response, she bit down all the harder. As a rule, he despised the articles, but his career with the Brethren had proven the benefits, and he gave thanks for the barrier between his palm and the hellcat.

"Mmhm—gnah." His hand muffled the words, which, by the fire flashing from her eyes, were really more an order than anything. She renewed her struggles.

"Have a care, love, or you're going to do lasting harm to your ankle." The dire warning managed to quiet the lady's efforts.

Sweeping her up, he did an inventory of the chambers he'd entered a short while ago. He located her cane and then paused, the scrap of wood conjuring another similar one, used by a different woman. He swallowed hard. Silently cursing the maudlin sentiments, he swiped up Chloe's cane and stuffed it into her palm.

Her fingers curled around it, and the scrap dangled awkwardly over his shoulder. Mayhap these recent remembrances were the sins of his past at last catching him. "Will you set me down?" Chloe urged, thankfully forcing him back to the present.

Leo started over to the four-poster bed with its nauseatingly innocent white coverlet. "White," he muttered, coming up short. Ivory. What a dull, colorless existence this one lived.

The lady tugged at his sleeve. "White is a perfectly splendid color. It is associated with purity and light and goodness." They were all fallacies believed by naïve misses touched by evil—like this one. "Why, there is a reason Homer uses the color in his works."

"Yes, there was," he muttered, carefully setting her down. He grabbed a nearby pillow and arranged it under her foot. "Because the bloody sod couldn't see color properly."

She opened and closed her mouth several times, giving her the look of a whiskered barbel he'd fished out of Spanish waters. "How would you know that?" she blurted.

Bloody hell. Cursing that carelessness, Leo snorted. "You'd provide me with a versed lecture on the color?" he taunted.

"I take it you, the black-hearted, sulking rake, despise all things white and innocent?" she shot back, neatly steered away from her previous query.

"Sulking?" Indignation crept into his voice. "I certainly do *not* sulk." He was indolent and carefree and menacing to the *ton*, but he was assuredly not one of those brooding gents.

"Sulking," she confirmed with a brusque nod. She arranged her skirts about her, smoothing her palms over her lap. "And sneering at anything white?" Lady Chloe peeled her lip back in a derisive sneer and, when she spoke again, dropped her voice to a low contralto. "Cliché, love. Very cliché."

He frowned as she tossed back the accusation he'd hurled at her in Waterson's corridors. "Are you... *mocking* me, madam?" People in Polite Society, as a rule, despised Leo. They spoke poorly of him and wished him to hell on a good day. And the rest avoided him. They did not, however, make light of him.

The lady did a dead-on impression of his leer. And then, holding his gaze, she gave him the same exaggeratedly slow wink he'd mastered long ago.

He narrowed his eyes. He'd far grander reasons for being here than debating her opinion of him, or her hideous preference for white. Leo would be damned, however, if the saucy minx wore that triumphant ghost of a smile. "There is, madam, one area where you are wrong," he murmured in silken tones. Resting his right knee on her mattress, he edged closer.

The lady swallowed loudly as her earlier bravado flagged. "Indeed?" she squeaked.

"Indeed," he repeated, wrapping those two syllables in velvet. "Very wrong."

"I assure you, I very rarely am." She edged her chin up a notch. "Wrong, that is."

The minx. Despite himself, Leo felt a smile pulling on his lips, which he swiftly concealed behind his usual mask of coldness.

With her palms as leverage, she propelled herself backward until she knocked into the headboard. "In fact, I'd wager that after just one meeting, I have mastered that which has surely taken you a decade to perfect."

He paused in his pursuit.

How incredibly close she danced to the truth. Unease stirred in his belly. She'd smartly identified the façade he'd crafted—the mask that had eventually become real.

Warning bells went off. *Leave. She's too clever to ever be your wife.* One such as Chloe would never be complacent. She would never be content until she'd unearthed the dangerous secrets he kept—from all outside the Brethren.

She waggled her thin, perfectly arched golden eyebrows.

And yet… it had to be her.

For she was the woman with whom he'd been caught.

Leo continued coming, crawling toward her like a panther. "Your words, uttered in those sultry tones, are ones that tempt, entice, and seduce," he whispered, stopping before her. He framed his palms on each side of her, effectively trapping her against the headboard. Leo hooded his lashes and then lowered his mouth close to hers. "No, you can never be confused for a bounder such as me."

The lady's throat moved frantically. He detected a brief flash of desire, melded with confusion, and then—

She brought her right, uninjured leg up. He easily caught it, preventing the strike.

"U-unhand m-me," she said, her voice breathless. She made no further move to fight him.

"Do you promise not to try and unman me again?" he countered, lightly stroking her through the thin fabric of her modest night shift.

She clamped her lips into a tense line that drained the blood from the corners of her mouth.

He would hand it to the lady. Leo had encountered all sorts of women in his work for the Brethren. Some vipers as ruthless as he was, who'd think nothing of gutting a man… or a woman in the name of country, all of whom had never gone toe-to-toe with him. With her show of spirit and resolve, this spitfire put all those adversaries to shame.

Lowering the delicate limb slowly back to the mattress, he set her free.

Chloe immediately shoved herself to the corner of the bed. "What do you want?" she demanded in hushed tones.

"To speak to you."

"This," she waved a frantic hand between them, "is hardly the manner in which a respectable gentleman goes about speaking to a lady."

He flashed an indolent grin. "I've never been accused of being a gentleman."

They locked gazes in a silent battle.

In countless missions, Leo had relied on the nuances of a person's body to determine how to go about handling the individual. The rise and fall of a person's chest, the emotions revealed in their eyes, the tension in their bodies—all of it dictated his next move.

Lady Chloe stared back at him warily.

She was afraid.

Palpable terror rolled from the lady's slender frame. However, when any other respectable miss would have been reduced to tears and wilted like a flower, Lady Chloe Edgerton cloaked herself in pride and courage.

"You said you wanted to speak to me," she gritted.

An unexpected admiration for the lady stirred.

Leo retreated to the opposite end of the bed. If she felt cornered, she wouldn't hear a single word he uttered, and his efforts would be in vain.

Some of the tension eased from her narrow shoulders, but remained rich in her gaze.

"As I said before, Chloe—"

The lady wrinkled her nose. "I've most certainly not given you permission to use my Christian name."

"Given our intertwined circumstances, I felt we might dispense with formalities," he said dryly. When was the last time a lady he'd kept company with adhered to such dictates? Another face flashed behind his mind's eye. Haunted eyes, hurt by him, at his hand.

Unnerved by the unwelcome intrusion of the past, Leo went on in the same gentling tones he'd used with angry husbands who'd rightly called him out for his transgressions with their wives. "It was my hope in coming earlier today that we might converse. Your brother, however, forbade it." A proud woman such as she would forever chafe at Waverly, or any man, dictating any terms of her life. As such, he wielded that admission with the same skill as a master swordsman.

"And what did you intend to say at this… meeting?" The gruff query came as though pulled from her.

He spread his palms. "Why, it was my intention to make an offer for your hand and do right by you."

She blinked like an owl startled from its perch. "*You* do right by *me?*"

The slightly derisive emphasis was wholly deserved.

Leo nodded once. "Marry," he clarified. "I'm offering you marriage."

He waited.

And waited.

And more than forty ticks of the clock later, he was still waiting, while Lady Chloe stared at him like he was a scientific oddity.

"No," she said succinctly.

When nothing more than that single syllable left her mouth, with no further explanations or details, he frowned.

Well, that was certainly… decided.

He'd spent the whole of his adult life avoiding the marital trap, clinging desperately to his bachelor state, only to now be filled with a restiveness at the lady's rejection. It was a singularly odd state for a rake of his black ilk.

With an air of finality, she edged closer and made a grab for her cane.

Leo handed it over. She eyed his fingers the way that fabled Red Riding Hood had looked upon her wolflike grandmother. "That is it, then? Just 'no'?"

"No, *thank you?*" she supplied. Her words, a question more than anything, startled a laugh from him. "Now you really need to get yourself gone."

This was going to be vastly more difficult than he'd anticipated. Leo dusted a hand over his jaw. Chloe Edgerton was not one of those desperate ladies who'd had too many Seasons and remained unwed, still. He measured his words. "Given our unconventional meeting, I trust this… my appearance in your chambers and my proposal provide you with a good deal to consider. However, you haven't even heard me out."

Lady Chloe shot an eyebrow up. "What is there to consider? You are a rake. You're in dun territory."

He shuttered his expression. By way of gossip, his financial matters were common fodder, and yet, to have her toss those transgressions in his face needled. "You're in want of a fortune to sustain your gaming and whoring. Have I missed anything?"

A better man, even the rakes with a modicum of respectability left, would have, at the very least, flushed at having those sins
hurled at him the way Lady Chloe did now.

He scoffed. "Though accurate by Society's standards, that perfunctory, if uninventive, list includes all the reasons you should *not*
marry me."

The spitfire folded her arms at her chest, plumping the small
mounds of flesh, drawing his appreciative gaze downward. A soft
light cast by the hearth bathed her in a soft glow, and a bolt of lust
went through him as he strained to make out the shade of her
nipples. A dusky brown. Or mayhap a pink. Or—

Lady Chloe gasped and squeezed her arms all the closer to her
chest, merely plumping the flesh all the more. "And you believe
there are reasons I should wish to marry you?" she hissed.

Reluctantly lifting his gaze from the great mystery that was the
lady's breasts, he favored her with an innocent expression. "Do you
mean other than salvaging your reputation?"

She flinched.

So she was not totally immune to the ramifications of having
her name sullied with scandal. Interesting. Until now, the lady had
shown remarkably little concern for what anyone might say about
being discovered with him.

Leo stood. "I'll not make myself out to be anything other than
what I am," he said matter-of-factly. "I'm the ruthless rake and
black-hearted scoundrel Society takes me for. Marriage to me,
however, would come with certain benefits."

She nudged her chin, silently urging him on.

He proceeded with a methodical accounting, ticking each one
off on a gloved fingertip. "I'm not one of those stodgy, oppressive
sorts who'd seek to control your movements and demand you
answer to me. I'm not looking to transform you into a biddable
bride." What he desired was an invisible wife.

Chloe drew her shoulders back ever so slightly. "Continue."

He'd found the hook. He invariably did. It was why he'd survived countless missions and triumphed over lesser adversaries.
Encouraged, Leo went on. "Why, I don't even require an heir."

She was shaking her head before the words had left his mouth.
"*Every* nobleman wishes for an heir."

That was the case for most bloody toffs. "No," he amended.

"Most do." He pointed to his chest. "*I do not.*" His was the ultimate triumph over the bloody rotter who'd given Leo a name
and legitimacy. He'd gladly kick up his heels and watch the title
pass on to some distant, distant relative tucked in the corners of
Northumberland.

Suspicion sparkled in the lady's pretty blue eyes.

"I would, however, require a short period of," he shuddered,
"monogamy." It was too much. "At least discretion," he corrected.

She scratched at her brow. "You require me to pretend at a love
match."

He shook his head. "No." Not even that. "I need you to make
me respectable."

"Make you…" The lady laughed until tears streamed from her
eyes… and then stopped. "You're serious," she remarked, dusting
back the evidence of her hilarity.

"Afterwards," after Society believed the farce of a whirlwind
love affair he'd perpetuated with the lady, "you'll be free to carry
on with whomever you wish, whenever you wish, as often as you
wish." And should her affairs become a matter of discussion, he
could by that point craft a new image—that of broken-hearted
husband—and from there, resurrect his reputation as a rake. All
would be right with the world, and he'd be free to conduct himself as he always had for the Brethren. He grinned. "Well?"

Her expression instantly darkened.

Blast and damn.

He'd lost the very hook he'd dangled.

Propelling herself closer, she moved toward his spot at the side
of her bed. "If the greatest gift you can grant is turning a cheek to
my faithlessness, then I must… decline."

Bloody hell. Every woman he'd carried on with over the years
would have leaped at that offering.

Lady Chloe pointed her cane toward the doorway. "I've heard
what you had to say, and I'd ask you for a final time to please
leave." She swiftly lowered her arm. "Wait," she called out quietly,
and hope stirred, and then was promptly dashed. "How did you
manage to sneak inside my family's residence? A disloyal servant?"
she pressed.

That assumption would spare him from her further probing and
allow him to maintain the image of sloppy rake. "Every man and

woman can be bought." He supplied that truth instead.

"Not those in my family, nor our household," she shot back. She again motioned to the door.

"Then you prove yourself to be entirely too trusting, my lady."

"Get out," she said again.

An unfamiliar sentiment simmered within, threatening to consume him—desperation.

This woman and marriage to her were all that stood between him and his position with the Brethren. *Who am I without my work?* His late father's memory slipped in.

... You are nothing Leopold Aldwyn Bromley Dunlop... and nothing is all you'll ever be... My only son died, when it should have been you...

Chloe scowled.

And God help him, the charm he'd perfected and used only to wheedle desired information eluded him with this one. "You are clever, my lady," he said quickly, too quickly.

Suspicion deepened in her eyes. "You've known me but a day. That is hardly enough time to make any kind of determination about a person."

Actually, one could gather the most meaningful aspects about a person's character, strength, and skills from but the first handful of moments in an exchange. Witty, fearless, and courageous, she was not a woman who'd be pacified or won with empty platitudes.

"I know you aren't an empty-headed, simpering miss." In this, he didn't hand her lies. Leo gave her nothing but the truth born of their two exchanges. "What I propose is a business transaction," he continued, appealing to her logic. "I'm not a romantic, Chloe," he murmured, drifting around the bed.

She followed his every movement with a world wariness better suited to an aged matron than a young woman. "Are you a rake?"

He abruptly stopped, carefully considering her question. No value could come in lying to her. Not her. "I am."

"Is there merit to the stories said about you?"

Her direct, no-nonsense questioning could have earned her a place within the ranks of the Brethren. Leo flashed a half-grin. "Undoubtedly."

The lady stitched her golden eyebrows into a single line. "You don't even know which gossip I speak of."

He lifted his shoulders in a lazy shrug. "Because I am deserving of my black reputation, Chloe. I'm a cheat, liar, whoremonger, and bastard. What use is there in me contradicting that gossip?" Gossip that had only proven beneficial to him and his role.

"Hmm."

He struggled to make sense of that noncommittal reply. He resumed his path around the bed, stopping when he reached her side.

The lady wet her lips, and of its own volition, his gaze clung to that subtly seductive gesture that highlighted the plump, red flesh. Visions of the pleasures to be had with that mouth enticed him. *Focus. You've worshiped many, many plump mouths, experienced ones that didn't require tutelage.*

Drawing on his skills at seduction, he slid onto the mattress beside her.

"Wh-what are you doing?" she demanded, faintly breathless. The fragrant whisper of jasmine filled his senses, oddly tempting in its innocence.

He swallowed hard as he, the predator, suddenly became prey. "I am trying to sway your opinion, Chloe," he confessed, lowering his mouth close to hers. He saw the long, graceful column of her throat move. He heard her audible intake.

She wanted him. The essence of her desire was wrapped in her every breath.

And he had no intention of failing at securing her hand.

He stroked his knuckles tenderly along her jaw. "I'm logical in terms of life and marriage. I don't want love. I don't want children." Some unfathomable glitter sparkled in her eyes. What accounted for it? Was it a desire for a small babe? That was something he'd not give her… or any woman. He tightened his jaw. "I don't even want your loyalty." He simply needed… her. "You have one day."

And after that, there would be no need for marriage to her—his fate would be set by the Brethren.

Leo jumped up and started for the doorway.

"I already declined your offer," she reminded.

"Yes," he agreed, not breaking his stride. He paused at the door and shot a glance over his shoulder. "But you are not one who is usually impulsive. You're one who carefully thinks out everything and plans." It was how he knew the moment he left, she'd be turning his offer and her answer over in her mind.

"You cannot know that about me," she called out quietly.

He knew more than she could ever believe. "One day," he warned.

And with that, Leo left.

CHAPTER 11

"ONE DAY," CHLOE MUTTERED. LYING on her bed, she made a face at the cherubs dancing merrily overhead in the frustratingly cheerful mural. "Giving me an ultimatum," she railed in the quiet.

Whether it was one day, one week, or one hundred years, she would never, ever bind herself to Leo Dunlop, the Marquess of Tennyson.

How damned cocksure he'd been as he'd slipped silently from her rooms with an ease that only a rake accustomed to a late-evening rendezvous could manage.

He'd gone three hours ago, and the audacity of the gentleman, her outrage and annoyance burned even stronger.

It was useless. Sleep this night was futile. Just as it had been the previous night when her reputation had been destroyed in the arms of a rake.

She contemplated the errant specks of dust floating overhead. How dare he invade her rooms, further risking her reputation, arrogantly presuming that marriage to him would salvage her future?

It was preposterous. It was presumptuous. It was… "True," she breathed.

Heart hammering, Chloe surged upright. No, it couldn't be true. There could never be any good in marriage to Leo Dunlop. Nay, there could be no good in marriage to any gentleman—but *especially* not him.

Except—

Chloe chewed at her nail.

He hadn't presented her with false words of affection or empty praise. As a desperate wastrel, eager to escape dun territory, he could have coaxed and cajoled. Nor would she expect or believe the Marquess of Tennyson beneath lies and deception. Instead, he'd spoken to her of a business arrangement with a bluntness that should have horrified her—and yet, did not.

Nay, those cool, pragmatic terms enticed, seduced, in a way that no pretty words ever could.

Freedom.

It was what he'd largely promised. Freedom of movement, freedom to make her own decisions. Why, the gentleman didn't even wish for an heir.

She let her hands fall back to the bed.

"A lie," she whispered. "It has to be."

All gentlemen desired those tiny souls to carry on familial names and titles, and to whom fortunes would pass.

You are useless. What use do I have for a daughter? You should pay for simply being born…

That hated voice echoed around her mind, melding with her own screams as a child, bringing her eyes shut. Her back throbbed with the remembered agony of the lash. She clenched her eyes tight, willing her demons gone.

But when he slipped in, he retained a grip only the devil could break.

Not this night. Not any night. "Leave," she rasped, forcing her eyes open.

Chloe's breath came loudly in her ears. Sweat dampened her skin. *He is dead. He cannot harm you ever again.* She hugged herself tightly, finding solace in that reminder. But if she married, another person could.

She shivered as a cold stole through her, freezing her from the inside out.

"I cannot do i-it." Chloe's teeth chattered. Not Lord Leo and not any man.

The day her father had cocked up his toes and gone on to

join Satan's army in the fires of hell, she had been freed. At that moment, she'd vowed to never become her mother and never subject herself or any child to the cruel whims of a mercurial man. With the hell she'd endured, and the liberation she'd known with her father's death, she could never marry.

The rub of it was, she'd so determinedly committed herself to avoiding marriage that she'd not given thought to the fate that awaited her as an unmarried woman.

Until now.

She slowly lowered herself back down.

Now, she was forced to confront how little power and control an unwed young lady truly had. And there was even less for one who'd been discovered in a compromising position.

Chloe pressed her palms over her face. Lord Tennyson had come here offering her freedom—through shackles. He'd allow her to live her life without interference on his part.

Surely it was exhaustion that made her pause on the offer he'd made.

Or mayhap it was simply madness.

For there was a dangerous allure to the offer from Leo Dunlop, the Marquess of Tennyson. Oh, it would be foolish to ever trust a word that dripped from his hard, cynical lips. But what if he'd spoken in truth? What if he truly would provide her a formal arrangement where they were business partners, joined for their own self-interests?

She'd feared a marriage that would have her under a husband's thumb. But this, this was altogether different. The arrangement put forward by the marquess would allow her invisibility.

Yes, there was something so very appealing in such a marriage.

But what would happen when he drank? Or changed his mind on the matter of an heir? Chloe firmed her jaw. She could not, would not ever subject a child to the same fate she and her siblings had known. That was one element of her life she could control as an unmarried woman. No doubt, everything he'd presented had, in fact, been a lie.

Which left her future uncertain.

For in moving on from the marquess' cold proposal, she was forced to confront her precarious circumstances and the limited opportunities available to her.

I'm logical in terms of life and marriage. I don't want love. I don't want children. I don't even want your loyalty…

Rather, he'd stated his need for… respectability. To what end?

All he'd require of her was her brief discretion in carrying on affairs.

Had he been any other man, she'd have clobbered him in the temple for daring to impugn her honor with the belief that she'd break any vow she took. But with him having gone and her having run through their meeting over and over, her mind latched on to one single sentence he'd uttered: *I would, however, require a short period of monogamy—at least discretion.*

Those words were significant for what they conveyed, and yet, oddly still a mystery.

She puzzled her brow as new questions surfaced.

He had his own reasons for offering her marriage, ones that his words suggested moved beyond the need for her dowry.

Why…

"*He* needs to marry *me*," she whispered. But *why*?

If it were solely for her dowry, then her decision was simple. Control of her funds was not part of the bargain. But if it was not about her monies, then his offer was, at the very least, something to be understood and then, mayhap, accepted.

Her stomach churned rapidly, sending bile surging to her throat.

Surely she was not truly considering marriage to him—the Marquess of Tennyson?

But if you can turn Society's most heartless cad into one who's polite, respectable, and… a proper gentleman, any post would be open to you…

"Mrs. Munroe's," she whispered. For not only would she have achieved the seemingly impossible task of reforming a rake, she would be a marchioness who—fair or not—would be acceptable.

A dull, throbbing ache settled at her temples. Chloe dug her fingertips into them and massaged in small, slow circles.

No, she was not contemplating marriage to him. Not truly.

She'd never been one of those wilting misses content to hide away in her rooms and pray for the scandal to fade, all the while bemoaning her fate. She'd not become one because of a misunderstanding stumbled upon by her family and a handful of strangers. She would, however, hear him out, present her terms as she would have them in a hypothetical arrangement, and from there…

Her mind shied away from traveling any further down that path. Wiggling out of her wrapper, she tossed the garment aside.

It sailed to the floor in a sad, fluttery heap.

Grabbing her cane, Chloe leveraged herself to a stand. Placing all her weight on her uninjured limb, she limped over to her armoire. With painstakingly slow movements, she tugged out her under-garments. She shoved aside gown after gown—white ones, ivory ones, pink ones. Now she wished she'd instructed the modiste, Madame Claremont, to construct one of those dark, scandalous ones.

Lord Leo had looked upon her white night wrapper with dis-dain.

She smirked. Which was precisely the reason that when most debutantes and young ladies lamented white garments, Chloe had quite happily donned those dresses. Rakes, rogues, scoundrels, and in truth... *most* respectable gentlemen barely spared a notice for a woman outfitted as a proper miss.

Her smug grin slipped.

Of course, leave it to Lord Leo to prove wholly contrary. For despite his lamentations about her largely white-adorned room, he'd studied her night wrapper with a lascivious gaze better suited for an outrageously clad widow. His stare had burned through those modest garments and scorched her skin.

Her skin heated at the mere memory.

She'd heard tales of rakes and rogues, but never had those atten-tions been turned on her. And in her bedchamber, no less.

Chloe reached the back of the armoire and continued digging around. A curl fell over her eyes, and she pushed it back. "Where is it? Where is it?" she mumbled, squinting. "Ah." Her fingers col-lided with the high-waisted, puff-sleeved dress buried away there. She yanked out the gingham monstrosity, briefly eyeing the tiny brown and ivory squares. The enormous bow.

This was, unfortunately, the closest to dark her gowns came. Why, oh why, had she never prepared for clandestine meetings?

She sighed. This would have to do.

Balancing her garments in her opposite arm, she carried them over to her bed. Chloe perched herself on the edge of her mattress and proceeded to dress.

While she squiggled out of her night shift, she stole a glance at the clock.

One o'clock.

Setting her jaw, Chloe forced herself up and, this time, made one more journey—to her desk.

Sitting down, she dragged out a sheet of parchment and a pen and then dipped the tip into the crystal inkwell.

She proceeded to write.

Leo was in desperate need of a drink.

More specifically, he was in need of a whole damned bottle. And then some.

He gave his uncle's well-stocked sideboard serious consideration. His mouth went dry from the need to tip a bottle back and let the slight burn of liquor blaze a path down his throat and dull the sharp edge of panic that had dogged him these last two days.

A sound of frustration escaping him, he continued to pace before his uncle's desk.

Drinking wouldn't do him any good now. Spirits served specific purposes: for celebrating raucous times, for lapping off a wanton beauty's lush, naked frame, for wallowing in one's miseries, or for dulling any hint of feeling.

As such, no bottle of fine French brandy could help him now.

He scraped a hand through his tousled hair. Nothing could help him now. Nothing, and no one.

It did not mean Leo was above trying and begging once more. Or praying for a miracle to a God he'd long ago learned was false.

Where in the blazes was his uncle? He yanked out his watch fob, consulting the timepiece. As a rule, his uncle despised balls and soirees almost as much as Leo did. "Everlasting bloody hell." Every moment that passed stuck a nail in the coffin of Leo's life and career.

"Miss me, dear boy?" a voice drawled from the doorway.

Leo cursed. The gold chain slipped through his fingers, leaving the timepiece twirling at his waist. "At last," he muttered, stopping midpace.

His uncle shrugged out of his jacket and entered the room.

"Didn't hear me coming?" He made a tsking sound as he closed the door. "You're becoming lax," he said with a light twinkle in his eyes.

Yes, he was. The past two days were testament enough to that. As it was, Leo would wager his uncle's stealth and years of service to the Brethren had more to do with his silent footsteps than Leo's distraction. "Bloody hell, where have you been?" he demanded as his uncle flung his jacket aside with an infuriating casualness. "I've been waiting for you."

"You were due here this afternoon, Leo," Uncle William noted dryly, taking up his usual post behind his desk. He motioned for Leo to sit.

Leo slid into the folds of the leather chair opposite the desk. "I was otherwise detained," he said brusquely.

"I told you..."

"I came as soon as I was able." To admit anything more than that about his meeting with Chloe would mark him as a failure—once more.

His uncle steepled his fingers. "Did you come to an agreement with the lady?"

Leo let his silence serve as his answer.

Abandoning his casual pose, Uncle William gave his head a sad shake. "I can promise you that Rowley will not back away from the ultimatum he set forth."

Leo surged forward in his chair. "I need more time."

"I cannot get that for you. You had today. You know better than anyone the essentiality of—"

Leo jumped up. "I'm not here for a bloody fucking lecture on punctuality," he snapped, slamming a fist on the edge of his uncle's desk.

The other man fixed a ducal stare on him, and in an instant, he was the same man who'd first trained Leo within the organization.

Forcing himself to draw in a calming breath, Leo reclaimed his seat. He tried again. "Did you speak with them?"

His uncle folded his hands and rested them on the immaculate mahogany desk. "Regarding your scandal? Of course I did, Leo."

"And?" Leo tugged the chair closer to the desk as anxiety roiled in his chest.

"And how do you believe they responded? Rowley called for

your immediate expulsion."

He'd been braced for it. He'd expected it. Even so, all the air exploded from his lungs. "Of course he did. The bloody sod." He raked an unsteady hand through his hair. It was all coming apart. His future. His life. The Cato case. Some pompous peers would continue to subvert the government from within, all to advance their own agendas. And Leo would be on the fringe, unable to stop it as he had so many past crimes. His pulse raced, deafening as a drumbeat in his ears. "He is trying to silence me." And he had been since Leo's suspicions on the Cato Street Conspiracy.

"He's trying to *punish* you for seducing his wife," his uncle corrected.

Leo's ears went hot. "If you believe that is all that motivates Rowley, you've been out of practice too long, Uncle."

His godfather flared his nostrils, but did not rise to the bait.

Leo continued to press him. "Every last rake and rogue in London has made a cuckold of the viscount. The viscountess has bedded anybody that is warm. Yet, my actions should be met with such outrage?"

"You've always gone toe-to-toe with the man, Leo," his uncle accurately pointed out. "It was only a matter of time before you crossed some until now invisible line with him."

He squared his jaw. He'd not make apologies for any of his actions within the Brethren and with his superiors. Leo had lived a ruthless existence, taking down countless men and women in need of taking down and leaving broken hearts and shattered people in his wake. And he'd certainly not drum up even false remorse for his disdain for the man in the organization he answered to. "If it's as you say, and Rowley is making this about a supposed slight, he's putting his own petty resentments ahead of the Brethren."

His uncle sighed. "Leo, you made the man a cuckold."

His patience snapped. "I've made cuckolds of lots of men." Even as there was truth to what his uncle said, something in hearing it from the one person who'd believed in him and given him purpose grated.

His uncle lifted a finger. "This is different, Leo." He grimaced. God, how he despised that name. The man Leo truly was bore no hint of the great saint his mother had named him after. His godfather let his arm fall to the desktop.

Leo's stomach sank as the thick tentacles of dread wrapped about him. "That is all, then?" he asked hoarsely. They'd simply dismiss all the work he'd done for the Brethren? All the plots against the Crown he'd foiled? The case he currently worked on to flesh out traitors to the country? He slumped in his chair.

"I did mention yours might be a whirlwind love affair with the lady," his godfather put forward. "I suggested that she might be the one to tame you."

"How easily you still manage a lie," he credited. The skills one employed on behalf of the Brethren remained with one forever, even with a loving marriage and family.

"Mayhap there can be truth to it."

"Truth to it?" he scoffed. First, the lady would have had to say "yes" for it to even be a possibility. And second, he'd have to be capable of that sentiment. "You've gone soft." His heart had been black since before he'd entered this world. He'd made the mistake only once of believing himself somehow… different than what he was.

The piercing intensity of his uncle's stare was one that saw too much. Leo slid his gaze to a point beyond his uncle's shoulder. "I've no intention of walking that perilous path." He'd made that mistake in his youth. He'd not do so again.

"Would it be so very bad?" his uncle suggested with a gentleness that set Leo shifting in his seat. "Being in love?"

Leo could handle direct talks about the Brethren and his reputation as a rake and pleading for help. His mouth went dry. When it came to this warmth, he didn't know what to do with it.

"Marriage has changed even the most hardened rakes." His uncle flashed a wry grin and gestured to himself.

"You've taken a misunderstanding between me and a young lady," one who, until two days ago, had been nothing more than a stranger, "and gone now to imagining a love match." A fate Leo was incapable of. One that he had no interest in. Not any longer. Love weakened a person. Destroyed and shattered. Yes, he was better off without that or any other weakening sentiments.

The duke hooded his eyes, the earlier warmth gone. "Then it seems you must also fake being in love… and well. It was not only Rowley who was doubting, but Higgins as well."

Because they wisely knew Leo for what he was.

"They plan to visit with me tomorrow afternoon. They'll... we'll make a decision about your fate and determine..." The duke stared pointedly at Leo.

Puzzled, he shook his head.

His uncle gave a nod.

"What?" Leo snapped. Given the precarious state of his future, he really did not have time to sift through his uncle's word riddles.

"Do pay attention, Leo. We'll determine whether you are, in fact, in love with the lady and pursuing a path of respectability now."

Leo's eyes slid closed as, with those words, his uncle put the death knell in his last hope.

"Oh, bloody hell," his uncle muttered. "You didn't speak to the lady."

"Of course I spoke to her," Leo said defensively.

"And?" His godfather leaned forward in his chair. "What was her response?"

"No, thank you." Despite the precariousness of his increasingly dire situation, a grin curved his lips.

His uncle leaned forward. "My God, are you... smiling?" He whistled. "The lady said yes."

Leo's grin instantly died. "She did not."

Uncle William dragged his hands over his face. "Oh, hell, Leo."

"I still believe I can convince her." It was a bald-faced lie. He'd gauged the lady as one who would value her independence and freedom... and made the greatest appeal to those desires, and she'd turned him down flat.

His uncle shoved to his feet, signaling the end of their meeting. "They're coming tomorrow. They've asked that I attend the meeting. Beyond this?" He shook his head again. "There is nothing more I can do for you."

Nothing more I can do for you...

Only Leo could help himself now.

Nay. Not Leo.

The spirited minx who proved clever enough to know marriage to him could yield nothing of value.

"Thank you, Uncle," he said tightly, smoothing his features, hiding his panic.

After he'd taken his leave of his uncle, Leo made the short ride to his own residence, frantically searching his mind for a solution that would get him out of this latest scrape.

I could kidnap the lady. Ride off with her for Scotland and…

As soon as the thought slid forward, he killed it.

He might be an immoral blackguard, but even he drew the line at abduction.

That was, abducting an innocent lady for his own gains.

He brought his mount to a stop outside his white stucco townhouse and leaped down.

A servant came forward to collect the reins.

Leo started up the steps and then froze. Would it solely be for his own gains if he abducted the lady? If marriage to her would salvage his career, then he'd be permitted to continue his work for the Crown. As such, wouldn't it be more a sacrifice to the country that the lady was unwittingly forced to make? He closed his eyes, contemplating the possibility… and then abandoning it. "Bloody bastard," he clipped out, taking the last two stairs as one.

Why did he have to develop a bloody conscience now, of all times?

The only hope for him was that, by some miracle, the stubborn minx set aside her disdain and accepted his offer.

Leo loosened the hooks at his cloak.

The doors were thrown open by his waiting butler, his usually affable features now stretched with discomfort.

"What is it?" he demanded as he shrugged out of his cloak. What in the blazes could it possibly be *now*?

"You have a visitor, my lord." Tomlinson pursed his mouth. "A lady."

Leo tossed the black wool garment into the man's capable hands.

The bloody tenacious viper. She was unrelenting. "You were instructed to throw her out if she were to come here again," he gritted. Wasn't it enough that she'd destroyed his career? Did she truly believe he'd welcome her in his bed? "So do it." Stalking across the Italian marble foyer, Leo started up the steps.

"Yes, my lord," his servant acknowledged. "That is correct." He cleared his throat. "But it is not *that* lady."

"I don't care who she is. I'm not receiving visitors." Nor did Leo care how the man handled the nuisance, as long as he rid the household of her presence.

"But, my lord." Tomlinson cleared his throat. "She insisted you'd want to see her. She insisted she'd wait until you arrived."

What manner of cheeky baggage entered his home and ordered about his servants? "There is no lady I want—" He stopped. There was one tart-mouthed miss who could order about even the most seasoned member of the Brethren. Furthermore, there was one respectable lady he cared to see. His heart increasing its rhythm, he wheeled slowly around. Given the whores and widows he'd bedded over the years, there could be any number of women who'd invaded his private residence at this late hour. But he'd not had any recent entanglements. His efforts had largely been focused on the Cato case.

It was far more likely that it was some discontented wife asking him to debauch her. And yet… hope stirred in his chest. "Who is she?" he demanded, bounding back down the stairs.

"She didn't give a name, my lord," Tomlinson informed, handing the cloak off to a liveried footman. "The young woman refused to relinquish her cloak and didn't remove her hood."

A woman bent on secrecy. Given the nature of his work, it could really be anyone. Given instincts that had saved his miserable arse more times than he deserved, he knew it was her.

It had to be. He'd given her a day to consider his offer. Mayhap she'd contemplated her future and reasoned that marriage to Leo was preferable to her shattered reputation.

"Where did you put her?" he asked, excitement spilling into his voice.

"I showed her to the Gray Parlor," Tomlinson explained. "I've stationed Michaels outside the rooms."

Of course, the loyal servant who'd been in his employ since Leo had begun working with the Brethren would know not only to bar anyone's entry into his offices, but also to set a guard on her.

Leo felt something he'd believed himself incapable of feeling— hope. He started down the hall.

"Oh, my lord? There is one more thing."

He paused. "Yes?" he asked impatiently.

"She had… has a cane. The lady walked with a limp and—"

Leo broke into a near run. He'd ceased to believe in God long ago, but it seemed the fellow might be real, after all.

Because nothing short of divine intervention from the Lord Himself could convince an intelligent miss like Chloe Edgerton to visit Leo in the dead of night.

CHAPTER 12

¶If it were discovered that Chloe had sneaked off and now sat in the home of London's most notorious scoundrel, she might as well pack her valises and prepare for a life abroad. There would be no recovering from such a scandal.

Or her mother's ire.

Still, with the threat real and her already tarnished reputation at risk of further tattering, she found herself oddly fixed not on the servant who'd been stationed at the doorway as a sentry of sorts… but rather on a fish.

An inanimate one, that was.

Just as she had been for the past thirty-three minutes since she'd been shown to the Marquess of Tennyson's Gray Parlor.

Seated on the silver satin sofa, she squinted across the room.

Or she believed the object was a fish.

Even after the footman who'd systematically lit the sconces, flooding the room with light, she still could not make out the creature.

Regardless, the bronze piece had held her transfixed the whole of her time here. At first, it was the one splash of oddly contrasting color to the otherwise sterile room that had called her attention. But the longer she stared and the more time lapsed, her focus had shifted for altogether different reasons.

Reaching for her cane, Chloe leaned her weight over the head of it and pushed herself up. Favoring her injured leg, she limped across the parlor.

What in the blazes was it?

She stopped at the Italian marble hearth. Leaning in, she examined the object that had kept her wondering, taking in the details that had, until now, escaped her—the open-work tail fins. She cocked her head. Or were they feathers? Regardless, they arced around the top of the creature's head.

Chloe stretched her fingers out and trailed them along the bit of patina at the base of the cool metal that hinted at its age. Everything, from the high quality of the casting, to the foreign craftsmanship, marked it as an exotic piece.

Why hadn't the marquess already sold the piece to cover some of his debts?

Her curiosity piqued, Chloe did another quick sweep of the desolate rooms. Gray curtains, gray Aubusson carpeting, a pair of tilt-top side tables absent of any baubles. In fact, the only ornamental item was the peculiar sculpture atop the mantel. What had made the marquess retain it, when the barren parlor spoke to items that had surely been sold?

Investigating the item again, she attempted to lift the statue.

She grunted as it remained firmly rooted to its spot.

Chloe attempted to lift it once more.

"Never tell me you've come to pillage from me, Chloe."

That droll interruption rang a gasp from her lips. Heart thundering, Chloe whipped around. Lord Tennyson lounged casually against the doorjamb, one broad shoulder propped.

How did a man of his size move with such stealth? "How did you…? When did you…?" Her questions rolled together, forming incoherent ramblings. "How long have you been here?" she blurted, and then her cheeks promptly fired.

Of all the blasted questions to manage to squeeze out.

"Long enough to wonder if you intended to make off with that piece atop my mantel," he drawled. Straightening, Leo entered the room.

Reaching behind him, he drew the door closed, shutting them in alone. The faint click and turn of the latch added a dangerous finality to her decision to come here.

There should have been a modicum of fear.

And yet, she followed his every movement, measuring his steps as he made for the corner of the room. Had the gentleman intended to harm her, he could have done so in Lord Waterson's offices and then again a few short hours ago when he'd entered her bedchamber.

With his back to her, the marquess contemplated the half-empty bottles before selecting a crystal decanter from under the mahogany drink cart.

"What is it?" she called over to him.

He paused, sparing a glance over his shoulder.

Chloe gestured to the peculiar artwork.

Returning his attentions forward, Leo proceeded to uncork the bottle. "It's a lamp." He tossed aside the stopper, and it clattered noisily upon the surface of the table.

"I gathered as much," she clarified, glancing back and exploring the piece with her gloved fingertip. "What I meant is... *what* is it supposed to be?"

"It's a swan," he said impatiently.

Her breath caught in a noisy inhalation as she whipped around. Chloe hurried to right her precarious balance. All the while, she clung to that annoyed utterance. "A swan," she breathed. *It was a sign.* Surely it was no mere coincidence that, of all the adornments in his sparsely decorated residence, the Marquess of Tennyson should have... a swan, the creature that had brought scandal down on Mrs. Monroe's Finishing School and opened the coveted post of headmistress.

"You insist on being on your ankle, madam?" he observed, calling her back to the moment.

Fighting to settle her thoughts, Chloe made her lips move. "It is feeling marginally better."

It wasn't altogether a lie. Though the ache lingered, the mind-gripping pain had receded.

The clink of crystal touching crystal and the steady stream of liquid as he poured his drink intruded, resurfacing the dangers posed by this man—and all men. Making a mockery of the bronze swan. This was real. This man's dependency on spirits. "I hardly..." As he spoke, his voice drifted in and out of focus.

She fought through the humming in her ears to make sense of

his words.

Unbidden, her gaze fell to his glass and lingered upon the reddish-brown liquid contained within.

The potent stench of brandy assaulted her senses as another man, a hated one, flashed to her mind, haunting as he invariably did.

I know you're herreee... I'm not happy with you, girl. Time to pay the price...

Chloe clung to the head of her cane, welcoming the bite of the carved handle as it dug into her palm, keeping her on this side of sanity.

"Chloe?"

That heavily impatient baritone pulled her back from the precipice.

What had he been saying? And more... why had she come? And then it all slammed into her again: Lord Waterson's ball, the gossip, Mrs. Munroe's.

"Why do you want to marry me?" she asked, getting to the heart of the question that had brought her here.

Lord Tennyson froze, his glass halfway to his lips. "Beg pardon?"

Nay, not Lord Tennyson. *Leo.* At the very least, given that she was even entertaining the prospect of marriage to him, she should muster the use of his Christian name.

"Well, it is just..." She paused and gestured to the chairs. "May I?"

"Please do." He waved his drink in the general direction of the silver upholstered sofa.

With those brief utterances and the veneer of politeness, one might believe they were any proper lord and lady engaged in a casual discourse, and not a pair who'd rocked Polite Society with their scandal and sought to come to an agreement amenable to both. Settling into the seat she'd vacated a short while ago, Chloe rested her cane against the nearby side table. "Why do you want to marry me?" she repeated.

"I don't. I *need* to. And it is in your best interest to marry me."

Her lips twitched. That honesty she could appreciate. "It is that 'need' that I'm most curious about."

He trailed a finger distractedly around the rim of his glass. "It would be enough for any lady that I made you an offer to spare you from scandal."

He was hedging.

Chloe smiled wryly. "I am not 'any lady,' my lord." She was a woman who knew her mind and what she wanted, and whose reputation mattered only for what it represented—her freedom.

"No, you're certainly not," he groused under his breath.

And mayhap it was a trick of her ears, but they pricked up at the hint of appreciation in that reply.

Nor did it escape her notice that time was marching on as he evaded answering her.

Collecting her cane, Chloe thumped it on the hardwood floor, the plush Aubusson carpet muffling the sound. "Well?" She didn't know what drove him, but she knew that he was no honorable gentleman hoping to rescue a virtuous lady from ruin. "A rake with your reputation must have been discovered in countless similar situations, and you've remained unwed. Why should you marry me now?"

Something dark flashed in his eyes. Leo tossed back his drink, downing it in one long, smooth swallow. The column of his throat worked quickly. Instead of setting the glass aside, he reached for the decanter.

Her black-hearted father had subsisted on spirits, a poison that destroyed.

"Must you do that?" she asked quietly.

Leo followed her stare to the bottle dangling between his long, gloved fingers. He hesitated, and for a long moment, she believed he intended to pour the next glass. She believed he'd do it as a testament to his power and to thumb his nose at her insolence for daring to question him.

And when he did, her reputation be damned, she'd walk out. She'd turn on her heel as quick as her still-aching ankle allowed, accepting that Mrs. Munroe's would never be hers and that her future would be forever set. She would be the eccentric aunt whose name had been ruined in a scandal that had shaken Society and, as such, marriage, employment, or any other opportunity would be denied her.

Leo returned the decanter to the table. His glass followed suit.

Chloe's lips parted, and she swiftly closed her mouth, schooling her surprise at the marquess' unexpected show of control.

No one could have impelled her dead sire to put aside his spirits.

The one time she had pleaded with him to stop, he'd thrashed her so that not a spare expanse of skin on her back had been anything but black, blue, or purple.

"Very well." The gentleman moved out from behind the drink cart. "You wish to know why I offered marriage to you?" He strolled over with his sleek, pantherlike steps.

She shook her head. "No, I want to know why it is so important that I shape you into a respectable gentleman."

With his thick, hooded lashes and hard lips, he was a predator hunting his prey, the perfect lion his namesake professed him to be. And mayhap if she were wiser, she'd be fearful. But he'd set aside his drink. He'd exercised restraint and revealed his hand. Lord Leo, the Marquess of Tennyson, might be ruthless and single-minded. But he was not a monster.

Monsters cared not for the wishes or whims of anyone, not children or wives, and certainly not strangers, and she took strength in that.

He stopped at the back of her sofa and leaned over so close his breath fanned the back of her neck, eliciting dangerous shivers that tingled through her.

Chloe's mouth went dry, and she desperately tried to make the muscles of her throat move so she might swallow. *He is just a man. He is just a man.*

And she was not a woman to be seduced by forbidden whispers and touches.

So why did her body continue to react to his nearness?

"Would you rather have pretty words, my lady?" he purred, wrapping that slowly drawn-out question in velvet. "Or mayhap you crave seductive ones? Shattering kisses? Forbidden touches." He slid two fingers between the slight gape at her cloak, further parting the noisy fabric.

Drawing in a shaky breath, Chloe slapped at his hands. "I've no desire to be shattered by anything." She hated the threadbare quality to that retort. Hated even more the masculine triumph that glittered in his blue eyes. The arrogance indicated he'd heard her falter and, worse, reveled in it.

"Which can only mean you've never known the pleasure to be had in a man's arms, Chloe," he enticed. "Because, if you did, you would gladly surrender to it."

Leo dusted his gloved fingertips along her shoulder. Back and forth. Over and over. It was a light, barely discernable caress. Yet, even through the protective fabric of her muslin cloak, her skin burned from that fleeting touch. It both tickled and tempted.

Chloe swallowed. And she, who prided herself on not being one of those silly misses who could be led astray by a ruthless rake or rogue, confronted her own fallacy with nothing more than the stroke of his knuckles. "Y-you are attempting to distract me."

He brushed his lips along the nape of her neck. The delicate kiss was so quick, with muslin a barrier between them, it might have been conjured of her own shockingly hypnotized musings. "Is it working?"

Chloe grinned. His teasing reply restored her mind to rights and reestablished the purpose of their latest meeting. "No." Scooting to the edge of her seat, she deprived him of the ability to bestow any more of those quixotic kisses. Chloe held his gaze. "You gave me a day to consider your proposal. I'm giving you even less. This is the last time I'll ask. Why? If you truly wish for me to entertain the possibility of marriage to you, I want an answer." One that he desperately clung to, which only further fueled her curiosity.

Leo flattened hard lips into an unyielding line. "My uncle."

She tipped her head. His uncle? Of all the reasons she'd expected—her dowry, his whoring, drinking, or wagering—the last she'd expected was that. "Beg pardon?"

"I have an uncle who has…" A vein bulged at the corner of his eye in a fascinating tell of his discomfort. "He's indulged my ways and assisted with my creditors. I was warned to be more discreet. If I failed to become," he grimaced, "respectable, he'd cut me loose."

It all made sense. "And then we were discovered together."

He sank onto the back of the sofa and folded his arms loosely at his chest. "Precisely."

He'd lost the benevolent support of his uncle due to an imagined indiscretion.

"He's cut you off, then? Unless you… that is… w-we," Chloe stumbled over the word that united them in a horrifying intimate way, "m—"

"Yes," Leo cut her off.

How very funny to find herself wholly unlike this man in so many ways and then to find common footing on their shared loathing of marriage.

Before her courage deserted her, Chloe spoke in a rush. "I would have certain terms met."

He shook his head once.

"If…" She lifted a finger. And it was still a gigantic, nearly insurmountable *if*. "I marry you, I have expectations."

She'd come to him with terms.

And if nausea still didn't roil in Leo's belly at the prospect of marriage to her—or anyone—he'd have managed a grin.

As it was…

She is actually considering it. She is here, of her own volition, to discuss a union with me.

The lady was either madder than the late King George or desperate.

Only desperation could have sent her from her rooms, injured ankle and all, to seek him out in his residence, and lay out… terms, as she called them.

Leo slowly lowered his arms. "Terms?" he repeated back, to be sure he'd not misheard.

Chloe nodded. "Ten of them." She sucked in a loud breath. "If you agree to all of them, then I'll help you become… respectable."

Intrigued, Leo straightened. He joined her on the sofa.

The lady cleared her throat. Reaching inside her cloak, she fished out a folded scrap and turned it over.

His fingers reflexively curled around the thick parchment. He glanced between the sheet and his early-morn visitor and then back again at the page. "You've written them down?"

She frowned. "If we are discussing a business arrangement, then it should be properly handled as all business arrangements are."

"And you have conducted very many business dealings?" He was unable to keep the smile from creeping into his question.

"You're teasing me." A pretty blush stained her cheeks.

Leo snorted. "I assure you, I don't tease anyone." That light repartee was reserved for foppish young pups, the manner of one he'd been a lifetime ago.

She spoke as though she hadn't heard him. Or mayhap it was that she didn't trust his word. Clever girl. "As you wish," she clipped out with a crispness to rival the queen's speech. "If you'd rather make light of me and my wishes—" She made a grab for the rough contract she'd come with, but Leo held up his arm.

"Forgive me," he said, angling his back to keep the page from her reach.

"You don't sound apologetic," she groused as he began to unfold the sheet.

"It's because I'm not." Glancing back at her, he softened that with a wink.

Chloe pointed her eyes skyward, pulling another grin from him.

Returning his focus forward in a bid to hide his amusement, Leo made a show of opening the intricately folded note.

He was having entirely too much fun with the lady. More fun than he'd had in years. The extent of his dealings with women entailed wicked bedroom activities and torrid affairs, and he'd never desired anything more than physical release. Verbal sparring was not something he engaged in with women, because it had never served a purpose. Only, now he found himself very much enjoying it with the spitfire beside him.

It had been years since he had engaged any woman in banter not born out of his sexual pursuit.

A lifetime ago.

"Well?" Chloe urged at his back, breaking the recollections of the first and last woman he'd let too close.

"I'm reading," he lied. Snapping the page in his hands, he directed his efforts to the requests inked there.

Marital Requirements of Chloe Edgerton

He flinched. The lady had put her name in bold upon the page, a sheet that could be picked up by any servant or nosy lady and bandied about by all. She'd have made a rotted spy. Sighing, Leo read.

1. I am granted ownership and total control of my dowry.

2. I will maintain relationships with my family and friends without interference.

He paused, glancing back. "You don't have a high opinion where men are concerned."

With an arch look, Chloe gave him a thorough up and down, and his ears went hot at the pointed recrimination. *My God, hell hath frozen over and chilled the whole of England with it.* He, Leo Dunlop, was capable of… blushing.

Shifting on the sofa, he faced forward again. "Uh… yes." He shook the page. "Continuing on." Even as he set to resume his reading, however, questions swirled around his mind about the mysterious lady who'd invaded his home. What gentleman was responsible for her world weariness? The same one now responsible for the spitfire's still-unmarried state?

"Are you reading?"

"I'm reading," he groused.

"Your eyes weren't moving on the page."

My God, she missed nothing.

Taking care to again present the too observant minx with his back, Leo pressed ahead.

> *3. I will maintain residence where and when I would—also without interference.*

"I'm beginning to notice a trend." He directed the dry observation at the page.

> *4. I will not be required to organize, host, or attend any ball… unless I so wish it.*

"It appears we have something in common," he muttered under his breath.

The rustle of muslin and the nearness of her voice when she spoke indicated she'd moved closer. "What was that?"

"I said…" His words trailed off as he snagged on the next item upon her list.

> *5. At my discretion and choosing, I shall be permitted the selection of a dog.*

"A dog, madam?" That was one of her requirements? He faced her. "You want a *dog*?"

She nodded. "Indeed. My family was never one to have them. Not even for hunting. Except…" Leaning around him, she snatched the sheet from his hands. Speaking softly, her mutterings wholly imperceptible to his ears, she scooted to the end of the sofa. He stared on with bewilderment as she fished around her cloak. Snaking something free, she leaned over the arm of the seat.

The rhythmic click of a pencil striking the table echoed in the quiet. A moment later, she handed back the sheet.

As Leo read her amendment, his eyebrows came together.

"Specifically, a mastiff," she clarified, as though he couldn't read the words written there and needed further elucidation. Which, in fairness, he did.

> 5. At my discretion and choosing, I shall be permitted the selection of a ~~dog~~ *mastiff*.

He had stepped into some farcical play. There was nothing else accounting for what this morning had dissolved into. Leo scrubbed his hand over the day of growth on his face.

Mistrust flickered in Chloe's eyes. "Do you have a problem with dogs, my lord?"

So she was "my lording" him… and her suspicion had been restored with force.

"I have more problems with the two-legged type."

A startled laugh burst from Chloe's perfectly bow-shaped lips. That mirthful sound was not the practiced, sultry ones affected by past lovers. It shook her slender frame and knocked her cloak further agape.

He stared on, transfixed. With her twinkling saucer-round eyes and flushed cheeks, she was transformed from the original common English miss he'd taken her for into a siren.

Her laughter abruptly faded. He grieved the loss of that oddly enticing innocent expression of joy. "What?" she asked, narrowing her eyes.

Leo dug around for some flippant, rake reply to earn another of the lady's eye-rolls. But God help him, for the first time in twelve years, he who'd never been without a retort—even a cruel one— came up empty. "It is nothing," he said in even tones, grateful for the diversion presented on her page.

Hurrying through the remainder of the items drafted, he stored away each detail. "A dog, then," he muttered.

Her interest in those four-legged creatures provided another intimate detail. With every reveal, she became less a stranger and more a peculiar woman who wished for dogs and isolation and… control. Her list evidenced a woman desiring of control… but also one who naively believed that charitable works mattered.

> 6. I am free to conduct my time at any charitable venture I deem important. I am also free to use my funds as donations to those unstated organizations.
> 7. We shall maintain separate lives.

Leo paused on item seven. Chloe wished for a separate life, wanted a dog—a mastiff, to be precise—and she preferred solitude.

Nay, that wasn't altogether true. He shifted his gaze to item two. Part of her demands included the freedom to maintain relationships with family and friends without interference from him. He tapped that telling item in her neatly scrawled hand.

Again, his earlier wondering surfaced.

"A broken heart?" An inexplicable curiosity pulled the question from him before he could call it back.

She went still.

Leo shook her list. "Was it some rogue who offered you pretty words and wrote poems to your beauty and then broke your heart?" It had been a role he'd played once with another woman. Only, it hadn't begun as such. It had begun as more…

The parchment crinkled noisily in his tightening grip.

Something in thinking of Chloe so hurt by a bastard such as Leo roused a primal fury in him. Which was ironic, given that he, as a rule and in reality, no longer felt anything… for anyone.

The lady wet her lips. Her expression guarded, her eyes unreadable, she proved him wrong in this instance. A lady who could dissemble in that coolly aloof manner could very well find her way in the Home Office. "Keep reading." The clipped command only served as further proof.

Leo resumed scanning the page and choked a bit on his swallow.

Feeling Chloe's eyes on him, he looked up slowly. With unhurried movements, he folded the sheet back into the neat little square she'd handed it over in.

She grabbed it and drew it close.

Coming to his feet, he yanked off his gloves and cast them aside. The soft leather landed with a thwack on the nearby console table.

"Well?" she pressed, fiddling with her cane.

"Yes. Yes. Yes. Yes. No. Yes. Yes. No. And nine?" He shrugged out of his jacket, tossing it on the sofa. It landed next to her. The midnight wool fabric crushed against her dark, muslin skirts. "Is an emphatic *no*." Leo rolled his tense shoulders. "Ten, however, is a yes." A peculiar one at that.

The lady wanted the freedom to take employment should she desire. It was a wholly foreign concept to both Leo and Society, especially the privileged beauties Leo took as his lovers. They wanted baubles and fripperies and a life of ease. Who was the bizarre lady he'd stumbled upon in Waterson's corridors?

While he contemplated her even now, the spirited minx silently counted and then consulted her list.

"No dogs," he clarified. It was the easiest place to begin their negotiations. "I'll not have one in my residence."

"Well, if I were in London when you are also in London, it would be *our* residence." She favored him with a generous smile that dimpled her cheeks.

Our residence. His palms went damp, and he scrubbed them on the sides of his pants. There was a permanency to their being melded as one, joined forever, until death did they part.

Nonetheless, he glanced covetously at the drink she'd challenged him to put down, needing it more than ever, but refusing to relinquish that control.

"No dog," he repeated.

"Very well." She grabbed her cane. "It appears our negotiations have broken down and—"

"A bloody mastiff," he snapped.

Her smile widened all the more, meeting her eyes. "Splendid," she said. With a pleased little nod, she settled back into her spot.

Leo sharpened his gaze on her. If his career and the Cato case weren't dependent upon his making a match with the lady, he'd have tossed her out on her delectably rounded arse. The minx was going to prove troublesome, and he had his own matters of trouble—ones that affected the whole of the bloody kingdom—to focus on that were vastly more important than an unbending Chloe Edgerton.

"I remain a firm nay on items eight and nine."

"Those are nonnegotiable." Another rush of color flooded her cheeks, turning them a deep crimson.

He looped his arms at his back. "Then it seems we are at an impasse, Chloe." He allowed those words to roll from his tongue, tempting her. For, her item nine—he was not to place his hands upon her, in any way—ran counter to every dark, carnal urge of his being.

The lady struggled to her feet. "Th-then we are truly done."

He closed the distance between them in four long strides. Sliding himself into her path, he cut off her retreat.

Five or six inches past five feet, she was taller than most women.

With no more than a handbreadth between them, he saw all: the rapid rise and fall of her chest, her flushed cheeks, her quivering mouth. Whether she wished it or not, her body responded to him.

Leo stroked his knuckles in an errant caress down her cheek. "Do you know the problem, Chloe?"

"I was unaware I had one." Her voice emerged breathless, the whisper of lemon and mint tantalizing in their innocence.

"Oh, yes. You do." He shifted his touch lower, along her slim jawline, dusting it across her delicate chin. "You've not yet discovered all the splendorous pleasures to be had from a man's touch." Her lashes fluttered wildly, and she leaned into him.

He reveled in the evidence of her hungering. "I'll show you all the pleasures you've not yet explored. I'll open your body to a passion that will sear your soul and leave you hungry and craving the rhapsody to be found in my arms."

The lady's throat moved.

She abruptly stepped back, stumbling a bit, and then she righted herself. "I'm not looking for a lover."

The soft flush on her skin made a lie of that pronouncement. She knew it. He knew it.

As such, he offered a half-grin. "A compromise, then?"

Chloe thinned her eyebrows. "I am listening," she said gruffly.

"I'll not put my hands upon you," he said as he caressed his gaze over her slender frame before returning his stare to hers. "Unless you wish it," he enticed.

She snorted. "I wouldn't."

Not *I won't*. But rather, *I wouldn't*. Which spoke to her eventual capitulation. Triumph was nearly his.

And, with it, shackles. Instead of the earlier horror that had turned his gut and caused a cold sweat, there was an eager antic-ipation.

Leo dipped his head. "If," when, "you want to know pleasure in my arms, Chloe, your term number eight is dissolved." He'd not debate that point with her now. Soon. After they were married, he'd have her in his bed, begging for him.

The lady drew in a shaky breath and nodded. "Very well. But I'm inflexible on my terms for item nine."

He jerked erect. "No."

"That is not an emphatic 'no.'"

"This one is." What she asked was impossible. "You'd ask for my f-f-f—"

"Fi-de-li-ty." She stretched out the syllables, sounding the words out the way a tutor might deliver a language lesson to a slow-to-learn student.

"And…" He strangled on the word.

A mischievous twinkle lit her gaze. She snapped her page out and waved it under his eyes. "I expect your faithfulness."

Leo ripped the page from her hands and gave it a shake of his own. "Why should it matter to you whom I bed?" Particularly when she'd requested a marriage of convenience.

"I'm incapable of," he curled his lip, "sexual purity."

The lady gave a flounce of her golden curls. "Then you, my lord, are incapable of marriage to me."

He opened his mouth to debate the inherent foolishness of her contradictory requests—a marriage of convenience with an imposed celibacy—and abruptly stopped. He snapped his lips closed and contemplated her requests.

Why… why…

She believed he'd deny her requests. It was the reason for the eccentric items scrawled in her neat, swooping letters.

Releasing some of the tension in his frame, he rolled his shoul-ders. "Very well," he conceded.

She choked. "Wh-what?"

He reached out and thumped her between the shoulder blades. "I'll agree to your terms."

Suspicion turned her sky-blue eyes dark. "It can't be that easy," she said slowly, backing away from him.

"Don't trust me, love?" He waggled his eyebrows.

Chloe laughed, a clear, bell-like quality that echoed around the room. "I'd be mad to." Her amusement immediately faded. "As such," she went on, no-nonsense once more, "prior to our wedding, the formal arrangement will be carefully laid out in a contract."

The farce continued. "A contract?" he parroted. "You want me to put into writing—"

"All items we've agreed upon?" She nodded emphatically.

Actually, he'd been about to mention their conjugal relationship once wedded.

As he studied her, his wariness grew. A lady who'd dictate his movements and actions, and who was far too clever by half, was one he'd be best running in the opposite direction from. And yet, there was no choice.

He took a step closer. "I'd also have certain promises from you."

"Oh?" she asked cautiously.

"In addition to your helping me attain respectability," or at least helping him craft that thin veneer, "I do not want any personal questions about me or my past or my present or future. Nothing."

She wrinkled her nose. "That hardly establishes a companionable match."

"Because it is not companionable," he reminded. "By your own terms, it is a business arrangement."

"But you also wish to bed me?" she returned.

The lady was still an innocent. She believed the two could not be mutually exclusive. She expected that with sex came intimacy. She'd learn—in time.

"What is your answer, madam?"

"Very well. I'll not ask you any questions. What else, then, my lord?"

Did he imagine the hint of disappointment in her tone? Regardless, they were strangers. He'd marry her, but ultimately wanted her to remain a stranger. Any emotional entanglements were dangerous ones. They prevented a man from fully devoting himself to a case.

"My office is off-limits. If you desire offices of your own, madam, I'll have the servants prepare one. I'm not to be disturbed when I'm in there, and you are not to enter, whether I'm in there or not. Is that clear?"

She scowled. "I'm not a child."

With her nipped waist, flared hips, and breasts made to fit his palms, no, no, she certainly wasn't. "Do you agree?"

"Very well." Chloe nudged her chin. "What is your next requirement?"

"You are not to fall in love with me," he said gravely. It had been the folly only one other woman had committed before. He was unworthy and unwanting of those sentiments.

A fulsome laugh exploded from Chloe's lips. Her mirth shook her frame until tears streamed down her cheeks.

Another would have been offended. Leo's shoulders sagged with relief.

The lady dusted off the remnants of her amusement. "I can offer an emphatic 'yes' on that term, my lord."

"Then it is settled," he said, starting across the room. There was much to see to, and quickly—before the lady's brother returned, or before she came to her senses and changed her mind.

"That is all?" she called out.

Leo didn't even break stride. "Would you prefer I ask you for more?"

She wisely fell silent.

"I'll have the contract drawn up and—"

"No."

Oh, bloody hell. She'd already changed her mind. Or, more likely, she was as greedy as every last lady in London. "What now?" he snapped.

"I want my family's solicitor to draft the document and be present for the... the..." *Wedding.*

He shook his head. "The moment your brother discovers your intentions, our arrangement will be at an end, madam." Leo stole a glance at the clock. As it was, with dawn rapidly approaching, the gentleman would soon discover her gone. Impatience snaked through him.

"My brother is gone to retrieve my mother," she supplied, neatly following his thoughts. "He left this morn and will likely return within two days. I'll not elope. As such, a proper betrothal is our only option."

Stalking over to the sofa, Leo retrieved his jacket and found the officious document tucked away. "I've already secured the special license."

The lady's startled gaze went to the document allowing them to wed and then back to his. "You secured a special license from the archbishop?"

"That is generally the way one goes about it, as long as one desires a legal union."

Accepting the document he held out, Chloe skimmed the sealed pages.

Yet, with his notorious reputation and black heart, she'd sufficient reason to doubt how one such as he had earned that fellow's approval. His work for the Brethren, however, would remain the eternal secret between him and his almost bride. Given her list of requirements for their marriage, it should be a secret easy enough to keep from her.

Striding over to the bellpull, he gave the slim string a tug. "I'll have you shown to your rooms."

"My rooms? Surely you jest. I c-cannot s-stay here," she sputtered.

"Provide me the name of your family's solicitor, and I'll have him summoned. We'll be married as soon as the documents are drafted."

A knock sounded at the door. "Enter," he boomed.

Chloe whipped her gaze toward the door. The alacrity of that movement dislodged several curls and set them to bouncing above her eye. "But—but..."

"Tomlinson," he instructed. "If you'll show the lady to the rooms next to mine?"

The lady blushed a crimson hue that could have set her afire.

"As you wish, my lord." To Tomlinson's credit, that revelation earned not even the slightest crack in the older man's composure. Or mayhap it was more a mark to Leo's wickedness these years that the servant wouldn't so much as flinch at a young lady invading Leo's home and being assigned the room beside his. "My lady?" his butler urged, motioning to the doorway.

Chloe remained rooted to the floor, immobile. Her quickly rising chest provided the only movement to her still form.

As time ticked by and she remained unmoving, Leo expected her to renege and bolt as fast as her "marginally better" ankle would allow. That all this had been a brave show on her part, but when push came to proverbial shove, she recognized the folly in both trusting him and wedding him.

Chloe exhaled slowly through her compressed lips. With a slight nod in Leo's direction, she turned on her heel and ambled off.

He stared at the empty doorway long after she'd gone.

It would seem this was, indeed, the day pigs had flown over the Thames.

And despite the fact that Leo was just a short while from abandoning his bachelor state, he smiled.

CHAPTER 13

With Leo's uncle, the Duke of Aubrey, and the Edgerton man of affairs as witnesses, Chloe and Leo were married one hour and eighteen minutes later.

For all the impossibilities of the terms she'd put to Leo and the unlikeliness of the timing to secure a license, witnesses, and a vicar, he'd managed to secure all… and in that short time.

It was another incongruity that didn't fit with the rake barred from more than most of Polite Society's functions.

It was far easier to focus on those puzzles and make sense of them than the fact of what she'd just done.

I'm married.

Her pen skidded, leaving a squiggly line of ink upon the marriage documents she now signed.

"My lady?" Clarke, the gray-haired, heavily wrinkled solicitor, asked in pained tones. "Are you all right?"

Blinking slowly, Chloe looked up at the loyal Edgerton servant. Leo had located the solicitor, dragged the man to his residence, and set Clarke to work on a contract.

"Fine. I am fine," she managed.

Clarke winced.

Yes, *fine* was hardly the attitude a bride should have on her wedding day. One was expected to be joyful and blushing and beaming… just as her friend, Imogen, had been and sister, Philippa, had been with her latest marriage.

"His lordship is going to have my head," he whispered, his jowls moving with his spasmodic swallowing.

That he'd assisted Chloe, without regard for whether he'd earn his employer's wrath, spoke volumes about the man's character.

She patted his hand. "He'll not." Chloe wouldn't let Gabriel have his pound of flesh from a man who'd merely sought to help her. "I'm happy," she said belatedly. "I wanted to marry the marquess." At least that much was true. In a sense. Marriage to Leo represented freedom and control of her future.

Clarke perked up. "Y-you're certain?" he asked. Hope tinged his words.

She wasn't certain of anything anymore. Which way was up, down, sideways, or in between. "I am." For, at least this decision belonged to her.

A marriage of convenience to a gentleman wholly uninterested in her.

Mr. Clarke's attention was called back by the vicar. As they conversed, their discourse was lost to the words now reverberating around her mind.

I'll show you all the pleasures you've not yet explored. I'll open your body to a passion that will sear your soul and leave you hungry and craving the rhapsody to be found in my arms…

Her heart galloped, and a warmth settled low in her belly. No, those were not the promises of a man who wanted nothing to do with her.

And she didn't know what to do with that realized-too-late consideration. She'd always had more than a distant curiosity of those forbidden acts that so many women explored. But she'd not given thought to experiencing any of those feelings herself.

Until now.

From where he stood conversing with the Duke of Aubrey, Leo paused mid-discourse. She braced for the lascivious grin or leer he'd donned during their first chance encounter at Lord Waterson's.

Instead, a question filled his eyes.

Had he sensed her nervousness? And more, why should a professed heartless rake even care?

Disquieted by the unexpected response, Chloe swiftly dedicated all her attention to the next page requiring her signature. The marquess' sensual grin would have been safer. Indolent lords weren't supposed to note the squeak of a pen or the unease raging in the breast of a mere stranger. And she'd wager it was unlike him to concede to the very points she'd put to him, plus agree to the use of her family's man of affairs.

"Ahem." The kindly, fleshy-cheeked vicar smiled. "If you would place your mark here, my lady." He motioned to the requisite space on the forms.

While she continued signing, Chloe peeked out the corner of her eye at Leo—her husband—and his uncle, the powerful Duke of Aubrey. That had been the benevolent uncle whose favor he needed to curry in order to have assistance with his debt and creditors.

And yet, as they spoke, they carried on easily with a familiarity and almost warmth that was neither strained nor for show. Oh, there was the perpetual bend of cynicism to Leo's lips, but there was an ease in his shoulders and entire frame as they spoke.

Riveted by the unexpectedly companionable exchange between uncle and nephew, she boldly watched. She cocked her head. Theirs was hardly the stilted tension and simmering fury she had expected of Leo and the uncle who'd threatened to not pay his creditors.

Just then, the duke caught Leo's upper arm and gave it a slight, affectionate squeeze.

A dull flush stained the younger man's rugged cheeks, giving the marquess an almost boylike quality. And for the first time since he'd stumbled upon her in the corridors, she saw beyond the rake he was. Who had he been before he was Society's most scandalous scoundrel? People were not born hardened, but rather they were shaped by life and all its hardships—just as she had been. What had made Leo Dunlop, the Marquess of Tennyson, into the man he was now?

I do not want any personal questions about me or my past or my present or future. Nothing…

As she turned his demand over and over in her mind, her intrigue doubled.

Both gentlemen looked in her direction.

Oh, bloody hell. Her cheeks fired hot.

"My lord?" The vicar called Leo over, and she gave thanks for the timely rescue.

Leo joined her, standing so close their legs brushed.

Chloe fiddled with her skirts. Aside from her brothers, she'd never stood so close to another gentleman. In fact, as a rule, she'd made it her mission to avoid those unpredictable sorts—whenever she could.

As such, she didn't know what to do with her body's reaction to this man. The intimate press of his thigh and the sandalwood cologne that clung to his person did odd things inside her belly.

And she, who'd never given thought to being in a man's arms, wondered. Wondered what it would be like to be with this particular gentleman.

While the marquess quickly and methodically slashed his bold letters upon the page, she inched away and knocked into a solid wall.

Gasping, Chloe wheeled around, steadying herself with her cane.

"My apologies," the duke murmured.

She pressed a hand to her racing heart. Was it a familial trait to move with such stealth? "No apologies required. I'm afraid I was woolgathering, Your Grace."

He held out an elbow. "Accompany me on a walk about the room, Lady Chloe."

There could be no taking that as anything less than a ducal command.

Leo paused. "The lady suffered an injured ankle," he said tightly. The duke widened his grin. "Then I'll escort the lady to a seat."

Uncle and nephew were locked in battle… that ultimately the duke won.

Chloe placed her spare palm onto the duke's sleeve and allowed him to escort her to the same sofa on which she'd worked out the terms of her arrangement with Leo.

I am married…

All the oldest fears she'd carried for the whole of her life resurfaced. They slammed into her, freezing the air in her lungs until a deep pressure built there.

She'd been so fixed on her hopes for the future and freedom and Mrs. Munroe's that she'd not allowed herself to linger on the price.

The duke took up the King Louis XIV chair closest to hers. He steepled his fingers and rested them upon his flat stomach. "You are the young woman who's managed to bring my nephew 'round to marriage."

She didn't delude herself into believing that a man of his power and prestige wouldn't have heard the details surrounding their hasty union. "We were discovered in a compromising position, Your Grace," she said carefully, studying his deadpan expression. She couldn't make out a hint of what he was thinking.

They sat, gazes trained forward on Leo, his back presented to them while he continued to sign the marriage documents. "When Leo was ten, his father purchased him his first horse," His Grace said quietly, unexpectedly.

Chloe blinked slowly and glanced to the older, but handsome, duke. "Your Grace?" she ventured. Her husband had forbidden her to ask for any information—from *him*. Therefore, every piece offered by his uncle was an unlikely glimpse.

The duke stared off at his nephew. "My brother-in-law was insistent that Leo learn to, at last, ride. Leo declined the offering. He was quite content with his books and studies, and little else interested him."

She started. "His books and studies?" She was unable to keep the shock from creeping into her tone.

A glimmer lit the duke's eyes. Leaning toward her, he dropped his voice to a secretive whisper. "From before the sun rose to the moment it went down, Leo could be found with his head bent over a book. He was quite the student."

Chloe whipped her gaze back to her husband, and she tried to imagine him with these new, unlikely strokes painted by his uncle: Leo, as a boy, burning the midnight oil. "Indeed?" she murmured.

The duke chuckled, bringing her gaze reluctantly away from her husband. "Don't let him convince you otherwise." He winked. "He's kept that secret rather close."

The Duke of Aubrey paused for a moment before he continued the story. "He refused to go near that horse, no matter how many times his father demanded it." A palpable fury flickered in the duke's eyes. "So, he took Leo's books away, one at a time. He found out which were Leo's favorites from the boy's tutors. He started there. And he systematically moved on through all the books in their household."

A sharp pang struck her heart as that imagery called forth a young Leo watching all those gifts he loved carted away. "But why did he not simply ride the horse?" Why, when nearly every English boy yearned to ride, had he fought his sire at the expense of his own pleasures?

"Because he's Leo," his uncle said matter-of-factly. "He wouldn't ride and had nothing to read… so do you know what he did?" Incapable of words, Chloe shook her head. "He wrote five books that summer."

Her mouth fell open. How odd was this explanation of Leo's youth compared with the rake Society knew him to be. "How did his father respond?"

The duke swiftly schooled his features. "That is a question for your husband." He intended to say nothing more, and she wanted to stamp her foot in frustration.

"We are done here."

They looked up. Leo towered above them, suspicion heavy in his gaze.

"Lady Chloe," the duke acknowledged, coming to his feet.

Grabbing her cane, Chloe stood.

"It was a pleasure," he murmured, gathering her fingers. He raised them to his lips for a kiss. "My wife will insist upon a wedding breakfast."

Leo snorted. "There'll be nothing of the sort."

"It was a pleasure speaking with you, Your Grace," Chloe said softly. There had been a calming reassurance to both his presence and the tale he'd told about her husband that had made Leo *real*. But then, mayhap there was a greater danger in that…

The three men who were witnesses to her wedding departed in a flurry, leaving in their wake a weighty silence.

Alone. She was alone with this man—her husband.

Chloe clenched and unclenched the head of her cane, searching for something to say, a question, an observation, a casual utterance. What was one to say? Or how was one to be?

"You've gone quiet," Leo observed in that seductive purr she despised, for its effect on her and its falsity. He drifted closer.

"Did you practice it?"

Her question brought him to a staggering stop.

"Your speech, that is," she clarified. "It's dark and cynical and is surely the stuff of practice."

"It comes with experience," he said. This time, his words were spoken in his smooth, melodious baritone.

Her heart fluttered. There was far greater danger to a lady's sensibilities than those natural tones that infused warmth and realism grander than the icy veneer he so often wore.

She wet her lips. "I should…" Her mind raced. What should she do? The immediate answer was… run. But from what? Her body's response to him? Their marriage? The uncertainty of both? Of all?

"What should you do?" he enticed, lightly cupping her nape in a tender grip that allowed her all the power. One that she was free to separate from—if she wanted. "Leave?"

So why did she not draw back?

"Or do you wish to remain here, with me, so I can show you what *we* should do?" he whispered against her mouth.

Shake your head. Push him away. For, with every sway of her body closer to him, she broke the terms she herself had set forth between them.

"We've not yet sealed our arrangement."

"H-haven't we?" she asked weakly. "I… we signed our contract, and there were the marriage documents and—"

Leo flicked the pad of his thumb over her lower lip, quelling those ramblings. Her breath quickened. It was just a small touch, and yet, that subtle caress seared her flesh. "Where is the fun in merely inking one's name to a sheet of parchment?"

His uncle's earlier revelation drifted forward.

He wrote five books that summer…

"You once enjoyed writing, though, didn't you?"

It was hard to say who was more shocked by her question— Chloe, for letting those recently shared words tumble free, or Leo, who stumbled back a step.

His previously heavy lids snapped open. "You were speaking to my uncle," he said bluntly.

Unease gripped her, and she retreated, as every age-old fear she carried resurfaced. "He volunteered information, and I listened." Gladly listened. She'd be mad to turn away information about the gentleman she'd wed. "You enjoyed books." He jerked his gaze about, as if he feared they were being spied upon even now, and his reputation would be ruined from that reveal. "There is no shame to be had in that. Nor should you make apologies for—"

Leo cupped her nape and slammed his mouth onto hers.

Heat.

Burning, searing heat, hotter than the summer sun on its warmest day, scorched through her as he slanted his lips over hers again and again.

Chloe stilled. Then, with a moan, she released her cane and gripped the front of his jacket. He devoured her. His lips molded with hers, and God help her, this was what he'd spoken of. *Passion*. She melted against his chest, absorbing his strength, clinging to him for purchase as he parted her lips and slipped his tongue inside.

That hot, velvety flesh stroked hers in a primitive meeting.

She tentatively touched the tip of her tongue to his.

A masculine groan of approval filtered from his lips, vibrating her mouth, emboldening her. And Chloe let herself go, turning herself over to the desire within.

Climbing her arms about his neck, she looped her hands there and clung to him for all she was. She'd never known it could be this way. Hadn't bothered to think of what a kiss could be beyond a curiosity about women who traded their freedom for a man's embrace.

Leo broke away, and she whimpered at the loss. But he swept her into his arms and guided her back down upon the sofa. He swiftly lowered himself above her. The springs of the sofa squeaked under the weight of his knee as he anchored it between her and the back of the seat.

It was time enough for reality to intrude, but God help her, she wanted more of him… and this. He trailed slow, lingering kisses from the corner of her mouth, lower, to her neck. Gathering the flesh between his lips, he gently sucked and suckled at the place where her pulse pounded.

She panted and tangled her fingers in his lush golden hair.

"I've wanted to do this since I had you in Waterson's offices," he rasped against her.

Chloe closed her eyes and angled her neck so he could better access her. "In-indee—shsh…" Her speech dissolved as he pressed a hot kiss to her modest décolletage.

All these years, she'd prided herself on taking control of her life… and living for herself, when her mother and sister had once existed only for another. Now, lying in Leo's arms, she reveled in the exquisite bliss of knowing this passion.

Reaching between them, Leo guided her skirts higher and higher. A blast of air slapped at her stocking-clad legs, providing a welcome cool to the conflagration he'd caught her in. That relief was short-lived as Leo caressed a searching hand from her calf all the way to her thigh. Then, sliding his hand under her, he filled his palm with her buttocks and drew her exposed lower legs around his thighs.

A keening moan spilled from her, wanton and shameless and wholly foreign as he pressed the rigid length of his shaft to the flimsy barrier provided by her undergarments. He rocked against her, and the heavy ache at her core deepened.

"Leo," she pleaded, unknowing of what she begged for, but trusting implicitly that this man could show her.

A proper lady would have been riddled with horror for the reminder that they were largely strangers.

Chloe had never been proper, nor had she aspired to a decorous state.

His mouth found hers once more, and she wrapped her arms about him. She eagerly met the bold thrust and parry of his tongue.

He continued that quixotic movement, grinding himself against her until her hips lifted and fell of their own volition. The pressure grew—

The air hissed from between her lips as he palmed her center.

"You are so wet for me," he purred as masculine pride dripped from that revelation. He parted the slit in her undergarments and slipped a finger inside her.

She cried out, reflexively clenching around that long digit.

He took her mouth again, his fingers moving in time to the stroking of his tongue.

Moisture beaded on her brow as she lifted into his touch.

He was a stranger. He was a rake. But her body didn't give a damn for propriety. It knew only what it wanted. And Chloe wanted him.

Panting, Chloe frantically arched. The yearning between her legs needed to be sated. She was so close. So close to some unknown goal.

"Let yourself go," he ordered hoarsely.

His urging pulled her across that invisible barrier. Chloe exploded in a flash of blinding white light. A scream tore from her, echoing from the rafters in a symphony of keening moans and rapture. He continued to stroke her, wringing every drop of pleasure from her lips.

Her breath coming hard and fast, Chloe collapsed into the comfortable squabs of the sofa.

As the tremors abated and the remnants of her pleasure went with it, reality intruded, and horror seeped in.

Leo removed his fingers from between her legs, and she shrank against the sofa.

She'd demanded a pledge from him, one that he'd given, and she'd faltered not even thirty minutes after being married.

Gripping his shoulders, Chloe used all of her body to roll him off of her.

He grunted, landing hard on the floor. From where he lay, Leo trailed an appreciative gaze over her naked limbs.

She gasped and swiftly lowered them into place.

If he uttered one triumphant word. If he spoke one single, rakish jest, she'd clout him. "There is the matter of my family," she said quickly. "I have to let them know... That is, I must..."

He lingered his eyes on her legs before meeting her stare. "Should I accompany you to—"

"No," she squawked, her own surprise reflected back in his eyes. "That will not be necessary. My brother is gone to gather my mother, and I should speak to them alone. When the time comes. When they return. Simply because..." *You are still rambling.* She went silent.

He leaped to his feet. "Of course," he said stiffly, adjusting his cravat. "I will... if you'll excuse me?"

And as though the devil himself were at his heels, he bolted.

A short while later, in her wrinkled brown skirts that had served as a wedding dress and curls freed from her plait, Chloe took the coward's way out—and sent her family a note.

CHAPTER 14

Oᴡʜᴇɴ ᴘʀᴇsᴇɴᴛᴇᴅ ᴡɪᴛʜ sʜᴀʀɪɴɢ A residence with his new wife or fleeing as fast as his legs could carry him, Leo chose the latter.

Since his uncle had ushered him into an existence where he served the Crown, sparing him from further abuse at his now-dead sire's hands, Leo had resolved to be the best at what he did. When the Brethren had ordered him to transform himself from the pathetically weak scholar he'd been into a hardened rake whose womanizing and drinking were such to rival Bacchus, he'd done so.

And through the havoc of the past two days, he'd found a diversion where he always had—in his work for the Brethren.

Or he attempted to.

Seated in his offices at Aldenham Lodge on the fringe of London, Leo stared at the files opened before him. Just as he'd been staring for the better part of the hour.

He tapped the tip of his pen in a staccato beat on the corner of the folder, reading and re-reading the information contained within.

The Cato Event

Initial Opinion—a product of the London Irish community and trade societies; a scheme concocted by merchants and com-

moners.

The Cover—a scheme crafted by members of the peerage, in effort to see through the passage of the Six Acts.

Evidence:

It was too damned obvious. With a sound of frustration escaping him, he tossed down his pen, the thick file muffling the thwack of his quill. Despite his earliest opinions, it could not be so easy as proper gents bent on controlling legislation. It was always about money and power... always about what a man could get...

Think... think...

He dug his fingertips into his temples. It was futile. Just as it had been since he'd fled his household.

Oh, Leo had been forced into the role of a liar since his days at Oxford, but he was at least truthful enough to acknowledge his flight to the Brethren offices and his distractedness now had more to do with the minx who'd come undone in his arms ten hours ago.

Each case consumed him. His investigations drove him. No detail went ignored.

Until now.

Chloe's visage flitted forward, teasing, challenging, tempting, as she'd been since their first meeting.

"Bloody hell. Enough," he muttered, gouging his temples with his fingertips, wanting to rid his thoughts of her, drive back whatever pull had him so entranced.

Only once had he made the mistake of believing he could have both a devoted wife and eventual family... and keep his role as a spy for the Brethren.

One youthful misstep had nearly cost him the latter.

It was a mistake he'd never make again.

From that point on, he'd become precisely what his uncle and the Brethren wished him to be. Nor had he ever had a single regret after that. Any vulnerability was perilous, be it the mewling sentiments of *love* or the affections of a woman.

Leo bedded women. He reveled in the release he found in their arms.

After he was sated and his lover well-pleasured, he didn't give another thought to her.

Which was what made the whole of these last ten hours so fucking confusing. For when he'd brought Chloe, his bride, with her lists and logic to a release that still left her cries of surrender pealing in his ears, he'd not thought of his own pleasure. His own sexual gratification hadn't been the ultimate urge that had compelled him, but rather the satisfaction of seeing her come undone.

Reaching back, Leo gripped his neck and rubbed at the sore muscles there. After riding at a breakneck speed for his offices off Watling Street and spending hours bent over his work, he was tired to the core and in dire need of a hot bath. A hot bath, a brandy, and the clever massages he'd received from beauties in the Orient. Those sessions where the soreness was dissipated with an expert touch and then, afterward, dissolved by a hot, violent round of lovemaking.

Except, when he thought of bedding just any faceless, nameless woman, it was his wife's face that slid forward.

With a groan, he lowered his head and knocked it silently against his desktop.

A knock sounded on his office door.

Leo jerked his head up. "Enter," he barked, welcoming the distraction.

His clerk, Lathan Holman, a bespectacled, tall, gaunt youth very much an image of the weak pup Leo had been a lifetime ago, ducked his head inside. "Is there anything you require, my lord?" He was also endlessly devoted after Leo had coordinated the young man's placement with the Brethren. If Leo sneezed from one end of the establishment, Holman would be there with a kerchief and a blessing.

"A drink," he muttered, and the boy sprang forward. "A woman."

That brought Holman up short. A fiery blush suffused the clerk's pale cheeks. "Uh... I..." Apparently, Leo had determined the one task the boy was unwilling and unable to carry out. "I-I'll s-see to it, my lord," he stammered, breaking for the doorway and then stopping. "Or should I fetch your drink first?" He feinted left, toward the sideboard. "Or would you rather I see to the..." Holman's large Adam's apple bobbed. "To the..."

"It is fine, Holman," Leo mumbled under his breath and shoved to his feet. "I was jesting." There was only one lady he wanted. And it was a wholly foreign concept for him, a man who'd eased himself in the body of the nearest, most eager, and inventive woman.

Registering the absolute still to descend, Leo paused in his journey to the sideboard and glanced back.

A pair of crimson brows lifted above the spectacles. "A... jest, my lord? But you don't—" Holman immediately went tight-lipped.

His neck hot, Leo hurried the remaining distance to the bottles of fine French brandy and Irish whiskey. "Did you need me?" he asked impatiently.

"Oh, right. Of course. I've copied the notes pertaining to Waterson's business contracts and..." His detailed accounting rambled on and on.

Leo's world had turned upside down, and insanity had begun. Grabbing the nearest bottle, he splashed several fingerfuls in a glass, thought better of it, and added another fingerful.

Must you do that?

Chloe's quiet recrimination as she'd sought to negotiate the terms of their marriage intruded.

Leo stared down into the pale brown contents of his glass.

He answered to no woman. Nor persons, if one wished to be truly precise. His loyalties were reserved for the Brethren.

As such, her barely concealed disappointment and annoyance at his drinking shouldn't grate. Her words should have rolled off his back, along with every other dark insult that had been hurled at his head over the years. A groan of impatience rumbled up his throat, and he set his glass down hard.

"When I obtain the information, I'll be sure and deliver it to your offices, my lord," Holman finished.

Leo creased his brow. What in the blazes? What had the man been saying?

"Married not even a day and hard at work as you always are, I see."

Oh, bloody hell on Sunday.

His uncle's booming voice echoed around the room. Blast. He was everywhere. Everywhere that Leo was, rather.

"You," he groaned, waving off his clerk. The young man dropped a respectful bow for the duke and then hurried around him. Needing liquid comfort, after all, Leo grabbed the glass and carried it to his desk.

Uncle William closed the door behind him. "That's hardly the warm greeting for a beloved godfather."

"Don't you have a beloved *wife* to see to?"

His uncle arched an eyebrow. "I would ask the same of you."

"I hardly believe our hasty union constitutes the blissful marriage enjoyed by you and my dear aunt." Nor was it one he aspired to. As a young man who'd been captivated by an unconventional young lady new to London, he'd allowed himself the fantasy of what his aunt and uncle enjoyed. No longer.

His uncle claimed the seat close to Leo's desk. "Following your wedding," he began, setting his cloak on the back of the empty chair, "I met with Rowley and Higgins."

He stiffened. "Oh?" His pulse accelerated. It was the meeting he should have been thinking of since he'd exchanged the vows that had ended his bachelor state. Not the breathy moans and pleas of the delectable Chloe Edgerton... Dunlop. She was a Dunlop now. "And how did the meeting go?" he asked with feigned disinterest. This time, as he reached for his glass and took a sip, it was liquid fortitude he desperately required.

"Higgins was incredulous."

Higgins required less swaying. As one of the heads of the organization, he well knew how crucial Leo's role had been over the years. He'd lull himself into believing the lie. "And Rowley?" he asked, swirling the contents of his drink. That son of a sod.

"He called your hasty marriage the weakest act you'd yet perpetrated." The hint of a smile ghosted his uncle's lips. "They want to see you together."

He stitched his eyebrows into a single line. "How do you propose I explain my relationship to those gentlemen?" Those starchy, proper lords were never the manner of men Leo would keep company with. "She's too clever to not ask questions about that connection."

The duke reclined in his seat. "Indeed?"

Leo's ears fired hot. "Don't make more of that statement than there is." The lady, with her retorts and unwitting ability to lay command of her... and his future, had proven herself more intelligent than any woman—of any station—to whom he'd linked himself.

"Hmph." *Do not rise to that bait.* His uncle had been more a parent than the man Leo had called Father. He'd always known precisely what to do and say to elicit a reaction. "I said… hmph."

"I heard you." Leo downed another quick swallow, grimacing at the fiery burn. He set his glass down hard and grabbed his file.

"Higgins expects you and your clever wife to become a pillar of respectability. Attend *ton* functions." *Bollocks.* "Maintain connections with proper ladies and gentlemen." *This was bad.* "Host balls and soirees."

The thick folder slipped from his hands. "Absolutely not." Absolutely not for so many reasons. The least of which was that he hated balls. "Chloe despises balls." It had been one of the remarkable terms set forth that further stirred his intrigue with the peculiar minx.

His uncle laughed. "A lady who despises balls and soirees as much as you do? I do believe you have found your match." The duke's amusement faded, and he gave Leo a long once-over. "Furthermore, when was the last time you let another person's feelings get in the way of what you want or need?"

It had been thirteen years. Thirteen years since another person's misery had cut him to the core.

Had there been a stinging recrimination there, it would have been easier to take than that pragmatism. And he hated that his uncle's opinion should still matter when nothing else did.

"It's not about how the lady feels or what she wants," he said coolly, reinforcing the walls he'd kept up. "I signed an agreement promising I wouldn't expect Chloe to attend or host a bloody function. I cannot very well go about asking to alter the terms less than one day into the union."

"Your dear wife also detests them," Leo felt inclined to point out, needing to make that unique fact less important… for reasons he didn't understand. Nor cared to consider.

"Your *dear* aunt is displeased," his uncle segued, loosening the clasp at his throat. He removed his cloak and rested it over his arm. "She wants a celebration between our family and Lady Chloe's."

Leo scraped a hand through his hair, the noose tightening. "I don't have time to play at proper husband." The sole reason he'd entered into marriage with Chloe was so that he could continue his work for the Brethren. He cursed blackly. "It's more vital I focus on the Cato case. I believe I was wrong in my original supposition—"

"Leo," his uncle interrupted.

He continued over his uncle. "I think there is more at play here—"

"Leo."

"My research revealed vast sums that were siphoned to Lord Ellsworth in exchange for—"

"Leo, enough," Uncle William said firmly. "I'm not here about your assignment. Your role in the Brethren won't even exist without a legitimate marriage accepted by the leadership."

That silenced Leo.

"Now, I'll remind you one last time: The *reason* you married her was to convince the world—particularly your superiors—that you'd turned from rake to respectable gentleman." He glanced pointedly at the cluttered desk. "So, I suggest you get on your horse and put the same effort into your marriage that you did creating your façade as a rake."

"It's not a façade," he gritted out. Not a single lord or lady in all of London would ever call him anything less than a scoundrel.

Uncle William leaned over and gripped the sides of the desk. "Then, if you managed to go from bookish scholar to this, I trust you can also fall as easily into the role of honorable husband changed by the influence of a young, respectable lady." He jumped up with an agility better suited to a man twenty years his junior. "Go home, Leo. That," he slashed a hand at Leo's work sprawled out before him, "is dependent on your ruse with Lady Chloe."

After his uncle had gone, Leo remained in his office.

Go home, the duke had advised.

Yet, he sat rooted to the familiar folds of his leather chair.

Dropping his forehead into his palm, Leo stared blankly at the Earl of Waterson's name scratched at the center of the page with an enormous question mark alongside it.

"I'm a bloody coward," he muttered.

"What was that, my lord?" Holman's query came muffled from the other side of the oak panel.

"Nothing," he called out. "I don't require anything else this evening."

"As you wish, my lord."

Except…

"Holman," he called after his clerk. "There is something you can do." If he had to cede his efforts and energies to his pretend marriage, he could, at the very least, have Holman conduct the most basic forms of research on his behalf.

Eager-eyed, his clerk trotted back over.

Fishing out several pages from his file, Leo turned them over to the younger man's hands.

Holman's eyes devoured the sheets the way a child did a puff pastry at dessert. He cradled them close, covetously.

Yes, Leo himself had once been that energized at the hint of a role in any case. A lifetime ago, he'd been that boy. "I want you to look into the financial accounts and business dealings that are in direct contradiction with Lord Liverpool's Cabinet." The best way to identify those who'd wish to do away with the prime minister's Cabinet was to determine who had the most to gain by their absence.

"Yes, my lord." Holman knocked his heels together. "As you wish. Is there anything else?"

He waved the young man off. "That is all."

His clerk all but tripped over himself in his haste to be free of Leo's office.

Snapping closed his file, Leo abandoned all earlier efforts to lose himself in his work. He then confronted, head on, the reason for the tightness in his chest.

His wife.

That morning, when he'd taken her in his arms, Leo's sole intention had been to silence her. He'd kissed Chloe Edgerton—nay, now Chloe Dunlop—to stop her intimate flow of words about his past.

The moment he'd tasted her, however, his insecurities and annoyances... and clear-headedness had all faded away, to be replaced with a fierce hungering to explore her mouth and then discover all of her.

And that need for her had scared the everlasting hell out of him. So much so that he'd fled to the Brethren estate and shut himself away.

Because Leo was a man who gave pleasure... but also expected it in return. He wasn't so selfless a lover that his partner's sexual gratification was enough. Or, he hadn't been.

But while exploring her tight, hot sheath and feeling her desire for him, all he'd wanted in that instant was for her to come undone because of his touch. Her pleasure had mattered to him more than his own. Not only had he hungered for her release above all else, he'd offered to accompany her to her family.

And he'd gone into hiding because of it. Leo snapped his folders closed and neatly stacked them. As his uncle had properly pointed out, Leo could not hide with his work. Not if he wished to convince Society and his superiors that he was capable of restraint and respectability. No, Leo could not accomplish that essential goal here on the fringes of London. As such, he needed to return home to the wife who terrified him more than any ruthless nemesis he'd faced in his line of work… even more so than the man Leo had called Father.

So why, as he took leave of his office and traded out his mount for a rested stallion, did it feel his return had nothing to do with his work and everything to do with a restive excitement to tangle words—and more—with the woman he'd made his wife?

CHAPTER 15

HER BROTHER HAD RETURNED MORE quickly than she'd expected.

As soon as Leo's butler drew the door shut behind Gabriel, he spoke on a rush. "My God, Chloe. What have you done?"

She opened her mouth.

"It doesn't matter," he said hoarsely as he strode over. He grabbed her by the arms and did a methodic search.

She grunted. "Gabriel, I am fine," she said gently, stepping out of his reach. "I wrote you because—"

"You asked for help." He brandished the note she'd penned. "I'm here now. I'll fix this. I'll—"

"I'd like our family to smooth Leo's entry into Polite Society," she interrupted, bringing his words to an abrupt halt.

He cocked his head. "What?" he blurted.

Chloe motioned to the letter he held. "As you are probably aware," she went on with a little flounce of her curls, "Society's opinion of Leo is not the most favorable."

A growl worked its way up Gabriel's throat.

She forced a smile, refusing to give in to the unease stirring in her belly. "Oh, very well," she said with a beleaguered sigh. "Their opinion is not at all favorable. But we, the Edgertons, that is, and the Brookfields can help with that."

"What?" Gabriel bellowed.

She jumped. And for Chloe's incorrect estimate on the time of her brother's return, she had proven wholly correct in one estimation—his fury.

To hide the slight tremble to her fingertips, she smoothed them over the front of her skirts. She forced her most winning smile. "You're taking this a good deal better than I expected," she drawled.

"This is not a matter to jest about, Chloe Edgerton," he exploded. "You marry a bloody blackguard like… like…" Oh, dear, things were dire if Gabriel was cursing and losing control of his temper. "Like…"

"The Marquess of Tennyson," she supplied calmly, refusing to be cowed. "And he has expressed a desire to reform." Which wasn't altogether untrue. She, however, took care to leave out the self-serving goals that motivated the gentleman. "As such, I'd like to solicit your help."

Gabriel resumed his tirade. "You sneak off, marry in my absence, and summon me to… to… help that bastard? *That* is the reason for your note?"

She mustered a smile. "Given I married the gentleman, I summoned you to help us." Not to save her like some wilting damsel.

Her brother froze and then slammed his fist onto the rosewood sofa table. "You are bloody mad. Mad, Chloe."

Heart pounding, Chloe fisted her hands.

This is Gabriel. Not your mercurial dead sire who'd smile one instant and clout you in the temple the next.

Except, this was Gabriel as she'd never seen him: in rumpled garments, smelling of horses and sweat, his face unshaven, his eyes bloodshot.

Her teeth chattered in the silence, and she immediately clamped them tight. The day she'd thrown dirt upon her father's casket as it was lowered into the ground, taking him on the path to hell, she'd made a vow to herself. She would allow no man to so terrorize her. Not again. Not her brother. No man.

"Dunlop," she said quietly, her earlier bid at humor gone. She edged her chin up, meeting her brother's gaze unflinchingly. "My name is now Chloe Dunlop."

Crimson splotches stained his cheeks. He said nothing for an interminable moment.

It is coming... just as all explosions of fury invariably did.

Gabriel thundered, "What have you done?" He proceeded to pace, his movements frenetic, jerky.

Even as she'd been expecting it, terror lanced through her.

"He is a *rake*."

"He is my husband."

"That doesn't change what he is, Chloe," he shouted, his anger echoing from the walls. "You know *nothing* of him."

No... and yet. "I know he agreed to a legal contract allowing me to retain possession of my dowry. He agreed to let my family's solicitor oversee the documents when you yourself orchestrated your own wife's future."

Gabriel stumbled and quickly righted himself. "Are you saying *Tennyson* is more honorable than me?" he choked out, shocked hurt dripping from that query. "That dastard? That... drunk?" With every allegation, fury grew in his tone. "A despoiler of innocents?"

She flinched. "You can't know that. You're basing that opinion on rumors."

Her brother scraped a hand over his face, muttering words that might or might not have continued to call into question her sanity.

Chloe frowned. Surely her husband wasn't... that manner of rake. *What other types are there?* They took their pleasures when and where they would. *And your rake of a husband has been gone for more than ten hours now.*

As if he'd followed the unwelcome path her thoughts had traversed, Gabriel dropped his arms to his sides. "Very well. This," he sneered, "*gentleman* wishes to reform his rakish ways and set himself on a path of respectability? Where is he now? At his club? Drinking? Wh—" He stopped, pressing his lips into a hard line.

The rub of it was, she and Leo had struck an agreement that was to be mutually beneficial. Why then did her insides twist in vicious knots at the likely possibilities dangled by her brother? "Enough," she said, as much for herself as for Gabriel. Shoving aside the unpleasant question about her husband's whereabouts, she nodded. "You will focus on the ugliest rumors you've heard about him. I'll, instead, focus on ways in which he's proven honorable." She stared at her always proper sibling who'd made it his life's mission to coordinate other people's lives based on what he thought was best for them. "Leo," her brother blanched, "allowed me to dictate the terms of our marriage. I am the one in control of my future, and he accepts that." How many other gentlemen would have so willingly ceded those controls? Certainly not her own brothers.

Gabriel gave his head a pitying shake. "If you believe that, you are a bloody fool," he said quietly. The calm to that pronouncement cut sharper than any charge he'd shouted.

The thin thread of her patience snapped. "How dare you?" Grabbing her cane, she propelled herself into a stand. "First, you'd dictate to Philippa whom she should wed. And even though she found herself in a miserable marriage to a man who didn't appreciate her or her children, you continued to play the role of one who knows what it is best for all your female siblings." The color leached from his skin, leaving it an ashen shade of gray. Fueled by her indignation, she took a step closer.

"Then you attempted the same for Jane. Lying to her... you *lied* to her, Gabriel, about her inheritance in order to *protect* her." She gave her head a hard shake. "That was not your choice to make, nor is it your role to save me from my own actions." Rather, she'd wanted Gabriel, her mother, all her siblings, to see her as her own individual deserving of her own decisions.

His throat worked. "I only sought to help."

He still couldn't understand. How could she make him see? "I know that, and I appreciate it, Gabriel. This, however, was my decision." Her marriage to Leo had been a well-thought-out grasp at a future she wished for, for herself.

Sadness filled her brother's eyes. "And it is one you'll live with forever," he said with an air of ominousness that raised the goose-flesh on her arms. "For there can be no undoing this." Hope blazed in his eyes. "Unless an annulment is immediately obtained."

Even meaning well, as he did, he could not relinquish his role as head of the family. "There are no grounds for an annulment," she lied, determined to quash his relentless attempts to maneuver her future.

Gabriel's cheeks went red. "Oh, God." He sank onto the edge of a nearby needlework side chair. The colorful tableau of doting mother and father beside two small children stood in mocking irony to the cold agreement she'd struck with Leo. "This is my fault," Gabriel whispered. "I should have never left. I was so concerned with fetching mother."

Their mother.

Chloe gripped the head of her cane. For, in the whirlwind of these past days, she'd not truly allowed herself to consider the moment her mother discovered that, in her absence, Chloe had wed the most scandalous of gentlemen. "How is Mother?" She forced the question out.

Her eldest sibling raised distressed eyes to hers. "How do you *think* she is, Chloe? When I handed her up into the carriage, she believed she would be dealing with a daughter who'd landed herself in a scandal because of that bastard, not one who'd gone and married him in haste."

She brought her shoulders back. Rumors be damned, she... and her Edgerton siblings were, if nothing, loyal. As such, she'd not tolerate her brother disparaging Leo. "That bastard,' as you refer to him, is now my husband," Chloe said coolly.

He groaned. "When our mother arrives home..." His gaze did a search of the room before settling on the enamel table clock beside him. He paled all the more. "Which will be any moment. And when she finds you're gone and married to..." Gabriel buried his head in his hands.

Chloe's attention, however, remained fixed not on him... but upon the intricate, repetitive pattern engraved upon the clock beside Gabriel. Pieced together in gold and silvers, the odd piece stood out as the only non-furniture item within the drawing room. She drifted closer, running her fingers over it. Yet another piece, foreign and unlike the usual adornments in English drawing rooms, and he'd not sold this one. Why? She searched her mind, desperately trying to reconcile that incongruity with the wastrel in debt and in need of his uncle's intervention to keep from floundering.

"This is my fault," Gabriel repeated on a tortured whisper. "I'm responsible for this."

He still didn't understand. "You'd take ownership even in this?" she challenged.

Gabriel might have always meant well, but that did not excuse high-handed behaviors that assumed he alone knew what was best for her or her sister simply because he'd been born a male and heir.

"What about your secrets? Have you shared them with the man... your... husband?"

She went silent. Her insides twisted.

"You didn't?" her brother rightly predicted, standing up.

Unable to meet his eyes, Chloe looked away.

"Did you think it did not matter?" her brother entreated. "Did you allow yourself to forget?"

"Of course, I didn't!" she exploded. Chloe stole a glance about, more than half fearing the man whose worth they debated lurked in the shadows. She dropped her voice to a hushed whisper. "One does not forget one's megrims." The debilitating headaches forced her into darkened rooms, away from anyone and anything—people, noise—where even the rasp of her pained breathing proved torturous.

"How can you not see?" Her brother took her by the shoulders. "A man like Tennyson would commit you faster than you could say 'dun territory,' Chloe," he whispered, "and then those terms would be moot, your dowry becoming his, and—"

"Stop it," she cried, spinning out of his reach. "Just... stop," she repeated, her voice a broken whisper. "You don't know that about him. You don't know—"

"Can you say with absolute confidence that he wouldn't, just to rid himself of you?"

Nausea roiled in her belly. Turning away from Gabriel's sad gaze, she pressed her fingertips into her temples, rubbing.

And just like that, the great terror she'd long carried assaulted her. As a girl, it had been the fear that her father would wash his proverbial hands of her by throwing her into a hospital. After his passing, as a young woman who entered Polite Society, she'd feared the very threat her brother now dangled.

The arrangement Leo had proposed, one that was mutually beneficial, had represented the greatest hope of her freedom and control... and through that, security. Naïvely, she'd allowed herself to forget the dangers of trusting a husband—Leo or anyone else—with her headaches.

Did you forget? Or did you force the thoughts from your head? Did you only see that which you most craved and deliberately omit the demons that will forever control you?

Chloe sucked in a slow, uneven breath.

For the truth remained: She could not predict what Leo would do if... nay, *when* her megrims struck.

"Come home with me," Gabriel cajoled.

Did he sense her faltering?

"I will hire the best solicitors, and we will find a way to free you from this mistake," her brother said quietly. "He is not to be trusted."

Mayhap it was fatigue after the upheaval of the past three days, or mayhap it was her need to ease the worries raised by her brother. But she could not reconcile the ruthless man her brother spoke of, a debaucher of innocents, as he'd claimed, with one who'd cared for her ankle, even as the risks of discovery would have been, and had proven, calamitous for him.

Staring into the small fire burning in the hearth, Chloe worried at her lower lip.

Who was the Marquess of Tennyson? And why did she suspect there were many layers and secrets to the man she'd married?

After a three-hour journey back to his Mayfair residence, Leo desired a drink, a bath, and his bed—in that precise order.

And cowardly though it was, he was grateful to arrive in the dead of night when his wife would be abed and—

"There is a visitor." Tomlinson spoke as he drew the door open, admitting Leo.

Alas, peace and solitude were not to be. Leo let fly a black curse. "Who in the blazes is here to see me at this hour?" Leo snapped. Aside from the like rakes within the organization, members of the Brethren, as a rule, generally avoided meetings at his townhouse. Connections between the lords and ladies who served had to be carefully orchestrated.

He made to unfasten his cloak.

Tomlinson's next words stayed his movements.

"You misunderstood." His butler cleared his throat. "*Her ladyship* has a visitor."

He removed his cloak and handed it off. "The brother?"

Tomlinson gave a jerky nod. "He arrived almost an hour ago.

They've been meeting in the Silver Parlor."

Bollocks. He glanced in the direction of the hall leading to that room. Leo had miscalculated the speed with which Waverly would return and seek out Chloe. No doubt to try to end the brand-new marriage. "I trust you've listened in?"

"Of course," Tomlinson said, as if it were the most common thing in the world for an employer to expect his servants to eavesdrop on private discussions. "The gentleman has spent the better part of his visit disparaging you," he shared in his clipped and proper tones.

"That is hardly surprising." Leo had come to expect nothing less. His butler had always been too loyal.

The older servant inclined his head. "Her ladyship has launched an admirable defense."

"A defense?" He cocked his head. "Of *who?*"

Tomlinson's lips twitched in the faintest whisper of amusement. "Of *you,* my lord."

That, however, was surprising. His bride was loyal. She was also naïve, placing trust where it wasn't deserved.

He again briefly contemplated the path leading to his wife and new brother-in-law. The lady had been clear that morning when she'd stated her desire to speak with her family alone. "That will be all." He dismissed the servant, starting up the stairway.

His butler cleared his throat.

Leo froze midstep. "What is it?" he asked impatiently.

"I should also mention, Lord Rowley arrived this morn when her ladyship was out at Hyde Park." Tomlinson dropped his voice to a low whisper. "Very early, my lord. Considerably earlier than could ever be fashionable."

And his wife had been out at Hyde Park… alone. Leo's hackles went up. "What in the hell did Rowley want?"

Tomlinson shrugged. "He insisted on waiting until her ladyship returned. I showed him to the Silver Parlor, but after an hour, he abruptly showed himself off."

Leo frowned and mentally stored away that peculiar detail about his superior. What reason would he have to come here? Nor did Leo believe for one bloody moment it had been to pay a visit to Chloe. No, his superior would have known she wasn't at home… just as he'd known Leo wasn't. He'd wanted inside Leo's household. "Thank you, Tomlinson," he said distractedly. "That will be all."

His butler shot a hand up. "That is not all. The other matter of importance pertains to the Marquess of Waverly."

"Oh, hell, what *now*?" he snapped, wanting his brother-in-law gone. Wanting his own bed. Wanting the peace and predictability of his rakish existence of just days ago.

"It is just, my lord, I should also make mention that the gentleman is *angry*."

Leo stiffened, rejoining his servant. "What was that?" he asked in measured tones. He tugged free his gloves and handed them off to a footman hovering in the shadows.

"He's been shouting intermittently at her lady—"

"And you're only just telling me this *now*?" he barked. His superior's odd call forgotten, Leo stalked off. With each step, fury built inside of him. How dare Waverly? The bloody pompous bastard would enter Leo's home and berate his wife?

This need to protect was new, in ways that it hadn't been since...

He growled, increasing the length of his strides.

As he turned the corner, only silence reigned in the corridors, bringing Leo to an abrupt halt. He stared at the doorway to the Silver Parlor and the path he'd just traveled when the nearly inaudible exchange from within the room reached his ears.

"He is not a good man, Chloe..." The statements to follow were too muffled to make out. "...deserve better."

Well, Waverly was right on both those scores. Clever, spirited, and courageous, the lady certainly deserved better than a bounder such as Leo. Why did the idea of some stuffy prig like Waterson as her husband rouse a primitive masculine fury? *Because the lady is your wife... whether either of you wished it or not...*

Of course, that hadn't stopped him from bedding other men's wives. As such, that loyalty ran counter to all Leo was and believed.

Uneasy with the warring sentiments, he gave thanks for Chloe's restrained response, which interrupted his musings. He strained to catch a glimpse of his wife through the minute crack they'd left in the door. "I'll not continue to debate you. He is my husband, your brother-in-law. Whatever he was before, you have no right entering our home and disparaging him."

He stared at the oak panel. She defended him to her brother?

"You'd defend him?" Waverly demanded in an echo of Leo's thoughts.

"I would," she said emphatically.

He drew back. When was the last time anyone had defended him? And with good reason. His own uncle and aunt, the only people in his life who'd cared for him in any way, readily acknowledged precisely *what* Leo was. As such, he didn't know what to do with his wife going toe-to-toe with her brother on his behalf.

"Think, Chloe, think!" Waverly's furious whisper reached him. "Can you truly trust that he won't send you on to Bedlam the first chance he has at his freedom?"

Leo's muscles went taut, and his entire body strained under the weight of his fury. Call Leo a rake and blackguard and scoundrel, as he was. But he wasn't so unprincipled that he'd commit a wife— unwanted though she might be—simply to rid himself of her.

The parade of silence that descended stood out starkly in the night quiet, a testament to his wife's reservations.

"Come with me," Waverly cajoled. "We will sort this out." The protective brother sought to spring Chloe free. And if Leo himself had had a sister and she'd married a miserable blackguard like him, he'd either end the man at dawn or spirit her away as Waverly was attempting. "I'll pay him off so that you can travel or live in the country. With his debt, he'd leap at the opportunity."

Leo curled his hands tight.

He braced for the lady to leave with her brother. And the only reason he would give a damn was because of what it would mean for his role with the Brethren.

Wasn't it?

"You are doing it again, Gabriel," his wife finally said, sadness laced in that rebuttal. "You are trying to orchestrate my life."

Leo released a breath he hadn't realized he'd been holding.

"Because you've gone and made a bloody mess of your life," the other man thundered. It was an explosive display for the proper marquess.

Energy thrumming in his veins, Leo shoved the door open, admitting himself. "Tsk, tsk. Hardly gentlemanly entering a man's home and shouting at the lady of the house."

Chloe gasped as she and her brother looked over to the doorway. "Leo."

He tried to gather information from those two syllables, but came up empty.

Instead, Leo took in the other man's hands gripping Chloe's shoulders, and primal bloodlust surged through him. He offered a cold, hardened grin. "Waverly, if you know what is wise, you'll take your hands from my wife before I separate them from your person."

Waverly followed the pointed stare leveled at his hold on Chloe. His new brother-in-law paled and swiftly jerked the offending hands back. "I wouldn't... My God, for you to even suggest..."

"Suggest that you've lost control of your temper?" He quirked an eyebrow. "Generally, berating a young lady and grabbing her is the mark of one who has already lost control." Leo leveled a glare at him.

Waverly stumbled back and swung his gaze to his sister. "I wouldn't... Chloe, you know I wouldn't..."

"I know, Gabriel," Chloe assured her brother softly.

Except, it didn't escape Leo's notice that she took several steps closer to him.

With falsely calm strides, he joined his wife and her brother. "I trust you've not come to offer your warmest felicitations, then?"

His wife shot him a dark, sideways glance.

Waverly's face crumpled. "Go to hell, Tennyson."

What the other man couldn't realize was that Leo had been there and survived, as only Satan's spawn could.

"Enough." Chloe turned a warning governess glare on both of them. "Gabriel, Leo is my husband."

Her brother recoiled.

Was it the use of Leo's Christian name or her marital state that horrified the man more?

Chloe smoothed her skirts. "I would have us present a united front, and help... launch Leo back into Society as a respectable gentleman."

Lord Waverly snorted.

She continued over her brother's derision. "I expect you to support us." Brother and sister were locked in a silent battle. Those were the terms Leo had secured from her, and she'd presented them to her family on his behalf?

The marquess slid his eyes closed. "Chloe," he implored. "Is there nothing I can say?"

The lady settled her hands on her hips.

The marquess slid his gaze away, landing it on Leo. "This is your fault." So much hatred poured from the other man's eyes, it would have burned a lesser man. One who was unaccustomed to such disdain. That antipathy, however, had greeted Leo the moment he'd slid into the world, a squalling babe who'd killed his mother in the process.

Chloe took a slightly labored step closer to Leo in an unexpected show of solidarity. "It is as much mine as it is Leo's, Gabriel."

At last, Lord Waverly turned his stare back to Chloe. "I will advise Mother that you will come tomorrow." A muscle ticked at the corner of his lip as he glanced briefly once more at Leo. "Both of you."

With another hate-filled glower, the gentleman took his leave.

Giving his lapels a tug, Leo rocked on his heels. How was a man to be with a respectable lady out and about? One who'd undeservedly defended him. It had been more than ten years since either had happened.

In the end, it was his fearless bride who broke the silence. "Well, he handled that a great deal better than I thought he would," she said, the strain at the corners of her mouth belying her droll response. Any other lady would have dissolved into a flood of tears at having earned the stinging disapproval handed down by her family.

"He's a pompous bastard," he returned, eyeing the sideboard and then recalling her challenge of earlier that morn. Had it truly been just fourteen hours since she'd invaded his home, accepted his offer, and then married him? He strode to the hearth and stretched his hands, still chilled from the long ride back, toward the fire. "He always was."

"You knew him?" she asked, surprise in her tone.

"There was a short while where we both attended Oxford at the same time." He rubbed his palms together. "He was bookish, devoted to his studies." With those once-shared interests, back then Leo would have welcomed a friendship with Waverly.

"And you were wild and outrageous?" she ventured.

He shrugged, allowing her the erroneous opinion. For he'd eventually become precisely that.

His wife perched on the ribbed back of a nearby sofa. "Thank you."

He eyed her warily. "For what?"

"For coming to my defense."

Leo waved his hand dismissively. "You didn't require any intervention from me in handling Waverly. I'd wager no one, not me, not your prig of a brother, nor the king himself, could orchestrate your life." In fact, she commanded with an ease that would have seen bloody conflicts ended or averted.

Her eyes softened. "Oh," she said breathlessly.

Terror clawed at his chest. He scoffed, the sound harsh to his own ears. "You make more of my response than there is."

"Perhaps." Chloe ran a finger back and forth along the carved wood. "Perhaps not." She ceased the distracted movement. "He called you a debaucher of innocents."

At that abrupt shift, he stiffened. "And?"

"Are you?" Chloe held his stare. "Do you seduce innocent young women?"

I've never tupped a cripple before...

Leo's hands curled into reflexive fists. The hateful words he'd uttered blared through his mind, conjuring the memory of another woman.

He shuttered his expression, eager to disabuse her of the dangerously enchanted glitter in her revealing gaze. "I have."

Her stricken eyes rounded, and he braced for her inevitable contempt. Welcomed it. "Oh," she said, the utterance nearly soundless. Who knew one syllable, barely a word, could contain so much emotion? Disappointment. Disgust. Regret. All sentiments that were so very familiar. Those words had followed him since his birth. So why did his gut clench?

His wife reached for her cane—and then stopped.

"I have," she blurted, the way agents who'd stumbled upon the clue to a complex case.

He shook his head tiredly. "You have what?"

"Not me. *You.*" She slowly straightened. "You didn't say you *do* debauch innocents. You said, 'I *have*,' which implies you no longer dally with virtuous ladies."

His body jerked ramrod straight. By God, the chit saw *everything.* He recalled all over again the perils in having married her.

"You do not dispute it," she observed, moving closer with her slightly unsteady gait.

His palms moistened, and he dragged forth a lifetime of experience within the Brethren.

"Do you want the truth about the man you married?" He wrapped the query in a jeering whisper that managed to halt his wife's movements. "Your brother was correct. In *everything* he said."

Her mouth formed a small moue. "You were listening at the door."

"That is the least of my crimes, Chloe," he mocked. "You'd be wise to recognize the truth in your brother's accusations and not attempt to ever make anything more about me or the decisions I make. I've never proclaimed to be anything other than a black-hearted scoundrel, because I'm not." Leo spread his arms wide. "What you see is precisely what I am, madam. The sooner you realize that, the better off you'll be. We're playing the part of respectable couple. I'd advise you not to lose focus of that arrangement."

All warmth faded from her eyes, leaving him peculiarly chilled inside. "Very well."

Good. The walls between them were safer than any warmth or pathetic softening on the lady's part toward him. Except, as he stormed off, quitting the rooms and his new wife, why did it feel like a lie he told himself in the hopes he might believe it?

CHAPTER 16

HE'D BEEN AVOIDING HER.

And more, her new husband had lashed out at her because of the prying questions she'd put to him. Having become a master at delivering an evasive answer in order to spare her skin from her father's blows, she'd come to well recognize the tactic in others.

And coward that she was, Chloe was grateful for the distance. For how was one to be around a man who'd been a mere stranger days ago and who'd strummed her body to exquisite bliss? Who'd managed to do so when she'd set specific terms that maintained control of her body and his rights to it? But in that moment, in his offices, she'd ceded all to him.

Now, she sat across from that same man who, once more, had disappeared during the day. He had returned at night only for the express purpose of attending a dinner with her family.

Seated on the opposite bench from him, Chloe kept her hands folded and tucked within the clever pocket sewn along the front of her cloak. The coach rumbled along, the rapidly churning wheels the only sound to fill the quiet.

Leo sat, his body positioned toward the window, his shoulder presented to her. The lines of his face reflected in the lead window revealed his usual mask—perfectly carved, wholly unreadable.

Chloe cleared her throat.

He remained immobile.

Chloe tried again. "I said, 'Ahem.'"

Her husband angled a cool glance over his shoulder. Gone was the rake bent on seduction. In his place was absolute... nothingness. Odd, she should find herself mourning the absence of that urbane figure.

"I created this for you." Removing her hand from her pocket, she held out the page she'd worked on that afternoon.

He flicked a glance at her. "What is this?" he asked frostily.

"Well, if you'd simply read it, you can see for yourself." She flashed a smile.

Leo narrowed his eyes and then glanced at the page. As swift as he'd looked down, he was already handing it back. "Duly noted."

Chloe folded her arms in an obstinate display. "You asked me for help in making you respectable." A feat she was learning every hour was nigh impossible. "I cannot help you if you're unwilling to take my guidance." Annoyance filled her. "Read it."

"I already did," he gritted out, shaking the page.

Chloe pointedly ignored it. "*No one* reads that quickly and certainly not well enough to process and properly contemplate any meaningful advice or ideas. As such, if you'll not take my guidance, I cannot—"

"Keep respectable hours. Quit my clubs. Give up wagering and drink." She opened her mouth, but no words came out. He'd read all of the notes she'd made for him with nothing more than a glance? "Ah, and what was the last item? Conduct gentlemanly *pastimes*." A rakish grin iced his lips as he ogled her with a leer that suggested he could see through her satin cloak. Which was preposterous. No one could undress a person with their eyes. Nonetheless...

Chloe adjusted the garment. "Not *those* gentlemanly pursuits. The *other*, respectable sorts, that is."

Shrinking the space in the carriage, he leaned forward and dropped his elbows onto his knees. The carriage became impossibly small, sucking all the air free. It had to be that. Because the alternative was that it was his body's nearness, and she could not, would not become one of those breathless sorts. Even telling herself that, Chloe felt her breath quicken. The masculine glint in his eyes hinted at a man who knew the exact effect he was having on her.

"Tell me, Chloe." He stretched the two syllables of her name out on a silken caress. She struggled to draw sufficient air into her lungs. "Do you know so very much about the disreputable gentlemanly pursuits?" he purred, the warmth of his breath fanning her cheeks.

Chloe trembled. *He's merely trying to unsettle me. He's using a rake's charm that has, no doubt, seen countless women in his bed. Don't give him that power.* "I do now." He stilled. "That is, after our morning tête-à-tête," she casually tossed.

She squeaked as he wrapped his gloved palms about her waist and gently lifted her onto his lap. The tender consideration of her healing ankle was a contradiction to the aloof rake who didn't give a damn about anyone. That realization made her awareness of him all the more perilous.

He whispered teasingly against her ear, "That is what you're basing your carnal knowledge on, love?" Her head tipped reflexively, allowing him access to the sensitive skin where her neck met her lobe. "One stolen exchange?"

"In your a-arms," she pointed out. "A-are you doubting the quality of that e-exchange?" Because it had been the single most erotic, heady moment of her five and twenty years.

"Doubt my own prowess?" he scoffed. He worked his hand up her skirts. She gasped. *Swat him away. Demand he...* "Never," he said as he moved his palm higher. The rub of his gloved fingers against her stockings lent an air of the forbidden to the exchange. She could no sooner stop his pursuit than she could muster a glib retort. "But that was just a taste, Chloe." He brushed his lips against her neck. Her pulse accelerated. "A taste of what I will show you... when you surrender."

What I will show you... not what I could...

So wholly different, the implication clear. Turning her body over to him in the most intimate of ways was inevitable.

Two days ago, she would have laughed confidently in his face. Now—

Leo drifted his hand higher, to the inside portion of her thigh, and lightly squeezed the flesh.

Chloe bit the inside of her cheeks as he turned the tables upside down. "I-I will simply add this to my knowledge of disreputable gentlemanly pursuits," she said as matter-of-factly as she could. He sucked at the place where her pulse beat, lightly grazing her skin with his teeth. Chloe's eyes slid closed of their own volition. Oh, God.

"What of this?" He palmed her between her thighs.

Her head fell back against the squabs of the bench. "C-certainly that t-too should make the list."

He grinned, applying pressure with his hand. An ache settled at her core, a desperate yearning for his touch—

Leo caressed his lips along the side of her mouth, a hint of a kiss that further ignited her longing.

The carriage hit a jarring bump, knocking his mouth free, clearing her senses. Chloe shoved at his hand. "Enough," she said tightly, for herself as much as for him.

He frowned. But it did not escape her notice that he didn't persist in his efforts at seduction.

"You are very... skilled," she settled for, "in the art of—"

"Disreputable gentlemanly pursuits?" he supplied with heavy sarcasm. That drollness was belied by the haze of passion in his eyes.

Chloe smiled. "Well, I was going to say 'lovemaking,' but that shall suffice."

He laughed. The expression of mirth was rusty and raw and so very real that her heart tripped several beats.

They both started. Her own shock was reflected in his gaze.

As quick as his composure had cracked, he reassembled the façade. "You were saying?" he urged gruffly, hurriedly setting her from his lap.

To give her shaking fingers purpose, she patted at her previously tidy chignon. "Yes. You do not wish me to ask questions about you or your past."

"No."

"It was a statement," she felt inclined to point out. "And yet, you'd freely..." She gestured between them.

"Make love to you?"

A wave of heat washed over her from just four words asked as a question. Words he'd undoubtedly uttered countless times with legions of women. Only, spoken in that husky whisper, there was an intimacy that also suggested a specialness. No doubt, this was what made rakes the legends they were. "You won't accept questions or share any parts of yourself. You attempt to push me away to prevent me from asking anything that forces you to reveal any true part of who you are. All of this—your kisses, your touches— they're all a distraction. Because as long as I'm off-balance, I don't get too close to whatever secrets you're so determined to keep." His expression grew shuttered. Chloe angled her chin up. "And *that* is why I'll never make love to you."

His lips curled up at the corners. "If that is what you desire… then that is hardly the business arrangement you spoke of."

"We can be friends." Where in thunderation had that come from?

He laughed again. The sound was brittle and coarse. "I don't have any *friends*."

Chloe's heart tugged. His, too, had been a lonely existence. As a child whose family had been determined to keep their darkest secrets private, she herself had known a solitary existence. Her eldest siblings had been… older, and they'd all been fixed on surviving. Because of that need for preservation, she'd not known just how important and cathartic a true friendship was—until she'd been sent away to finishing school and found her first true friend. Chloe bent and retrieved her forgotten instructions for him. "We must add that," she said, tucking the page back inside her cloak pocket. "You require friends. Respectable ones," she hastily added.

He snorted. "I'm quite content *without*."

One might say it was a fate he was surely deserving of. However, one might also say that not everyone, not even the hardest, darkest rake, had been born evil. With that pronouncement and jaded laugh, she learned more about the man she'd married than she had in any previous exchange. "Of course you are," she said softly.

The carriage rolled to a slow halt.

Leo smoothed his palms down the double-breasted plait on the front of his cloak. "First task, respectability," he muttered to himself. He reached for the door handle, but Chloe shot a hand out.

"I promised I would not probe—"

"But you intend to anyway," he ventured warily.

"If you answer me one question, it will be my last." But she needed to know.

"Very well."

She widened her eyes. He'd capitulate that easily? Before he changed his mind, Chloe opened her mouth.

"I'll allow you that question as long as you are willing to welcome me into your bed."

Chloe promptly closed her mouth.

"I take that as a no, then?" he drawled.

"A firm no, my lord."

"Then no questions." With that reminder, Leo opened the door and jumped down.

While Chloe gathered her cane, she stared contemplatively after her husband, a man so determined to hold on to his secrets. A man she'd taken to be an emotionless, hard-hearted rake. And then he'd revealed his was a friendless existence, changing everything.

Yes, she'd committed herself to a distant business arrangement that would earn Leo the respectability he needed. It would also earn her the post at Mrs. Munroe's.

But as he reached inside and helped hand her down, she acknowledged there was no reason she couldn't help her husband in other ways, too.

Hiding her smile, she allowed him to escort her along the pavement to her former home.

Leo had fought adversaries in the darkest alleys of the Continent in exchanges less tense than the meal he now suffered through.

Surrounded by his wife's eldest brother and elder sister, along with their respective spouses, and the dowager marchioness, Leo rather thought he'd prefer a walk down one of those darkened alleyways.

It was silent in the room. Only the clank of silver utensils striking porcelain plates provided any sounds to fill the Marquess of Waverly's dining room.

Carefully slicing a portion of his fillet of veal, Leo cheerfully popped the bite into his mouth.

Alas, he'd encountered far more loathing amongst members of Polite Society. His new family's opinion of him mattered less than even his dead sire's. Leo set down his fork and reached for his half-drunk glass of wine.

Thrumming the corner of the glass with the tip of his finger, he took a long swallow. "Quality wine, my lady," he said for their hostess.

The Marchioness of Waverly lifted her head in acknowledgment. Her curious gaze was surprisingly devoid of malice. She studied him with clever eyes. Probing. Piercing.

Life, and his work with the Brethren, had long proven the peril in both.

He lifted his glass in a salute and then downed his drink.

Feeling hostile eyes on him, he glanced down the length of the room.

With hatred burning from within his eyes from his place at the head of the table, Lord Waverly carved up the veal on his plate. All the while, he did not take his venomous gaze from Leo. Favoring his brother-in-law with a mocking lift of his head, Leo abandoned his glass in favor of another bite of veal.

A growl sounded at the opposite end of the crowded dining table.

The Dowager Marchioness of Waverly pressed her napkin to her lips, burying yet another sob. From over the white fabric, her bloodshot eyes avoided Leo.

Leo could certainly commiserate with that response. Had he a daughter—which he decidedly would not—and she married a bounder like Leo, he'd have a like reaction and then would promptly make a widow of the girl.

Humming a tavern ditty, he moved over to his cauliflower à la Flamande.

A slippered foot collided with his shin. He grunted, the food slipping from his fork.

Across from him, his wife scowled. "Behave," she mouthed.

"I'm not doing anything," he silently returned.

His wife arched an eyebrow. "*The. Rakes. Of. Mallow?*" she silently enunciated.

He sat up. "You know it?" Was there no end to the surprises around his wife?

Chloe tipped her head back and forth. *"Beauing, belleing, dancing, drinking, breaking windows, cursing, sinking. Ever raking, never thinking, live the rakes of Mallow."*

Leo grinned and joined her noiseless rendition. "*Spending faster than it comes, beating waiter's bailiffs, duns, Bacchus' true begotten sons, live the rakes of Mallow—*"

The screech of metal scraping across glass cut through his wife's singing of those lyrics.

Leo and Chloe glanced as one to a glowering Waverly.

The bastard he'd been these past years, Leo wanted to flip a finger up in a crude mockery of the man's upset. His wife kicked him under the table.

"Respectability," she mouthed.

Oh, bloody hell.

The whole of his mission and his career with the Brethren was dependent upon the very reminder his wife now uttered. That word, and all it implied, ran contrary to all he was. He didn't know how to be respectable. Hell, he didn't know how to be anything but one who inspired fear from protective mamas, loathing from every distinguished matron, and sexual interest from women.

His wife's elder sister cleared her throat, calling his attention. "We regret that we were unable to be present at your nuptials, Lord Leopold, but I can attest that we all wish you and Chloe the utmost happiness."

And with that, she was officially the first of the Edgertons who'd not skewered him with her eyes or words.

Leo shifted in his seat. "My lady," he acknowledged. It was simpler dealing with the loathing. He didn't know what to do with this warmth... from anyone. It was as foreign as the Arabic language spoken so quickly about portions of Spain.

The table fell into silence once again, which was far preferable, and yet...

He glanced across at Chloe.

Oddly, he'd been quite enjoying the back-and-forth with his wife.

After a never-ending stretch, the courses came and went, the dessert was cleared from the table, and the guests began to file from the room.

Leo tarried behind his chair. Oh, God, this was a special kind of hell. Adjourning for—he shuddered—brandy and gentlemanly discourse with Waverly and his equally stodgy brother-in-law, the Marquess of Guilford.

And by the quick path all the Edgertons took, they were as thrilled at his joining their ranks as he was to join.

His wife hesitated in the doorway. With the benefit of the cane, she brought herself back around to face him. "Leo?" she asked quizzically.

He held his palms aloft. "I've dined. I draw the line at anything further."

"Joining respectable gentlemen for brandies?" She tapped her cane. "Gentlemen who also happen to be your brothers-in-law."

"I trust I'm doing them a greater favor if I allow them their company without me being a part of it." In fact, he'd be doing them all the greatest favor—Leo included.

Chloe sighed. "You really need to consult the instructions I provided earlier."

They waged a silent battle. Any other woman would have backed down under the dark glare he shot her. He should have known better where his wife was concerned.

She thumped the floor again with her cane.

"Oh, bloody hell." Leo scraped a hand through his hair. "I'll join them."

His wife smiled. That grin faintly dimpled her left cheek. "Splendid."

So it was, a short while later, after being escorted to Waverly's billiards room, he found himself alone with his brothers-in-law. Both already engaged in a game, they didn't spare him even a glance.

"Gentlemen," he called from the doorway.

The crack of Guilford's targeted ball served as Leo's empty greeting.

He sighed.

His wife was still too naïve to realize her hopes for the Edgertons welcoming Leo into their folds were as unlikely as the queen's terriers taking flight over Kensington Palace. Had Leo truly ever been that innocent?

"Your shot," Guilford murmured to Waverly.

Uninvited, Leo did a turn about the room, surveying the space. If he were going to have to suffer through this, he'd require a damned drink. He settled his gaze on the mahogany tantalus. Crossing over, he attempted to open the glass doors. *Locked.*

"Tennyson, what the hell are you doing?" Waverly snapped.

He paused. "I thought it should be fairly obvious," he drawled over his shoulder. "I'm availing myself of a glass of brandy. Or trying to." He looked pointedly at the stand.

"You ruin my sister and wed her without my consent, and think to drink my spirits?" his brother-in-law asked, his tone steeped in incredulity. Tension spilled from the Marquess of Waverly's broad shoulders.

He was on the cusp of snapping. Leo had countless experiences with men—and women—close to losing control. "I did speak with you first." He smiled. "Though, in truth, your answer never meant anything." It had been the lady's cooperation he'd required.

Chloe's brother stiffened. Then, with a sharp bark of fury, he surged forward.

Lord Guilford grabbed his brother-in-law by the shoulder, holding him back.

"This continues to be a game to you, Tennyson," Waverly hissed.

"Pfft, hardly that." Leo gave a mock shudder. "No game ends in marital chains."

Waverly fought against his brother-in-law's hold. The vein bulging in his forehead and his mottled flush showed his anger. "And yet, you married her anyway," he cried. "You whoreson. You wed a woman whose slippers you aren't even good enough to kiss, for what? To pay your debt and bed your whores?" he spat.

"I suggest you leave," Guilford said quietly.

For an infinitesimal moment, he considered remaining. He contemplated riling the deservedly outraged marquess in a defiant show.

And yet, to do so would create additional unrest for his wife.

He started. Where in hell did that worry come from? Leo shook his head hard. The sole reason he was concerned was because he required the Edgerton connection to Waterson... and respectability. Of course. That was the sole reason. Familial unity for his wife merely aided those efforts.

Leo released a beleaguered sigh. "Oh, very well. Gentlemen." He touched the brim of an imagined hat and then quit the billiards room. As soon as he'd stepped out into the hall, he glanced up and down the corridors.

Humming *The Rakes of Mallow*, he strolled the length of the silent corridors. As he walked, he took in the ancestral portraits hanging upon the walls: ones of marquess' past, bewigged gents alongside powered ladies. With each painting he passed, the passage of time was marked, giving way to more recent Edgertons.

His whistling faded to a slow stop.

The portrait of a little girl with golden curls and cornflower-blue eyes beckoned. Despite the white frock and tender years, there could be no doubting the figure reflected back was his wife. Leo glanced about and, finding himself alone still, examined the rendering. The artist had captured the likeness when Chloe was nine or mayhap ten. And yet, for all the remarkable likenesses that marked her as the woman he'd wed, there were shades that revealed a wholly different person.

He peered at a young Chloe Edgerton.

Unlike the mischievous glitter that lit his wife's eyes now, there was an uncertainty in the girl before him. Shoulders hunched, eyes downcast, she was a shadow of the woman who'd invaded his household and presented terms of their marriage.

"Are you the rotter?"

He wheeled around. Two little girls stood several paces away. The elder of the pair lifted one of the rapiers in her hand. "Well?"

Oh, bloody hell. Proper dinners and now… discussions with children.

The world had gone insane. He yanked at his suddenly tight cravat. Children were innocent. As such, he'd not a bloody clue as to what to do with them.

The girl trotted over. "Is something wrong with your hearing?" she asked excitedly.

He bristled. "Certainly not." His keen hearing had, in fact, saved his miserable hide scores of time from discovery.

Her face fell.

"Faith can't." The other curly-headed girl skipped over.

"Be. Quiet," Faith gritted, nudging the garrulous one in the side.

Do not ask. Do not ask. He would only regret it. Alas… "Cannot?"

"Hear," the smaller child piped in.

Her sister growled, "I can hear."

"Not out of your right ear, Faith," the smaller child insisted, pointing to her left lobe.

Ah, the girl was deaf.

While they bickered back and forth, Leo contemplated a path to freedom over his shoulder.

"I'm only partially deaf," the older girl cried, stamping the tip of her rapier into the hardwood. The metal thrummed back and forth, forcing his attention back.

"Pfft," he scoffed. "Beethoven is now nearly deaf in both ears, and he composed his Second Symphony in the state."

The eldest child widened her eyes. "Who?"

"Beethoven?"

Both girls looked blankly back.

"The *Sonata quasi una fantasia?*"

"Mm. Mm," the eldest child confirmed with a shake of her head.

Weren't young ladies tasked with music lessons? "DaDaDaDa-DaDa—Da-Da—Da—Da-Da." He waved his finger in time to the beat.

"That's horribly dreary," the eldest child whispered.

Leo drew back. "Surely you've heard his works?" "Da. Da. Daaaa. Da-Da." He proceeded to sing the lyric-less tune.

The different-aged girls, who could only be sisters, glanced at each other and dissolved into a fit of giggles.

"*That* is dreary," he corrected. "Not knowing Beethoven," he mumbled. "A splendid chap." One Leo had met in his travels to Austria. "I'll leave you ladies to your own pleasures." He swept a bow and marched off.

He made it no farther than three paces.

"He was deaf, you say?" Faith called after him. Her voice echoed in the emptied corridors. The pair of girls instantly trotted over and stood side by side, blocking his path toward escape. The eldest sister pointed her rapier at his throat.

His lips twitched. "Chloe's nieces?" Their stubbornness and spirit marked them as smaller versions of his Edgerton wife.

They nodded.

"The husband?" Faith countered.

"The same." He sketched a bow.

"Hmph," she said noncommittally, in a reply that might or might not have been an insult. In the end, her curiosity won out. "About this Beethoven. He was deaf in both ears, you say?"

"This Beethoven *is* deaf in both ears. He's very much alive, I assure you. And," he felt compelled to advise, "only one of the greatest musical minds of this time."

"Never gave much attention to music lessons because of my ear," Faith said quietly, lowering her rapier.

Disquieted by the emotion that lit the girl's eyes, he tried to step around her. She stuck her rapier out, once again, blocking his escape. "Do you fence?"

"Do I…" he repeated slowly, feeling like one in the midst of a play without the benefit of his lines.

"I'm teaching Violet."

"Shouldn't you be abed or… or… doing whatever it is children do at this hour?"

The girl grinned widely. "We are. I fence."

"Of course you do," he muttered.

"And I'm learning." Violet waved her fingertips.

Her elder sister went on as though she hadn't spoken. "You could return to Uncle Gabriel and have him yell at you some more." Faith lifted her little shoulders in a shrug. "Not really sure what else you are going to do, since my uncle threw you out."

"Fair point," he said under his breath.

When presented with joining his brother-in-law or interacting with this tenacious imp, he found himself seriously debating a plea for a truce with Waverly.

"What's a pony son?" the small girl asked curiously.

"A pony… son?" he echoed. What in the blazes?

Faith sighed. "A whoreson. Uncle Gabriel called him a whore-son."

His ears heated. *Oh, bloody hell.*

"Fencing it is, then," he muttered and allowed the small pair to lead him off.

CHAPTER 17

THROUGH HER MOTHER'S NOISY WEEPING, Chloe puzzled through one question: Just how many times could her mother utter a single word before Chloe's patience snapped?

"M-married," the dowager marchioness gasped out for a fourth time. From where she sat before the hearth, she buried another sob in her palm. "M-married."

Five. That was now the fifth time she had thrown out that forlorn utterance.

Seated beside her on the damask sofa, Philippa, who'd long been the one to appease their mother, proved wholly incapable. She caught Chloe's gaze, an apology in her expressive eyes. "I'm sorry," she mouthed.

Chloe turned her focus to the window. What was the remorse for? Pulling back the curtains, she peered down at the streets below. Their mother's endless round of tears? Her family's unpardonable rudeness at dinner? *Or fear that you've found yourself in a miserable marriage like their mother's… and Philippa's first union?*

Her sister-in-law moved into position just beyond her shoulder. "She is worried about you," Jane murmured.

Ah, Jane, ever the peacemaker. "As is Gabriel. As is everyone. That does not give anyone permission to be rude." She'd expected more from her family. Instead, throughout the dinner, not a single member of her family had uttered a word to Leo.

"Married," her mother repeated.

Chloe drew the line at that sixth utterance. She let the curtain slip from her fingers and faced her weeping parent.

"Given you've spent the past eight years trying to maneuver me into that very state, I'd expect you'd conduct yourself with a modicum of delight," she called over.

Her mother flew to her feet. "Yes," she cried, slashing the air with her wrinkled handkerchief. "I wished to see you wedded to a good man. A kind one. Instead, you've gone and tied yourself to a brute like—" Chloe's father. The marchioness broke down, wilting into the sofa. Covering her face with her hands, she wept copious tears that shook her frame.

Philippa folded their mother close and made nonsensical soothing noises.

Chloe bit the inside of her cheek. "Leo's not like him." Was that assurance given for her mother? Or Chloe herself? Because, did she truly know him? Did she know him in any way?

Her mother drew back from Philippa. "How do you *knowww* that?" her mother pleaded, echoing her very thoughts. "He is a blackguard."

I've never proclaimed to be anything other than a black-hearted scoundrel, because I'm not…

She hugged herself in an involuntary embrace. For the truth was, she *didn't* know that.

"He is a man who wishes to be better," she finally said into the quiet. Which wasn't untrue. Her family, however, didn't need to know the reasons for his request. "A gentleman who offered me marriage and forfeited all rights to my dowry, who asked for little in return."

"A man like Tennyson does not do anything because he has a heart, Chloe," her mother shot back, fury adding strength to her previously weakened timbre. No, he'd had a need in marrying her. Just as she'd had her own reasons to wed him.

Her mother drew in a breath and made a show of smoothing her skirts. When she again spoke, she was a master of her emotion. "I've always admired you, Chloe. Despite… everything." The Monster Marquess of Waverly. "You were strong and clever, and you learned how to smile and laugh. But this?" She shook her head sadly. "This decision, I can never understand. It goes against all you are and all you have adamantly stood against as a woman."

The damning words echoed in the quiet of the room long after her mother finished her measured diatribe.

Jane and Philippa stood in like measured silence, an affirmation of the dowager marchioness' charges.

Chloe looked to each of them, the women in her life. "I came tonight to enlist your support in smoothing Leo's entry into respectable Society. I never expected you, my family, of all people, should so pass judgment that you'd be incapable of extending that to him." Bitterness lined her words. "Whether you approve or disapprove, despise him, or find me foolish for wedding him, he is my husband." She squared her shoulders. "If you'll excuse me?"

"Chloe," Jane said, rushing over.

Chloe held a hand up. "I'd rather not discuss this any further. Not now." Presenting her back, she marched off—albeit at a slower pace that her still slightly aching ankle allowed.

She exited the parlor and continued on through the corridors she'd raced as a child. And when she'd placed a sizable distance between herself and her mother, sister, and sister-in-law, Chloe let a stream of curses fly.

How dare they?

Regardless of whether or not they believed she'd made a mistake, the Edgertons had proven a loyal lot… extending kindness to those in need and forgiveness of each other. Now, they should meet Leo's entry to the family with coldness?

Chloe scowled. She hadn't expected them to be effusive with false joy. But a polite welcome and casual dialogue were the least they could manage for strangers at *ton* functions.

Outrage fueled her steps, pushing her onward and leaving her to muddle through her predicament.

As part of their arrangement, she'd promised Leo entry to Polite Society. She, however, had taken for granted her family's assistance. What now?

The peel of children's laughter split into her worried musings. Compelled toward the innocent expression of her nieces' mirth, Chloe started for the ballroom. How many times had she herself sneaked about while her parents, a leading patron and patroness of the *ton*, had entertained guests? She reached the double doorways that hung wide open and abruptly stopped.

All the outrage and fury that had fueled her earlier movements fled.

Her niece Faith raised a rapier into position, facing her expertly positioned opponent.

"*En garde*," Leo called and, leading with his front leg, thrust.

Faith retreated, moving sideways and parrying. "Like this?"

He shook his head and stopped. "It's like a dance. One—"

"I don't dance," Faith interrupted.

"So no music lessons and no dance," he noted, brushing the loose, golden curls that had tumbled over his brow back. "Another shame. Dancing is good fun."

"Are you going to show Faith how to dance?" Violet called from where she sat at the edge of the ballroom, her legs stretched out before her. "Because I want to learn to dance. Will you show me?"

"Dancing will have to wait for another day," he promised. "Assume your *en garde* position." Pivoting on his heel, he rocked back, demonstrating the proper positioning. "Now, lead with your dominant leg," he instructed.

While Faith followed the quick commands, Chloe muddled through, trying to make sense of the unlikely exchange between Society's most-hardened rake, a man called heartless by her own family and by himself on numerous scores... and her young nieces. For men who were heartless didn't deliver fencing lessons to young girls.

"Now, retreat," he ordered, pushing forward. He lunged, his unconventional yet effective upward positioning highlighting the power of his lithe frame.

Chloe's mouth went dry, her body heating at the mere remembrance of his touch... his kiss...

Faith just missed the tip of his rapier and went on the attack.

"Good," he praised. "Those are the precise movements."

A warmth spread throughout Chloe's chest, quickening her heart. And God help her, it was disastrous and would prove problematic from this moment on, but a small scrap of that wildly beating organ slipped away, forever lost.

"Aunt Chloe!"

Leo stopped midlunge, his gaze alighting on Chloe.

Faith's rapier found its mark, and it vibrated upon his shoulder.

"You were distracted," she called out excitedly.

Violet hopped up, cheering her elder sister's triumph.

Leo flashed a bashful half-grin that softened him. "My lady," he greeted, touching the tip of his blade to his forehead.

Smile. Be casual and breezy and all things nonchalant. Chloe forced her lips up into a grin, praying that it wasn't one of those silly, fawning ones surely worn by too many women around her rake of a husband.

Leo said something to Faith and then, handing his rapier to Violet, sprinted over. "Have the ladies and gentlemen rejoined one another's company?" he asked, ushering in the stark reality of her... *their* situation.

She shifted her weight over her cane. What was she to say to him about her mother's explosion? And worse, the lack of support from Chloe's family? It was the one major request he'd put to her.

She opened her mouth and then stopped. "Why aren't you with my brother and Miles?"

He flashed another wry grin.

"Uncle Gabriel yelled at him," Violet piped in from the middle of the ballroom floor.

Chloe whipped her gaze back to Leo's. "What?"

"I was advised that your family wouldn't take kindly to my being there." Leo lowered his lips close to hers. "With good reason, love."

She frowned. She'd not let him flirt her out of this discussion. "He was unkind to you," she predicted, letting those words sink in. At his silence, fury rooted around her belly once more, spreading out.

Her husband chuckled. "It would hardly be the first time, and it will certainly not be the last, that I've earned some proper gent's ire."

"He called him a pony son," Violet gladly supplied.

"A pony son?" Chloe echoed blankly, her mind racing. "What is a..." She gasped, slapping a palm to her mouth. Not only had her family been unpardonably rude with their silent treatment, they'd also hurled insults. Moving her hand, Chloe grabbed one of Leo's. "We are leaving," she gritted. Drudging up a smile for her nieces' benefit, she waved with her and Leo's interlocked fingers. "I'm afraid we have to leave."

"Noooo," the girls moaned in unison.

"Can Leo stay?" Violet pleaded.

And if rage hadn't been spiraling through her, she'd have laughed at that honest and more than slightly disloyal willingness to cede Chloe's company as long as it meant Leo remained. "I'm afraid not. Another time," she lied, even as a ball of fury and pain stuck in her throat. For who knew if or when there would ever be another time?

She dragged her husband from the ballroom. As fast as her ankle could manage, she limped along the halls toward the foyer.

"The carriage please, Joseph," she advised as soon as the old butler appeared.

His wizened features strained, he swallowed hard. So he knew of the tension that filled the household. Of course, as one who knew the darkest secrets to dwell in these corners and corridors, he'd be aware of her family's less-than-discreet censure of Leo. "But his lordship—"

"The carriage, Joseph," Chloe bit out.

"I cannot, my lady. Your brother would not want you to leave without…" He wisely let the remainder of that go unfinished. Over her shoulder, Joseph glanced at a footman, who rushed off.

She narrowed her eyes. "You'll fetch my brother, then?" To what end? With the exception of her nieces, she'd heard enough from every Edgerton present. Chloe brought her chin up a notch. "You can tell my brother that unless he has an apology, there is nothing I care to speak with him about." Releasing a still silent Leo's hand, she ambled over to the door and yanked it open.

"But, my lady," Joseph called after her.

Not bothering to wait to see if Leo followed suit, she marched off as quick as her ankle would permit.

Her husband immediately fell into step beside her. "I'd advise we wait for the carriage, madam." He cast a pointed look at her ankle. "I've never been one so proud as to bite my nose to smite my face," he drawled.

"Well, I have." And she absolutely drew the proverbial line at allowing insults to be hurled at her or Leo.

Her husband took her gently by the forearm, forcing her to a reluctant stop. "I still must insist we wait."

Chloe scoffed. "Come. It's but a few streets between your residence and my family's."

He sighed. "Very well, then." Leo swept her up by the knees, startling a squeak from her.

"What? You cannot…" Chloe sputtered. She shoved against him.

Leo tightened his hold around her. "If you insist we abandon our carriage, then I can't allow you to go walking the streets of London on your injured ankle," he remarked, not breaking stride. As calmly as he spoke, he might as well have strolled at a lazy pace through Hyde Park, rather than carry her through Mayfair.

"I'm too heavy," she protested once more, struggling against him.

"We could return," he suggested without inflection.

Chloe fell silent.

She could not return. Nor could she confide in Leo the full extent of the disastrous exchange with her mother. How did Chloe possibly tell him that the one thing she'd promised, she no longer could help him attain?

Laying her cheek against his chest, she stared out at the oddly quiet streets. *I'm unable to fulfill the terms of our contract.* Her mind shied away from the implications of what that meant for every other agreement struck. It merely highlighted every last warning her family had lashed her with again and again—Leo was a stranger.

Her husband broke the silence. "Your discourse with the ladies went as splendidly as mine with the gentlemen of your family?" he asked dryly.

For a brief moment, she contemplated glossing over the grimness of her exchange. She nestled against him, the beat of his heart steady, calming, with just the faintest acceleration because of the chore of carrying her. As a girl, however, she'd learned to appreciate the benefits of a direct beating. One didn't spend minutes and hours and days with dread building when the outcome remained inevitable. "My family will not help with your entry into Polite Society," she brought herself to say.

He stiffened. His biceps strained the fabric of his jacket. "I see."

I see. Just that.

Two words that revealed… nothing. Silence stretched on as they made the slow journey home.

Home. That was not what it was. Not truly. Nor, however, had been the townhouse that she and her siblings had grown up in.

"I trust this is the first time you've earned your family's disappointment."

Chloe stiffened. Grateful that he could not see her face, lest he uncover the secrets she kept, she burrowed closer. "Because I'm a proper lady?"

"Because you're a proper lady," he confirmed.

Fencing? Shooting? By God, you are not a street slattern…

Leo knew nothing about her. And those demons, the ones that belonged to her, known only in parts and pieces by her family, would be shared with no one. Yet… she chewed at her lower lip. "It isn't so much my family's disappointment that… cuts," she finally acknowledged into the quiet. "But rather… a shattered illusion of who they are." In her mind, she'd built the Edgertons into an unconditionally loyal lot who'd blindly support one another's decisions simply because of who they were to one another… and what they'd shared.

"People will always let you down, Chloe. The sooner you realize that, the better off you'll be," Leo said in somber tones that, prior to this moment, she would have said he was incapable of.

He is speaking of himself. It was a warning of sorts that she'd have to be deaf not to hear.

"Now have your one question," he said tiredly.

Her one? "Why?" she asked. Angling back in his arms, Chloe searched his face. "Why would you do that?"

"Is that your question?"

And lest he withdraw the opportunity on a technicality, she blurted, "How many innocent women have you debauched?"

His body went to stone. It wasn't the question he'd been expecting. That much was clear in his coiled muscles.

For a long moment, she believed he wouldn't answer.

And then…

"One."

One. There had been just one innocent woman. Rakes, by nature and reputation, were men who despoiled innocents and seduced widows in equal measure. Yet there had been just one virtuous young woman. A million questions swirled.

"That was your one question," he reminded.

Just then, a carriage rumbled along the intersection.

It jerked to a stop. The team of snow-white horses pulling it whinnied their annoyance.

"We have company," Leo murmured, adjusting his hold on her.

The occupant, a gape-mouthed Lady Jersey, blinked repeatedly. She pressed her forehead to the pane, gawking at them.

Leo lifted his hand in salute. "My lady," he shouted into the London quiet. "A pleasure seeing you here. Wave," he said from the corner of his mouth.

Wave? Chloe shot a palm up, waggling her fingers.

Lady Jersey's black barouche sprang forward, resuming its course. They watched as it disappeared around the corner.

Chloe giggled. For the rot that the evening had been, there had been something—

"Freeing, isn't it?" he perfectly supplied. "Not giving a rat's arse on Sunday what the world says."

"It is," she murmured to herself. "Do you know," she started slowly, "I always prided myself on being one who thumbed my nose at Society's conventions and lived without a worry about anyone's opinion. And yet, I didn't live that life. Not truly." Despite her loathing of *ton* events, she'd never said *damn all* and refused to attend. "I went along to whichever ball or soiree my mother or brother wished me to attend." All the while, she'd taken secret triumph in the knowledge that she wouldn't marry. "Where is the triumph in that?" she spat, unable to keep the bitterness from creeping in.

Leo slowed his stride. "If it is any consolation, I went through my entire life flipping a middle finger to Society's rules and expectations, and that is why I find myself... where I am."

Married to me. A small pang struck somewhere in her chest.

It was foolish to feel anything from that revelation on his part. Neither of them had wanted this... And yet, it was there, a sharp disappointment.

It's solely because you loathe the idea of being incapable of fulfilling your respective portion of the agreement.

Strengthened by that realization, Chloe stared contemplatively ahead. She didn't need to rely on her family's assistance in smoothing Leo's way among the *ton*. Oh, it would be vastly easier with their help. But she herself—until now—had lived scandal-free. She could guide Leo so that he was... respectable, and then surely certain polite doors would be opened—to the both of them.

Enlivened, she mentally crafted her next plan.

Mayhap all was not lost, after all.

CHAPTER 18

THE FOLLOWING MORNING, ARMS LINKED, Leo and Chloe made their way, of all places, through Hyde Park. With a maid trailing behind them, no less.

Leo gave his head a wry shake. He'd gone from bedding widows on empty paths to respectable walks with an unwanted servant underfoot.

"*This* is your strategy to make me respectable?"

Leo grunted as Chloe jammed her elbow into his ribs. "You needn't sound so skeptical."

He rubbed the wounded area.

"And unless you want all of Polite Society to know this," she discreetly motioned between them, "is a ruse, then I'd suggest you have a care with your words."

Being called out by a lady… With a sea of lords and ladies in the crowded Hyde Park looking unabashedly on. And yet, blast if the lady wasn't right. Carelessness wasn't a sin that had belonged to him.

Still…

"I still do not see how this will help with anything," he gritted through a forced smile. What he required was entry to polite events hosted by Waterson's circle and other stodgy members of the Whigs.

"It will. Trust me." As they continued down a graveled path, he resisted the urge to point out that he, as a rule, trusted no one, and to encourage her to use the same discretion.

The lady would eventually have her eyes opened to the reality that was life. They all did, inevitably.

"I must confess," she began almost hesitantly, bringing his gaze briefly over. "I'm surprised that you are not more… upset by my failure to fulfill my portion of the agreement."

Given the access to Waterson he'd hoped to have, and invites to like respectable households, he should have been filled with a teeth-gnashing rage. He'd traded his freedom on the hope that it would benefit his career and the Crown. So where, as she'd aptly pointed out, were those sentiments on his part? Disquiet swept through him, and Leo trained his attention on the path ahead. "I trusted you'd crafted another scheme that would prove equally beneficial," he countered, needing to shut her questions down, because they only stirred unwelcome ones in his own mind. Ones he didn't have answers to. "Are you now doubting your abilities?"

Chloe bristled. "Undoubtedly not." She stopped at the shore of the Serpentine, forcing Leo to a halt. Loosening her bonnet strings, she tugged the straw article from her head. "If doors aren't opened by my family, we'll simply see them opened ourselves."

"You're an optimist," he murmured. Had he ever been so naïve?

Yes, yes, I was. I once smiled and read and fashioned a future for myself different than what my life was and then what it became…

Smiling, Chloe lifted that silly bonnet and shook it at him, killing his melancholic reverie. "I am *determined.*"

And as he was the wagering sort, by the glint in her eyes, he'd place bets on her ultimate success. Which would only mean his triumph, as well.

Marriage to her would still allow Leo to reshape his image and appease the discontented leadership within the Brethren.

Why did it feel that the silent assurance was more an afterthought and nothing else?

"Leo?" A question colored Chloe's tone.

Removing the blanket tucked under his arm, Leo snapped the fabric open. It caught an errant early afternoon breeze, the edges of the gingham cloth fluttering and then settling into place as he lowered it.

A maid came rushing over with a small basket and turned it over to Chloe.

Accepting it with a word of thanks, Chloe set it on the right corner of the blanket, anchoring the cloth in place. She tossed her bonnet to the ground next.

"Now, we sit." She settled herself onto the blanket. Singing *The Rakes of Mallow* quietly under her breath, she proceeded to fish around in her basket. She withdrew a book, followed by another and then another.

What in the blazes?

Chloe paused. She tipped her head back, staring expectantly at him. "Well? Do you intend to stand there all day?"

"You are mad," he muttered, dropping to the ground.

"Am I?" His wife discreetly motioned to the crowd of onlookers gaping at them from a nearby walking path. "They are no doubt saying, 'Lord Tennyson... he is not at his clubs or foxed or... or conducting some scandalous activity. He's simply in the park. Reading.' Nothing says respectability quite like reading." Beaming, Chloe jammed a small, leather tome into his hands. "So *read*."

Leo glanced at the book, then back to Chloe, and once more to the title. "What is *this*?"

"Well, generally what one reads... a book."

"I can see it's a *book*, madam. I mean what do you have me reading?"

His wife pursed her mouth. "Mary Darby Robinson."

Ahh... he fanned the pages. The verses paraded quickly before his gaze, a kaleidoscope of words, as a hated voice rose from the grave at the back of Leo's mind where it forever dwelled.

You pathetic excuse of a man... reading women's works? It's not natural... You are no son of mine... but then, we've always known that... You are nothing, Leo... nothing. A bastard undeserving of the name Dunlop...

Chloe tipped her chin up in silent challenge. "Do you have nothing to say?"

The memory of the late marquess vanished under his wife's lilting voice, a welcome lifeline back from the past that he clung to. "Do you think I take umbrage with your selection? Madam, I'm a hedonist. I live for my own pleasures. I engage in wicked delights and forbidden acts that would set you into a perpetual blush." Her cheeks pinkened, a pretty, innocent stain of color that he should have shuddered at. But he found it oddly right on this woman, and not unappealing. "As such, I'm not one who'd begrudge anyone taking one's pleasures where they would." With every word uttered, her eyes softened and her thick, golden lashes swept lower. "Though, there are far headier pleasures I could show you." He lowered his mouth close to hers, reveling in the quick intake of her breath and the flush of desire on her skin. "Would show you. If you'll but let me." And she would. In time, he'd join his body to hers and awaken her to the passion that thrummed within her.

Chloe wet her lips. "Y-you will cause a scandal. We are striving to shape you into a respectable gentleman."

Were those reminders for the lady? Or for him? "If we're to be the madly in love pair who set off a scandal throughout London, we must play the part. Place your head on my lap, madam."

She hesitated, and then, to his surprise, she complied.

"Your Mary Darby Robinson, then." He snapped the book open and skimmed poem after poem, words that portrayed the harsh reality that was London life and marriage. This was what Chloe should read. "Most ladies are fans of Lord Byron."

"If one prefers the wild, reckless, womanizing sort."

Leo didn't blink for several moments. By God, had she just insulted him? He glanced down.

His wife stared innocently back.

"Minx," he muttered, even as a grin pulled at his lips. A gust of wind played with the open page, and he smoothed his palm over it.

> *"O! How can LOVE exulting Reason queil!*
> *How fades each nobler passion from his gaze!*
> *E'en Fame, that cherishes the Poet's lays,*
> *That fame, ill-fated Sappho lov'd so well."*

All teasing faded in Chloe's eyes. Her bow-shaped lips parted with each verse.

> *"Lost is the wretch, who in his fatal spell*
> *Wastes the short Summer of delicious days,*
> *And from the tranquil path of wisdom strays,*
> *In passion's thorny wild, forlorn to dwell."*

While he recited the words, he stroked the pad of his thumb

along the puff of her sleeve, grazing her skin, eliciting faint but audible inhalations.

Yes, his wife might laud herself on being practical and logical and turn her nose up at romance and passion, but she was born to both.

> *"...Where holy Innocence resides enshrin'd;*
> *Who fear not sorrow, and who know not guile,*
> *Each thought compos'd, and ev'ry wish resign'd;*
> *Tempt not the path where pleasure's flow'ry wile*
> *In sweet, but pois'nous fetters, holds the mind..."*

As he finished, he lowered the book, facedown, on his lap.

"I... I had not read that one yet," she whispered.

Leo caressed his thumb along her slightly fuller lip. "There is much you have not done yet." He lowered his voice. "Many things I want to show you." His gaze fell to her mouth. A bolt of lust shot through him. *I want to kiss her... I want to lay myself between her welcoming thighs...*

And just like that, the tables were flipped and the world turned upside down as the seducer became the seduced.

"Are people watching?" she whispered.

Hyde Park had slipped away except for them... with her query pulling him back to the moment... and reality. He snapped his head up and looked around.

Lords riding by, young women off with their maids, gentlemen strolling with ladies all watched on. As they'd intended.

Because it was all for show, on this, Leo's quest to be a proper gentleman.

Only, somewhere between pretend and a poem, the purpose of their being here, his assignment, all of it had become muddled.

Chloe stared quizzically. "Leo?"

"They are staring sufficiently," he answered belatedly. He lay the book beside them. "So tell me, Lady Chloe Dunlop, how is it a lady comes to be reading Mary Darby Robinson?" he asked, a question that benefitted the Brethren not at all and had nothing to do with his assignment or the quest to reshape himself in Society's eyes. But it was one he wanted an answer to anyway.

Chloe turned her head on his lap and looked up at him. "My parents insisted Philippa and I only read proper, ladylike texts, books on deportment and decorum."

He imagined the clever imp of a child she would have been. Such texts could have never satisfied her curiosity, even then. "Interesting stuff."

She laughed. "Precisely."

He tweaked her nose. "And here I'd imagine you would spirit away some forbidden texts tucked away on your family's shelves."

Her expression darkened, ushering in a solemnity that made him yearn for the bell-like mirth that had spilled past her lips. He ached to call back what he'd meant as teasing.

"Our mother read romantic novels," she shared in quiet tones. "Philippa and I would sneak them into our chambers. Until…" A shadow fell across her eyes, ushering in a cold that touched Leo to his core.

"Until?" he urged gruffly.

His wife snapped upright. "I don't… we just stopped… reading them, that is. Philippa didn't. Or rather, she reads them now." Chloe dug her fingertips into her temple. "I don't. Sometimes I do. But not…" Chloe caught his gaze on her hands. She swiftly dropped them to her lap. Her ramblings drew to a cessation.

Leo examined the brittle, white lines at the corners of his wife's mouth and the thin thread she clung to. What secrets did Chloe hold? And why did he, who didn't give a horse's arse about anything or anyone, want to know them? "Where did you discover your love for Mrs. Mary Darby Robinson?" he asked gently.

His wife drew her legs close and looped her arms loosely around them. "Jane arrived a few years ago as my companion. *She* introduced me to Mary Wollstonecraft and the other great philosophers."

The puzzle piece slid into place. "And their views on marriage." It's why she'd wished to retain a desperate grab on her freedom.

His wife stretched her palm to the grass and dusted her fingertips over the blades, setting them into a back-and-forth sway. "My mind was set against marriage long before Jane arrived with her Mrs. Wollstonecraft," she said cryptically and then went silent.

Leo stared at her bent head as she attended her own distracted movements.

Someone had broken her heart. Her sudden somberness was proof of her pain.

He frowned, and a need filled him to bloody senseless the blighter who'd hurt her, to drive back Chloe's melancholy and restore her to her usual cheer. Incapable of the former, he settled for the latter.

It was foreign to Leo, this need to see another person happy. And yet, there it was.

A gust of wind tore through the park, rippling the waters. That same heavy breeze tossed several golden curls across Chloe's eyes.

Catching the silken strands between his fingertips, Leo gently tucked them behind the delicate shell of her ear. "Where were we, Lady Tennyson?" he asked, startling a laugh from her, and the sheer sound of it filled his chest with a lightness.

Chloe arched her neck back, finding his gaze with her own. "I never took us for the couple who would refer to one another by our titles."

He tweaked her nose... and lied through his teeth. "There is the whole respectability thing to consider," he said, even as a question surfaced. What kind of couple had she taken them for, then? The immediate answer was... none, as their time together was limited, and their futures never meant to truly be tangled as one. The teasing in her voice, however, had contradicted the practical and put forward an enticing vision. Unnerved, he grabbed the book and quickly turned the pages before settling on a sonnet.

> "Is it to love, to fix the tender gaze,
> To hide the timid blush, and steal away;
> To shun the busy world, and waste the day
> In some rude mountain's solitary maze?"

As he quietly spoke, Chloe's eyes slid closed. Unable to shift his gaze from the image she presented, resplendent in her ease and calm, he continued the recitation.

> "Is it to chant one name in ceaseless lays,
> To hear no words that other tongues can say,
> To watch the pale moon's melancholy ray,
> To chide in fondness, and in folly praise?"

A wistful smile danced on her perfect bow lips. Desire rippled through him. An aching to lower his head and take her mouth under his, to taste her, overwhelmed him. "I haven't read either of those yet." She slowly opened her eyes. A contemplative glitter sparkled in their cerulean-blue depths. "I never took Mrs. Robinson as a romantic. She lived apart from her husband and wrote about the rights of women and—"

"And she also saw that advancing rights of one did not preclude her from abandoning her passions." Leo rubbed the pad of his thumb along the seam of her plump lips. "There is no shame in exploring the pleasures our bodies *should* derive, Chloe."

Her cheeks turned several shades of red, the color reaching the roots of her hair.

Since he'd turned his back and soul on good, he'd sneered at virtuous ladies such as his wife. Now, he saw that innocence in a new light, tempting and enthralling, like Eve in the garden of sin. And he sat before her, hungering for that fruit.

He leaned down to take that which he craved. A breeze gusted across the Serpentine, whipping Chloe's bonnet up and hurling it toward the shore.

His wife pinched his thigh.

"Bloody hell," he groused, rubbing the wounded flesh.

"This is where a respectable gentleman rescues the bonnet."

"I was going to kiss you," he said bluntly.

Her shoulders shook with a laugh. "I know," Chloe confessed on a whisper. She plucked the book from his hands. "The bonnet better serves your purposes than a public kiss."

In this instance, he didn't give a jot about his reputation. The need to have her in his arms superseded all.

Blanching, Leo surged to his feet. *My God, what am I thinking?* "The bonnet it is," he croaked, jabbing a finger in the air.

Chloe grinned that impish, blindingly bright expression of mirth that sucked the breath from his lungs.

What madness had befallen him? *It is merely that she is an innocent.* Rakes were enticed by innocence. Except, he hadn't been. After he'd broken one lady's heart, he'd despised any hint of it. "My bonnet, dear sir," Chloe said in modulating tones suited to an aging matron. The teasing repartee slashed across his panicky musings.

He sprang into movement. "My lady." Leo took off after the straw bonnet as it hopped along the shore. The article came to a gradual rest and then took off tumbling again. Grateful for the distance, he struggled to resurrect long-built walls.

All these years, he'd prided himself on being fearless. He'd faced head on the threat of death, danger, and dying with equable measure. Only to find himself racing away from a spirited minx with mischievous eyes and a too-clever mind.

Not for the first time since he'd married, Leo acknowledged the dangers posed by being married to Chloe.

As Leo tripped over himself in his haste to retrieve her bonnet, laughter spilled from Chloe's lips, free and honest and so very wonderful.

If she hadn't signed an agreement with the gentleman outlining the business terms of their union, she might, in fact, see more in their afternoon outing.

And if she didn't know Leo was one of Society's most outrageous rakes, Chloe could *almost* believe he was a tenderhearted gentleman. One who doled out fencing lessons to small girls and who'd gallantly carried Chloe through the streets of London to spare her ankle further injury. And one who asked her what she read and why, and who in turn recited romantic poetry—and recited it as though the verses meant something to him.

But she did know precisely what had sent him sneaking into her family's home to offer her a marriage of convenience.

Regret struck unexpectedly at her breast.

Chloe clenched the book in her fingers tightly, leaving crescent marks upon the pages.

For she knew, ultimately, Leo was a rake solely bent on a path of respectability to please his uncle and settle his debts.

She ripped her gaze from the man responsible for her suddenly unsettled world and absently glanced at the poem he'd read.

> *"Ah! wherefore by the Church-yard side,*
> *Poor little LORN ONE, dost thou stray?"*

Chloe stared at the page. Puzzling her brow, she skimmed the verses. *"Thy wavy locks but thinly hide. The tears that dim thy blue-eye's ray…"*

Nay, those *unfamiliar* verses.

"What?" she whispered, trying to make sense of it.

Mayhap he'd simply handed the book over at a different place from where he'd read. Of course. That was no doubt what he'd done. Frantic, Chloe flipped to the front of the book, searching the titles, searching, searching...

It is not here.

Which meant... he'd recited the poem from memory. Two of them. Nay, not by just any poet, but the English Sappho, who'd crafted feminist treatises and championed the rights of women.

And Leo had read her.

Her mind raced with everything he'd revealed in his questioning of her, his familiarity with Mrs. Robinson's works and past and life—

"What's that, love?"

Chloe jerked her head up with such alacrity the muscles along the back of her neck screamed in protest. "I didn't say anything," she blurted.

Leo arched a golden eyebrow.

Heart hammering, Chloe scrambled to her feet. "Nothing," she squeaked. All the while, her mind raced. "It is nothing." But why did it feel very much... like something?

Or did she, in her need to want him to be more, simply make castles out of sand?

That dangerous half-grin still affixed to his firm lips, he moved his eyes over her face like one who searched for secrets and who'd ultimately find them.

"I said we should go," she lied, snapping the book closed. Chloe cradled it close to her chest. "I... trust we've spent sufficient time here."

Did she imagine the flash of disappointment in his blue eyes? "Of course." He sprang into action, gathering up the blanket and basket with such speed that it slayed any such silly ponderings.

A short while later, after the short trek to his curricle, Chloe and Leo sat in a stilted silence for the slow journey back to their townhouse.

Seated on the bench beside him, Chloe examined the small tome, flipping past poem after poem, searching in vain for a sonnet that was not contained within the leather bindings.

Nothing.

Chloe snapped it closed. As Leo expertly guided the conveyance along Oxford Street, Chloe absently surveyed the passing West London scene and tried to make sense of Leo's recitation of Mary Darby Robinson's sonnet.

The easiest explanation that slid the puzzle piece that was Leo Dunlop into place was that rakes and rogues and scoundrels alike all used poetry as a tool of seduction.

But what of the other pieces that did not make sense where her husband was concerned? She ran through every encounter, every exchange they'd had, looking at them through new lenses: his memorization of the ten detailed terms she'd brought to him, the list of rules for reform he'd glanced briefly at and acknowledged.

Leo Dunlop, the Marquess of Tennyson, might have rightly earned his reputation as a rake, but he was keenly intelligent. Nor were the two traits mutually exclusive. So why did it feel as though there was more at play here, after all?

In the end, her attempts at restraint were in vain.

"You knew the poem," she charged.

Leo clenched his fingers around the reins and then relaxed those digits. "Is that a question?"

Ignoring the droll edge, she lifted the book. "You read poetry." Nay, not just any poetry. "Poems written by female poets and philosophers."

She searched for some hint of response. His face was a careful study in stone that even a marble sculpture would struggle to emulate.

"I don't read poetry," he finally said emphatically, guiding the pair of whites around a corner.

"You've *read* it, then," she surmised. It was all that made sense in a world that was suddenly without stabilizing clarity. Except... "That is a question about your past, though, isn't it?" One of the secret parts of himself he'd demanded complete control of.

"What does it matter my familiarity with a bloody poem?" he groused. "I'm a rake. One of those gents who uses glib words, hooded stares, and," he lowered his voice to a husky purr, "scandalous touches to seduce." Shifting the reins to one hand, he slid his other palm along the side of her hip.

"Stop." Chloe shoved his hand back. "You're attempting to distract me," she noted. A dull flush stained his cheeks, but he did not deny it. "You would have me believe that of all the romantic verses and poems you might have used to seduce a lady, your choice was that of *Mary Darby Robinson?*" Chloe turned on the bench and looked squarely at him. "Most women prefer Lord Byron," she said, tossing back the observation he'd made in Hyde Park. "You said it yourself."

"I know what I said," he clipped out, his gaze trained directly forward. "Do you want to know the truth?" he snapped. "Do you want me to tell you how my father ridiculed and mocked me for reading feminine works? How he burned those volumes as a punishment for my not being the son he truly wished for?"

"Oh, Leo," she whispered. Her heart buckled under the power of the revelation. For the suffering he'd known. All along, she'd seen them as two very different people, surely incapable of having anything in common. They had both suffered at the hands of a cruel sire. Chloe covered her husband's hand with her own. He stiffened, but did not pull away.

His Adam's apple worked.

Silently, Chloe willed her husband to look at her. To tear his focus from the crowded streets that slowed their progress through London and see that they were the unlikeliest pair of like souls. Selfishly, she longed for him to let her in, while she herself was unable to share the ugliest horrors of her past.

"My father hated me," he said softly, a man who'd forgotten anyone else was near. In this moment, Chloe could have owned the admission made by her husband. His lips parted on a laugh filled with self-loathing. "I was a bastard, and he hated me for it."

She made a sound of protest. "Your father was the bastard." The exclamation was ripped from her, from a place of knowing.

Leo chuckled, the sound devoid of mirth. "You misunderstand me, Wife. I was a bastard child sired by another man. A babe that didn't have the decency to join its mother in death and, instead, lived on to forever remind the marquess of his wife's infidelity. When his *real* son, my *brother* who wouldn't even acknowledge me, kicked up his heels."

Chloe gripped the bench to keep steady as the enormity of what he revealed robbed her of breath. What a horrid existence it must have been for him, a motherless babe surrounded by hatred and loathing.

Oh, Leo.

How she despised the passersby and carriages clogging the roads. She yearned to be alone with Leo and this revelation so she could fold him close and weep for what he, too, had lost.

Tension crackled between them, and she weighed her next words. "Your birth, your mother's death, her infidelity, none of that was your fault, Leo," she said quietly.

Leo expertly handled the reins, guiding the carriage down the busy thoroughfare. They might as well have been any of the other lords and ladies in passing conveyances. Except, the gravity of the secrets they shared set them in an altogether different hemisphere. Chloe roved her gaze over Leo's face, the chiseled planes carved in stone. "The only one to blame for wrongdoing was the man who treated you with such cruelty for actions that belonged to others and who was too cruel to give love to a babe." Who desperately needed it.

"Pfft. He knew what I was."

And, at last, it made sense. The truth came to her with a staggering clarity. Leo had spent his life fulfilling every low expectation the late marquess had of him. Chloe had long ago come to peace with the fact that she hadn't been responsible for her father's sins... but Leo had never come to that realization. If the late Lord Tennyson were alive, she'd gladly plunge a stake through his black heart. "Leo?"

With a stiff, reluctant turn of his head, he faced her.

"He was the monster. You never were," she said, willing him to see.

He sneered. "You know *nothing* about monsters, madam."

"I know more than you think." She, however, was unwilling to shift their discussion to her own suffering. Leo would only slam shut the small window he'd opened into his mysterious life. "He's gone, and you are free of him. You don't have to hide your true intellect from the world, Leo." He never had. "And you don't need to present yourself as a coldhearted rake."

He laughed. To her ears, the sound was brittle and forced. "My true intellect, madam?" Leo scoffed. "Present myself as a cold-hearted rake? That is rich." Her husband jerked on the reins, and she registered belatedly that they'd arrived.

A servant came rushing forward, but Leo held up a staying hand, and the man immediately made himself scarce.

Leo leaned close, shrinking away all the space between them. He angled his body in a way that cut the world out and conveyed intimacy, a stolen moment between lovers.

Chloe shivered. The display of warmth was belied by the icy glint in his eyes and the hardness of his lips. It was a coldness she was all too familiar with. She knew how simmering rage so easily became blinding violence. "I want to go inside," she stated with a calm she desperately hoped to feel.

"You are free to leave any time… as soon as the terms of our arrangement are met, my lady."

Chloe flinched. The casual willingness to set her free shouldn't cut, and yet, it did.

"But before you do," Leo said as he captured her chin in a grip that was both unrelenting and gentle. It was a bewildering contradiction. "Let us be clear. Perhaps you wish to convince yourself that the man you've bound yourself to until death do we part is more. Mayhap it will help you slumber more peacefully to see a poor, snot-nosed babe crying for a father's affection, who learned to conceal his love of poetry, and not a man who took a virgin against a library wall in Lord Ackerland's precious library in the middle of a bloody ball."

Her stomach pitched, and she shrank away from his touch. For having him say it in those plain terms was a confirmation that the allegations made against him were, in fact, sins upon his soul. It ripped a hole somewhere inside Chloe. "Stop it," she ordered quietly. Was it him she commanded to stop? Or herself? "You are just trying to push me away. You became who he professed you were, but you don't have to be that person any longer. You—"

Leo shook his head. "You'll hear this first. That rake… the one that has your mother weeping and your brother ready to duel me at dawn? That is precisely the man I am. So do not make me out to be more."

Leo swung his leg over and leaped down.

He could have stormed off in the rage that now gripped him and left her to the waiting servant. Instead, her husband reached up and scooped her around the waist like she was the most delicate of treasures and set her down.

They started for the steps.

"Leo?" she put forward as the butler swept the doors open.

Her husband cast her a glance.

"The lord doth protest too much, methinks." She lifted her palms. "There is always more… to all of us. It's just oft times easier to look upon the surface and accept that which is so obviously displayed."

His golden brows stitched into a single line.

"Ahem," Tomlinson interrupted.

"What is it?" Leo snapped.

"Her ladyship has guests. I informed them you were out, and they insisted they would wait." They? "Until you returned." Tomlinson presented a silver tray, and Chloe collected the card. "I showed them to the Ivory Parlor."

"My sister and sister-in-law," she said, lifting her head. No doubt, after her flight last evening, they sought to make peace.

"And this arrived for you, my lord." Tomlinson handed over a small, folded scrap.

In his peculiarly speedy manner, Leo glanced at the page, folded it, and tucked it in his pocket faster than it would have taken most men to read a single sentence.

Leo sketched a bow. "I will leave you to your visit, then." And just like that, Chloe had been summarily forgotten. He called for his horse.

He is leaving…

Questions swirled. And ugly, unwelcome possibilities about the author of that note slipped forward. He'd pushed her away. She'd asked too many questions, and he'd shared too much of his past, and now he'd turned from her.

"My lady?" Tomlinson ventured.

"Yes, thank you." Forcing her legs into motion, she hurried to greet the two ladies who awaited her. Given the gulf that had developed between Chloe and her family since she'd married, she should be grateful at their arrival. And yet, she wanted them gone. Wanted to plant her feet and demand Leo hear her, and more… keep him with her so he couldn't fill his days and nights with a woman who wanted nothing more from him than a brief diversion from her own miseries and tedium.

Chloe reached the parlor.

She found Jane and Philippa, backs to her, at the hearth, examining the same piece that had so riveted Chloe days ago. Had it truly been mere days since she'd wed Leo? Surely a lifetime had passed.

"Hullo," she called out from the doorway, drawing the door shut behind her.

Both women spun to face her.

"Chloe," they both exclaimed, perfect ducks in tandem from each step and movement.

They stood, a strained silence between them. One that had never been there before. It was ultimately Jane who took control. "We came to speak with you. May we sit?"

"Of course," she said stiffly. Chloe settled herself on the edge of a King Louis XIV chair directly facing the Edgerton women. If Philippa and Jane had come to lecture and admonish her over her decision, she'd ask them to leave. There was no undoing what had been done. Nor would their misery or anger do anything but hurt.

"He knows Beethoven," Philippa blurted.

Chloe slowly raised her brows. What was she on about?

"Your husband, Lord Tennyson, that is," her elder sister went on to clarify. "He knows both *of* him… and knows him personally."

Chloe widened her eyes. Of anything and everything she'd expected Philippa or Jane to say, that had decidedly not been it. "I don't understand," she said, trying to make sense of her sister's revelation.

Philippa spoke in a rush, gesticulating wildly as she spoke. "He shared with Faith that Mr. Beethoven has lost most of his hearing. That he's, in fact, been without full use of his ears for a number of years and composed music anyway and…" She stopped abruptly and pressed a hand to her mouth. From over her gloved fingertips, tears welled in her eyes.

"And this… upsets you?" she asked, confused, desperately attempting to follow along.

Philippa recoiled. "Of course not." Reaching across the table, she gathered Chloe's hands and squeezed. "Chloe, he was reassuring her. About her hearing."

Warmth spread throughout Chloe's chest. Her husband had been threatened and ridiculed by his host, and where had he gone? What had he done? He had joined two little girls, sharing the accomplishments of one who was hard of hearing with a girl whose greatest insecurity was her partial hearing loss. Chloe bit her lip. The man he'd proven himself to be was again inconsistent with the angry figure who'd stormed off.

One who was even now likely at one of his scandalous clubs.

From where they sat, Jane and Philippa exchanged a look. Her sister-in-law stood and joined Chloe. "I'll not make excuses for Gabriel. He was wrong. He is worried about you," she added. "But that does not give him leave to treat either of you as he's done." Calm, rational, and in possession of one of the purest hearts—there was so much to love about her sister-in-law. "Unless we're given evidence that you are... unhappy, I explained to Gabriel how it is to be." With each statement, she stuck a finger up. "You're *both* to be met with warmth and kindness when you are in our home. We will provide a united front to Polite Society."

Philippa nodded. "We will help you gain access to societal functions, as we can." Her sister peered at her. "Which is odd, as you've never before expressed an interest in societal acceptance. But if that is what you wish?"

They stared at her, matching questions in their eyes.

"Yes," she said hoarsely. Emotion clogged Chloe's throat. It was not what she or Leo wished, but what they required. And now her family, as devoted as they'd always been, had responded with that usual Edgerton support.

Jane nodded. "Very well." Fishing inside a pocket along the front of her gown, she withdrew a small, leather notebook and pencil. "We'll begin with Philippa's unveiling at the Ladies of Hope."

Philippa nodded. "In two days, there will be a gathering of the benefactors and benefactresses. You and Lord Tennyson will attend."

"Mother?"

Her sister looked away, but not before Chloe caught the flash of regret in her eyes.

"She returned this morn to Imogen's side. In time, she will come 'round," Jane promised. She locked a stare on Chloe. "As long as she is able to see that you were right about Lord Tennyson. That he is worthy of you. That he is loyal and eventually, in time, loving."

And while her sister and sister-in-law proceeded to plot, Chloe stared absently off at the peculiar piece atop the mantel.

She wondered which wicked haunt her husband had gone off

to… and why, in a marriage of convenience, should it matter so very much?

CHAPTER 19

Marriage to Chloe was going to be a problem, and not for reasons Leo could have ever foreseen.

When Leo was around Chloe, he alternated between a maddening hunger to make love to her… and *admiring* her for being more damned clever than any tutor and Oxford instructor he'd had combined.

But this cleverness, her innate ability to see everything, was something far more perilous than a simple lust that could be sated with sex and sinning.

He'd shared parts of his past with her. He'd discussed the late marquess with no one—not even his uncle, who'd finally wrestled Leo away from any further torture at that bastard's hands—yet, Leo had let Chloe inside, and he'd shown her too much. More than could ever be safe.

Leo urged his mount on to a faster gait through the fashionable streets of London. Again, she'd called into question what he was.

The lord doth protest too much, methinks…

He'd been careless in what he'd revealed, and because of it, Chloe insisted on seeing something in him beyond a callous rake. Nay, it was more than that. She questioned gossips and wondered at his knowledge of literature and his ability to memorize a page at a mere glance. Under his gloves, his palms grew moist. For God help him, until her, he'd forgotten that there were other pleasures to be had outside the carnal ones. There had been just one he'd let close enough to see… back when he was a boy just out of university, romantic and foolish enough to believe he could have a life within the Brethren and a bucolic life with a loyal woman.

And after the blunder he'd made one night with that woman, Leo had turned his back on the bookish pup he'd been and fully embraced the life he'd been born to.

Chloe, however, was different than any other woman before her.

Leo gripped his reins hard. What had he done? He'd been a fool to believe he could perpetuate the lie that was his life so long as Chloe resided under the same roof.

Guiding Sin down St. James's Street, Leo brought the loyal horse to a stop.

After fleeing his wife, her family, his townhouse, and his upheaved life, Leo found himself outside the last place he ever cared to be—White's.

In fact, he'd made it a point to avoid the damned establishment altogether since he'd been beaten to a pulp and nearly strangled to death by the irascible Earl of Montfort two years earlier. Montfort had been summarily banned afterward, so there were no worries of another encounter. It had been a deserved thrashing, but one he'd rather avoid a repeat of, nonetheless.

Yet, respectability called—for his mission, anyway. Leo had been summoned. Leo tossed his reins off to a nearby street urchin, with a coin and promise for more. As he strode up the steps, his attention should be solely focused on his upcoming meeting.

Instead, Chloe retained a tentaclelike grip on his thoughts.

A servant admitted Leo and accepted his cloak.

All eyes within the club swiveled to the front of the establishment, settling on Leo.

A resounding silence fell, and then the room dissolved into a flurry of whispers.

Bloody fucking nobs. Leo yawned. Fortunately, he'd grown well accustomed to the tediously predictable response to his presence. Infusing a deliberate laziness into his gait, Leo started for the infrequently visited tables reserved for him. Given his lecherous reputation, the doors of White's should have long been closed to him… and would have been shut to any other man. The empty-headed sots who sipped their brandies and played their dull games of whist didn't have the sense to question the oddness of Leo maintaining a membership. Leo reached his table and waved off a servant coming forward to drag out his chair.

"Leo!" A booming voice broke across the still-buzzing whispers. "My dear boy."

On cue.

Leo hesitated a long while, deliberately stretching out the length of his insolent pause. And then, with feigned reluctance, he faced the owner of that cheerful greeting. Seated at his tables in the far left corner of the club, the Duke of Aubrey was joined by Higgins and Rowley, two of Society's most respectable, proper gents.

"Why the hesitation, dear boy?" Uncle William shot a hand into the air and waved him over. "Come, come! Join me."

Abandoning his table, Leo cut a path through the club, kicking up frenzied whispers in his wake.

"Uncle," he drawled when he reached the trio.

They went through the false show for their audience's benefit. Leo, the reluctant, slightly disrespectful nephew; the duke, a benevolent and expecting-to-be-obeyed uncle; and two lords, who remained seated as the nephew joined them, because it would be unpardonably rude to quit a duke's company.

In all, it was the perfect ruse and one that had proven exceedingly helpful through the years.

Hiding in plain sight, as his uncle called it, allowed one more freedom and security than even the darkest corner.

"I understand congratulations are in order," Higgins remarked. The graying man gestured over a footman.

A moment later, a glass was set before Leo. The Delegator poured a snifter full and handed it over.

"I never thought I'd see the day." A patent disdain dripped from Rowley's words as each gentleman held his drink aloft in a formal toast to the end of Leo's bachelorhood.

"Ah, but that is the power of love, is it not, Rowley?" Uncle William waggled his eyebrows. "That even the most hardened rake or rogue can be reformed by its power." The duke smiled at Leo, again lifting his glass in his nephew's direction. "And when the Hellings fall, we are known to fall hard and fast. Isn't that right, Leo?"

How different the requisite reply to his uncle's assertion would have been just days ago. Now, Leo played a new part: devoted husband to a delectable spitfire. He smiled loosely. "My wife is unlike any other woman," he said quietly. Except, the layer of truth contained within those words made them spill forward easily. His fingers curled tight around his glass, and he took a long, desperate swallow, letting the spirits blaze a sharp trail down his throat. He'd set his glass down hard and reached for the bottle to add another fingerful when he felt three sets of eyes boring into him.

Neck heating, he swiftly released the bottle.

Rowley's expression set in a smug knowing... when the sod couldn't see anything with clarity. For Leo himself couldn't make sense of the murky cloud of his life. Sitting back, he lazily cradled his glass between his fingers to keep them steady.

"From what I hear, you were seen carrying the lady through the streets of London," Higgins remarked.

The Delegator or not, his superior could go hang before Leo revealed the abrupt departure and fight that had sent Chloe fleeing her family's residence. "The lady wished to walk, but I was unwilling to allow her to strain her ankle after a recent fall."

"Hmph," Rowley grunted, tossing back his drink.

"And I also hear," Uncle William leaned his elbows on the table, "you were seen reading to the lady earlier today in Hyde Park."

There was more than a question there, one that moved beyond this façade they carried out for the benefit of the crowd. Leo shuttered his expression and cursed the duke's ability to see below anyone's surface, including Leo's. A smile ghosted his uncle's lips, and he winked.

They maintained the casual dialogue until the other patrons' attention throughout the club drifted away from them.

Lord Higgins picked up his glass and raised it to his lips. "We've uncovered proof you were... are correct," he said without preamble.

Even as every last muscle in his being jumped at the admission, Leo gave a casual roll of his shoulders. "Oh?"

"As you know, the Home Office was unwilling to use spies in court to bring down all those involved in the Cato Event. Criminal charges were dropped as long as Adams and Monument," two leading figures in the conspiracy, "supplied evidence to convict the rest of the gang. Which they did in the form of names names. George Edwards was never called to bring forth information on the event."

Leo sat up straighter, homing in on that latter admission. "They never *interviewed* him?"

"No, they did not," Uncle William said, his glass carefully held close to his mouth, hiding his lips as he spoke. "One of the Brethren tracked him down and conducted that long-overdue interview. And with some persuasion, he proved… cooperative."

Leo glanced around the table. "I trust he had information to share that was of value?"

Lord Rowley pursed his mouth like he'd sucked on a rotted piece of fruit.

Triumph pumped through Leo's veins. It was a great thrill as potently strong now as when he'd been proven correct with the information he'd ferreted out as a young man. He'd been right in his suspicions.

"Immeasurably," Higgins intoned. "There were forty men recruited for the plot. Only seven and twenty took part. Edwards insists he was given bad information about the Cabinet meeting taking place at Lord Harrowby's residence."

"It was meant to trap Edwards and those determined to overthrow the government," Leo murmured, the pieces of the puzzle sliding into place.

"Precisely," Uncle William confirmed. "Not only would this group of Tories focused upon radical reforms to oppress the masses take full blame for the Cato plot, but it would also allow them to enact their legislation."

Leo silently whistled. It was masterful. What men didn't realize, however, was that ultimately no secret was safe. And when there was one bent on subversion, the truth inevitably came to light and justice attained. "Did he offer the names?"

"Lords Waterson, Tremaine, Ellsworth," Rowley grudgingly volunteered, the names coming as if forcibly pulled from him. "They were the greatest proponents of the Six Acts inside and outside of Parliament."

Leo smirked. This was why there had been so little a battle required for him to retain his post with the Brethren. "This must be difficult for you, Rowley." The bastard had to swallow that he'd been not only unsuccessful in his efforts to oust Leo from the Brethren, but also had to admit Leo was correct in his suppositions.

"Go to hell," the viscount returned through a tight-lipped smile.

"Gentlemen." Higgins thumped the bottle, leveling a sideways glance at each of them. He made a show of refilling each gentleman's glass and then held his up in another false salute. "We don't have time for your petty rivalry. Tennyson, you've done a convincing job with your recent bride. Keep at it. Her family is close to Waterson. Her sister-in-law was an instructor for Ellsworth's daughter, but the connection isn't strong enough to reach the family that way. Another agent will handle Ellsworth and Tremaine." As he proceeded to fire off commands, he rolled his snifter back and forth between his fingers. "You'll need another invitation into Waterson's home, so you can continue the search you started." Before Leo had been caught with Chloe. "See that you secure that. And you'll host a soiree with the respective gentlemen present as guests."

"Taking advantage of her familial connection may not be as… easy as we had anticipated."

Higgins' brows pulled together. "In what way?"

Leo measured his words carefully. "The lady's family has proven less forthcoming with their support."

"What family would be elated with a wastrel like you in their midst?" Rowley muttered under his breath.

That insult rolled off Leo's thickened skin. He focused, instead, on his uncle and the Delegator.

"Bloody hell," Higgins muttered in an unusual public display of his frustration. "The whole reason you wed the damn woman was for entry and access to Waterson—"

"And the appearances of it all," his uncle interrupted, a frown marring his lips.

"If she cannot provide you with *all* of that, she is useless to us," Higgins stated with a brutal candor that sent Leo's hands curling into fists on his lap.

The lady was many things: clever, determined, spirited. Yes.

"I'd have a care," he warned Higgins on a steely whisper. "The lady is my wife."

"Then see that your *wife* gets you that which we need." The Delegator stood, with Rowley falling into like step. "Tennyson,"

Higgins called loud enough for those at nearby tables to overhear. "Again, congratulations on your recent nuptials."

Leo nudged his chin up in the expected insolent acknowledgment, fighting the urge to lift a crude finger instead. After his superiors had gone, he swiped his drink up and stared at the half-empty amber contents.

Both men had been, in fact, correct. The sole reason he'd wed Chloe had been with the Cato case in mind. But that had been before, when she'd been nothing more than a chess piece upon the board, used to maintain order and right for the Crown.

Now, she was a spirited miss who read the works of female philosophers and aspired to... work, when ladies of the *ton* aspired to nothing but their own pleasures and pastimes.

"That bad, eh?"

"What?" Leo directed the curt utterance at his glass.

"Woolgathering," his uncle said with entirely too much amusement.

Leo sat up in his seat. "I'm not... woolgathering." That was what innocent misses and lovesick swains did. Not devils with black souls.

"Defending the lady," the other man persisted. "As one who has also been bewitched by a young bride, I'd say you are smitten."

Smitten. Leo recoiled. "Impossible. Never." Why, that would have to mean he, Leo Dunlop, was capable of caring for someone. Which he wasn't. "Egads, you're... m-mad," he sputtered.

His uncle dissolved into a very unducal-like round of laughter. His broad frame shook with the weight of his mirth. "Methinks he doth protest too much."

At having that quote so glibly tossed by his wife a short while ago thrown in his face by the man opposite him, Leo felt his skin go hot. "You don't know a thing about it," he said tightly. He'd never before shared with a soul any mention of the one woman he had mistakenly opened his heart to... and all the ways he'd broken it and been reborn from that folly. "I'll never be one who's smitten or falls in love. That is not who I am." But it had been... back when he was a boy and hoped for that sentiment... nay... a family. He'd wanted a family. The cynical set of his features reflected in the his brandy. What a fool he'd been.

All hint of amusement fled his uncle's face. He dragged his chair closer and, anchoring his elbows on the table, leaned forward. "You think I don't know anything about it? Loss? About choosing... other obligations before my own wants? I've lost as much as I've won. I have your aunt, but..." Pain contorted his features. "I knew loss before her."

Leo sat in silence. The late Duchess of Aubrey's death at the hands of foes to the Brethren was known as a cautionary tale to all who entered the ranks of the organization, but the details of her demise remained a long-held secret shared by none.

"Sometimes, Leo," his uncle said gravely, finally speaking again, "it is easy to become embroiled in that life that you forget to live. I don't want that for you."

"My work is all I am," he said automatically, without inflection, and only as a matter of fact.

"Ah, but it doesn't have to be. Mayhap Chloe... will be good not only for your assignment, but for you."

A flippant denial hung on his lips, but he could not force the words out.

His uncle fortunately let the matter rest and was, once more, all business, which was good. "In the meantime, you'll need to gain her family's assistance. Like Higgins, I recommend a soiree. The only one you require in attendance is Waterson."

Leo filed away each recommendation. It was safe. Familiar.

"Keep your invitations to those Waterson would be most comfortable with. Tories."

Leo grimaced.

"That way, the gentlemen will converse freely about their politics."

There was, however, one dilemma. "I still have to convince Chloe to host an event." For he'd found the unlikely—the one lady in all of London who despised balls and soirees.

His uncle snorted. "If you convinced that girl to marry you, Leo, I trust managing to elicit her cooperation for a formal affair will be effortless." He finished off his drink and set his glass down. "Like you, I have a lovely wife awaiting," he said, heavily obvious with his insinuation. His uncle stood. "My congratulations, Leo."

Leo made his goodbyes and stared after his uncle's retreating form. The duke cut a swath through the club, earning respectful greetings and calls from the gentlemen he passed. And then he was gone.

Leo pulled over the bottle and added brandy to his glass.

His uncle had urged him to return home. Leo, however, was not too proud to admit he was bloody terrified. His wife had begun to probe… and only a few days into their marriage. How was he to maintain the secret of his role within the Brethren when Chloe saw secrets in details everyone else before her looked past?

Where every other lord and lady was content with the image he presented to the world, his wife challenged it. And he was torn between admiration for her intelligence and frustration for the danger it posed. Regardless, one thing was certain, it was far safer in his club than returning home to her further questioning.

Nay, that isn't all. You're terrified out of your bloody everlasting mind. She is the only person, aside from your uncle, who knows you're a bastard in every sense of the word.

He tossed back a long swallow.

Hours later, after night had descended and his wife was surely abed, Leo finally shoved back his chair. There was nothing else for it. He was a bloody coward, and it hadn't been a damned assignment that had set him running and humbled, but a slip of a spitfire.

Leo had made his way to the front of the club when a servant opened the door, admitting a patron.

Leo stopped in his tracks as his stare collided with the gentleman's. The other man drew back, his mouth agape, his muscles tense, like one who'd seen a gorgon.

Oh, bloody hell on Sunday.

Leo mustered a smile. "Montfort," he greeted jovially. "I see they've renewed your membership. Drinks, perhaps?"

With a roar, the Earl of Montfort charged him.

Every part of him thrummed to life with the primitive need to fight. Cursing, Leo stepped aside, avoiding the earl's hurtling body. "It is not my intention to fight with you," he murmured, placating.

"You bastard," Montfort hissed, throwing a punch.

Leo angled his head quickly, dodging the blow. He had taken a beating from Lord Montfort, his former rake compatriot turned reformed rake, in the past. Largely because he deserved it. Nonetheless, Leo would rather avoid a repeat performance. With the patrons eagerly watching, Leo planted his feet. "You don't want to do this, Montfort."

"Trust me. I do." Montfort muttered and then slammed his fist into Leo's cheek.

Pain resonated throughout his entire face, with agony exploding from his jawline to his temple. A slow trickle of blood seeped from his nostrils. "Oh, bloody hell," he mumbled, yanking out a kerchief. He held it to his face. "Bad form beating a man who—"

Montfort let another punch fly. This one collided with Leo's stomach with such force it sucked all the air from his lungs. His legs swayed under him, but he fixed his feet, refusing to go down.

"Fight me," the earl shouted.

"Montfort!" someone exclaimed from beyond Leo's shoulder.

"I'll not fight you, Montfort." And it had nothing to do with the earl and everything to do with the one sin Leo would take back but never could.

Montfort took another swing. And this blow connected with Leo's other cheek, effectively bringing him to his knees. The fabric in his hand fell to the floor.

He dimly registered the Marquess of St. Albans rushing over and gripping the irate earl by his shoulders. His murmurings, however, were lost to the buzzing in Leo's ears. Not that he gave a rat's arse what St. Albans had to say this day or any other. Blinking wildly, fighting off unconsciousness, Leo struggled to his feet.

"My lord." The butler came rushing forward, outrage written in his stern expressions. "Your membership—"

"Is revoked?" Montfort growled, spitting on the carpeted floor. "With bastards like this one allowed entry," he said as he jerked his chin in Leo's direction, "I've no interest in membership to your," he peeled his lip in a sneer, "esteemed club." On that, Montfort stalked off, St. Albans at his side.

"My apologies, my lord," a servant was saying to Leo. Someone pressed fabric into his hand—a kerchief.

His mouth throbbed, already beginning to swell. Leo took the scrap with a word of thanks. Forcing a smile around the kerchief, he lifted his other hand in parting. "Gentlemen," he called jovially and strode forward.

He stumbled.

Concerned whispers and gasps went up.

Gritting his teeth, Leo steadied himself. He accepted his cloak and, clasping it at his throat, took his leave of the club.

Of all bloody days for Montfort's membership to be restored.

He did a sweep of the streets for the boy he'd tasked with watching his mount. The child came springing forward. "Oi, sir, ya look bloody awful."

"Undoubtedly," he drawled, passing off a heavy purse for the child.

The street urchin's eyes formed wide circles. As if he feared Leo might change his mind and snatch back that gift, the boy bolted.

Sucking in a slow, steadying breath, Leo turned his attentions to dragging himself atop his mount. He winced as he settled into the saddle. By God, his ribs burned like the devil. Urging his mount onward, he made a slow, agonizing journey home.

CHAPTER 20

Leo HADN'T RETURNED HOME.

Knees drawn close to her chest, Chloe sat on the sofa in the Ivory Parlor. Laying her cheek to her night skirts, she rubbed back and forth, absently contemplating the bronze sculpture atop the hearth.

Chloe might be a virtuous lady, but she had a former rogue of a brother and enough sense to know that when a gentleman disappeared for hours on end, and into the night, there were few respectable places he might be.

You'll hear this first. That rake… the one that has your mother weeping and your brother ready to duel me at dawn? That is precisely the man I am…

Her stomach muscles clenched, and she hated herself for caring that he was off doing… doing… rakish things. While she? She sat here, alone, as she'd been sitting, waiting for his return.

Yes, waiting. Because she was not one who'd lie to herself… on either score.

She hated the idea of Leo off with one of his scandalous ladies, exploring the curve of a cheek and a hip that belonged to another, as he had done hers.

The soft tread of footfalls punctured the quiet.

Chloe swung her legs over the side of the couch and quickly

rescued Mary Darby Robinson's works that rested beside her. From over the top of the leather volume, she peeked. Her heart beat harder.

Leo strode past, and then his footfalls stopped.

She yanked her attention downward.

"Chloe," he greeted with not even the barest hint of enthusiasm.

"Leo," she returned, lowering the book. "I didn't—" She gasped. Abandoning all attempts at nonchalance, she tossed aside the leather tome. It tumbled to the floor, forgotten. "My God," she breathed, rushing over to where his powerful figure was framed in the doorway. The fire's glow played off the macabre blood staining his face and the beginning shades of purple and blue bruises setting in. She pressed a hand to her lips.

"You are still awake," he noted tiredly.

"What happened?" she demanded. Taking him by the hand, she tugged him forward. Before he could reply, she pressed her palms against his shoulders and gave a slight push. "Sit," she ordered. Chloe ran her gaze over his face, assessing his bruises. His right eye had already swelled and showed faint hints of purpling. A faint crack in his left cheek seeped blood. Having suffered through endless rounds of torture at her father's merciless fists, she well knew the agony of those blows, how a strike to the temple caused a brutal ache. "Oh, Leo," she whispered.

"It is fine," he assured.

She was already moving. Reaching the bellpull, Chloe tugged the string. Perhaps he'd been off with another woman and been discovered and beaten by an angry husband. And perhaps she was a pathetic ninny, but Chloe could not turn a cheek to his suffering.

Tomlinson materialized almost instantly. He glanced from Chloe to Leo and then back to Chloe. "My lady?" The absolute composure at seeing his employer in his existing state spoke of one who'd seen Leo in this condition before.

"You needn't worry, Chloe," Leo called from behind her.

"I require two bowls of water, a pitcher, and scraps of cloth," Chloe instructed, ignoring the useless assurances from her husband.

Dropping a bow, Tomlinson set off.

Chloe rejoined her husband at the sofa. Resting one knee on the cushion, she examined his injuries more closely. Her stomach pitched.

"Never tell me you're going to faint, love," he drawled, his voice slightly strained.

He was hurting.

Tentatively, she probed a knot at his temple. "I don't faint." He winced, and she gentled her touch. Were his injuries a product of a lover's irate husband? A fight at the gaming tables?

"Of course you don't," he muttered.

Chloe paused in her examination. "Would you rather I be the wilting sort?"

Leo captured her wrist, staying her movements. Drawing her hand close, he placed a lingering kiss on the place where her pulse hammered. Delicious shivers radiated from that butterfly-soft caress. "I wouldn't change you, love," he murmured, his brandy-tinged breath wafting over her. That always hateful scent, now wrapped in words so beautifully tender, exploded warmth in her breast.

She bit the inside of her cheek hard.

Fool. Fool. Fool. Fool.

Even now, she hurt for a man who neither wanted her fidelity, nor wished to give his to her in return, who likely wore the bruises he did because of another woman.

But mayhap not.

A pair of servants rushed in with the requested items. Chloe jumped up, directing them to set the pitchers and bowls down. While they organized the materials on a rose-inlaid table, she hovered at the fireplace, alongside the bronze sculpture.

She absently trailed her fingertips along the peculiar creature's face, using the servants' presence to rein in the sick knot low in her belly at the thought of Leo off whispering in his husky baritone words meant to seduce another. Chloe curled her toes so tight, the arches of her feet ached.

When they'd gone, she returned to Leo's side. Giving him her back, Chloe grabbed a white cloth and dunked it in one of the bowls. She wrung out the excess water and applied the compress to the worst of his bruises.

Leo flinched.

"I'm sorry," she murmured, knowing firsthand that the pain of a beating came not just in the act, but in the body's healing.

His gaze pierced hers, eyes that could see through her, if he so wished. But she'd wager her soul on Sunday that there was no woman whose heart or soul Leo would ever have a use or want for. Why did that leave her bereft? Chloe slid her attention back to his injuries.

"You really do not have to—"

"I know I don't have to," she interrupted, removing the cloth. "I want to." Ever so gently, she applied the damp fabric to the cut on his cheek. "How did the other gentleman fare?"

"Immensely better," he said with a droll edge. He grimaced, and murmuring her apologies, Chloe gentled her ministrations.

He wrapped a hand loosely about her wrist, briefly halting her efforts. She stared at him with a question in her eyes. "I should not have shared what I did this afternoon."

Chloe didn't pretend to misunderstand. Contained within his gaze was an insecurity she'd never before seen from him.

Lightly brushing the luxuriant gold strands back from his brow, she tangled her fingers ever so gently in the faint curls. "Do you take me as a woman who'd judge you for your birthright? Who your father was does not define you." *Any more than my father defines me.* And yet, she'd allowed the ghost of the late Marquess of Waverly to determine her future—whether or not she would marry or have children of her own. Leo had shown her that. And how very freeing it was. "Who you are is what matters, Leo," she said softly.

Leo's throat worked. "Thank you," he said gruffly.

She offered him a tremulous smile.

A comfortable silence fell, a companionable one that defied the earlier tension that had sent him fleeing the townhouse… to wherever he'd gone. Chloe soaked the rag again and reached for another. All the while, her skin prickled with the feel of Leo's eyes on her.

"You've experience with this," he noted when she touched the damp fabric to another injury.

She applied a light pressure. "Is that a question about my past?"

A devastating half-grin curled his lips. "Those were my terms, love."

Just like that, the tension that had throbbed between them since their carriage ride vanished. Chloe pointed her eyes to the heavens. "You're insufferable."

"As I've been told."

"Countless times?"

His smile deepened, dimpling his left cheek. "Vast in its sum."

They shared a smile.

There was a boylike quality to Leo's teasing that made the cold scoundrel who'd come upon her four days… four years… a lifetime ago at the Earl of Waterson's a distant figure who might as well have been conjured of one's imaginings.

Chloe soaked the cloth again and reapplied the compress to his right eye, obscuring his vision. "My brother Alex was often nursing bruises and breaks," she said softly. Vicious injuries doled out gleefully by their miserable sire. How many times had she been nursed this way by a loyal maid? Or tended wounds left upon Gabriel?

"Your brother Alex would have been better served with better friends," Leo drawled.

Entranced by the smallest cut at the corner of his right eye, she stared on, transported back to like marks worn by her brothers… and herself. "A better father," she whispered.

Leo shook his head slowly.

She sucked air in through her teeth. The revelation did not shake the foundation of her world as she'd long expected it would. Chloe stole a peek at him.

"Your father beat your brothers?" he ventured in grave tones.

And me… Her mouth went dry. But God help her, she could not make herself utter that truth. "He did and often."

"He was the monster you spoke of."

You shameful, lying bitch… reading smut not fit for a whore…

Chloe's fingers curled reflexively into the rag, digging into the split on his cheek.

Leo winced.

"My apologies," Chloe murmured, unclenching the digits. An ache settled at the base of her skull. The ache proved to be a weighted pressure that wrapped around the whole of her head. She bit the inside of her cheek, willing the familiar pain gone.

It was inevitable. Her megrims had been with her the whole of her life, and eventually they would come, and Leo would know and—

The cloth slipped through her shaking fingers, landing with a noisy thwack in the bowl. Water splattered over the rim.

"Chloe? Are you all—?"

One time, her father had dealt her swift blows, simultaneously, to both ears. She'd collapsed, all noise and sound coming from a distance, muffled and muted. Mouths had moved, but the words had emerged murky.

She blinked, settling her gaze on Leo's mouth. This moment felt very much like that one, and yet not. For this voice was not raised in anger, this face was not mottled with rage, and she clung to those differences in a bid to anchor herself to reality. Chloe struggled to bring her husband's melodious baritone into focus.

As it had then, all sound and noise came forth on a whirring rush.

Leo palmed her cheek, and she leaned into that gentle touch, one of tenderness and warmth, wholly removed from violence. His hooded gaze swept over her face. "What is it?"

Chloe shook her head slightly. "M-my sister and sister-in-law visited earlier," she said in a desperate need to shift them to safer discourse.

His hand froze on her. "Did they say something to upset you?"

The hard edge there sent a chill scraping along her spine.

"Did they…" she processed slowly.

He stood.

"No," she said on a rush. He'd misunderstood the reason for her unrest. "They came to make their apologies and offer us their assistance."

The tension ebbed from Leo's frame, and he let his arm fall to his side. "I see," he said, his brow wrinkled with befuddlement.

"Sit." Chloe urged him back to his seat. Recovering the cloth she'd dropped, she returned it to the bowl and reached for another. Chloe dipped a new rag into the slightly cooler water. "We spent the day strategizing how best to help with what you require— being respectable. And… Was it over a woman?" The question tumbled forth before she could call it back. Chloe bit the tip of her tongue.

Leo stiffened.

"Yes."

Her husband didn't even pretend to misunderstand, and the

automaticity of that reply hit her like a fist to the belly. He met her gaze squarely. She searched, wanting… nay, needing to see remorse, regret. Something. Just not this impenetrable emptiness.

"Was it the lady's husband?" she asked quietly. Why did she continue to torture herself?

He nodded once.

"I… see." With shockingly steady fingers, she set the cloth down. She braced for him to hurl those reminders about the type of man he was and how she needed to accept that she'd wed a rake, and other useless reminders.

His silence, therefore, stood out stark, more potent for its solemnity.

Flustered, Chloe tidied the makeshift medical station. She was wringing out wet rags and laying them to dry, folding untouched ones into neat, methodical squares. All the while, Leo watched her.

When she'd finished, she put several steps between them.

At last composed, she looked at Leo. "I agreed to help you, my lord." He stiffened. Was it the fact that she was even now calling him out or her use of his formal title that he took umbrage with? "H-however…" She faltered slightly as he unfurled to his full height. Quickly regaining her composure, she went on. "Anything I do will be in vain as long as you are off seducing other ladies."

He took several steps closer. Those steps were the sleek, pantherlike ones of a man on the prowl. The seducer had returned. She knew it by the way he lowered his thick, long, golden lashes and the curve of his hard—and damn him, tempting—lips. As he spoke, the sough of his breath fanned her cheeks. "So I'm not to seduce *other* ladies, which begs the question…"

"Th-the question?"

Leo placed his mouth close to her ear, and she slid her eyes closed. All her senses and nerves went on alert, vibrating and alive. Because of him. For him. "Who is the lady I should be seducing?" His lips caressed the shell of her ear in a fleeting silken kiss.

Chloe remained trapped in a web of desire only this man was capable of weaving. She was the prey trapped by a spider, wrapped and twisted, to be devoured by him. As if he'd sensed her weakness, he curled his palms under her buttocks, shifting her closer.

Chloe tipped her head back, wanting him, wanting his kiss, and his touch, and everything that would lay her bare and open before him. She yearned to taste desire and passion in his arms. He lowered his mouth to hers. And yet—

Chloe turned away. His kiss landed sloppily, grazing her cheek.

She'd not humble herself before a man who that very night had been beaten for the attentions he'd bestowed upon another woman.

She stepped out of his arms. "In two days, there is a ceremony at my sister's institution. She has asked us to be there."

"Very well. I would ask that we host a soiree."

Of anything he might have said, that certainly hadn't been what she'd expected. She eyed him warily. "You promised I wouldn't be required to host any events." With the unpredictability of her headaches, the din of a crowded ballroom and crush of bodies within formal halls had always proven perilous.

Leo gathered her hand and drew it to his mouth. He placed a lingering kiss upon her knuckles. "I'm not demanding it, Chloe. I'm asking you," he said simply.

She bit down on her lower lip. Damn him for not making demands and being so blasted... polite with his request.

"There is nothing that demonstrates more clearly to Polite Society that I've reformed my ways than our hosting, as a newly married couple, a formal gathering. A respectable one," he tacked on, almost as an afterthought, a reminder that he was known for throwing scandalous affairs whispered about behind closed doors.

Chloe chewed at the tip of her index finger. Leo was correct. Establishing themselves as a leading host and hostess among the *ton* could only benefit him in his quest, and Chloe in her goal of becoming headmistress.

She didn't blink for several moments.

For she hadn't, since her marriage, given much thought to her hopes for Jane's school. The muscles of her stomach knotted. How had the role of headmistress, the single-minded goal she'd set for herself, become singularly forgotten since she'd wed Leo?

It was simply because of the whirlwind of her marriage. Her whole life had been thrown into an upheaval. Yes, that was surely the reason for it all.

Calmed by the reassurance, Chloe conceded the point. "Very well. We'll host a small soiree."

"We need to act quickly. The event must take place next week at the latest."

She sputtered. "At the latest?" She'd never personally thrown a function and had avoided her mother's planning of them like the Great Plague. But Chloe knew enough that such events were certainly not thrown together in a week's time. "It's impossible, Leo. There are the invitations and the orchestra and flowers and... People likely already have commitments by this point, anyway."

He snorted. "Not a single lord or lady would neglect an invitation from Society's most scandalous couple."

She wrinkled her nose. "I wouldn't say we are the *most* scandalous. Simply that we were caught in a scandalous situation."

"Chloe?" he prodded.

Goodness, he was determined.

"Do we even have the funds for such a venture?"

"You'll have what you require in terms of monies."

Questions sprang to the tip of her tongue about how, but she set them aside for the more important matter at hand.

Chloe released a beleaguered sigh. "You ask too much."

"It needs to take place within a week, Chloe." Her husband reached inside his jacket and drew out a folded sheet of paper. "I've taken the liberty of assembling names of the dullest gents I'd never dare entertain," he explained, handing over the scrap, his notes written in pencil. "However, for the sake of what I require, I'd like these gentlemen and their families invited."

Not taking the sheet, she ran her gaze over the rough list. At the top, the Earl of Waterson's name stood out with those of other, less familiar yet notoriously stodgy, lords underneath. "You've given this a good deal of thought," she finally said, briefly lifting her head.

"Indeed." Leo waved the scrap. "There are my debts to consider."

"Of course," she said, bitterness creeping in. Chloe accepted the sheet, and her fingers brushed Leo's. The familiar electric warmth tingled at the point where they touched.

She made to draw her hand back... and then froze.

Chloe stood motionless, her gaze riveted upon his hands.

Her husband promptly let his arms fall to his sides, clasping them behind his back. He cleared his throat. "I thank you for agreeing to host an event." My God. *He is rambling.* Always composed and smooth and unaffected, his words now rolled together. "Again, it needs to be soon. No more than a week's time." He dropped a quick bow and, without another word, left.

Chloe stared at the doorway long after he'd gone.

Despite his hasty flight, she'd already seen that which he'd clearly attempted to hide—his hands had revealed not a hint of evidence of one who'd beaten another gentleman. Surely there would have been a cracked or bruised knuckle, something to indicate he'd delivered a blow himself.

She frowned.

How many secrets did her husband carry? As she quit the room and sought out her chamber, Chloe resolved to find out.

CHAPTER 21

ꟾN THE DAYS THAT FOLLOWED, a distance had grown between Leo and Chloe.

Leo locked himself away in his offices, poring over the Cato file without interruption, while his wife remained off… seeing to her own affairs.

Occasionally, Tomlinson shuttled notes back and forth between mistress and master of the household. The notes outlined details and questions about Leo and Chloe's first formal soiree as husband and wife. In sum, that was the extent of their communication.

It was the ideal arrangement. The one Leo hoped for when he offered her marriage: each of them carrying on separate lives with separate purposes.

So why, as their carriage rolled to a halt outside the impressively constructed stone establishment belonging to the Marchioness of Guilford, did Leo once more feel this blasted lightness at being in close quarters with his wife?

Yet, that lightness was short-lived.

His driver pulled the door open and held a hand out.

Without a backward glance, Chloe allowed the liveried servant to hand her down.

He frowned. Accustomed to the always garrulous and teasing Chloe, he didn't know what to do with this laconic and distant woman. And blast if he didn't prefer the former.

Leo jumped out and smoothed his lapels. He held out an elbow, and his wife wordlessly placed her fingertips on his sleeve.

They continued along the graveled path that led to ten long stone steps. "It is an impressive structure," he finally said lamely.

Chloe cast him a curious look. "You are an aficionado of architecture?"

No, he was a man interested in talking to her. One who wished for the pleasure of her clear, teasing tones. "I… uh… studied it in my university days," he lied.

"Hmm."

Chloe redirected her gaze forward. Allowing him to guide her up the stairs to the front of the establishment, she settled into that bloody aloof state.

A butler opened the door, allowing them into the sun-drenched foyer. He then led Chloe and Leo along white-and-pink-striped, satin-wallpapered walls.

The slight heel of her silk shoe tapped a staccato that echoed the discordant beat of his footfalls. Two people out of step, when the previous days they'd gotten on… why, almost as friends.

Leo gritted his teeth and damned himself to hell for wanting her to speak to him and wanting to speak with her.

But why should she? a voice taunted at the back of his mind.

For all intents and purposes, when he'd returned late the other night, he'd all but confessed that his battered face was the consequence of his attentions for another woman. Oh, she'd never explicitly asked, and he'd never explicitly explained, but his meaning had been there all the same… his wounds had been caused by some other woman's irate husband. In a way, Leo had given her facts, and they'd contained more truth than anything else he'd uttered. In doing so, he'd managed to erect an impressive wall between him and Chloe.

And damn it all, if he didn't want to kick that barrier down.

For Chloe treated him as more than a rake. She didn't stare down the length of her pert nose or eye him with disgust. In fact, she was the only one—in more years than he could remember—who'd not treated him so. He'd become so immune to that disdain that he'd ceased to care about those ill opinions… had reveled in them, in fact.

Only to find he—God help him—enjoyed simply being someone other than a scoundrel with her.

Leo's stomach lurched. There it was. He... liked his wife. He genuinely, sincerely, with a depth he hadn't believed himself capable of any longer, liked her.

He abruptly stopped.

Chloe continued on several steps before slowing and then looking back. "Leo?" she asked.

The butler glanced back and forth between the couple and then slipped off, allowing them a semblance of privacy.

"I'm sorry," he said quietly.

A small frown puckered the place between her brows. She came back over. "What?"

Leo dropped his voice. "I allowed you to believe... something that was not wholly true." He glanced about. When he ascertained they were alone, he dropped his voice to a hushed whisper. "I haven't been unfaithful. I just... wanted you to know that," he finished lamely. For reasons he didn't understand, and didn't care to explain, he needed her to know he'd been faithful—at least for now.

Though, since she'd stumbled—quite literally—into his life, he'd not given thought to anyone... but her.

His hands shook, and he looped them at his back in a bid to steady them.

Chloe smiled. "Shall we?" She held her fingers out, and he hurriedly supplied his elbow.

They resumed their walk through the Ladies of Hope. A natural calm overtook him. A semblance of order was restored with all somehow... right.

It is because of her.

An invisible weight slammed into his solar plexus, nearly knocking him off-balance. What madness was this? He liked his wife. Surprisingly enjoyed her company... but he'd never before needed anyone to maintain order over his logic-driven world.

"Breathe, Leo." Her soft whisper carried up to his ears. "It is merely a small gathering of respectable families."

She'd sensed his unrest and wrongly attributed it to their presence in this place.

Breathe, he reminded himself.

It was vital advice. He repeated it in his mind as a mantra.

To focus on something, anything, other than the tumult inside, he took in their surroundings.

"It is magnificent, is it not?" she murmured as they strolled down another corridor. This one's walls were lined with bucolic paintings done in cheerful shades of pale greens, pinks, and blues.

Of its own volition, his gaze traversed a path over the delicate planes of her face. "Magnificent," he murmured.

"It is her second one," she continued in animated tones, excitement coloring her words. "There are more than thirty young girls cared for at Philippa's first institution, and now there will be forty more here. Girls of all ages. Some just babes, and others seven and ten years." Her expression darkened. "They've been cast out because Society has deemed them unfit by their standards."

As she spoke, Leo slowed his steps, pausing to finally truly take in his surroundings and contemplate the institution.

"Here, come with me." His wife took him by the hand and tugged him off in the opposite direction.

The servant held a hand up. "Uh… the ceremony, my lady, is this…"

Ignoring the older fellow, Chloe urged Leo on until they reached a doorway that hung open. She held a finger to her lips, urging him to silence.

Leo studied the cheerfully bright room. Six young girls, mayhap three and ten years of age, sat around on pink, upholstered tub chairs arranged in a neat circle and better suited to a lord and lady's formal parlor. Each child held a book.

"Mary Wollstonecraft," Chloe mouthed.

The girls spoke animatedly to one another. There was an organized chaos to what was ensuing. An older woman in steel-gray skirts looked on, as more of an observer, only periodically pausing to direct the discourse.

He furrowed his brow. The makeshift classroom bore little resemblance to the staid and silent rooms he and other dutiful English boys and girls sat within.

Chloe motioned for Leo to follow. He gave one last curious look back at the gathered children and fell into step.

"They hold Socratic circles," he noted as they made their return to the still waiting butler.

His wife shot her eyebrows up. "You're familiar with them."

"Only insofar as I read of them."

"Of course," Chloe interjected with an emphatic nod. "Because dutiful English boys and girls are hand-fed information as fact and expected to believe it. Here, my sister has encouraged those who Society would scuttle away to use their minds and think." She tapped a gloved fingertip to her forehead. "And, just as importantly, to challenge."

Prior to this instance, the only matter of relevance surrounding the Ladies of Hope Institution had been the role it served in crafting a façade the *ton* could believe.

His existence had solely been focused on hedonistic pursuits so that the world saw only that. And he was able to conduct his investigations freely outside the scope of suspicion. Ultimately, however, the Brethren had always been his focus. Now, he stared in a whole new light at the world Chloe's sister created here. Saw that there were others who made equally, no less important, contributions to the world.

Understanding dawned at last.

"Terms six and ten," he murmured.

Chloe stared up at him, puzzled.

Leo shot a glance back, motioning to the classrooms they'd just abandoned. "Term six: *I am free to conduct my time at any charitable venture I deem important. I am also free to use my funds as donations to those unstated organizations.* And term ten: *I am free to take employment.* It's this place, is it not?" She wished to teach at her sister's school. "This is the reason for those provisions in our contract." It now made sense.

Chloe lifted her shoulders in a little shrug. "Not this place, but another."

So that was what she intended after their time as a proper, respectable couple came to an end and they went on to live separate lives. An image slipped in of a time in the not-so-distant future when she'd go off and he'd resume his solitary existence. A hollow emptiness carved a spot in his chest. "Why not this one?" he made himself ask through the tumult.

"My sister has committed to hiring young women who've known like struggles, ones who cannot find employment." Chloe joined her hands and briefly studied the interconnected digits. "It is my sister-in-law Jane's establishment I wish to oversee—Mrs. Munroe's. It is a finishing school for ladies whose circumstances have not been the kindest. They have been without a steady head-mistress. and I'd like to fulfill that role."

So that was where she'd soon go, not off with a lover or to travel abroad through Europe, but to a finishing school... in some part of England. The hollowness grew as their inevitable severance morphed into a new reality that he could see laid out before him.

The butler brought them to a stop outside a great hall. Its double doors gaped wide, and an impressive gathering of guests could be seen. An odd mingling of small children and fancily clad patrons interacted throughout the rooms.

"Chloe!" The Marchioness of Guilford's happy cry went up. From where she stood across the room with her husband, brother, and sister-in-law, the kindly woman waved.

Leo stiffened as his new family started through the crowd, fast approaching.

Chloe took a step to meet her siblings.

"Chloe?" Leo shot a hand out, lightly collecting her shoulder and forcing her back.

She looked up, a question in her eyes.

"Why not one of your own?"

Chloe shook her head. "What?"

"You've spoken of your sister's and sister-in-law's establishments and the visions they have, but what of your dream? With your funds and cleverness, you can also create something of your own."

Her lips parted, and a whispery sigh slipped out. "I didn't... I..."

"Chloe!" The warm, welcoming voice of his sister-in-law piped in, shattering the moment. "Lord Tennyson."

Chloe's family joined them—the Marquess and Marchioness of Guilford and the Marquess and Marchioness of Waverly.

His wife's brother glowered openly at him.

"Lady Philippa, Lady Jane," Leo murmured with a bow. "Gentle-men," he greeted tightly.

A stiff silence fell among the group.

His wife slid her fingers onto his sleeve in a tacit mark of her support. When had been the last time anyone had come to his defense? Had stated for the world that they stood beside him? Emotion stuck in his throat.

Waverly was the first to break the silence. "Tennyson." He held a hand out.

Leo eyed that offering for a moment and then shook the other man's hand.

"Come, come. Join us," Lady Philippa encouraged and, linking her arm with Chloe's and Jane's, led the way through the guests, leaving the gentlemen to follow.

Chloe shot a glance back in Leo's direction. Worry creased her delicate features.

He flashed a smile for her benefit and waved her on.

"Chloe says you wish to be respectable and honorable," his brother-in-law said after the women had gone. "Though I have my doubts, I'd invite you to join me for drinks at White's." Waverly's mouth hardened. "That is, if you're capable of visiting the club without being delivered a proper thrashing by an irate husband?"

"Gabriel," the Marquess of Guilford warned.

Drinks with his brother-in-law, one of Polite Society's stiffest, stodgiest lords. All was progressing as hoped.

He smiled. "Thank you for that gracious invitation," he drawled.

"We're welcoming you into the family, Tennyson," Guilford explained.

"Why, thank you. That is certainly unexpected. Appreciated," and beneficial, "but—"

"But be warned," the other man interrupted. "You hurt her, and one of us is going to kill you."

"We'll all vie for the privilege," Waverly said crisply.

"Chloe would likely slay me herself, saving you all the trouble, if I did." When he did. Ultimately, he'd hurt her. He hurt everyone. Why, his first act upon entering this world had been to take his mother's life. Leo sought his wife, finding her at the front of the room speaking with her sister and several young children.

As if feeling his focus on her, Chloe glanced over. "Come," she mouthed, gesturing.

He lifted his hand, wanting to join, feeling like an intruder.

A small girl in white skirts tugged at his wife's hand, tearing Chloe's attention away. She sank to a knee beside the child, and with whatever words were uttered, she pulled a wider and wider smile upon the girl's lips.

But then, wasn't that the effect his wife had on people?

Leo grinned wistfully.

His skin pricked, and he found both men eyeing him peculiarly.
"What?" Leo asked defensively, shifting on his feet.

"Nothing at all," the other man murmured. "Drinks tomorrow,
then," the marquess offered in what felt like the first true olive
branch extended by his in-laws.

CHAPTER 22

FOR ALL INTENTS AND PURPOSES, Chloe and Leo might as well have been any other respectable couple.

Nay, rather, more.

They might as well have been any happy, devoted husband and wife. Through the unveiling of the new establishment, they remained at each other's side, meeting children, speaking with patrons who arrived to assess the newly resurrected establishment. And when Chloe was called off to see the chambers the young ladies would call home, leaving Leo to his own devices, she found herself restless to return.

A short while later, Chloe located him in one of the classrooms. Hovering on the edge of the doorway, she freely observed Leo as he spoke to Faith and Violet. By their motions and movements, they were in the throes of a discussion about their last fencing round.

Something Violet said earned a booming laugh, and he ruffled the top of her niece's black curls.

Another portion of Chloe's heart wiggled free and slipped dangerously outside her grasp.

"I will admit," Philippa murmured, joining her in the doorway, "I have been skeptical and fearful of Lord Tennyson's intentions."

Chloe stiffened.

"But seeing him with Faith and Violet and hearing them speak of the night he visited, I must acknowledge the wrongness in my own prejudices."

Yes, everyone had judged Leo—Chloe included—a man who flaunted his indifference at all those opinions. Did he do so in a bid to protect himself? It was as though he embraced the derision. Why? "There is more to him," Chloe said softly. He might insist otherwise. "I do not say that because I need to see it, nor because I wish to reassure myself that I've not made an egregious mistake, but because I see it," she said to her sister.

Philippa smiled and called out a greeting. "The children are assembling for desserts. I thought—"

Faith and Violet squealed and took off running, knocking into Chloe and Philippa in their haste to pass by. Laughing, Philippa hurried after the girls.

Alone in the newly constructed classrooms, Chloe called out to her husband. "I've been looking for you, my lord."

Grinning, he strode over. "Alas, my attentions were stolen by two lovely ladies. Two *faithless* ladies who prefer treats," he added, pulling a laugh from Chloe.

"One may say you even enjoyed your first foray into respectability."

He set his features in a somber mask. "I'll deny it to the end of my rakish days."

Through the teasing, Chloe was filled with regret that the day had come to an end. Oh, it had been a success, and yet, she'd enjoyed the interlude of pretend. "We should have the carriage called," she said quietly.

As they wandered the lengthy halls to the foyer, not another word was spoken.

Chloe waited off to the side as Leo conversed with one of the footmen. Just then, another set of patrons entered through the massive double doors—the gentleman strikingly handsome and the crimson-haired lady at his side a stunning perfect counterpart. The Earl and Countess of Montfort. The countess had gone from being one of Philippa's instructors to being a great benefactor.

The couple froze. Their expressions ran a gamut of surprise, horror, and then outrage.

Frowning, Chloe searched for—and found—the source of their

fury.

An ashen-faced Leo stared back at the pair, and then a quick grin was firmly back in place. "My lady—"

The Earl of Montfort lunged. "Not another word," he thundered.

The countess cried out and made an ineffectual grab for her husband's arm.

Leo took a blow to the chin. Through a resolute strength, he managed to maintain his feet.

Jerked out of her dazed shock, Chloe went sprinting forward. Holding her palms up, she placed herself between Leo and the earl's wrath. "Stop," she cried out.

Or was that the countess? Everything had become a blur of noise and confusion.

Fury burned from the earl's eyes, and for a terrifying moment, she believed he'd knock her down. Palms sweating, Chloe rooted herself to the floor and glowered at him.

"Chloe," her husband bit out, making an attempt to push her behind him.

She fought off his efforts, locked in a silent battle with Lord Montfort.

"We're leaving," the Earl of Montfort seethed.

"No need, Montfort," her husband smoothly supplied. "We were just leaving." Wordlessly, Leo tugged a cloak-less Chloe through the gaping doors and into the London streets.

Not a word was uttered until they were ensconced in their carriage.

Leo sat on the opposite bench, his gaze firmly trained on the window at the passing scenery.

"Well?" Chloe finally shattered the quiet.

With bored movements, he glanced over. "Well?" he drawled in tones she'd learned early on were false.

"Are we going to speak about what happened?"

"No."

She dropped her brows. "No?" Did he think they'd say nothing about the fact that another gentleman had dealt him a violent blow at nothing more than a glimpse… and the fact that he'd made no attempt to deflect or fight back?

Leo reached inside his jacket and withdrew a flask. "Nothing to

talk about. Montfort and I used to be friendly, and now we're not."
He removed the stopper.

Chloe leaned over and plucked the drink from his fingers just as
he'd raised the silver flask to his lips. She set it beside her on the
bench.

He frowned and opened his mouth.

"Do not ask or demand your spirits back."

Leo's lips instantly compressed into a tight line.

Chloe folded her arms. "What happened?"

"We had a falling-out."

There. At least he hadn't pretended to misunderstand whom
she'd been speaking of. Chloe waited for him to say more.

And waited.

Leo hummed the discordant tavern ditty he had broken into at
her family's dinner party.

As a small girl, she'd had a tenacious tooth that had refused to fall
out. The dratted thing had hung by a bare thread, and no amount
of wiggling or yanking or pulling had managed to snag it free. Her
husband, with his secrets, was very much like that stubborn tooth.

"Is he the same gentleman who sent you home bloodied two
days ago?"

He gave a brusque nod.

"And yet, both times you made no attempt to defend yourself."

Leo grunted. "You don't know that."

"I know what I saw today, and I know the effects of one lifting
one's fists to defend oneself. I know a single punch will land a man
with bruised or cracked knuckles, and yet, yours were not."

He brought his eyebrows together. "How does a young lady
come to know so much about prizefighting?"

Chloe faltered as the tables were abruptly and unexpectedly
turned. "We're not talking about me, Leo," she neatly sidestepped.
"We are discussing the history between you and the Earl of Montfort."

Her husband wiped a tired hand over his face. "Let it go, Chloe."

She shook her head. "No. I will not."

The carriage hit a large bump, and she caught the upholstered
bench to keep steady.

"Do you have a history with the countess?" Her question slipped
out on a shaky whisper. It was a question that she, in her coward-

ice, didn't want an answer to.

"Don't do this, Chloe," Leo entreated, pleading when neither God nor the devil himself could coax a grin that Leo didn't wish to give.

Chloe sank back on the squabs. The metal springs pinged noisily under the pressure added by her weight. "You do," she answered for him. "You seduced the Countess of Montfort." A leading patroness, who was a friend to Philippa and had earned a reputation as kind, clever, and tenderhearted, had been one of Leo's lovers? That realization soured her mouth and knifed at her belly. "You don't deny it," she blankly noted. It had been easier to imagine a caricature of a rake than one who had lovers… like Lady Daphne.

"You've already figured it all out, Chloe." He turned his face away, but not before she caught the glimmer of some emotion, stark and indistinguishable, in his blue eyes. "Why should I bother you with any of the other predictable details?"

"Is she the innocent you seduced?" Whom did Chloe seek to torture with this questioning? Him? Or herself?

All the color bled from Leo's cheeks, leaving him a sickly shade of white. And that was when she knew that it wasn't a rake's seduction that had left an indelible memory upon him and the Winterbournes. "You care for her." Chloe worked her gaze searchingly over his face.

"I don't care for her." He paused, that beat of silence meaningful and significant. "I did."

All the air went out of Chloe, exhaled as a breathless, "Oh." His revelation knocked into her chest and pinned her to her seat. "She is… the one." The one innocent he'd confessed to having debauched. Only, he'd cared about her… which was not altogether the same thing.

"I was young," he murmured. "A pup just beginning to sow my oats, and she was recent to London."

He went silent.

"That is all you intend to say?"

"There's nothing else *to* say. It was a long time ago, Chloe. Let us leave it at that."

She would not. She *could* not. The carriage hit another uneven cobble, knocking her against the wall. Chloe planted her feet and steadied herself. "If you cared about her, why did you not wed her?" she persisted.

Her husband raked a hand through his hair, tousling those curls into an endearing golden disarray. "We came from different circumstances, but our interests were the same. She enjoyed literature, and I'd recite poetry." He grimaced. "I was young."

The pair had shared a love of literary works, which was a bond greater than mere lust and physical passion. A little niggling of discomfort worked around her breast. "What happened?"

His mouth hardened. "I was unable to marry. My... family did not approve." Did she imagine the slight hesitation there? The tensing of his mouth, the muscle that jumped by his eye? "They made it clear that it would not be in the lady's best interests if we wed. Hers would not be a comfortable life." Ahh, so that had been the reason. They had been young lovers separated by the expectations placed upon a young heir.

It was another glimpse he'd offered up about his family, and she despised the lot. She'd wager that the man he'd become would have flipped a finger and his nose to any of those dictates on whom he should or should not wed. As a young man? Well, Chloe knew enough from her own experience what one would do in the name of self-preservation. She reflexively reached for his hand and then forced her palm back to her lap. "And so, you set her free."

Leo stared through her. "All our meetings were clandestine, a secret that I had to keep from her. I was warned that she would pay the price of our relationship... I had to end it. She was innocent, tenderhearted, clever—stolen meetings were far less than she deserved."

That intimate recounting of the character of his first—and no doubt only—love left a mark upon Chloe's heart. "Wh-what did you do?" she asked, a pressure weighting her chest as she imagined a young Leo and Lady Daphne stealing away, young lovers with stars in their eyes and happiness in their hearts.

Leo blinked and looked to Chloe as if he'd forgotten her presence. A spasm contorted his face, a rippling of grief so stark that it sent her pulse skittering. "I asked her to meet me in our host's library with the intention of severing our connection," he whispered. "I took her in my arms, telling myself I sought a final embrace. But I was young and lacked the restraint I do now. Everything happened so quickly."

Oh, God. She silently begged for him to withhold the details of him making love to another. It was even worse so because this was a woman he'd loved. One who clearly mattered to him still. "You do not have to tell me anything more," she said quietly, selfish and cowardly in that request.

"And deny you the true depth of my ugliness?" A coarse laugh shook his frame. "Do you know what I did?" He didn't pause a beat for an answer. "I took her against the wall like a whore."

He hoped to shock her with his crudeness, and yet... "Lord Ackerland's libraries," she murmured as understanding set in.

He gave a curt nod.

Of course. That was why he recalled the precise room where he'd taken a woman's innocence... because the act had been significant to him.

Leo sucked in an uneven breath. "And then in the cruelest of ways, I assured afterward there would never be any warmth or forgiveness left when I walked out of her life."

Her heart sped up, and she braced for whatever horribleness that had unfolded that accounted for resentment almost fifteen years later. "What did you do?" she whispered.

His face hardened, and he stared directly at Chloe. "After we made love," he said as her heart spasmed, "I told her that I'd never rutted with a cripple. I laughed at her."

A gasp burst from Chloe's lips.

He grinned. That empty, macabre rendition of mirth left a coldness in the carriage as he turned his stare out the window.

He'd painted an image so clear of that long-ago day between him and a woman he'd loved. There could be no doubting, by the pain that seeped through the weak veneer of cynicism, that he regretted that day, that he was haunted by it, still.

Chloe sank back in her seat. "You were trying to protect her."

Leo whipped his head back. "Don't do that," he rasped.

"And you hurt yourself as much as you hurt that young woman," she continued.

He surged forward, gripping her by the shoulders. "What manner of woman are you that you'd make excuses for that?" he asked hoarsely, giving her a slight shake. "For who I was? For what I did?" His voice rose, echoing around the carriage.

She winced.

His body recoiling, Leo released her. He flexed his fingers. "What will it take to make you see I'm a man who doesn't care about anyone's well-being or happiness other than my own?"

Chloe gathered his hands in hers and squeezed. "A man that was truly soulless wouldn't remember the lady all these years later. And he certainly wouldn't feel guilt for what he did… and said, Leo."

They continued the remainder of the way home in silence, and through it, Chloe sat contemplating her husband and all he'd revealed.

It was as she'd once said to him… Not all men were born evil, but rather shaped by life. Now, how to make her husband see that and help him return to the carefree young man he'd been of long ago?

CHAPTER 23

¶IT WAS SAYING A GOOD deal that Leo was eager to visit White's… with his deservedly livid brother-in-law for company.

The man was respectable, staid, and dull as shite, and yet, after yesterday afternoon's carriage ride with Chloe, Leo preferred Waverly's torturous company to his wife's.

For a second time that week, Leo found himself entering through the distinguished doors of White's. Removing his cloak, he did a sweep for the other man, determined to advance his efforts as respectable gent.

And then he found him.

Leo paused for the minutest stretch of time. Then all his senses went on the alert as he joined his brother-in-law… and the Earl of Waterson.

Waterson is here.

All earlier tedium vanished. He'd been handed a meeting with Waterson, with no maneuvering required on Leo's part. He forced aside thoughts of his troubling fascination with his wife and the dangerous proclivity of sharing his past with her.

"Tennyson," Waverly greeted as he and the earl shoved to their feet.

Respectable and honorable, even when hatred for him likely sang in their veins.

"Gentlemen," he returned with an affable grin.

They settled around the table with an awkward pall descending.

Meticulous with his stratagem, Leo drummed his fingertips on the arms of his chair in a deliberately grating staccato. With a bored gaze, he glanced about the club. From the corner of his eye, he spied the look shared by Waverly and Waterson.

"At last," Leo murmured as a servant appeared with a crystal snifter. Snatching the glass from the young man's hands, Leo helped himself to the bottle and proceeded to pour a healthy amount of Waverly's brandy.

Registering the silence, he glanced up. "Not a problem, I hope."

"Not. A. Problem," his brother-in-law gritted out.

Waterson buried a grin behind his hand. Interesting. Leo had taken the earl, given his voting record in Parliament, as one incapable of even the slightest humor. Leo kicked back on the legs of his chair and rested his glass upon his belly. "So, what is it respectable gents spend their time talking about? I trust it's not delectable widows—" If looks could kill, Waverly would have smote Leo to ash as he spoke. "So mayhap wagers and cards?"

"*They…*" He'd have to be deaf as a post to fail to hear the slight but distinguishable emphasis on that word. "They speak on horseflesh and politics and one another's families," Waverly said pointedly.

"Haven't got two coins of late to rub together for a quality thoroughbred," Leo acknowledged. "I've seen your family just yesterday. Our family." Red splotches suffused his brother-in-law's cheek. "So, nothing to talk about there. Waterson, you've sisters on another London Season, do you not?"

"Let us not speak about my sisters," Waterson clipped out.

Leo sighed. "Very well." He rolled his glass between his palms. "Politics it is, then. God, how I do love when Parliament is in session."

The earl flared his eyebrows. "Indeed? I never took you for the political sort."

"*The political sort?*" Leo chuckled. "Egads, no. Parliament being in session is the reason for the London Season and thus the wicked engagements that keep a gent from going out of his goddamn mind with boredom."

His brother-in-law growled. "Tennyson," Waverly snapped.

"Oh… uh… yes." Leo lowered his chair so that all four legs touched the floor. "My apologies. So… Waterson… bravo on your work with the Blasphemy and Seditious Meetings Act."

"The *Blasphemous* and Seditious *Libels* Act," the earl corrected, like one schooling a child. "Nor am I capable of claiming credit for that particular legislation. I was the push behind the…" Leo yawned and did another bored search of the club.

"Training Prevention Act," Waterson finished impatiently.

"I was never a parliamentary man," Leo said, taking a long swallow. "Never fancied myself in a powdered wig and black robes."

Waterson's lip curled derisively.

"Oh, it's not just that," Leo rushed to assure the other man. "It's all the endless ramblings from stodgy gents—" He stopped and gave his companions a sheepish look. "Uh… no offense intended."

His brother-in-law's brows dipped. "Why would we be offended, Tennyson?"

"Yes, well… it is just…" He pointed a finger from one gent to the next. "You and… Waterson. Your reputations…" Two pairs of eyes bored into him. Leo coughed into his fist. "I digress. You were saying about your act?"

"It is not *my* act," the earl said impatiently, setting his brandy down. "It is for the people. My portion was written with the purpose of ensuring the Crown maintains the safety and efficacy of military trainings."

"What is in it for you?"

"What is what for me?" the earl echoed dumbly.

Leo might as well have asked Waterson to snuff out old George himself for all the horror there. "Well, every man, present company not excluded," he waved at himself, "desires something. Land… money." He paused as something stirred at the back of his mind. Words spoken by another. "It was business, and common citizens and do-gooders in Parliament need to stop interfering…" Forcing his attention back, he continued his questioning. "What do you care who has arms or when?"

Waterson sputtered. "How dare you? My work in Parliament is only to benefit the Crown." The man's indignation and outrage were no mere ruse.

Leo filed that important detail away. The question it begged, however, was how far would the other man go to maintain order…

in the name of the Crown? He probed. "Well, there's no surer way to preserve the Crown than to stifle the masses, eh?" He laughed, lifting his glass in toast.

Stony silence met his show of amusement. Forcing another sigh, Leo lowered his drink.

"I'm not looking to stifle the masses, but rather maintain prosperity and peace for all."

"Very noble. Then you," he saluted the earl, "are unlike most men who'd build their fortunes on the backs of..." He stumbled. "Others," he forced himself, his mind swirling. "Some would argue the masses would prefer to say their piece and do as they would without interference from some bewigged gent in Parliament."

"That's why Waterson spoke out in opposition to the Seditious Meetings prevention and the Blasphemous and Seditious Libels," Waverly defended his friend, "which is something you'd know if you'd bothered to visit the chambers and listen behind closed doors where legislation is worked out." With that set-down, his brother-in-law neatly handed Leo the most helpful piece of information he'd gathered yet about his suspect.

It wasn't Waterson. Leo didn't require so much as another interview to confirm it. "My apologies," Leo murmured, bowing his head. "I should not have taken you for a total prig."

"Thank—" The earl blinked. Waterson stood. "I'll leave you gentlemen to your drinks. Waverly."

"I trust Chloe and I will see you at our soiree?" Leo ventured when the earl turned to go.

Too polite to decline, even though loathing spilled from the earl's eyes, he nodded. "Tennyson," he said grudgingly, dropping a bow.

Without a backward glance, he left.

"I'd say that went well." Leo quirked his lips in a grin. "My first venture into gentlemanly topics."

His brother-in-law dusted a hand over his eyes. "I understand you are trying, for reasons that I don't understand, to be respectable. I'm not sure why but trust it has something to do with a wager or funds?"

At that supposition, Leo schooled his features.

"But, by God, have a care to learn something before you open your mouth and insult a man. Waterson isn't one of the damned pompous lords you'd lump him in with. He's one who's been loyal to me and kind to my wife despite the origins of her birth. When he says he wishes to make England safer and better, he speaks true." The marquess lowered his voice. "One of Waterson's sisters was traveling through Manchester at the time of the Peterloo Massacre." Leo absorbed that revelation. "His interest in maintaining arms and peace stems from that." The marquess climbed to his feet. "Next time, before you hurl out shameful charges about what drives a man, know something about it first."

Waverly quit the table.

Following the other man's retreat through the club, Leo leaned back in his chair. On the whole, the day had been a resounding success. He'd not only secured details about Waterson's efforts behind closed doors in Parliament, but discovered the source of his political pursuits... and his character as a loyal friend saw him.

He'd secured everything else he needed this night. Leo fought the urge to also quit White's. The desire to see his wife hit him like a physical hungering. Forcing himself to finish his drink as the world expected, Leo strode lazily through the club.

After an endless ride through the crowded streets of London, he found himself at home.

Home. How very peculiar that word was, foreign to his vernacular. It was a state he'd not even known as a child, and yet, somehow, with Chloe under the same roof... in his life, it was more a home than any place he'd been. Ever.

Whistling *The Rakes of Mallow*, Leo took the steps two at a time. His cloak whipped about his ankles.

"Tomlinson, my good man," he called as the servant pulled the door open. "Where may I find my lovely lady wife?"

The other man avoided his gaze. "She is not here," he demurred, scurrying off.

"Halt." The servant came to a shuddery stop and reluctantly faced Leo. Warning bells went off, and Leo froze with his fingers at the clasp at his throat. "What is it?" he asked slowly. Unease stirred as the intuition that had yet to fail him reared its head.

"She isn't here, my lord," the butler squeaked.

"Yes, you've said as much," he said with an admirable calm. "Where is she?"

Tomlinson gulped audibly and darted his bulging eyes around.

"Tomlinson?"

"She is gone for a… visit."

"And that merits this nervousness?" Something did not add up. The warning bells became a clamoring symphony of chaos portending trouble. "Where did my wife go?" he demanded a third time, taking a step toward his tight-lipped butler.

The servant held his palms up. "The… Earl and Countess of Montfort's, my lord."

Leo went motionless, his mind moving infuriatingly slow. "She went to visit the Earl and Countess of Montfort?" he repeated dumbly. "Why in the blazes would she go…" His words trailed off. *You were trying to protect her, and you hurt that lady as much as you hurt yourself.* "Bloody hell!" And with a curse, he thundered for his horse. He found himself heading for the last place he had any right to be—the Winterbourne residence.

Chloe sat with a cup of tea balanced on her knee. Her fingers kept the cup steady.

Across from her, the young countess went through the motions of pouring herself some of the tepid brew. The cane used by the countess to help her walk, rested beside her, forgotten.

Chloe used the distraction to study the woman her husband had been in love with.

He had made love to her. Dreamed of a future with her. And broke his heart because of a need to protect her from his family. Despite his insistence to the contrary, did he love her still?

Chloe's fingers shook. A lone drop of tea splashed over the rim and landed forlornly upon her white skirts.

How was it possible for a heart to break twice, in two different ways, at just one thought? She hurt for what Leo had cost himself in his youth… and she was ripped apart inside thinking of him with this woman, longing for her, wanting her.

Chloe hurriedly set down her cup.

Lady Daphne glanced up from her efforts.

"You must wonder why I'm here," Chloe finally said. She'd never been one to dance around details. Directness served a person well.

The countess set aside the teapot. "I'm thinking perhaps your visit has something to do with Philippa and her school?" the other woman ventured. Picking up her cup, she raised it to her mouth.

"No, that is not why I've come."

Several little creases puckered Lady Daphne's brow. "It is not?" she ventured, slowly lowering the delicate, floral, porcelain piece between her fingers.

Chloe shook her head. She'd spent the whole of the morning plotting and planning what she would say. And yet, it was difficult to call forth the script in her mind. *Just have out with it.* "I understand there's a history between you and my husband."

All the color bled from the countess' cheeks, leaving her freckles stark. She turned to stone before Chloe's eyes.

"I… I don't know the meaning of this visit," the other woman finally said. "Or what he's told you or—but perhaps it would be best if you left." Setting aside her tea, she grabbed her cane.

"Wait!" Chloe held her palms up. "Please, I'd ask that you at least hear me out. I did not come to hurt you or force pain upon you… but to try and understand."

"It's not my place to help you understand anything about your husband," the countess said coolly.

The other woman's patience was wearing thin. Chloe had long ago become a master of knowing a person's breaking point. The Countess of Montfort had nearly reached hers.

"My husband is not a bad man." And he wasn't. One who fenced with children and unquestioningly allowed his wife the right to her dowry, funds, and future was not one who was cruel. There was good in him. She knew it. And she'd not let him flagellate himself over mistakes made a lifetime ago. Leo needed to forgive himself. Perhaps then he might shed the role of rake and become the person he'd spoken of in distant terms.

The countess drew in a breath through her tight lips. "I hope for your sake that he is kind, at least for you. But the man you would enter my home and defend is not one worthy of the defense."

I've never rutted with a cripple before…

Her heart buckled. How those words must have shattered this woman. Chloe tried to make her see. "He was a boy."

"Age does not excuse cruelty."

"No, but it *does* explain impulsivity and recklessness." Chloe smoothed her palms over her skirts. Lady Daphne made another reach for her cane. "I don't trust you could forgive him for what he did or said." The countess widened her eyes. Did she marvel that Leo had told Chloe about that long-ago night? "And it is not my place to answer for him. But he had reasons for both, and though those reasons will not erase those cruelties, please know that it wasn't all pretend."

"My lady—"

"Chloe. You are a friend of my sister," she reminded.

"Chloe," Daphne said gently. "I wish I could provide you what it is you seek—forgiveness of your husband—but I cannot offer that." The other woman glanced past Chloe to the clock atop the mantel. "If you'll excuse me? I have an appointment I'll be late for at the Ladies of Hope."

"Of course. Of course," Chloe said, hopping up.

Beside her, the countess struggled to a stand. Silently, they started from the room and made a slow walk through the halls to the foyer. Chloe adjusted her pace to meet the other woman's uneven gait. Everything was unraveling. Lady Daphne had misunderstood her point in being here... in helping her and Leo find peace... and forgiveness. Chloe hadn't come here for herself... but for Leo.

Frantic, she glanced about. Her gaze landed on a gilded frame. She stopped at the tableau of familial happiness etched upon the canvas.

"It is lovely," she said softly.

Eyeing her warily, Lady Daphne limped over to where Chloe rooted herself. "Thank you."

Chloe examined the trio in the portrait. The devoted husband had a hand lovingly upon the shoulder of the beaming young mother and countess, who cradled a babe in her arms. Each parent singularly focused on another. "So much love," she whispered. A terrifying yearning stirred in her heart, a great cataclysmic shift from a place she'd always been. A place where, in her need to protect herself and others, babes were tiny creatures who would never belong to her. Now she saw in her mind's eye a tiny boy with Leo's tangle of golden curls and boyish grin. *God help me. I want that.*

Chloe hugged her arms about her middle, and panic built inside.

For she'd come to care for her husband... a man who had no use for her outside their arrangement and whose heart would forever belong to the woman at her side.

That staggering realization brought her back to her purpose in being here. "I've been told your husband was once a rake," Chloe finally said, examining the portrait of the earl. "There have been shocking accounts of his... escapades." She briefly shifted her attention to the motionless woman Chloe's husband had fallen in love with all those years ago, and then back to the picture. "I've come to know Polite Society enough to find that there are, at best, gross exaggerations to most of what they say and, at worst, outright lies. But if there is even a scrap of truth to the things your husband did, and you're able to love him as my sister says you do, then mayhap you might see there could be good in others... like my husband."

"You care for him," the countess murmured, as one who saw too much.

"Yes," Chloe confessed. What good could come in denying that truth and suffering through it alone?

Lady Daphne sighed. "Caring for one against all logic and good judgment? That, I can understand." She smiled her first real smile since Chloe had arrived. It was a rueful expression of commiseration. "When logic and everyone around you question the wisdom in giving your heart to a man who wants nothing less than the heart of a lady, one is helpless anyway."

Giving her heart to... she couldn't... she didn't... love him. He'd become a friend. "You misunderstand," she blurted. "Leo and I are..."

The countess stared patiently back.

Chloe went tight-lipped. After all, the role she was to play was that of captivated lady in love with her husband. "I care about my husband," she said simply. "You are right on that score. It is why I needed to come and assure you that not everything that came to pass with you was a lie." The countess drew back, but Chloe pressed ahead. "There was a time he very much cared for you, but sometimes, life's circumstances make that which we truly desire an impossibility."

Lady Daphne placed both palms upon the top of her cane and leaned her weight over it. "And sometimes, wounds are left that are so great that they can never be completely healed."

Regret filled Chloe. "I understand that," she said softly. She could not make the other woman see, could not provide Leo and Lady Daphne peace from their past. Her failure here left her restless. "I shall not take up any more of your time."

Again, they fell into a side-by-side march.

"As friendship is an impossibility between you and Leo, it is, at the very least, a hope that the earl might refrain from beating my husband whenever their paths might cross," Chloe ventured. It was the least of the offerings she'd hoped to secure this day.

Lady Daphne's lips twitched. "I will speak to my husband. I can promise those exchanges are to stop."

They reached the foyer, and the countess sent a footman off to fetch Chloe's cloak. "I will say," Chloe went on when the servant returned and helped her into the garment, "there was at least one benefit to…" She waited until the servant had gone. "What did happen in the past. Had Leo not severed your connection, then you would not even now be wedded to the earl." *And I would not be married to Leo.* How odd that in just a matter of days in knowing him, the idea of that had her bereft.

"You're determined to bring peace between my family and your husband," the other woman marveled.

Chloe smiled. "I am."

"I—"

A pounding at the front door broke across whatever the countess had been about to say. Both women looked to the oak panels.

"What in the blazes?" the Earl of Montfort muttered, striding forward.

Chloe started. The earl had been following them, then. How much had he heard?

"I have it, my lord." The Winterbourne butler rushed past and drew the door wide.

Leo stumbled through the entranceway. His gaze collided not with the woman who'd snagged his heart all those years ago… but Chloe.

Her heart did a somersault. He…

The fury in his eyes scorched her. "Leo!" she greeted with false cheer and a jaunty wave.

"Tennyson," the earl growled. "What in the blazes are you doing here?" That question was cast to both Leo and Chloe.

"Montfort," Leo muttered. "Nothing," he gritted out, taking

Chloe by the hand. "We were leaving. Both of us."

She dug in her heels. "But, Leo…"

"Not a word," her husband said under his breath. "Not a single, bloody iota of an utterance."

With a gape-mouthed earl stopped in his tracks and the countess watching on, Chloe hurried to keep up with her husband, lest she be dragged down. "Will you slow down?" she panted.

"No."

"I've secured Lady Daphne's promise that the earl will not plant you a facer anymore, so you needn't worry—"

"I. Said. Not. Another. Word." A primitive growl suited for a caveman rumbled from her husband's chest. This time, Chloe opted for silence.

As they approached Leo's carriage, the driver drew open the door.

Not breaking stride, Leo scooped Chloe about the waist and unceremoniously deposited her upon a bench.

She grunted, rubbing her posterior.

Leo turned back, and for a cowardly minute, she hoped he'd leave. After all, he had surely ridden here. Hope trickled in. Why, yes, it made more sense that he'd meet her at home. Which would, of course, only delay the inevitable. Nonetheless, she'd welcome even the brief interlude, so she might at least compose her thoughts.

After a handful of words exchanged with the driver, Leo joined her inside. The carriage grew suddenly small as Leo's tall, muscular frame shrank the space.

Leo jerked the door closed behind him.

Chloe jumped. Everything in her said to bow her head and meekly accept his inevitable berating. It was an age-old instinct she'd employed as a girl. But after her father had kicked his vile toes up, she'd vowed never to be cowed before another. "You are angry," she noted.

"Tell me, madam," he gritted out. With precise movements, he tugged his gloves off one at a time, drawing them off by the fingertips. "Whyever would I be angry?"

She puzzled her brow. How peculiar. "Oh. You *seem* angry and—"

"I'm livid."

"Then why would you ask—?"

"I was being sarcastic," he said tersely.

"Hmph." Chloe gave a flounce of her curls. "I hardly see why you're upset. I merely sought to coordinate peace between you and—*eek*."

Leo pulled her onto his lap. One of his large palms came up about her nape, and he touched his brow to hers. "You are the only woman in the whole of the kingdom who'd attempt to matchmake her husband with another woman."

She frowned. "I wasn't trying to matchmake you." Not really. Because even while she wished for peace between Leo and his first love—his only love?—she wasn't so magnanimous that she'd push him into the arms of Lady Daphne... or anyone. Chloe smoothed her hands along the wool fabric of his cloak. "She is not just 'another woman,' Leo," she said pragmatically. "She was once a friend. Nay, by your admission, more than that. She is—"

Leo kissed away the remainder of those words.

Chloe stilled, and then the spark of desire exploded within her. Pressing herself to him, she returned his kiss. She opened her mouth, allowing him entry.

He swept his tongue inside, and they dueled, a rising heat spreading like a slow-moving conflagration.

"You are mad," he rasped against her mouth. His right hand worked the bodice of her gown down, baring her to his eyes.

"Th-that is hardly a c-compliment to pay a lady when you are—ahhh," she moaned. She arched her neck back as he palmed her breasts, filling his hands with the oversensitized flesh.

"What was that?" His hot breath fanned her skin.

Biting her lower lip, Chloe shook her head. What had she been about to say? Everything was all muddled. Then Leo closed his lips around a swollen tip. She cried out. Her fingers went reflexively to his head, and she curled her fingers in the luxuriant strands. He suckled and teased. With every pull and stroke of his tongue, the ache between her legs built and built until, of their own volition, her hips came off the bench. Arching up, she was desperate to feel his hand there.

And then it was.

"Leo," she moaned against his temple as he found the thatch of curls shielding her femininity.

His only reply was to slide a finger inside her damp channel.

She keened wildly, lifting into his touch while the carriage rocked and swayed. The whole world was coming undone around her, and she was capable of nothing but—

Craaaack.

The carriage hurtled sideways, throwing Chloe hard against the wall. "Chloe!" Leo shouted. Her cheek slammed into the lead windowpane. Pain exploded throughout her face. The agony of it was distant to the frantic hammering of her heart.

She fought for purchase.

Leo dragged her into his arms. Hunching his body protectively about her, he kept her framed in the shield of his embrace while the conveyance hurtled along at dizzying speeds, swaying and shifting. A dreaded anticipation built to a noisy crescendo in her mind as she braced for the certainty of their crash.

A scream tore from her as the carriage flipped sideways.

Cupping his hands over her head, shielding her, Leo shifted her atop him just as the conveyance landed on its side, coming to a jarring and eerie stop.

Chloe lay there atop him, his arms wrapped about her, his heart beating hard and fast against her ear. She clung to him, holding tightly.

The world righted itself.

Leo struggled into a sitting position and brought her onto his lap. "My God," he whispered, frantically running his hands over her.

"I'm f-fine, Leo," she assured him.

"My God," he repeated hoarsely, again and again, searching her for injury.

And as her assurances fell on seemingly deaf ears, it occurred to Chloe that, for a man who continually insisted he didn't care about anyone's well-being or happiness but his own, he'd sought to protect her over himself.

CHAPTER 24

WITH ONE SINGLE CARRIAGE ACCIDENT, life had come crashing in with a reminder of the danger Leo danced with every day as a member of the Brethren… and the realization that Leo cared for his wife.

Nausea roiled in his stomach. Terror, panic, and horror combined to form a vicious blend that he fought to choke down.

Shaking still from his and Chloe's brush with death, Leo took the steps outside his uncle's Grosvenor Square residence two at a time.

The crash had been a reminder. There was no other way to explain why, at the precise moment he'd escorted Chloe from his former lover's residence, the axle on his carriage had *broken*.

The duke's staff, as officious as ever, drew the door open the instant Leo rapped.

"My uncle," he barked, glancing around the foyer.

"He is in his offices, my lord," the butler of middling years announced.

"I don't require an escort," Leo clipped out, rushing through the labyrinthine maze that was the ducal palace of his esteemed uncle. All his nerves and senses remained on alert, vibrating still from the attack. He reached the duke's offices and didn't bother with a knock.

Leo hurled the door open. "Uncle—" His words cut off.

The Duchess of Aubrey scrambled up from her husband's lap. Nearing her fiftieth year, there was still a youthful innocence to the willowy woman. "Leo," she welcomed, her cheeks blazing red as she rushed over.

Leo's neck went hot. Rake or rogue, a gent would still rather not discover a favorite aunt and uncle in flagrant dishabille. "Aunt Elsie," he returned, presenting his cheek.

His uncle reclined in his seat, a droll grin on his lips. "Given your intrusion, I trust this is important." A faint edge underlined that statement.

"Hush, William," the duchess chided. "Leo, you're welcome anytime. We're just happy to see you. Isn't that right?" she asked her husband.

The duke lifted his head in acquiescence.

"Now, what brings you here?" She dusted a speck of wood from Leo's right sleeve, those remnants lingering from his shattered carriage. Worry creased the place between her brows. "Never tell me things are not well with your bride, whom I've yet to meet."

"No. No. No," he hurried to assure. "Chloe and I are... well." Insofar as his aunt meant. "We're happy." How easily that slipped out.

His too-clever aunt peered at him. "It is business."

Leo managed a tight nod.

The duchess glanced over at her husband. "I'll leave you gentlemen to discuss." She pressed gloved fingertips to her lips and blew a kiss for her husband.

"What is it?" his uncle demanded as soon as the door closed behind his aunt.

Hand shaking, Leo stalked across the room. He grabbed the first decanter his fingertips brushed and sloshed several fingerfuls into a glass. "We were attacked." His fingers trembled so badly, liquid spilled over the side of the table, staining the gleaming mahogany floor.

Uncle William stood. "What happened?"

"Our axle was broken."

The duke grabbed the edge of his desk, but his efforts were in vain. He sank weakly back onto the edge of his seat. "Christ," he whispered, a prayer and a curse rolled into one. "You're..."

"I'm fine." Except inside, fear held him in its punishing grip.

"Your wife?" His uncle's voice emerged threadbare. "Chloe?"

"Shaken, but fine. I had Tomlinson summon Holman to act as guard. Until he arrives, Tomlinson will shadow her." Tomlinson, who was so fleet of foot, she'd never know he was there. Leo ran through a quick accounting of his and Chloe's journey from Montfort's. "It wasn't just a broken axle. It never is."

Uncle William wrung his hands together. "Leo, are you certain you aren't just..." At the look Leo leveled on him, his godfather wisely fell silent.

"I believe I'm close," he said cryptically, mindful that there could be passing servants, and *no one* could be trusted.

Surprise lit his uncle's eyes. The older man's entire body arched forward, revealing the inherent need that would forever be with a member of the Brethren for the elusive details on an assignment.

Leo gave a slight shake of his head. Until he had Chloe away and conducted his inquiries, he'd withhold his suspicions. "I want the most-trusted men following my wife... at all times."

"I'll speak to Higgins," his uncle promised in frustratingly calming tones.

Leo set his jaw. Surely his uncle didn't doubt Leo's instincts or the very real threat he and Chloe had faced a short while ago? "Someone knows of my role in the case," he pronounced, watching his uncle's face for a reaction... and finding none. Leo downed his brandy in one long swallow, welcoming the warmth that it left in its wake. And yet, the panic raged within.

The duke made a sound of protest. "You are assuming it is connected to your current case, Leo," he said gently. "It could be an irate husband—"

"It's not."

"Or a foe returned from banishment."

"It's not," Leo said vehemently. "I've never left a trail."

His uncle winced.

"I did not mean," Leo said quickly, setting his snifter down hard on his uncle's desk, "to suggest... to imply..."

The Duke of Aubrey brushed off the useless apology. "I know, Leo."

Leo had been—and was—a heartless bastard. But even he would never hurl the death of his uncle's first wife at him in insult, or in any way for that matter. He began to pace. Logic said Chloe needed to be sent somewhere removed from Leo and his investigation. Nay, logic said he should have never married the lady in the first place. In being wed to him, she would always be at risk. It was the reason he'd set Daphne free. In the blackness to which his soul had descended, however, he'd allowed himself to forget humanity and put his role with the Brethren before everything else—and now Chloe could pay the price.

He scrubbed his hands over his face. "Tell me what to do," he entreated.

"You need to complete the assignment. Ferret out those responsible for the Cato Event."

"I've gained access to Waterson, and feel confident he is not the traitor, but I'm not willing to embroil Chloe." He increased his frantic pace.

Any more than he had...

That damning revelation hung in the air between them, as real as if Leo had spoken the pronouncement aloud.

"You've been married to the lady less than a week, Leo," his uncle reminded him. "Society is just coming to believe the lie about your being ensnared by the young lady. You can't very well just sever the connection now."

Believe the lie...

There should have been a rush of triumph for what he'd managed to accomplish in a short time. And yet, his reputation and his fight to maintain his post within the Brethren had been the furthest afterthoughts in his mind since Chloe had invaded his household... and his life.

And now, she was at risk—because of him.

"What of the soiree? Has Waterson accepted your invitation?"

"He has."

His uncle nodded. "That is good. At that point, speak to him. Tell him about a business venture you'd like to propose between him and Waverly."

"I can't do this," he said quietly. "Put her at risk."

The Duke of Aubrey said nothing for a moment. "Leo, you already did when you wed her. There can be no going back from this now. I'm a duke, but even I couldn't manage to secure you a divorce." He steepled his fingers and stared over their joined tips at

Leo. "Would you even want that?" he quizzed.

Would Leo want that? Would he want to return to his bachelor state, free to carry on his rakish pursuits without a spirited minx underfoot who asked too many questions and teased with her eyes and smile?

He slid his eyes closed. God help him. It was all muddled. Unclear. For he couldn't need her in his life. He was content. Filled with the purpose of his work. Wasn't he? "I don't know," he said in truth. The answer knocked him on his arse as he slid into a nearby seat. "Just tell me what to do," he implored.

Send her away… just as you did Daphne Smith. Only, this time, before it was too late. Before he lost any more of himself to her… before he craved any more of her smiles and laughter and clever repartee…

His chest rose and fell with the frantic breaths he took.

The duke dusted his hands together. "You don't send her away, Leo. That is what you're thinking."

Did that ability to know precisely what Leo was thinking come from his own experience as a member of the Brethren who'd himself lost… and then found love with Lady Aubrey?

"At least, not yet. Hold your soiree, get inside Waterson's household—only, this time without being discovered—and then you go from there."

"What does that even mean?" he exploded.

"It means you can't know yet whether or not Chloe is best off without you until you find out precisely what in hell happened today. Mayhap it was just a carriage accident."

"It wasn't," Leo said automatically. If his uncle believed that, time away from working assignments had dulled his abilities.

"Go home, Leo… and be with your wife. There's no certainty about tomorrow for any of us," he said somberly as he came to his feet and joined Leo. "That is the only advice I can give you now."

Leo set his jaw. What his uncle suggested—Leo returning, without answers and without assurances that Chloe was and would be safe—was an impossible venture by a man who'd been outside the inner workings of an assignment for too long.

As he took his leave, one thing was certain—Leo was going to flesh out the conspirators behind the Cato Event and protect a woman who'd come to mean entirely too much. And after he

did, then he'd sort out what was to be done with his marriage to
Chloe.

CHAPTER 25

ℐT WAS FUNNY HOW IN the midst of a near tragedy a person saw the world and oneself with a startling clarity. When one's life flashed before one's eyes, one didn't have the time for mistruths or wonderings or useless self-assurances that life was one way or another.

As Chloe and Leo's carriage had careened over, breaking apart in a violent explosion of wood and glass, she'd seen not the past and everything she feared... but everything she wanted: a family... but one with Leo as her husband and babes of their own.

And as the conveyance had crashed to a stop, Chloe's world had continued on in a dizzying spin of mayhem.

For there could be no altering or recovering from what she'd discovered—she loved her husband.

She loved that he'd not so much as blinked at the prospect of ceding control of Chloe's future and funds, but accepted it as though it was her due. She loved him for fencing with her nieces and reciting verses of Mrs. Mary Darby Robinson... and blast, for simply knowing who Mrs. Mary Darby Robinson, in fact, was.

And she admired him as a man of restraint. Oh, the world saw a careless, thoughtless rake. But Chloe had witnessed in him a gentleman who'd not come to blows, not even to defend himself, because he took responsibility for a mistake he'd made in his youth.

That was why being abandoned by him after the accident had carved a hollow emptiness inside her chest. Seated in her husband's library, her legs drawn close, Chloe stared absently at the letter on her lap. The cryptic missive had been resting on the leather button sofa… a note that not a single member of the staff she had questioned had been able to account for.

She trailed her fingertips over the handful of sentences there.

Your husband is not who he seems. The carriage incident is a reminder that he should proceed with greater caution if he has a regard for your well-being…

What did it all mean? Leo was not who he seemed? She'd already seen flashes of truth about Leo Dunlop, but why should someone go to such lengths to harm her as a message to him?

What secrets did he carry? Secrets she'd long suspected and couldn't make sense of, but could make even less sense of now.

Glancing up from the note, she looked around at the rows upon rows of leather tomes. The sheer volume of books in this room was an incongruity that didn't fit with a rogue who couldn't be bothered with a book over his bedroom activities.

Furthermore—Chloe furrowed her brow—what did it say about Leo that, despite the grim state of his finances, he'd not sold those copies, still?

"Who are you, Leo Dunlop?" she whispered into the quiet. And why did she have this painful inkling that he'd never tell her? Not truly and not fully. He was a man bent on his secrets, who shared only the remotest glimpses of himself and then pushed her away whenever the wall between them began to come down. Pushed her away by seeking out his clubs and returning only in the dead of night, when Chloe should be sleeping. But she remained awake, unable to rest, fixed on the sounds of him entering his rooms and moving about the chamber next to hers. Until all was quiet.

At which point, sleep eluded her still.

She hated this gripping need to see him and talk with him. To share with him the contents of the note and face that unknown threat with him.

Because in that instant when they'd both nearly died, when he'd shielded her body with his own, there hadn't been indifference, but a fear in his eyes and a need to protect.

Footsteps sounded in the hall. Heavy ones, methodical in purpose, and definitively masculine.

Relief filled her. Note in hand, Chloe stood.

And her heart promptly sank as the door was opened.

"The Marquess of Waverly," Tomlinson announced. Tomlinson, whose steps were as stealthy as Chloe's husband's.

"Oh." The regret-tinged utterance slipped out.

Her brother grinned wryly. "A standard greeting I've come to expect from my dear sister," he drawled, pulling off his gloves as he walked.

A guilty flush climbed her cheeks. "I didn't mean... I wasn't expecting..." She hurriedly folded the letter and tucked it away inside her pocket.

He waved off her attempt at an apology. "As I've stated numerous times in the past, I long ago accepted that I am not the favorite of your brothers. Speaking of which..." He fished a note out of his jacket and held it out.

Chloe's startled gaze went to the officious-looking letter, folded and marked with a familiar signet. "Alex." As soon as the telltale admission came out, her blush burned all the hotter. "Forgive me," she spoke on a rush. "I didn't mean to imply—"

"It is fine, Chloe," Gabriel said gently.

Worry pitted her belly. "Imogen?"

"Has not yet given birth."

Since she'd wed, something that felt very much like homesickness struck when being presented with a link to the sibling who'd stepped between Chloe and her father's fists countless times. Accepting the note, Chloe clung to the edges and clutched it close, finding a lifeline in the connection to Alex.

Perching herself on the leather button sofa she'd abandoned, she slid a nail under the seal and worked the page open. She proceeded to read.

Chloe,

I won't begin by berating you. Knowing our dear mother and Gabe as I do, you've already suffered through quite enough chastisement.

A smile curved her lips.

When her mother and eldest brother had sought to shape Chloe into someone other than who or what she was, and would always be, Alex had encouraged her to thumb her nose at convention.

There had been a great void in the Edgerton household since he'd gone and wedded Chloe's dearest friend.

She continued reading.

I will not say, however, I'm glad over your choice of husband (Tennyson ran in too wild of circles for even me), or your being married without an Edgerton at your side. Particularly me. Because had I been present, I would have had an opportunity to threaten your husband with death if he even causes a wrinkle of a frown in your brow.

He'd always been devoted. Nor did Chloe believe for a single instant Alex's words were anything less than a promise based in fact. He would kill Leo if Chloe gave that order.

Alas, my face-to-face and threats must be saved until I return. Please, send me some indication of your well-being. If you need me now, say the word.

Your faithful servant and favorite brother,

Alex

Chloe carefully folded the note over. For that was the devoted brother he'd always been. Even expecting his first child and his wife in confinement, if Chloe cried for help, he'd be there.

"I learned you were involved in a carriage accident," Gabriel said quietly, unexpectedly. "A carriage accident, Chloe," he repeated, more urgent in his tone. He moved to the edge of his chair. "And yet, you didn't see fit to tell any of us."

She shrugged. "There was nothing to say. I'm—"

"Never tell me? You are fine?"

Well, she was. Chloe flashed a teasing grin. "Well, I was going to say all right. But that shall also suffice."

Of course, her most serious sibling merely frowned in return. "Do you truly think this is a matter to make light of?"

Her teasing and mischievousness over the years had been a crafted ploy to keep anyone—her family, the other girls at Mrs. Belden's—from seeing the scars she carried. Ones that would always be there...

Except, since you met Leo, you've not been haunted even once by those ghosts...

"What would you have me do, Gabriel?" she asked, impatient. "Dissolve into histrionics about an incident when I'm fine? An incident that happened yesterday and left me no worse for the wear."

"That accident was a product of your husband's funds."

She scoffed. "Don't be foolish. There's nothing wrong with my husband's conveyance." Or there hadn't been, until it had splintered into a million fragments and pieces. "The accident was a product of a broken axle. Nothing more."

"That same day, Tennyson and I met for drinks at White's. I invited him to join Waterson and me."

"How gracious of you." If Gabriel detected any of the sarcasm there, he gave no outward indication.

"Chloe," he went on in pained tones. "He admitted to not having two coins to rub together to buy a horse."

She bit the inside of her cheek. *I should know that.* She'd sworn never to be one of those wives who remained oblivious to the familial finances. As such, Leo's inability to purchase a horse if he so desired was a detail she should be privy to. Nonetheless, her own failing aside, she took umbrage to Gabriel's being here. Chloe arched a brow. "Is that why you've come, then? To tattle on my husband?" Her brother blushed. "I daresay it is in bad form to bandy about details shared among gentlemen."

A sound of disgust spilled from Gabriel's lips. "Again, you'd disparage me while blindly turning an eye to who Tennyson is." Before she could rush to her own defense, her brother pounced. "Tell me, Chloe. Where is this honorable husband you so staunchly defend?"

"My husband is otherwise engaged," she said smoothly, not missing so much as a beat. She'd too much pride to admit to anyone—family included—that she didn't know where in thunderation her husband was.

"Then ring for him. Invite him to join us."

Chloe bit back the urge to tell her brother precisely where he could go with his questioning. For, Gabriel knew. Her brother knew precisely what he was asking and where Leo was.

"He's not here, Chloe. He left following the accident and hasn't returned since."

"Having my servants spy upon me and my husband, are you?" Outrage sent her hands curling into fists. She made a tsking sound. "How impolite of you."

"Be upset with me, Chloe. But I know this is hurting you."

Damn him for being correct. "What do you hope to accomplish?" she asked tightly.

"I am looking after you."

"You are more than twenty years too late," she cried. As soon as that charge echoed around the room, she wanted to call it back.

Gabriel paled.

"Gabriel." She stretched a hand out.

"It is fine," he said gruffly.

"It isn't. I shouldn't have said that."

"No. You *should* have." Her brother dusted his hand over his jaw and, avoiding her gaze, spoke. "You are correct, Chloe. I have attempted to exert control over your life, but it is not a product of you or anything you've ever done wrong." His throat convulsed. "But because of every way I failed you. I should have been there. It should have been me who put an end to…" His gaze slid to the door, and he went silent.

It was those secrets the Edgertons carried and shared with none. Ones they guarded, even now.

"Oh, Gabriel. Your being here now will not erase any decision you made." Or, more important, the ones he *hadn't* made. It would be unfair to hurl accusations… even if she'd always resented him for not intervening when their father had beaten her. Now, with a woman's eyes, she saw the truth. "You were afraid," she acknowledged to herself, as much as for his sake.

"I was," he said, his voice as ragged as a graveled path.

He looked back to her. "Chloe." He stretched those two syllables into an agonized plea. "This isn't about me being right or you being wrong. This is about you deserving more than one like Tennyson."

"One like Tennyson," she echoed, her voice climbing. "And what does that mean, precisely?"

"Very well, you'll have me say it." Ticking off a list, he jabbed a finger in the air with each point he made. "One who's unfaithful. One who'll leave you for days on end while he goes off with scandalous widows." Chloe curled her toes so hard, the bottoms of her feet ached. "And the least of the offenses I'd level: He can't even hold a serious conversation about matters of importance, Chloe. You deserve, at the very least, an intelligent gent capable of matching your wit."

She wrinkled her nose. "I assure you, my husband is most clever."

Gabriel gave her an incredulous look.

And yet, he wouldn't know that Leo quoted Mary Darby Robinson and knew of the enlightened thinkers. Rather, he handed the world an image of who he wanted them to see, and all were content with that shallow view. Why was her husband so very determined to maintain that image?

"Chloe, Tennyson joined me and Waterson for drinks, and not only could he not string together a meaningful thought on politics or Society, but he insulted us both throughout."

Chloe stood. "Then mayhap you should give him reason not to insult you," she said matter-of-factly.

Gabriel winced. "I see." He rose. "I merely came to deliver that missive and remind you that when you tire of your circumstances, we are here, and we will help you."

"Thank you for the note," she said pointedly.

He nodded curtly and strode toward the front of the room.

Her family still sought to protect her from the folly of her decision. They still assumed she was incapable of looking after herself. And though she appreciated their love, she would not tolerate their constant efforts to control her.

"Gabriel," she called when he reached the door. "If it is as you said and you truly 'see,' I'd encourage you not to make another appeal for me to leave my husband."

After he'd gone, Chloe let her shoulders sag. She pressed her palms into her face and breathed deep. For in the privacy of her own company, she absorbed all the accusations her brother had hurled and processed them as she'd refused to do with Gabriel present. Why was she so determined to defend Leo? And trust him? And, as her brother had accused, turn her cheek to Leo's failings?

Because he'd proven himself to be more… and she yearned to hang on to that.

But she *was* deserving of more, such as an understanding of their finances and… respect. Blast it, she deserved his respect. And fidelity.

With renewed purpose, she set off at a brisk clip through her new home, not stopping until she reached Leo's office.

She twisted the handle, braced for the resistance of a lock. She was surprised when it easily turned. The well-greased hinges of Leo's door were silent and smooth as she stepped inside the darkened rooms.

You are not to set foot in my office…

The pledge she'd made reverberated in her mind.

"Yes, well, you promised fidelity," she muttered and hurriedly closed the door.

The hum of quiet pinged off the walls and rang in her ears as she took in the sterile space.

Leo's desk, a hand-carved walnut piece with double bookcases built in, sat slightly off-center of the doorway, as outrageously bold as its owner, a man whispered about by all Polite Society. But for a handful of chairs and a fully stocked sideboard, the room was wholly barren, evidencing one who'd sold off his fineries to appease his creditors.

Her brother's chastisement echoing in her mind, Chloe moved deeper into Leo's office, making a path for his desk.

Gripping the carved back of the Venetian grotto chair, she dragged it out and seated herself.

Chloe shifted back and forth, testing the comfort of the carved walnut seat. Again, even Leo's choice of seating, when most men set themselves up in comfortable leather winged chairs, set him apart. Was he merely determined to thumb his nose at conventions? Or was there more? Did he simply appreciate the obscure female philosophers and ancient bronze pieces?

Stealing a glance at the front of the room, Chloe verified she was still alone.

"Of course, one's husband would have to be home for me to fear the risk of discovery," she mumbled.

Not that she feared discovery. After all, she was the lady of the household and entitled to a full understanding of their dire financial straits. Why, mayhap she could even help Leo with his books.

Enlivened by that purpose, Chloe tugged the center drawer out by the garish gargoyle with a ring through its mouth. Wrinkled papers and parchments lay in a haphazard display with pens scattered about.

Chloe quickly set to work righting the untidy space. Removing the vellum and paper, she set them into neat columns, stacking blank page after blank page. Into the next pile, she placed sheets that contained markings with establishments she recognized as scandalous clubs.

She paused. Her gaze lingering on one.

Forbidden Pleasures. Debt to be paid: three thousand pounds.

Was it the drink he sought there? Or the wicked women? Or... both?

Jealousy slithered around her insides, an ugly serpent spreading its venom.

She'd known who she married. But seeing his pastimes laid out left her aching inside.

"Fool. You bloody fool." She repeated that mantra and forced herself to continue cleaning. After all the miscellaneous scraps had been neatly organized, Chloe peered down at the faded leather ledger resting crookedly at the bottom of the drawer.

With dread replacing jealousy, she forced herself to drag the book out. Loath to see the true state of her husband's and now—by their marriage—her finances, Chloe stroked the top of the book. She'd hidden long enough from the reality of her circumstances.

Compelled by that, Chloe opened the book.

Even prepared and expecting it as she'd been, unease tightened her chest as she read page after page of sloppy accounting that detailed the depth of her husband's wagering—and losses. The money gone to mistresses and drink and wagering went on and on. Dates crossed out, ink marring the pages, Leo's ledgers were a sorry glimpse of his reckless existence. Chloe pored through page after page until the recordings blurred before her eyes and her back ached.

She turned another page... and stopped.

Chloe sat slowly up in her seat. Absently rubbing the aching muscles of her neck, she fixed on the abrupt end of her husband's accounting.

It had been more than three weeks since he'd made a mark within the book.

Mayhap with his erroneous notations, he'd missed a page or two... or several. She flipped ahead.

Nothing.

A curl fell over her brow, and she blew back the errant strand. "Hmph," she murmured, setting the book down.

Chloe leaned back in her husband's chair and tapped the arms in a distracted rendition of *The Rakes of Mallow*.

Her gaze fell on the double doors along the sides of the desk.

She brought her fingers to a slow halt. Shoving back the chair, Chloe grabbed the ring.

The door held tight.

Locked.

Nonetheless, she tried again, and then each door, before ascertaining that her husband had, in fact, locked them all. Which could mean only that there was something contained within that he sought to hide.

Puzzling her brow, Chloe sank to her knees. She pressed her eye against the heart-shaped lock.

Disentangling a pin from her chignon, she jammed it inside, poking around.

She went on that way, blindly searching for the mechanism.

At last, the lock gave way with a satisfying click.

Triumphant, she tossed the pin aside, forgotten, and drew the doors open.

Empty? She peered around the space. That made even less sense than the locked doors. Chloe ran her palm through the space, which was one foot wide and one foot deep. She glided her fingertips around the corners.

An oak panel flipped up.

She gasped and yanked her hand back.

Hesitant, she sat there, motionless, more than half fearful about what she would find now.

Did he have an illegitimate child? A number of them?

With dread driving her movements, Chloe reached inside and found a stack of leather journals. Drawing out as many of the volumes as she could, she sat and rested the pile beside her. And then she proceeded to read.

They were… ledgers.

And yet—blindly reaching overhead, she fished around for the discarded book on the desktop.

Chloe dragged it down and compared the writings and the accountings.

They were all in Leo's hand, but wholly different. Marked with the same dates, these books revealed not a wastrel drunkard sloppy with his finances and careless with all, but rather—

"Have you had a good look, Wife?"

Heart lurching, Chloe looked up and found her husband's menacing, black gaze on her.

She swallowed hard.

Drat.

CHAPTER 26

BLOODY HELL.

He'd known from the instant she'd sneaked into his residence and put demands to him that Chloe would be trouble.

He could not, however, have predicted just how much.

"Leo," she said calmly, rising to her feet, maintaining a hold on his damned ledger.

His fury spiked. Nay, not solely his fury… panic and desperation.

What has she done? The question peeled around every corner of his mind.

He seethed. "You were ordered never to come in here."

She held his ledgers up. "You lied."

God, she was breathtaking in her bravery and resolve. Any other time, he'd have admired her for that showing.

"Quiet." He glanced back at the door. His staff had all been carefully selected by the Brethren, but that still did not mean speaking freely was safe.

Chloe jutted her chin out. "You are *not* in dun territory." He winced. "You are outrageously wealthy. Of course," she breathed. "It all makes sense. It is why you allowed me control of my dowry, and you have that bronze piece that any man truly in debt would have sold off long ago."

His mind swirled under her rapid ramblings as his panic mounted, staggering in its intensity.

His wife smiled, that pleased little expression that indicated pride at what she'd pieced together. And then it faded as she contemplated him. "It all begs the question, however, of why? Why do you go to such great lengths to present yourself as someone other than who you are?"

A loud ringing filled his ears as she raised the most dangerous question that not a soul before her had dared ask.

"I'm not discussing this with you," he bit out. "You violated the terms of the contract."

"With good reason. I have every right to know the state of our finances." She jutted her chin at a defiant angle. "And the secrets you carry."

Those five words sucked the air from his lungs and all life from the room.

"Who are you, Leo Dunlop?" she murmured, drifting closer.

He had to send her away. He'd realized as much when pieces had slid into place at White's. Her discovery here only confirmed the urgency with which he needed to separate himself from this woman.

Agony pierced him like a thousand dull knives being plunged into his chest. Oh, God, he didn't want to send her away. And yet, she couldn't stay. Not with what she'd uncovered. And not with what she was so very close to discovering—that his life had, in fact, largely been a lie crafted so he might carry out his work for the Home Office.

He snapped.

"You had no right," he thundered, slamming his fists down hard on the surface of his desk. The ledgers and his wife both jumped. Fury pumping through his veins, he surged toward her. "You had no right," he repeated on a furious whisper.

He took her by the shoulders and gave her a firm shake. "There are no secrets," he hissed. "Do you hear me? There are no secrets!"

With a cry, Chloe stumbled out of his arms. Terror bled from her eyes and spilled from her slender frame.

Good, she should be afraid. Mayhap then she'd allow him to keep the walls resurrected between them. Mayhap then she could be safe. Only, why did he want to carve out his own heart for daring to scare her as he was?

Chloe was bold, fearless, and courageous above anyone he knew… and he'd reduced her to this trembling, pale-faced shadow of herself.

Leo dragged a hand through his hair. "Say nothing about what you've learned here."

She shook her head. "You want me to let my family to continue to malign you and worry after me—"

"I don't give a bloody damn on Sunday what your family believes or does not believe," he bellowed.

Chloe recoiled, holding his ledgers close to her chest in a terrified embrace. He expected her to run, wanted her to so he could begin trying to set this all to rights.

Leo stalked over and, with crisp, angry movements, stacked the pile of books at his desk. He stuffed them back inside the secret panel. "Only you would know how to pick a damned lock." He belatedly recalled the copy she still held. Leo glanced back. "My book, madam," he snapped, holding out a hand.

Again, Chloe jumped and released the copy into his hand.

As he organized the pile and slid the lock back into place, he dug deep for calm and order of his thoughts.

So she'd discovered he had an appreciation for literature and healthy finances. Such discoveries revealed nothing about his work for the Brethren. Calmed by that, Leo slowly unfurled to his full height.

Chloe edged away from him, placing his high-backed chair between them as a barrier.

The muscles along his jaw went taut. Good, she feared him.

Why did that feel like the emptiest of victories?

"I prefer my finances a secret," he began, feeding her yet another lie. "So that the creditors I'm indebted to don't all come a'calling. So the mistresses I broke it off with who didn't receive so much as a parting gift aren't prodding me for baubles."

She worried at her lower lip. "I don't believe you."

Of course she didn't.

"You're not who you seem," she persisted. "I've always believed that. And then I received this…"

His senses on heightened alert, Leo fixed on her slender fingers as they dug around the front of her gown. She withdrew a small, folded sheet.

Chloe came out from behind his chair.

"What is this?" he demanded as she turned it over. Not bothering to wait for an answer, he unfolded it. Leo's stomach dropped. *Oh, God.* He stared blankly at the warning as terror peeled around his ears.

"Who would send me that? And what would they warn you away from, Leo?" She spit out question after question. "Tell me," she pleaded.

With an animalistic cry, he swept the contents off the surface of his desk, scattering them about. The inkwell crashed in a crystal explosion, spraying shards about his office.

Her entire body recoiled.

"It is not your business," he cried. He gathered her firmly by the shoulders again, crushing the damning note against the delicate white puff of her sleeve. "Why? Why must you probe?" he shouted. The page slipped in a whispery fall to their feet. "Why?" A keening moan filtered past his lips.

"Stop," she pleaded, wrenching back, but he tightened his hold.

"Do you want the truth?" he thundered, shaking her harder. "Do you?"

"Yes," she cried.

"I am an agent for the Home Office."

It was harder to say who was more stunned by that whispered revelation. His own shock was reflected in the pools of her eyes. "What?"

The question belonged to the both of them, spoken simultaneously from a shaken state.

He shook his head numbly. What? Where? Leo jerked his palms back so abruptly, Chloe tumbled back into his chair.

He flexed his fingers. His throat burned with the need for liquid fortitude. On unsteady legs, he stalked over to his sideboard. Not bothering with a glass, he grabbed the bottle of whiskey that was closest to his fingertips. Yanking the stopper out, he tossed it on the floor, where it bounced around.

Leo took a long swallow.

Chloe's eyes followed his every move. As the liquor burned a path down his throat, she sank farther and farther into her seat until she sat with her shoulders hunched in a protective posturing.

Lowering his bottle, Leo took a step toward her.

She held her hands up, an entreaty in her gaze.

That fear—of him—struck like a lash upon his soul. Leo dropped to his haunches, the decanter dangling between his fingers. The bottle was a crutch to cling to. Words stuck in his throat, making speech impossible. He swallowed hard and tried again. "I've been an agent for a special division within the Home Office since I was just eight and ten." He finally shared the truth with another soul, the first time in the whole tenure of his service to the Crown. "My role with the agency required I cultivate the persona of a rake." Leo chuckled, seeing the scared child he'd been. "It was so very easy," he said softly to himself. "My... father... I wasn't..."

He closed his eyes as every age-old sense of failure and insecurity battered at him, transforming him back into that stuttering, stammering, pleading boy. Leo forced himself to complete the telling. "I was never the child my father wanted." There, that much was true. Sharing with her the darkest truth of his existence, however, he still could not bring himself to utter. "My work gave me purpose, and I reveled in every moment of my instruction. Bedding whores, drinking spirits, learning whist and hazard and faro..." How very thrilling it had all been to him, a sheltered scholar.

Chloe wet her lips. "It's why you set aside your studies... and Lady Daphne?" she ventured, far more clever than could ever be safe.

"The agency had reason to believe I was compromised. I went off to meet with her and break it off..."

"It wasn't disapproving parents," she breathed, sliding the puzzle pieces he'd handed her into place. "It was—"

He again nodded. "After we'd made love, I discovered we'd been followed." And so he'd ended it in the cruelest way possible. "None of that matters. Your silence," *and your safety*, "is essential." Leo grabbed the missive she'd received. "Where did you get this?" he demanded, focusing on the one thing he'd always been able to control—his work.

"I came to the library, and it was resting on the sofa."

His home had been infiltrated. Impossible. That would have to mean there was someone on his staff, in his midst... nay, worse, within the Brethren who wanted him to abandon his efforts. Something stirred at the back of his mind. The thought proved a dark, unpleasant niggling. An impossibility... and yet... not.

How many men had betrayed the Crown in the past, and how many would in the future?

But why... Why?

Leo struggled to think.

"What is the mission they seek to steer you away from?"

For a moment, he weighed silence. But Chloe knew too much. And with her familial connection to Waterson, she might prove valuable in ways he hadn't considered. "I had reason to believe the Cato Street Conspiracy, the plan to—"

"I'm familiar with it," Chloe interrupted.

Despite the horror of all that had unfolded, admiration for this woman rose to the surface. Leo went on to provide the details about his investigation... and her role involved in it.

"So you wed me to be closer to Gabriel's closest friend," she murmured.

"It was a mutually beneficial goal," he said gruffly. "My superiors had expressed displeasure with my recklessness." He cracked his knuckles. "There were rumors that I'd bedded my immediate supervisor's wife."

"Rumors." Chloe ran her eyes over his face. "You did not, then, make her your lover."

He shook his head. "Any further scandals would have seen me removed from my post."

Understanding dawned in her eyes. "It is because we were discovered. We were the scandal."

"My superior was gleeful with the prospect of my being cast out."

A resentment he'd attributed to the other man's viper of a wife... and now something more sinister had reared at the back of his mind.

"Another lady would dissolve into a fit of tears at that betrayal," he noted.

"Ours was a business arrangement from the beginning, Leo. I had my own desires and expectations of a union between us. It would be unfair to resent you for your reasons."

Did that still hold true? Or had she come to care for him, as he had her?

His palms moistened with his aching need for an answer.

Chloe drifted closer. "You gave your life to the Crown, you gave up the woman you loved. And yet, the men you serve had so little faith in your loyalty," she murmured, stroking a palm over his cheek. "They wronged you."

His heart hammered. How did she see feelings he carried? Resentment he'd shared with none?

He shoved her hand back, and his always fearless wife shrank once more from him. "You make presumptions you shouldn't," he hissed.

From the corner of his eyes, he caught her inching toward the door.

He stepped into her path, wringing a gasp from her.

Leo caught her chin between his thumb and forefinger, tipping her gaze to meet his.

She winced.

"You think you just get to walk away, madam?" Leo placed his lips along her ear. The hint of jasmine flooded his senses. God, she was a siren, and he was helpless where she was concerned. Held in the grip of frustration, he seethed. "Your life is no longer your own." And how he hated that for her and loathed himself for stripping that anonymity from her. Nonetheless, he needed to open her eyes to the peril she would forever face. "When you walk outside, an enemy wishing to get to me knows you are there." Just as they had with the carriage accident. "When you attend a dinner party, the safety of your repast is no longer assured." With every possible threat he dangled, the color seeped more and more from her cheeks until her eyes stood out, stark, vivid pools of terror within her porcelain-white visage. "Rides in Hyde Park or outings to the modiste… no place is safe."

I'm going to be ill.

Leo's stomach roiled, vomit stinging his throat. He abruptly released her, and she tripped over him in her haste to put distance between them. Leo dusted his palms together. "I trust I needn't stress the importance of your keeping this information to yourself."

She narrowed her eyes. "Do you think me an empty-headed miss who'd bandy about your role and jeopardize your work?"

"You expect confidence in the lady who sought out my former lover to bring us both *peace*?" He smiled coldly. "Oh, with your tender heart, one couldn't say what you'd share, and with whom, to alter people's opinions of me."

Say something. Lash out at me. Defend yourself and send me to the devil as I deserve.

Instead, Chloe remained stoically silent.

Leo caressed a palm down her right shoulder, drifting it along her modest décolletage. He wrapped her in a loose embrace. "I expect you to play the role of perfect hostess tomorrow at our soiree, madam. You'll smile, because I need you smiling. You'll arrange discussions between me and Waterson and anyone else I require. Are we clear?"

"I don't break my word," she retorted with a faint quiver to her voice.

"Get out." The command whistled past clenched teeth.

And she did what she should have done at their first meeting— she fled.

After she'd gone, Leo stormed over to the door and kicked it closed with the bottom of his boot. The violent force set the frame to shaking.

Bloody hell.

It had been as he'd feared. A risk he'd realized too late—that Chloe would forever be in peril because of his work for the Brethren. He'd sent Daphne Smith away long, long ago. So many years had passed that he'd believed himself sufficiently deadened to feeling anything.

Only to be proven so wholly wrong—with Chloe at risk for that mistake.

He began to pace. All right. So he'd revealed the truth to her. This needn't be a bad thing. In fact, it had been wrong to keep her in the dark. Not knowing about the work he did and the enemies he had as a result would only see her an unwitting target.

Yes, at least she knew… and could be on alert.

But it did not erase the fact that when this was all said and done, he needed to send her away.

Leo rubbed uselessly at the ache in his chest. He'd believed himself heartless, only to find out that he very much did possess that dangerous organ and that it beat for his wife.

CHAPTER 27

As A CHILD, CHLOE HAD pitied her mother and all that went into the planning of balls and soirees. Aside from the lists and invitations that consumed her time leading up to the grand events, there were the floral arrangements and orchestra to be arranged, servants to be directed, and refreshments seen to and properly situated.

That was why the morning following a sleepless night, Chloe's inability to move, breathe, or think had come at the utmost worst time.

But then, she'd learned early on that her megrims were not discriminating. They didn't care whether it was a cheerful, summer day in the country or, say, one's presentation before the queen. They came when they would, dictating her every action. Or rather… her inaction.

Her maid moved about the room in a chipper manner, humming a discordant tune as she dragged the curtains open.

Sunlight flooded Chloe's chambers.

Groaning, Chloe placed her palms lightly over her eyes. Even that faintest pressure sent nausea churning in her stomach. "Stop," she entreated when Doris reached for another one of the gold tassels. The plea echoed around her brain like the hammering upon an anvil.

The maid stopped. "But you indicated I should wake you. 'Tis the day of the soiree and—"

God hated Chloe. There was no other accounting for her inability to so much as quell a rambling maid in her employ and spare herself the throbbing, vicious ache. She blindly fished around for one of the pillows until her fingers made purchase with the linen fabric. She dragged it over her face. The cool, feather-soft fabric blotted out all light and muted her garrulous maid.

When the misery came, one took any relief as a monumental triumph.

Chloe drew in slow, steady breaths.

She needed to make her maid stop. Needed her to go. Weighing the torture of speaking against that of the whine of Doris' speech, Chloe shifted the pillow slightly over her mouth.

"Go," she ordered.

The maid paused midsentence. "My lady?"

"I said go," she repeated, too loudly, and her eyes clenched reflexively at the excruciating sound of her own voice. Nay, everything was magnified under the onslaught of her megrims, the press of the door handle, the click of the panel shutting.

As soon as silence fell, Chloe removed the pillow and promptly wished she hadn't.

Her eyesight tunneled, canceling out her peripheral view as blinding, bright spots dotted her vision. Heart thudding in her ears, like the incessant beat of a drum, Chloe bit down hard on her lip.

The metallic tinge of blood filled her nostrils, flooding her senses. *No. No. No. No.*

Since she'd wed Leo, she'd allowed herself the illusion of forgetting the hell that would always be with her. She had been happy and focused only on them, together. She'd not given thought to this. A piteous moan escaped her, ratcheting up the pain that wrapped around the base of her skull.

Chloe forced herself upright. She held her hands up uselessly, fighting to steady the spinning room, and stumbled step by laborious step to the curtains.

After an endless journey, she collapsed against the wall. She borrowed support from the wall as, with her left hand, she searched for and found the gold tie.

Such a small task.

She tugged.

One her maid had so easily seen to.

Chloe tried again.

Flitting from curtain to curtain, unleashing the torture of the morning light on Chloe's hellish world.

At last, Chloe freed the tassel, and the heavy velvet fluttered back into place. Each whoosh and whir of fabric produced a magnified clamor in her ears. Hunching her shoulders, Chloe cradled her head in one hand. She moved from window to window until the room was doused in darkness once more.

Panting, she limped over to the four-poster bed at the center of her chambers and collapsed onto the mattress. That Herculean effort drained all life from her limbs as she lay with her cheek against the rumpled linen sheets.

Time ceased to matter or mean anything. It could have been marching on into eternity or standing still altogether, for when her headaches came, she dwelled only in a hell created by her mind.

A single tear popped out the corner of her eye.

Never before had she missed her family and staff who knew about the secret she carried. They had been there to tug the curtains, casting the rooms in darkness, forbidding noise, and offering absolute silence and still.

It had been inevitable.

The debilitating migraines that had haunted Chloe since she was a girl would always be there. They were the demons left behind by her father, torturing her still, lingering until she, one day, would draw her last breath.

And when her headaches struck, death was the most appealing of options. For then, there would be no suffering or pain… but the bliss of emptiness.

But death came only when it was ready, and Chloe was left to suffer through the misery that was life.

Drawing in a shaky breath, she pulled herself all the way onto the bed until she lay facedown in the center—and then she slept.

A frantic beating sliced across her uneasy slumber.

Where was she? What was that infernal banging?

Her eyes heavy, Chloe forced the lashes open.

She winced as an aura of white light danced before her vision.

That light was made even more acute by the pitch black of her rooms.

"My lady," a muffled voice was saying, "...come to ready you for..."

Ready Chloe for what?

And then she remembered: her marriage, Leo's volatile explosion, the soiree.

Oh, bloody, bloody hell.

The soiree.

RapRapRap

"My lady?"

The words muffled by the oak panel became all the more distorted by the high-pitched whine in her ears.

No.

Chloe turned her head toward the revolving clock, trying to make sense of time in her darkened quarters, the cherubs holding the crystal glass more like Satan's spawns as they shoved the cylinder in a dizzying circular movement. The numbers, as they pulled into focus, were obscured by the dancing ball of light behind her eyes.

Tears stole the remainder of her vision.

"My lady?" Doris called again, her voice shifting in and out of focus.

I cannot do this...

And yet, she had to. She couldn't very well renege on the agreement she'd struck with Leo. Furthermore, there would be a ballroom full of lords and ladies—her family included—and deafening noise and blindingly bright chandeliers, and—

Gritting her teeth, she swung her legs over the bed. Chloe's stomach turned over at the suddenness of her movements. "Just a moment," she forced herself to call out.

It was only one night. A handful of hours. Surely she could put on a show for everyone's benefit.

And then nausea assailed her. Bile climbed her throat, and she swallowed rhythmically, over and over. She could not do this. "T-tell his lordship I will not be coming," she rasped, praying her threadbare voice carried, praying Leo would leave her alone, praying for death.

Chloe knew the latter two were useless prayers that would never be answered. Leo had expectations and wouldn't—nay, couldn't—accept her refusal to attend.

"My lady?" Confusion wreathed her maid's question.

"I'm not attending," she managed to call. "Tell him I'm not feeling well enough to," she sucked in a breath, fighting to continue, "join him."

Oh, God.

A moment later, with the frantic footfalls of her maid rushing off, Chloe grabbed the empty chamber pot at her bedside and heaved the contents of her stomach into the porcelain bowl.

Where in the blazes was she?

Standing in the foyer, Leo consulted his timepiece for a third time.

The lady was furious with him.

As she should be... for any host of reasons. One, she deserved a respectable, honorable gent who'd offer her a staid but safe life. Two, he'd lied to her at every turn. All for valuable reasons related to his work, but lies nonetheless. The list really could go on and on.

Even with all that, he'd never considered that she might ever renege on—

Footsteps sounded overhead. *At last.* Tucking his timepiece into his jacket, Leo glanced at the landing. "I'd begun to think you weren't coming, l—"

Chloe's maid appeared at the top of the sweeping staircase. "Her ladyship sent me. She indicated that I should tell you... tell you..."

"Yes?" he barked, his already thinly held patience snapping.

"Her ladyship is not coming," the maid squeaked and scurried off.

Leo puzzled his brow. Her ladyship was not coming? "Halt." His command boomed around the sweeping foyer, freezing the trembling young maid in her spot.

The girl faced him. Even with the space between them, her audible swallow reached his ears. "I-is there something you wish, my lord?"

Yes. His wife. "What do you mean, she is not coming?" he called up.

Darting her nervous eyes about, the servant studiously avoided looking at Leo. As the one who oversaw all the hiring of Leo's very small staff, how in the blazes had the man seen to the hiring of this meek miss? There wasn't a scrap of Brethren boldness or fire in her. "I asked—"

"Her ladyship simply said she's not coming and ordered me to leave," she cried, fisting the front of her skirts. "Her ladyship claimed she isn't feeling well enough to attend."

He snorted. "My wife doesn't have a weak constitution." Which only meant... she was making a statement with her refusal. Leo cursed. He had been a bloody bastard last evening. Out of frustration and fear, he'd lashed out, ordering Chloe about... when not even the king himself would have the wherewithal to do so.

"Do you wish for me t-to deliver a m-message?" the maid ventured.

The girl sounded about ready to dissolve into a blubbering mess if he accepted that offer.

"I'll gather her myself," he gritted out. He'd not even finished his thought before the servant bolted.

"Is there a problem, my lord?"

Leo started at the unexpected appearance of his butler at his side. "Bloody hell, announce yourself, man."

Tomlinson grinned and then promptly hid his amusement. "As you wish," he demurred.

"And yes, there is a problem." Leo had had a scarcity of friends over the years and no real confidantes, and Tomlinson had played that de facto role. At least, he'd come as close as Leo could manage to—he grimaced—friendship. Or, that had been the case until his spitfire wife.

The same clever minx who'd invaded his office and gathered that all of Leo's life had been nothing more than a lie. The same minx who'd locked herself in her rooms. At the worst possible time.

"My wife is refusing to join me."

"That is a problem," Tomlinson murmured, his expression deadpan. "An apology after your temper last evening?"

Leo's ears went hot, and he felt himself blushing. Egads, blushing? "The staff is aware of that?"

Unapologetic, Tomlinson adjusted his already immaculate jacket. "I took the liberty of stationing myself outside your doorway."

A modicum of relief filled him, along with frustration at his own carelessness. Even as the other man had verified no one else would overhear all that was said, Leo's absolute lack of control had made him incautious.

"Afterwards, I had the maids tidy your office."

The broken glass, his false ledger. *Christ.*

Heat burned up Leo's neck. What was it about Chloe that made him lose control? What made him forget the Brethren and his responsibilities to that organization and worry only about her well-being? His mind shied away from a truth he could not... nay, would never confront.

"My lord?"

"How long until the guests begin arriving?"

"I couldn't say," Tomlinson said regretfully.

"Guess," he snapped.

"I would expect your and her ladyship's guests might begin to arrive any moment."

Leo cursed roundly. His uncle, his superiors, most important, Rowley and Waterson, and all the damned suspects for the Cato Street Conspiracy were to assemble in his household. His wife had picked the absolute worst time to pitch a temper. "And what in the blazes am I to do if they arrive with no host or hostess?" he demanded, yanking a hand through his hair.

"Again, I'm afraid I—"

"Don't know," Leo finished for him. "You're useless, Tomlinson," he muttered, taking the stairs two at a time. As soon as he reached Chloe's rooms, he pressed the handle.

The door refused to give.

Bloody hell.

She'd locked him out.

Leo curved his hands around his mouth and called through the panel. "I trust this is a jest, dear wife."

There was a lengthy pause.

"Go away."

Gnashing his teeth with frustration, he raised a fist to pound on her door. He stopped himself.

Regardless of the fear and worry that had assailed him yesterday, he'd been a miserable bear. It hadn't been Chloe's fault that she'd been embroiled in Leo's work for the Brethren and his current assignment. Rather, it was his for having married her without consideration of the peril he'd place her in. He lowered his arm back to his side.

"I apologize for…" He glanced about. He'd reassigned his assistant to shadowing his wife's movements. Though he trusted the man with his life, he'd still rather not bandy the details of his fight yesterday. "I am sorry for our last meeting, Chloe." He settled for vagueness.

Another pause and then, "It's fine, Leo," she said tiredly.

He waited for the click of the lock as she allowed him entry—that did not come.

"Do you wish for me to grovel, madam?" he bit out.

Because, damn it, he would. He had no other choice. He needed her. He needed them to present a united front of respectability and begin laying a trap for the real traitor of the Cato Event.

"I wish for you to go away."

The confession drifted through the panel, muffled and so faint he might as well have imagined it. And yet—

"You're accompanying me," he boomed. "I—"

A tortured moan slashed across his fury.

All his senses heightened, Leo grabbed the handle. "Chloe?" he asked, his alarm creeping up.

"G-go away."

The tremor there notched up his unease.

Leo shot a hand up. An instant later, Holman trotted over. "My lord?"

"When was the last time you saw my wife?" he demanded gruffly. His always steady, unaffected heart thundered an erratic, unfamiliar beat. *When was the last time you saw her?* a derisive voice jeered at the back of his mind.

"She's not left her chambers, my lord. Turned away meals."

Not left her chambers? Leo grabbed him by the shoulders, shaking him so hard he dislodged the smaller man's spectacles. "And you didn't think to report to me that she's been shut away?" he whispered.

"The maids saw her ladyship fleeing through the halls last evening," Holman squeaked. "Upset," he tacked on.

In other words, the entire household knew there had been a row.

Releasing his assistant so abruptly the boy stumbled back, Leo returned his attentions to his wife's door.

A groan wreathed in agony met his ears.

His pulse skittering out of control, he stepped back and, raising his leg for a high kick, slammed his foot into the unrelenting oak.

"No," she pleaded. "Please, don't."

"Chloe," he shouted hoarsely, kicking the panel over and over. Oh, God. Sweat beaded on his brow. Was it terror? His exertions? Desperation? In this instant, Leo couldn't sort through the cacophonic tumult of his mind. He gave another mighty kick.

The panel splintered. Leo continued battering at it until the wood gave way enough for him to squeeze a hand through. Shards of broken wood stabbed at his gloved palm as he pressed the handle, letting himself in.

Fishing a pistol from his boot, he frantically searched the chambers, pitched in black.

Chloe's sheets stood out, a stark tangle of snowy white in the otherwise dark space, without even the glow of a fire for light.

What in the hell?

"Chloe?" he shouted, raising his gun close to his chest.

Then he heard it.

A faint, animalistic moan.

Charging over, Leo skidded to a stop, and the earth fell out from under his feet.

He recoiled at the scent of sweat and vomit.

His heart skipped several erratic beats and then ceased to throb altogether. "Chloe," he whispered. The gun fell from his hand, clattering noisily on the floor. The sound pulled another moan from his wife.

Chloe lay in the same nightclothes she'd worn last evening. Her hair hung in a tangle of knotted golden curls about her hunched shoulders.

Prone on the floor, she clung to a porcelain chamber pot with a death grip that had drained the blood from her knuckles.

With a seeming Herculean effort, she lifted her head a fraction. Her bloodshot eyes, brimming with agony, met his.

All the air stuck sharply in his chest, trapping the gasp in his throat. "My God," he whispered, stumbling back. "Poisoned," he choked out, his speech dissolving into fragments of incomplete, panicked thoughts. Thundering for Holman, he raced to the door.

His wife's piteous moans punctuated the thump of his footfalls, and then a violent retching commenced at his back.

Holman stormed the doorway, his gun at the ready.

"A doctor," Leo boomed.

Those two words sent the man into flight.

"Noo," Chloe entreated, spitting into the bowl. "No doctor. Please, please," she begged.

Leo raced over and collapsed to his knees at her side. So this was fear, this mindless, numbing, soul-rending hopelessness that robbed a man of logical thought, action, and words. With hands that shook, he reached for her shoulders, hovering above them, afraid to touch her, afraid she'd splinter and break apart.

"It's not poison," she rasped, resting her head upon the porcelain bowl. "Though I wish it was." She spoke to the bottom of the chamber pot, her weakened voice pinging off the glass.

"Do not say that," he said harshly. Oh, God. Why had he married her? Why had he subjected her to every peril that went with being connected to him? "I've seen this before." Both men and women, who'd been sapped of their strength and who'd wasted away to emaciated corpses within hours.

His breath came fast in his ears. He yanked both hands through his hair, wanting to tilt back his head and rage at the merciless heavens. Even as all blame belonged squarely at Leo's feet.

"It's not poison," she insisted, her voice weak. So weak. His eyes slid closed. "Please don't send for a doctor. I get migraines. I don't want anyone to see. Please," she begged. As if that effort cost her everything, Chloe vomited. Her narrow shoulders shook. Her entire body trembled like a slender reed about to buckle under the slightest pressure.

"No doctor," he vowed. At this moment, he'd carve out his heart and hand it to her on his outstretched palm if it would stop her suffering. "Migraines?" he echoed. She'd not been poisoned. The relief of that assailed him, weighting his eyes closed and filling every corner of him. She would not die. And yet, the relief was short-lived.

Chloe heaved again. The groan that stole from her shredded his soul. The need to take away someone else's pain and make it his own was so foreign, so unfamiliar to him, a man who'd never given a jot about anyone's comforts but his own.

Leo only knew, in this moment, that he wanted to take away this woman's suffering. He would have sold his soul, assets, and role with the Brethren if it meant she was spared from the pain that gripped her.

"Shh," he whispered. Yanking free his previously immaculate cravat, he stuck it between his teeth. Then, gathering the mass of curls hanging limp about her shoulders, he gently drew the damp strands back so they exposed her sweaty nape. He made quick work of tying her heavy curls with the strip of satin fabric.

Loath to leave her, Leo stalked to the door. Tomlinson lingered in the hall. Ashen-faced and worried, as Leo had never seen him, the butler wrung his hands together. "Her ladyship?"

"When the doctor arrives, do not send him in. Keep him for the night in the event I require his services. I need pitchers of cold water," he spoke quietly. "Strips of cloth. Bring them yourself and leave them at the front of the room." The commands came easily, a welcome diversion that gave him a small sense of purposefulness. Otherwise, he'd descend into madness. "I don't want a single soul entering this room until I give the command."

Tomlinson rushed off to do his bidding. Leo returned to Chloe.

She was so still. So very, achingly, painfully still that, for a torturous moment, he believed she was wrong and her suffering was not the product of a headache, but rather vengeance carried out by someone Leo had brought to justice.

Chloe groaned, and he fell to his knees beside her. "What can I do?" he entreated. This helplessness was worse than paralysis. It gutted him in ways no blade or pistol ball had ever managed.

"Nothing. Just go," she begged. He'd sooner take off his own limbs with a dulled letter opener than abandon her. "The soiree."

He forced his lips into a smile. The strain on his facial muscles made a mockery of his efforts. "Not attending my own soiree is what all of Polite Society has come to expect, anyway."

"I'm so sorry," she whispered, her voice breaking under the effort it cost her to speak.

"Shh," he murmured. And as she again emptied the contents of her stomach, he held her gently by the shoulders. She continued on that way, spitting bile into the chamber pot.

Where in the hell was Tomlinson? Leo shot frantic glances back at the slightly gaping door. Never, not when faced with the late marquess' violent outbursts or on any assignment, had he felt this sense of helplessness. He, a man who, for the past twelve years, had been in control of his own fate and the fates of the people of the British Empire, could not help his own wife. This woman who mattered more to him than himself.

And mayhap later, he'd rail at himself for having lost so much of himself to Chloe. But in this, he could think only of her.

Tomlinson finally reappeared.

Jumping up, Leo rushed to meet him. With the butler standing as a barrier between the maids in the hall and Chloe, Leo accepted the offerings one at a time. "Have a hot bath readied in my chambers," he instructed.

"The guests have begun to arrive, my lord. Her ladyship's family is asking after the marchioness."

"Turn them away. Turn everyone away."

"As you wish." Tomlinson turned to go.

"Tomlinson?"

His butler wheeled around.

"Inform Lady Waverly that I require an appointment." Even as that meeting would usher in the end of the only happiness Leo had known… ever. For though there had been a fleeting time he'd shared with Daphne Smith, every moment had been cloaked in secrecy, with everything about him a secret. Chloe had slipped past his defenses and reminded him of who he had been. And who he wanted to be again… His throat convulsed.

"My lord?" Tomlinson prodded.

Leo gave his head a clearing shake. "I'll send word for her ladyship." Closing the badly broken door on that, Leo rejoined his wife, shedding his jacket and rolling his shirtsleeves as he went.

"Leo, go. You cannot miss your soiree." She spoke on the faintest exhalation. "My sisters will help—" She cradled the back of her head and buried her head again in the pot, retching.

"Stop talking." He issued the command in quiet, even tones. "We won't talk. No noise."

With that, not another word was spoken between them. Leo fetched a cloth. Dunking it in the bowl of cold water, he wrung it out and returned to Chloe. He placed the cool compress along her nape.

An appreciative moan spilled from her lips.

Fetching another cloth, Leo knelt in front of Chloe and ever so gently wiped her perspiring brow. He cleaned the corners of her mouth and then laid another compress over her eyes.

Taking care to not jar her, Leo scooped her under the knees and carried her from the fetid chambers and into his own. A steaming bath had already been drawn and sat readied beside the hearth. The fire crackled noisily within the grate.

Cursing himself for not ordering it doused, he placed Chloe on his bed and stalked over to the windows. Making quick work of the lock, he tossed the crystal pane open. The unseasonably cool spring air spilled into the rooms, immediately stealing the warmth provided by the fire.

Leo stalked over to the mahogany four-poster bed that dominated the room. Carefully balancing a knee on the mattress, he reached for the hem of Chloe's nightgown.

Her eyes flew open, and she immediately covered her face with her palms.

"A hot bath will help."

"It won't," she mumbled into her hands.

"It—"

"I don't want a bath, Leo," she begged.

In this moment, she could have asked him to duel Satan and God himself for mastery of the world, and he would have committed himself to that battle. "Very well."

Returning to her rooms, he fetched the strips of cloth and the bowl of water. Throughout the night, he placed cool cloth after cool cloth atop her brow, at her wrists, her neck, until the chill left the water and the fire faded in the hearth.

And when the faintest little snore escaped her, Leo pulled his carved walnut chair over to the side of the bed and sat. Settling into the olive-green leather folds, he stretched his legs out before him. Steepling his fingertips under his chin, he watched his wife until the fingers of dawn peeled back the night sky and ushered in a new day, and then he left.

CHAPTER 28

CHLOE KNEW WHEN A PERSON was up to something. After all, she'd invariably been plotting, planning, or scheming… something since she was a girl.

That was why, the following afternoon, with her mother returned from a still expecting Imogen's side, sister Philippa and sister-in-law Jane squeezed onto the double-peaked, camel-backed sofa wearing like unreadable expressions, Chloe knew this was no ordinary social visit.

Jane broke the silence. "You are… well?"

"Undoubtedly," Chloe said with false cheer. She reached for the tray of pastries that had been delivered a short while ago by a maid. "Is Imogen well?" she countered.

"Very much so," the dowager marchioness murmured. "Surely you did not believe I'd miss the first event hosted by you and your husband?"

There was an ill-concealed question about the event. "Refreshments?" Chloe offered quickly. She looked between the ladies assembled.

"Chloe," Philippa began gently. "You canceled your soiree."

"If one wishes to be truly precise, it was my husband," she pointed out. To give her fingers something to do, she plucked an apple dappy from the silver tray. Breaking it in half, she popped a piece into her mouth. Errant buttery flakes sprinkled onto her skirts, and she dusted them off onto the floor.

Her mother stared at her painfully. "Chloe," she said in agonized tones.

"My apologies," Chloe mumbled around a mouthful of pastry. Lifting a finger, she finished her bite and grabbed a small dessert plate. "There."

Her mother moved to the edge of her seat and, with an undow-ager marchionesslike grab, jerked the dish from Chloe's lap. "Do you think I am scolding you about whether or not you have a blasted plate, Chloe?" she demanded, setting down the dish in question with such force it rocked back and forth before coming to a slow, clamoring halt.

"Your husband sent word last evening."

"Did he?" she asked tightly. How she despised her impairment. How she yearned to be like any other woman, instead of living with a sense of dread of the inevitability that she would ultimately be brought low and crippled by pain and weakness. "I trust you'll have quite a time smoothing over the scandal of a canceled soiree, Mother," she said, fisting her skirts, wrinkling the ivory satin.

"Chloe," Philippa chided.

"Do you think I care more about your manners or that damned soiree than I do your well-being?" Their mother spoke quickly over her eldest daughter.

Over the years, Chloe couldn't have answered that very question with any real degree of confidence or certainty. Never once had her mother stepped between Chloe and the marquess' blows. "There was a time I felt that way," she said somberly. "When I was a girl…"

Tears formed a watery sheen over her mother's eyes. Angling her head down, she discreetly dabbed at the corners. "I deserve that."

"Now, I've come to peace with the fact that we each do the best with our circumstances." Leo had shown her that. The whole world had judged her husband. And though he was guilty of many sins, so many of them had been products of his existence. "How much easier it is to judge when we don't truly know a person's circumstances or the secrets they carry."

"I know I failed you," she whispered, pressing her gloved finger-tips to her mouth. "I failed all of you. He was a vile, cruel monster handpicked by my father, and I hated him, but I hated myself m-more." Her voice broke on a sob that tore at Chloe's heart. "I tried once… and beyond that, I was too much a coward."

The evidence of her mother's suffering and shame didn't bring Chloe any pleasure. Rather, it just highlighted the hold their father held, still. *It is time to let him go…* It was time for all of them to release the shackles and free themselves. "Mother," she began.

"N-no, Chloe. I need to say this." She drew in a shuddery breath. "I haven't been the mother you deserved. Not just then." She swiped angrily at her damp cheeks. Other tears quickly claimed their place. "But even after, when your headaches came, and it was so easy to shut your door and let you suffer through them alone."

Only, last evening, Chloe hadn't been alone. She hadn't been tended by a stranger or maid, or shut away alone until she was restored. Leo had been there, and he'd cared for her with a gentleness while preserving her dignity.

Her heart swelled to overflowing with her love for him.

"Are you well?" her mother asked, holding her gaze.

Chloe wet her lips. "They'll always be there." The headaches would always be a part of her. They could not be banished by wishing or hoping or even medicine. "But Leo, he was there. He cared for me," she said softly, wanting the women present to know precisely what manner of man he was.

Jane cleared her throat. "He paid me a visit this morning."

Chloe stiffened. "Indeed?" she said curtly. Having slept long past morning, she'd not known that. A million questions swirled in her mind, but only one sharpened into focus. Why had he called on Jane? A niggling suspicion slipped in. When it became clear that Jane was giving her time to make the next move in their dialogue, she asked, "And what did my husband have to say?"

"He explained the reasons you'd wed."

Betrayal slapped at her like a fist to the belly. "He had no right," she whispered. The terms of their marriage had belonged to them.

"He explained you wanted the post of headmistress at Mrs. Munroe's," Jane murmured. "I should have let you have it. I was the one who indicated your marital status mattered to the post. If it weren't for me, then you wouldn't have married Lord Leo."

Yes, it had been only because of a series of unexpected and unintentional moments that Chloe found herself married to Leo.

She stared beyond her family to the swan situated atop the mantel. Those gloriously devoted creatures represented what love should be. In this time, he'd come to matter so much to her. He'd snagged a heart she'd vowed she'd never trust to any man and filled her with a longing for so much more than she'd ever allowed herself even the dream of.

"Oh, Jane. You still haven't realized." Chloe glanced over to her mother and Philippa. "None of you have. Everyone has sought to protect me. And though I'll always be grateful to each of you for caring, never did I wish to be coddled." She scooted to the edge of her seat. "You should not have given me that post," Chloe said to Jane with a quiet pragmatism. "I have no experience and no right to ask or expect the post." She knew that now.

"But you deserve it now, Chloe. Not because it is a favor you or your husband asked, but because you will bring a wisdom and life experience to my students." Jane held her gaze. "I'm offering it to you."

There it was... everything Chloe had aspired to and dreamed of—a post at Mrs. Munroe's overseeing the instruction of young women who'd been shunned by Polite Society. The post would see her away from her marriage and safe.

How wrong she'd been. About everything. She didn't want safe. She wanted to feel again, without fear. She wanted a family of her own. *Leo. I want Leo.*

Her mother made a slight clearing sound with her throat. "Won't you say something, Chloe?"

"I am... honored," she finally said. For it was a gift her sister-in-law held out and a dream that Chloe's mother now accepted. But now she had new dreams. Ones Leo had opened her eyes to.

You've spoken of your sister's and sister-in-law's establishments and the visions they have. But what of your dream? With your funds and cleverness, you can also create something of your own.

"It is a lot," Philippa demurred. "And given you're only just recovering, one you should think on. We should let you to your rest."

Wrong as it was, Chloe was eager for her family to take themselves off. She wanted to be alone so she could seek out Leo and strive to know what he was feeling... about her and their marriage.

As Philippa stepped from the room, Chloe's mother lingered.

"Chloe, I was not altogether fair…" Her lips pulled in a grimace. "I was not at all fair where your husband is concerned." As she spoke, her voice grew wistful. "That he would allow you the life you dream of, an unconventional one that would raise a scandal, without a care for how the world views you or him, shows how very much more there is to Leo." Lifting a hand that showed the early signs of wrinkling and age, she caressed Chloe's cheek. "I don't think he'll ever deserve you. Nor will Gabriel or Alex think that. But no man will ever deserve you, and if you had to choose someone, it would be one who supports your dreams."

Chloe blinked back the sting in her eyes. She'd been filled with so much resentment over her mother's inability to accept her for who she was and then Leo. A lightness filled her soul, freeing in its power. Leaning down, she kissed her mother on the cheek. "Thank you."

A rosy blush immediately stained the dowager marchioness' cheeks. She coughed discreetly into her hand. "Yes, very well, then."

Chloe smiled. Her mother would never truly be at ease sharing her emotions, but time had changed her, as it changed them all. "I love you, Mother."

"I love you, too," she whispered. With tears falling, she swept out, leaving Chloe alone.

After they'd gone, Chloe wandered around this first room she'd been shown to by Tomlinson almost a fortnight ago. Then, she'd entered this household, fearful of a future with Leo as her husband and desiring only one thing—her freedom. And now he'd offered it. He'd not only offered it, but he'd gone to her family and secured not only the post of headmistress but peace with her headstrong kin.

Chloe stopped at the bronze swan. She absently trailed her fingertips over the elaborate wingspan.

So why could she not just take what was held out before her?

"Because I want him," she whispered, breathing life into that truth. And wanting a future with him did not make her weaker, or mean she was abandoning the dreams she'd carried. Rather, it marked a shift in how she wanted those hopes to play out… and whom she dreamed of at her side.

A healing light buoyed her like that first warm sun after the winter's retreat.

Yet…

Uncertainty intruded. It was dark, unwelcome, and unwanted. For, with it, came the question of what Leo wanted.

At no point had he shared any desire he had for a future with her in it. He had his work for the Home Office and had never been anything but clear that their marriage was a business arrangement.

It had been his actions that had shed doubt upon his indifference, the gentleman who'd read poetry to her in Hyde Park and encouraged her to follow her own pursuits. What had been real, and what had been pretend to serve his role?

She closed her eyes. Every memory and moment they'd shared clamored in her mind like a discordant symphony she sought to pluck a harmonic rhythm out of.

Or mayhap he doesn't want you, flawed as you are… A woman laid low by migraines that reduced her to a pathetic, quivering mass.

After all, he'd made no attempt to see her today. Instead, he had paid a visit to Jane with the express purpose of sending her on to Mrs. Munroe's.

Chloe rubbed the lingering ache at the back of her neck. She needed to know, even as she feared the answers. Giving the bronze swan a last caress, she forced herself from her spot at the hearth and wound her way through the halls until she reached Leo's offices.

She lifted her hand to knock and then lowered it to her side.

Chloe raised it once more. *You needn't knock. He is your husband. And he has seen you at your absolute worst.* Surely that intimacy merited more than a perfunctory knock suited to a stranger or a servant.

Before her courage flagged, Chloe pressed the handle and let herself in.

His jacket thrown alongside the back of a nearby chair, Leo sat in his crisp white shirtsleeves. Surprise etched on his face, he hastily shoved back his seat and stood. "Chloe," he greeted. Almost as an afterthought, he tossed down his pen, the thin scrap of black bouncing between two open ledgers.

"Leo," she returned, quietly closing the door behind her.

"Come in. Come in," he said gruffly, motioning to the chair opposite him.

Come in.

How very different that gentle encouragement was from the man who'd ordered her to never enter his offices or ask him questions.

Clasping her hands before her in a demure display Mrs. Belden would have found pride in, Chloe marched over to the indicated seat. With each step that brought her closer, she struggled to return to the easy camaraderie they'd developed. And yet, what did she say to this man who'd seen her at her lowest, humbled and broken and so very battered?

One who sought to send her away.

Leo cleared his throat. "You are... well?" he finally asked haltingly.

And this... this politeness was so much worse. For he didn't know how to be around her, either, and the truth of that stung every corner of her heart. An urge to cry overwhelmed her. "I'm fine." In the end, Chloe opted for the directness that had so often had her mother on the cusp of tears. "Jane indicated that you'd spoken," she said on a rush. Grateful for the high-backed chair that served as a protective barrier between them, she clung to the top of the seat. "That you asked her to provide me the post of headmistress of Mrs. Munroe's."

Leo remained silent, and she railed at him to say something, to offer anything other than this stoic indifference. Chloe nudged her chin up. "Is it because I'm broken?" Her voice emerged weak to her own ears.

His mouth moved, but no words came out.

Chloe bit the inside of her cheek, wounding the flesh hard enough to draw blood. Her fear of how any man would see her and that condition had been just one more reason she'd vowed never to marry. But she wanted the headaches to not matter to this man. "If you are sending me away because of your soiree, I can host another." She hated the desperate quality in the pitch of her voice, but couldn't stop the words from spilling out. "They do not come that often." *Liar.* "I, of course, understand why you are upset, because you relied on the gathering, but..." She faltered as Leo moved out from behind the desk. He stopped with just a handbreadth between them. "But I can—" He touched a fingertip to her lips, stifling her false promises.

"I am not worried about the soiree," he murmured and then lowered his arm to his side. He took a hasty step away from her. She ached to feel the heat of his fleeting caress once more. And yet, he acted as if he were afraid to touch her.

"Your assignment, then?" she forced out on a faint whisper, mindful of the need for circumspection. "You cared about the event for what it meant to your work."

"That was the only reason it mattered," he confirmed.

He hadn't disputed her claims of being too flawed for him to want. That realization left a gaping hole in her heart. "I see," she said dumbly. Unable to meet his piercing eyes, she glanced down at the hem of her white dress, that color of innocence he so hated. "I'm sorry for the," she grimaced, "inconvenience posed. I trust your uncle was livid and…" She wrinkled her brow. *Except…* "But that was also pretend. You needn't have gained his approval for his funds, so—" *Stop rambling.* This time, Chloe ended the flow of unending words. A knot formed in her throat. "I should leave you to your business," she squeezed past it.

Leo followed her gaze to the leather folios that lay open.

How had she failed to see the time he'd spent in his offices? Proof had been there all along that he wasn't the indolent wastrel Society thought him.

Nay, he was an agent for the Crown, with a sharp wit and dangerously smooth intellect. He deserved more than a wife who was endlessly flawed in every way.

Burying her fisted hands along her skirts, she turned to go. Her quick strides sent her skirts whipping angrily about her ankles.

"Chloe," Leo called out, halting her flight.

Her tongue heavy in her mouth, Chloe faced him and stared back with a question in her eyes.

With languid steps, he ate away the space she'd put between them. "You aren't broken."

Her heart thumped an erratic little beat, and she waited for him to say more. She wished for additional words, ones where he asked her to stay and make a life with him. Ached for him to take her in his arms. At his prolonged silence, those foolish musings shattered and tumbled to her feet. "I know what I am, Leo," she said, her voice steeped in exhaustion. "People who are whole don't lose control of themselves and need to be shut away."

"Shh." He raised a fingertip to his own lips. How odd she'd never known that exhalation could emerge from a person as so very pleading.

But he'd seen her at her worst, and she'd not allow him to escape the truth that was her reality. "People like me are shut away, Leo. Sent to Bedlam."

"I would never do that." Such a wealth of hurt was contained within those five words, they splayed her open.

"No." The muscles of her throat worked over and over. "But you would send me away, just to a different place."

"It is what you want," he pointed out with a quiet pragmatism that set her teeth on edge.

"Do not presume to know what I want," she gritted out.

A pained laugh escaped him. "Chloe, you stated it in our contract."

She spun away, frustration rippling through her at his throwing that reminder in her face. "Is that all we are, then, Leo? Is that all we'll ever be?"

"Chloe," he said, a frown marring his lips. "You're only just feeling better—"

She recoiled. "Don't do that," she rasped. "Don't treat me like a fragile piece of glass. You were the only one who never did." *Because he didn't know the truth of your frailty.* "Don't do it now," she ordered.

"I'm not."

"You won't even touch me," she cried. "You are acting as if I'm broken, and I—"

He covered her mouth with his in a tender joining of their mouths that immediately sapped the frustration, fear, and fury overwhelming her. They were replaced with a honeyed warmth.

"You are not broken," he whispered against her mouth. He shifted his lips, journeying them down her neck. Her head fell back. "You are whole and perfect in every way, Chloe Dunlop." Hearing her name joined with his surname squeezed a pleased little moan from her. Her every sense and nerve were heightened by the flick of his tongue upon her heated flesh. Her lashes fluttered shut as he gently sucked at the skin where her pulse pounded. Then he was flicking his tongue over her lobe, the sensitive place under the shell of her ear.

Her legs weakened, and he immediately caught her, cradling her buttocks.

His tumescence throbbed against the swell of her belly, igniting a forbidden longing. Reflexively, she pressed herself against his length. The feel of him, like steel, burned through the fabric of her satin gown. That pulsing, radiating heat scorched her with its intensity.

Leo groaned, burying his face in her shoulder. "If I were a gentleman, I'd set you aside." Her headaches. "But I've only ever been a bastard, and I want you more than I've ever wanted another."

Her pulse leaped as he devoured her mouth with his. All gentleness stripped away, he slanted his lips over hers again and again in a primal meeting, fierce in his possession.

Chloe moaned, meeting every thrust and parry of his tongue, tangling the tip of hers with his. He drew her atop his oak-hard thigh. Her skirts rustled like a naughty ballad in her ears as he rocked himself against her aching core. "Leo," she moaned. She wanted this. Had wanted this from the moment he'd first taken her in his arms and given her a taste of passion.

He responded to her unspoken entreaty by slipping the bodice of her gown down and exposing her breasts to his attentions.

A keening cry tumbled from her lips as he filled his palms with those orbs, bringing them together, caressing, worshiping. "So beautiful. So perfect." Then he closed his mouth around one pebbled tip.

Her legs turned to jelly, and he easily took over the effort of keeping her upright.

Time, reason, and reality ceased to matter. As he suckled at that sensitized tip, Chloe was capable of nothing but feeling. Tangling her fingertips in her husband's silken strands, she held him in place, wanting this moment to go on forever. Wanting more. So much more.

Dimly, she registered his hands making work of the handful of buttons at the back of her gown.

Reality washed over her, dousing the conflagration he'd set with a blanket of ice-cold emptiness.

Gasping, Chloe stumbled out of his arms.

His eyes heavy with unsated passion, Leo glanced up.

Struggling to hold her dress in place, she backed away. *So beau-*

tiful. So perfect. And yet, she was none of those things, not in body, mind, or soul. "I can't... I'm sorry..." she panted.

While agony wreathed her husband's features, Chloe pushed awkwardly past him and raced out into the hall.

She pulled the door shut and then leaned her head against the oak surface.

Her body trembled.

Coward. You are a coward. You expected... nay, wanted your husband to share all his secrets, and yet, you would hide every last part of yourself from him.

Tears stinging her eyes, she fought back the useless drops.

Before her moment of bravado faltered, Chloe reached for the handle.

CHAPTER 29

HE'D HAD NO RIGHT TO touch her.

It was best for both of them if she went on her way and he resolved his assignment and then went on to whatever next case the Brethren tossed his way.

His body, still throbbing with an aching need for her, cared not for honor or the Brethren, or logic. It cared only about this unfulfilled longing to bind his body with hers.

Standing precisely where she'd left him when she fled, Leo ran trembling palms up and down his face. Then he registered the faint click and press of a handle as Chloe let herself back into his office.

Silent, the twenty paces between them a great chasm, Chloe leaned against the heavy panel. Her gaping dress was gathered tightly in her palms.

"I'm sorry," she whispered, clutching at the satin fabric like a warrior would his shield in battle.

He wouldn't have her apologies. She'd been clear from the start that she'd not share his bed. "Don't," he said hoarsely, his voice still graveled with his hungering for this woman. "You are correct. It would be unwise for either of us…" His words trailed off as she let the bodice of her gown sag.

Leo's mouth went dry as she stripped away the thin barrier left by her chemise so that her breasts were bared before him. He took a step closer, like Adam aching for the fruit that would condemn all.

Chloe drew in a long, slow, noisy breath and then turned.

Leo froze. All the life went out of him.

A buzzing filled his ears. The sound of his heartbeat thumping furiously was deafening. His vision tunneled on the crisscrossing of faded scars upon Chloe's small, white back. The marks decorated her flesh in swirls and stripes of long-faded red.

"My father was a drunkard," she said softly, directing the admission to the door.

"He beat you." His voice faltered as he forced the truth past his lips, an acknowledgment of what she'd already confirmed with the scars upon her skin. This was the one who'd broken her heart. Not a lover, but rather… the man who'd sired her.

"Regularly," she said matter-of-factly. Her always proud shoulders sagged slightly under that revelation. Then, with her infinite spirit and strength, she straightened them. The tensing rippled the intersecting stripes along her spine.

A piteous moan filled his office.

Did that tortured sound belong to her? To him? It was all jumbled and twisted. He'd ceased to exist outside the evidence of the suffering stamped upon her, the eternal marks of the evil done to her. Leo made fists so tightly, his nails shredded the skin of his palms, marking sharp crescents that did nothing to ease the horror slapping at his senses. It sucked the breath from his lungs and the thoughts from his head and left him reduced to an agonized mass.

Chloe proved herself braver than he could ever be, answering the quiet with, "I was four the first time."

His eyes slid closed. She'd been a babe as small as the tiny child he'd fenced with in Waverly's ballroom. *Oh, God.*

"Philippa and I were playing hide-and-go-seek," she went on, a detachedness to her sotto voce telling. "Mother told me never to bother my father when he was in his office, but he wasn't there. So I made use of his desk. I heard his footsteps and was excited to let him share in our game. I darted out. I asked him to keep me h-hidden." Her voice quaked.

Oh, God. I cannot. He did not want to hear the rest. Didn't want to know that, as a babe of four, she'd discovered the depths of cruelty in the man who'd sired her. And yet, neither could he stop her.

"He slapped me across the face." One hand came up to cup her left cheek, and the sight of her in solitary suffering ripped a hole through his heart. "He hit me so hard, my feet left the floor and I landed on my back. I couldn't even cry," she whispered. "I couldn't make a sound. Everything was just sucked out of me in that moment."

"Chloe," Leo whispered, her name a prayer layered with the anguish eating away at him like a vicious, slow-growing cancer that devoured all in its wake. The evidence had been there. Leo just hadn't seen it. Nay, he hadn't allowed himself to see it. She'd told him of her father's abuse of her brothers, and Leo's mind had not entered into the darkened territory where she was also a victim of that heinousness.

"I was so afraid of him, but hadn't believed he'd hit me because I entered his offices." Chloe laughed then, the sound of it so bloody awful for the misery contained within. "The following day, I plucked flowers from my mother's gardens and placed them atop the morning papers that always sat in wait for him at breakfast." She angled a glance over her shoulder at Leo. Her eyes were distant and glazed, belonging to one who'd forgotten Leo's presence and lived in the hell of her own mind. "He always wanted everything just so. The flowers… they didn't belong. He found me, playing in the nursery. He didn't say a word. He just picked up my cup and ball and beat me with them over and over again." Leo could not bear this. His breath rasped loud in his ears. "That's when I learned about monsters and hiding and running, Leo," she murmured, calm once more. She smiled sadly. "I even learned how to pick a lock to get myself into empty rooms to escape him."

An agony unlike Leo had ever endured, even at his *own father's* hands, gripped him. It filled him with a physical hungering to strip away her sadness and drag the demon who'd dared put his hands upon her from the grave and kill him dead all over again.

She hastily drew the garment back into place. "That is why I didn't want to marry. I've had the headaches since I was a girl. My siblings and mother kept them from him. They eventually sent me to a finishing school so I might escape my father."

But the damage had already been done by that point.

Can you truly trust that he won't send you on to Bedlam the first chance he has at his freedom…

At last, that veiled conversation between his wife and an irate Waverly made sense.

Leo pressed a fist to his mouth as every last wall he'd built about himself came toppling down, leaving him open and exposed and so wholly shattered by this woman... because of this woman.

The sight of her struggling to pull her chemise and gown back into place slashed across his soul. Wordlessly, he crossed over and took the sleeves of those delicate garments.

She bowed her head, avoiding his gaze.

Leo dropped to his knees and placed his lips along the stark white scar that began at the crest of her buttocks. He followed the puckered mark, trailing a path of kisses that ran the length of her back.

A broken sob escaped her.

"So beautiful," he whispered, kissing each stamp of a pain that would always be with her, wanting to chase it off and leave it with only good. He, Leo Dunlop, a bloody wastrel without a clue as to how to do that. Only knowing he wanted it for her.

Chloe softly wept. "I'm n-not." This was the vulnerable side of her. She was a woman who'd gone toe-to-toe with him at every turn, and she continued to ravage him.

Leo gathered her hand and raised it to his mouth. "There is no one more magnificent than you." In any way. "You are an Athena in mind, beauty, and spirit." With his lips, he worshipped every expanse of flesh. Kneeling at her feet, he brought her slowly around to face him.

Leo gazed up at her, entrusting the decision to her hands. If she rejected him, he'd be forever incomplete for not knowing her in this way. Before she'd come into his life, making love to her would have only ever been a mere physical act meant to sate their mutual lust for each other. Now, it represented an intimacy he yearned to share with her. But selflessly, he would suffer the loss of that intimacy if it was what she desired.

Chloe bit at her lower lip and then nodded slowly.

Coming to his feet, Leo swept her into his arms, holding her so close their hearts met. Not breaking stride, he stalked from the room with purposeful steps for his chambers.

Several maids with linens and dusters in their hands blushed and bolted down bisecting corridors.

Chloe buried her face in Leo's shoulder. "Everyone will talk."

"Let them. Nothing matters but your happiness." It slipped out, steeped in a truth so utterly foreign and so wholly right.

Leo took the stairs two at a time. They reached his bedchamber, and Leo let them in. He shoved the door closed hard with the heel of his boot. The force of it shook the frame. With an infinite tenderness he'd believed himself incapable of, Leo carried Chloe to the gilt-bronze kingwood bed and laid her down on the silk, crimson coverlet.

She pushed herself up onto her elbows. Some of the earlier passion receded as she examined the room with curiosity brimming in her eyes. "I did not appreciate yesterday how very… wicked your chambers are," she murmured contemplatively. Chloe touched her gaze on the nymph carved at the center of the headboard and the sirens stretched out on each poster. She studied the matching satine nightstands and armoire. "Do you know, I think it is rather… pretty? Elaborate, but there is a poetry to them." She stretched innocent fingertips to the gilded skirts upon the closest siren.

His lips twitched. "If you're more fascinated by my bedroom décor, love, then I've failed as a rake."

"Oh, no, never," she said quickly, coming up onto her knees. "I was quite…" She blinked wildly. "You're teasing."

Leo shucked a boot. "Indeed."

"I thought you didn't tease, Lord Tennyson."

He paused, awkwardly balanced in his efforts to remove his other gleaming black Hessian. "I didn't…" Their gazes locked. "Until you." He hadn't felt, laughed, or loved completely until her.

Leo fell on his arse.

Scrambling to the edge of the mattress, Chloe peered down at him. A smile teased her lips. "Are you—"

"Fine," he muttered. His bruised ego ached worse than his posterior. With that, he wrenched the boot free and tossed it aside. The crimson Aubusson carpet muffled its fall to the floor. Kneeling, Leo met Chloe at the side of his bed and kissed the smile from her lips.

A breathy little sigh left her, allowing him entry, and he slipped his tongue inside, tangling that flesh with hers. Cupping her about the nape, he angled her head to better avail himself of her mouth.

Wrapping her arms about his neck, she met his kiss with a wild abandon. The tip of her tongue as it touched his was like a brand that seared him, left an imprint that would mark him as only hers until he drew his last breath and went on happily to the hereafter because of the joy she'd brought him.

His chest rising and falling, Leo crawled onto the bed. In synchronic harmony, she inched back so that they lay at the center of the feather mattress.

Leo slid the delicate puff sleeves of her modest dress past her shoulders, kissing a path down the silken softness of her arms. "I'll never look upon a white gown again without thinking of this moment," he rasped against her chest.

Her head fell back as a soft laugh shook her frame, the pale swells of her breasts rising and falling. "You despise white."

"Never," he said, filling his palms with those orbs.

Whimpering, Chloe bit at her lower lip. Several curls popped free, framing her damp brow. "O-oh, yes," she panted. He massaged her breasts, weighing the flawless feel of her against him. How perfectly she fit into his hands, as though she'd been made for him... nay, as though their bodies had been made for each other. "Y-you said as much at our f-first meeting."

"Surely not," he said as he closed his lips around a swollen peak. He drew the bud deep, suckling and teasing.

"Mmmmm." She encouraged him with the tilt of her hips. Her body's involuntary search for him sent another surge of blood to his shaft. Never before had he been consumed with this need. Before Chloe, it had been about sex... a surcease that offered an infinitesimal release from the ugliness of life. After her, everything had changed, because of her, and he would never be the same. And, God help him, he never wanted to be the same.

Turning his attentions to her neglected breast, Leo worked her gown over her hips. With the same spirit she'd shown since their first meeting, she kicked it aside. Next, Leo slipped her chemise off until she lay bare before him in all her naked splendor.

Chloe had known so much pain in the course of her life that she'd never known her body could also be capable of such splendorous… bliss, this heady, dizzying magic that robbed one of one's breath, logic, and sense. It transformed one, instead, into a bundle of nerves capable of only feeling.

Leo guided her back until a mound of pillows cased in satin met her. Not taking his hot gaze from her, he pulled his shirt overhead and threw it to the floor.

Her breath caught. From the rippling muscles of his stomach and his narrow hips, he was a study of masculine perfection. And yet… as he reached for the waistband of his trousers, Chloe came up on her knees.

He froze. There was a question in his gaze as she drifted closer.

Chloe's throat worked painfully as she trailed a fingertip lightly over the small, circular, puckered scar embedded within his right shoulder. "Who did this?" she whispered, reality intruding.

"It was a long time ago."

She shook her head. "That isn't what I asked," she scolded, lifting her eyes to his, wanting to know every secret he carried. Wanting to share in his life in every way.

"When Boney was in power, he sent men to sow the seeds of discontent here in England. It was my role to identify them… and stop them."

Stop them.

A chill scraped along her spine at the pointed reminder of the perilous nature of what he did. "They shot you," she whispered.

He lifted his lips in a wry grin. "One of them did." Chloe caressed the bullet hole left, that a few inches lower would have snuffed out Leo's existence and the reason for more light and happiness than she'd ever known.

Chloe continued her agonized search elsewhere to other jagged marks left upon him. How many other times had he suffered?

Her husband caught her wrist and dragged it to his mouth. "They are gone, Chloe. And I don't want their ghosts here now. I only want you." He came down over her once more, taking her lips as they went. The mattress cushioned her fall as she bounced within its feather-soft folds.

Leo stroked a hand up her stocking-clad thigh. She held her breath in anticipation of the touch that had the power to break her into a million useless shards of tingling sensation.

Instead, he rolled her knitted silk hose down, kissing each portion of her limbs as he exposed first one leg and then the other to the cool air.

Chloe's lashes fluttered. The act he performed was one she or a maid had seen to countless times, and yet, Leo transformed it into something so very different. It was heady, erotic, and scintillating. He drew her foot to his mouth and touched his lips to the sensitive skin of her arch.

A breathy half laugh, half moan pulled from her throat.

"Since I first had your ankle in my hand, I've dreamed of this, Chloe." His breath came labored, his chest rising and falling heavily. "I dreamed of exploring every nuanced curve of your body, discovering what makes you scream to the heavens, and then bringing you to pleasure after you climb that peak." Gently lowering her leg so her knee remained bent, Leo shucked his trousers, unrepentant and proud in his naked form.

Chloe's mouth went dry, and she ran the tip of her tongue over her lips.

He was… "Magnificent," she whispered, devouring him with her eyes. His long shaft jutted out high and proud amidst a thatch of dark, golden curls. It stood straight against his stomach. The sight of him drew forth images of Michelangelo's masterpiece David, but Leo was so much more beautiful for the life that rippled from his frame. "You are magnificent."

He grinned. It was a pleased masculine smile as he drew her naked body close.

Electric heat coursed through her, and she twined her arms about his neck, bringing him down for another kiss.

Their mouths danced in a passionate give-and-take.

And then he was moving lower, worshiping each breast, pulling pleading, incoherent whimpers from her mouth. He slid a finger inside her sodden channel, and Chloe mewled shamelessly, unapologetic in her desires. "Leo," she begged, and he slipped another long digit within her.

"Your body was made for this, Chloe," he crooned, sweat beading on his brow. "Spread your arms wide," he ordered, a man wholly in command. In this, she could deny him nothing.

She obeyed, stretching her fingertips out beside her.

"Do not touch me. Use your hands for nothing. Just feel."

He slid down her body until his face lay between her legs.

Chloe arched her neck in a bid to see… "What are you…"

"Shh," he instructed, his voice a sough upon her aching core. And then he buried his face between her legs.

Chloe collapsed against the mattress. All the air exploded from her lungs on a long, endless hiss. She moved her palms reflexively. Not shifting his attentions from the magic he wove, Leo stretched his arms beside him, capturing her wrists, forcing them back to her sides as he worked a slow, exquisite torture on her.

He teased her nub, flicking his tongue back and forth over the sensitive flesh until Chloe's hips, of their own volition, were rising and falling.

Leo laved her channel, stroking her with his tongue.

She bucked, fighting for all her worth to keep her arms as he'd instructed. But as his mouth continued its torture, the ache at her center was excruciating and splendorous all at the same time. Her feet arched, and she scrabbled with the sheets. Pleading. Begging. Weeping.

And then he drew back. The loss of him was so keen, she cried out.

Chloe dimly registered him lying between her legs and his length nestling at the gates of her femininity.

He thrust deep. Her sopping channel slicked the way for his entry, but still, the tearing of that thin scrap of flesh pulled a shuddery gasp from her.

Leo caught the trailing end of that sound, swallowing it with his kiss.

He stilled, his chest frantically rising under the restraint he showed.

Chloe caressed her fingertips over his lower back.

He placed a kiss at her temple. "I am so sorry," he whispered.

Laboring to keep her lashes open, she held his gaze. "There are no regrets here. Not between us, and certainly not now."

Heat blazed in his cerulean-blue eyes. With a primitive groan, he began to move. Slowly at first. In and out. Over and over. Until all pain receded and desire invaded every corner of her being, so all she was capable of was feeling.

Chloe lifted her hips, meeting his powerful strokes. With every lunge that found him buried deep inside her, she climbed higher and higher.

"Come for me," he cried. His hair fell across his brow, and he touched her to the quick.

Chloe screamed over and over and burst into a million shards of blissful, beautiful feeling. Leo cried out. His primal shout blended with her endless call of his name as he tossed his head back and poured himself inside her.

Gasping for air, Leo went limp and collapsed.

As he rolled off her and drew her into the nook of his shoulder, Chloe burrowed into him. And with a contented smile on her lips, she slept.

CHAPTER 30

LEO WAS SENDING HER AWAY.

It was a discovery that had come to her not as she'd awakened in his bed after an endless night of lovemaking to find him gone. Or to find the sheets beside her wrinkled and cold from one who'd long taken his leave of her.

Rather, it had been more definitive, in the form of an army of maids packing her trunks and valises the following morning.

Standing in the doorway, Chloe opened and closed her mouth, trying to bring forth questions for Doris, who made a point of avoiding her gaze. "What is going on?" she asked. All the young women came to a screeching halt with their activities.

The five servants looked between one another, before homing in on Chloe's lady's maid.

Doris gulped. "M-my lady," she squeaked.

A sick sensation pitted in Chloe's belly. "Nothing," she said tightly. Fury, hurt, and humiliation all roiled in her chest. "Nothing at all." She'd not make a cake of herself in front of her staff. Nor would she misdirect her upset.

Spinning on her heel, she stalked off.

Strapping footmen bearing trunks hurried out of her way, allowing her to blaze a direct path through the bustling halls, down the stairs, and onward to Leo's office. Not bothering with a knock, she shoved the door open. "What is the meaning of—"

Empty.

Chloe did a sweep of the room.

Empty of not just the man who called this his kingdom, but also... his sideboard.

Her lips parted, and she ventured deeper into the room, searching for the broad mahogany piece filled with bottles and decanters.

"May I help you, my lady?"

Chloe gasped and spun about to face the young servant. Pressing a hand to her racing heart, she stifled a frown. Leo's clerk, Holman, dogged her footsteps when Leo wasn't about. He was a shadow that she could not shake.

"I'm looking for my husband."

"His lordship has gone out." He stretched an arm out in an obsequious gesture that urged her from the room.

Chloe pursed her lips. As she was the lady of the household, his superior attitude grated. "Do you know when I can expect him back?" she countered, planting her feet on the floor.

The young man adjusted his spectacles, but not before she caught the flash of annoyance in his eyes. "I wouldn't presume to press his lordship for such details."

And yet, he thought nothing of steering her from her husband's offices like she was a naughty child underfoot. Chloe's days of being ordered about by any man had come and gone long ago. "Thank you, Holman. That will be all."

The clerk went slack-jawed at the dismissal. "I must really insist, my lady—"

"Holman, that will be all," Tomlinson called beyond the younger servant's shoulder.

Holman yanked at his crimson lapels and, with a deep bow, quit the rooms.

"My apologies for Holman, my lady. He meant no offense."

And yet, nonetheless, he'd caused it. "He follows me about," she said bluntly. Just as he'd done since the carriage accident days earlier.

"His lordship asked Holman to look after you." Tomlinson's gaze caught hers. "He takes pride in his work for the marquess."

Chloe opened her mouth and then registered the glint in the older servant's eyes. Why... Holman was in Leo's employ, but not as a mere clerk. Of course. The timing of his presence now made sense. And yet, the other implication was that Tomlinson also knew of Leo's role within the Home Office. What did that mean about the butler's role in the household? Was everyone more than they seemed?

"Is there anything else you require, my lady?" Tomlinson murmured, his expression guarded once more.

"No," she said slowly. "That is all. Wait," she called as he turned to go. Chloe motioned to the barren space at the opposite end of Leo's office. "Do you know where my husband's sideboard has gone?"

Tomlinson inclined his head. "He ordered it removed."

"Why would he do that?" she blurted. As long as she'd known her husband, he'd been comfortable with a drink in hand. Was it just another display of selling things off to cover manufactured debts?

"I'm afraid that is a question best reserved for his lordship."

His lordship, who'd ordered her belongings packed and then summarily disappeared. She clenched her jaw as her earlier anger surged forward.

"And what question is that?" the unaffected voice that had become so very beloved drawled from the doorway, pulling her attention from Tomlinson.

Wordlessly, the butler slipped past Leo.

Her heart fluttered.

This was the first time she'd seen him since they'd made love. She roved her gaze over him. His tan, front-button trousers clung to his long, powerful legs. "Leo," she greeted, priding herself on that steady deliverance. With a burgundy tailcoat accentuated by black sleeves, a midnight cravat, and matching brocade waistcoat, he had the look of a devil who'd come to tempt.

"Chloe," he murmured.

Only she knew there was so much more to Leo Dunlop, the Marquess of Tennyson. Her reasons for searching him out became mixed up as her body burned with the memories of the night before. The endless hours they'd spent learning each other's bodies, the pleasure he had brought her, and her discovering what brought him pleasure in return. Her cheeks warmed, and she damned that pathetic response... when he should be so... aloof. So somber.

He was framed in the doorway, his chiseled features bearing not so much as a hint of the teasing rake who'd stolen her heart. She hated him for so effortlessly slipping into this unreadable stranger.

They spoke at the same time.

"Where—"

"I have—"

Leo was quick to motion her on.

"Your sideboard is missing."

It was the most nonsensical of places to start—and yet, the safest.

Leo entered the room. "I had it removed… along with all the spirits."

Chloe fluttered a hand about her throat. "Why?"

"After what you shared?" He curled his hands. "You think I could drink again, knowing everything you shared?"

At that sacrifice, every last corner of her heart was lost to him. Tears clogged her throat. Not even her brothers had managed, or so much as attempted, that feat for her or the other Edgerton women. "Thank you," she whispered. Surely those were not the actions of one who wished to sever their connection.

A blush splotched Leo's cheeks, an endearing boylike flash of color that marked him so different than the rake who'd scandalized her with his words and actions in Lord Waterson's residence. "I've greater restraint and self-control than most know."

He cleared his throat. "I have something for you."

"Oh?" Surprise pulled that little exclamation from her. She'd never been one to want or seek out baubles and fripperies, but there was a tender intimacy in her husband going out and purchasing something with only her in mind. Relief drove away the earlier anger and unrest. Mayhap he wasn't sending her away. Mayhap they were going somewhere together. Mayhap—

Leo drummed his fingertips once again and—

Chloe's eyebrows shot up.

More than thirty inches in height, a fawn mastiff trotted forward.

Leo snapped his fingers once, and the dog sank onto his haunches at his side.

"You bought me…"

"A dog," he finished for her. "More specifically, a mastiff."

She cocked her head, and the dog, with enormous jowls and a black muzzle, matched her movements.

Leo strolled deeper into the room. The mastiff remained duti-fully frozen where he'd sat. Almost as an afterthought, Leo tapped his leg twice.

The dog sprang into movement. Trotting over, he joined Leo and waited expectantly. "You aren't pleased," Leo noted.

"I… am," she started, but words failed her. He'd never again spo-ken about that particular term of their arrangement, and the more she'd known her husband, she'd not wished to force him into that commitment.

Leo pointed a finger at Chloe. The mastiff quit Leo's side and walked over to Chloe. His nails were noiseless upon the Aubusson carpet.

"He is *big*," she finally settled for. A coarse tongue lapped her fingers, and she started. Big, brown eyes stared back.

"Down," Leo commanded. The mastiff immediately sank into position, resting his head between his paws. "He is large, but they are, by nature, a gentle and loyal breed," he informed as he strolled to his desk, shucking his black gloves as he went.

Chloe stared on, feeling like one who'd entered onto the stage without the benefit of her lines. "He is lovely," she praised, going to a knee beside Leo's gift. She stroked the dog between his ears, and he leaned into the caress. "I simply had imagined we would have a mastiff *puppy*." Not a dog that was surely fourteen stone and more than two and a half feet tall.

Leo stuffed his gloves inside his jacket. "He is the finest in England. It's taken me some time to find him. He's fully trained and will serve as a masterful guard dog for you."

"For me," she repeated dumbly. "Not 'us'?"

He winced. "Chloe," he began.

Her eyebrows snapped into a single line. Why… he was pawning her off on a dog. "Are you sending me away?" she demanded.

He paused a fraction of a moment. Then he enthroned himself in that miserable-looking chair, a king in command of all.

She sucked in a breath. "You are." It was as she'd expected. "It's why you bought me the *dog*."

Leo swiped a hand over his eyes. "His name is Henry."

Chloe rocked on her heels. "My God, you don't deny it."

He sighed. "There is nothing to deny."

His absolute indifference melted away the last of her pride, suffusing her breast with so much hurt, it left a sharp ache that would never go away. "I don't care what his name is," she cried.

Henry whined, shifting his head back and forth between his paws. Chloe stormed Leo's desk. Her skirts snapped noisily about her ankles. "How dare you?" she seethed, feeding the fury to keep from buckling under the hurt. She dropped her palms on his desk. "Do you have nothing to say?"

"What is there to say?" he asked in agonized tones. She celebrated them, for at least they meant he felt… something and not that absolute apathy. "I've given you everything you asked for, Chloe." He stood and placed his palms upon the immaculate surface of his desk so that they were like mirror reflections of wholly different images. "You desired your independence, Mrs. Munroe's, the dog—" Henry yapped once in canine affront.

"Is that what this is?" Her voice trembled. "You checking off items on a list?" Hurt bled from that question, and she could not hold it at bay. Nor did she want to. She wanted him to know everything that was in her heart. She wanted no more secrets between them. And more… she wanted a life… with him in it.

"I don't…" Leo lifted his palm in supplication. "I've never done this, Chloe," he said pleadingly. "Not with any woman. I'm trying to give you what you want."

"I want you. I love you." The truth burst from her, echoing in the quiet. Chloe and Leo went still. Terror, and some other undefined emotion, glittered in his eyes. She gentled her voice and sailed around his desk. "I love you, Leo," she repeated.

All the muscles of his face contorted. "No."

"Yes," she said again. Reaching up, she framed his face with her hands. "I love you," she said a third time, needing him to hear it. Needing him to believe it. Wanting those three words to matter to him.

His eyes slid briefly closed. "No one loves me," he said hoarsely, his words lancing at her soul. A pained chuckle shook his frame. "No one even likes me."

Her lips twitched. "I like you very much. I love you even more." Chloe's smile faded, and she lowered her palms to his chest. His heart pounded erratically, like he'd just run a great race. Even though she'd suffered at the hands of her father, she'd had a loving mother and siblings about. Despite the uncle he'd had about, he'd lived under the thumb of cruelty and hatred. She wanted to spend the rest of her days replacing those memories with ones they shared. Chloe smoothed her palms over the lapels of his burgundy tailcoat. "I see who you really are."

She braced for the protestations—that, this time, did not come.

Leo's throat bobbed. "I love you, Chloe. I never knew there was a woman like you. You taught me to laugh and reminded me of what it is to be human…" He tugged his fingers through his hair. The abrupt movement jarred her arms and sent them back to her sides. "And you're so bloody clever and spirited." Each beautifully sincere compliment that tumbled from him widened her smile. Leo touched his forehead to hers. "I love you," he echoed the pronouncement. Her heart lifted, soared, and then took flight. "It is why I need to send you away." And that wildly beating organ crashed to the earth.

"I don't want to go."

"You do," he begged. "It's all you've ever wanted."

"That was before you." Chloe caught his hands and twined them with her own, joining their digits. "Mrs. Munroe's was the dream I aspired to." Only, how little she'd thought of the post of headmistress… or anything or anyone since Leo. "You made me see that we can have that, together. A place where young girls… and boys can be educated and safe." He, with what he'd shared of his own past, had opened her eyes to the fact that young women were not the only ones in desperate need of an institution where people cared for them. "You can still make a difference," she told him as she glanced to the door and then lowered her voice. "Outside the work you've done." He'd given his life for the Crown. It was time he took for himself.

A resounding silence met her profession, stirring her nervousness. "Say something," she urged.

"You have to leave."

She firmed her mouth. "How long? Until your assignment is complete? A week? A fortnight?" Her voice climbed as she spoke. "A year?" How little she knew about his work. But she knew enough that she despised the whole damned Home Office, because its hold on him was greater than any mistress or lover.

Leo released her hands. The separation, telling and powerful for what it conveyed, split a hole in her chest. "Chloe—"

"Don't," she pleaded, laying herself bare before him. "I'll not let you push me away as you did Daphne. I'm not afraid. I can face anything with you."

"What if we had children?"

If.

Two letters and one syllable that ripped up her hope for a future.

"We would care for them and love them together."

"You and they would always be at risk, and I'm selfish." Leo slid his gaze past the top of her head. "I'm a bastard in every sense of the word," he continued in somber tones. "But you've shown me that I'm not so much a bastard that I'd put my happiness before your safety and well-being. I love you enough to let you go."

Chloe grabbed him by his lapels and dragged herself up onto her tiptoes so she could meet his gaze. "I do not want to go," she gritted out.

He offered her a sad smile. "The choice isn't yours. It never was."

She sank back. The weight of finality washed over her. It filled her with panic, left her in tumult. "What if I'm already with child?" she asked, her voice pitched.

A brief light glinted in his eyes, and then that glimmer was extinguished. "Send word if you discover you're increasing."

That was it.

He reached inside his jacket and handed her a sheet of ivory vellum.

"What is this?" she asked, already unfolding the page, seeing before he spoke.

"They are Henry's commands. He'll answer to each. If someone wishes you harm, the directives are at the bottom there." Leo pointed over her shoulder, and she slapped his hand away.

Fueled by anger and hurt, she stalked off, putting space between them. "You're a coward," she spat.

He shrugged. "I never professed to be anything more."

"What is the command for 'go to hell'?" she clipped out. Fumbling with the page, she ran her eyes over it and then patted her leg once.

Henry pushed up onto all fours. As she yanked the door open, he fell into step beside her.

Four hours later, after all the carriages had been packed, Chloe boarded her husband's conveyance.

And left.

Two hours later

Her body angled toward the window, Chloe stared out at the passing landscape as the London streets first gave way to the hint of countryside.

He'd sent her away. And she'd cajoled, pleaded, and given every reason in her heart why he should share his life with her, and none of it had mattered.

In the end, she'd proven no different than Lady Daphne.

Reflected back in the crystal pane was her brother, Gabriel, on the opposite bench.

Cramped on the carriage floor between them sat Henry, panting loudly. Head resting on Gabriel's knee, the dog drooled.

At any other time, Chloe would have been filled with amusement by her ever-proper brother being slobbered upon by a dog the size of a horse.

"Despite what you believe, I didn't want this, Chloe," Gabriel finally said, breaking the tense quiet that had followed them since they'd left London.

"Indeed?" Meeting his glance in the window, she arched an eyebrow. "This from the man who has done everything since I married to separate me from my husband?"

He winced. "I deserve that."

"You deserve more than that," she said coolly. She could forgive him for not having been the brother she'd wanted him to be while their father was living. But she could not forgive his absolute unwillingness to accept her marriage and try to forge a friendship with Leo.

"Damn it, Chloe," he snapped in a shocking break from his composure. "I made efforts with Tennyson." Henry's head snapped up, and he growled at Gabriel. Casting an uneasy glance at the dog, when he again spoke, Gabriel did so in quiet tones. "Surely you see that?"

If she were being truthful with herself, she'd acknowledge there was some merit to that claim.

As if he'd sensed a crack and sought to slip in, Gabriel edged around Henry's massive head so he sat closer to Chloe.

"He was singing tavern ditties at dinner," Gabriel reminded.

"Humming," she mumbled. Her heart tugged at the memory. "I was singing tavern ditties with him." That had been the same night he'd fenced with her nieces and first slipped inside her heart.

"And after our attempts to include him for drinks, he insulted Waterson."

For reasons her brother didn't know and couldn't understand. Leo had merely been playing the part of diffident scoundrel to gather information about the earl's possible role in the Cato Event. Chloe chewed at her lower lip. Leo had been fearful she'd attempt to come to his defense and expose his role. How well he knew her. For in this instance, with her brother's ill opinion of Leo, it was a battle to keep the secret.

Nonetheless, she'd pledged her silence. So she said nothing.

"I merely ask you to understand why I felt the way I did toward Tennyson. I do not, however, feel the same way I did."

She snorted. "It is far easier to profess yourself Leo's friend and speak of peace between you when you've gotten what you always sought—our separation."

The carriage hit a large bump, and the conveyance swayed. Lurching sideways, Chloe caught the edge of her seat and balanced herself.

"I never said I was a friend, per se," he drawled. "Just that I don't feel the same pressing need to see you widowed."

She glowered back.

Her brother sighed and swiped a hand over his face. "I was jesting. In part."

"Somberness suits you more than sarcasm."

All his earlier levity faded. "Yes, and happiness suits you. It always has," Gabriel said quietly. "You were always a scared, silent child, and I hated that for you because I remember," his gaze grew distant, "who you once were. I remembered when you laughed and smiled, and it was so very fleeting before..." His voice cracked, and he looked away. Henry nudged at his hand, and Gabriel automatically patted the top of the dog's head.

"Before Father beat all joy from me," she supplied, finally able to utter those words.

Tears formed a glossy shimmer over Gabriel's eyes. "Before that.

And somehow," he whispered, "you… found the ability to do all those things again… to laugh and be mischievous and spirited. I both admired that and feared it would be extinguished. I was so determined to protect that joy that I stopped truly considering what made you happy. Your books. Mrs. Munroe's."

Chloe traced a distracted circle on her skirts. "Mrs. Munroe's was just a dream. I know that now. It was an escape. Would I have been happy there… before?" Before Leo had entered her life and shown her the true meaning of joy? "I think I would have always been… content, but nothing more."

So why are you letting Leo send you away there now? Why should you surrender the hopes you truly carry for you and Leo? Why, when you know he loves you?

If she let Leo push her away, then she was no different from Daphne.

"Stop the carriage," she breathed. Heart thundering, Chloe shot a hand up and knocked hard on the ceiling. "Stop the carriage."

The conveyance came to a jarring, lurching halt that threw her against the opposite side of the vehicle.

With dust and gravel still settling outside the windows, Chloe sat motionless. "I'm not going, Gabriel," she said, smiling her first smile since she'd taken her leave of Leo. "I'm returning to Leo."

Her brother's lips moved with no words coming out for a long while and then, "Your husband insisted that I see you to Mrs. Munroe's," he said regretfully. "He paid me a visit and explained you would be in danger if you remain in London." Her breath caught. He'd confided that to Gabriel. "Chloe, your husband wants you safe. I don't know what threat he intends to keep you away from, but in putting your well-being before all, he's earned my respect."

That was why he'd sent her. Because of his assignment. Hope hammered a wild beat in her chest.

She narrowed her eyes. "Gabriel, have you ever known me to do what others expect of me?" she asked in her best Mrs. Belden's chiding tones.

"No," he mumbled.

Nor did she attempt to begin now.

The driver pulled the door open. Henry immediately sat up, his ears going up, as he fixed on Daily. "My lady?" Tugging off his cap, the servant darted a nervous gaze between his mistress and the enormous dog filling the carriage.

Chloe offered a cheerful wave. "We're returning to London."

That earned his full attention. "But his lordship—"

"Isn't here. I am. I'm her ladyship, and as such, I'm ordering you to return me at once."

Daily clutched his cap close. "But…" He glanced at Gabriel.

Chloe faced her brother. Their gazes locked.

He shrugged. "Her ladyship instructed you to turn the carriage around."

A wide smile turned Chloe's lips up at the corners.

A short while later, she was returning home to her husband… and their future, together.

CHAPTER 31

¶IT WAS DONE.

The single most difficult, excruciating assignment of his miserable existence—he'd set Chloe free.

And never before had he felt more miserable.

Seated in his office, just as he'd been since Chloe left, Leo steepled his fingers, rested them under his chin… and just stared.

Even the pain of losing Daphne Smith hadn't cleaved him in half. Not like this. That had been a whirlwind courtship. He'd not shared any parts of his past with Daphne, but had kept a safe barrier. When he'd sent her away, the knowledge that she was safe had been enough.

In this case, with Chloe… it wasn't enough. Greedily, he wanted every gift she'd held out. He wanted to give up the Brethren and have a marriage with Chloe and golden-haired girls with her spirit and smile. He grimaced. Mayhap not girls. Little girls grew into women, and women were prey to scoundrels like him.

And yet, there was the Cato case… which, if the information Holman had unearthed and turned over to Leo's care was accurate, represented a greater threat. For it would mean there were members within their midst who'd stood to profit from the assassination of Lord Liverpool…

It would mean there were traitors among the Brethren.

It was an earth-shattering discovery… and still, for the peril it represented, he could think solely of his wife—and how sending her away shattered a heart he'd not even known he was in possession of.

A knock sounded at the door.

He let his hands drop to the arms of his chair. "Enter," he called out, a nonsensical hope that she'd defied his orders and returned instantly crushed.

Holman stood framed in the doorway. "Viscount Rowley to see you, my lord."

Just like that, every thought of Chloe slipped to the back of Leo's mind as every sense went on alert. "Show him in and then shut the door," he ordered.

"As you wish." His assistant went rushing off.

Leo pulled open the center desk drawer and withdrew a stack of folded notes. Then, retrieving the folders from the locked nook built within the left side of the unit, he took out the towering files contained within. He positioned everything neatly before him, just as Holman reappeared.

"Lord Rowley," he announced.

"Rowley, to what do I owe the honor of this unexpected visit?" he drawled, reclining in his chair.

Leo caught the tightening of his superior's mouth at the blatant show of disrespect.

"Tennyson," Rowley greeted like one making his hello to a favored friend and not the agent who'd roused his fury for the length of their tenure together. But then, the viscount had always displayed a veneer of civility that fit with his image of respectable lord.

Ducking his head, Holman beat a swift retreat, closing the door in his wake.

As soon as the door shut, Rowley's façade cracked. "Mine isn't a social visit. I'd rather keep company with the slime in the streets than you, Tennyson."

"Business, then."

Rowley pulled the pistol out of his waistband.

All Leo's nerves went on alert. He made himself go motionless.

Crossing over, the viscount laid the weapon on the edge of the desktop and slid it forward, so the gleaming metal was mere inches from Leo's fingertips. Rowley sat. "Tomlinson must be getting old, ceding control of your household to a young pup like Holman. Or your judgment has faltered. Which is it, hmm?" he asked, folding his hands atop his belly.

Leo weighed his words.

Before he could reply, Lord Rowley made a clucking sound that set his jowls jiggling, giving him the look of a farmhouse rooster. "Come, come, dear boy. Where's the bluster and bravado you've shown? You're always ready with a snappy response. Hardly ever thoughtful." He jabbed a finger at Leo's desk. "You owe your placement to your uncle. But then, everyone within the Brethren knows that."

Leo scoffed. "Do you believe I give a damn what you or anyone thinks about me?"

Rowley drummed his fingertips in a grating rhythm. "Tell me, where is Lady Tennyson?"

His body tensed, and it took every lesson he'd been handed as a member of the Brethren to not lose his masterful control. "Why don't you say what it is you came to say?" he warned.

"Hmm." Leaning forward, Rowley picked up the gleaming pistol and passed it back and forth between his hands.

Leo sharpened his gaze on the deliberate movements meant to intimidate. He'd faced far greater threats and foes than the bastard before him.

"I credited the papers and gossip as rubbish. I assumed your marriage was nothing but an orchestrated attempt to maintain your position... but it seems there was merit to the claims. You've been tamed by a proper English lady."

Leo's fingers could have left marks in the wooden arms of his chair as the viscount stoked a volatile rage inside him.

The viscount abruptly stopped. He returned the gun to Leo's desk, pointing the handle directly at him. "You could not abandon the damned case, could you?" Rowley asked crisply.

At last, they'd stopped playing this game of cat and mouse. "You arrived sooner than I'd expected."

"You pieced together the truth about the Cato Street Conspiracy faster than... oh, hell, I trusted no one would gather the details, and certainly not you."

After Peterloo, none would have dared look further than insurrections against the government. Leo flashed a cold grin. "I realized I was only looking at the surface. That there was more there." Chloe's tenacity in uttering those words over and over had taken root in his brain in a way that had allowed him to see the obvious facts he'd been missing. One who'd made a fortune off the slave trade, Rowley would have always had reason to resent Lord Liverpool's push to abolish it. "Cut into your profits, did he?"

The viscount pursed his mouth. "What was it to him whether a man deals in the sale of savages?"

Leo didn't so much as flinch at that ruthlessness. It was the level of avarice and evil he'd confronted countless times in his career. "And he is coming next for your slaves altogether, isn't he?" he taunted, reveling in the splotchy color that filled his superior's cheeks.

"The king and Parliament had their scapegoats in those commoners, and the Brethren were content to close the case. I could have been free of that damned Liverpool." The viscount wagged his finger the way one of Leo's too-stern tutors used to. "You could not leave it alone. But no matter, after tonight, you will cease to be a problem for me."

Keep him talking.

"Lord Liverpool saw the slave trade abolished. Murdering him wouldn't see it restored."

"No, it won't. But my business ventures in India and the Caribbean are at risk as long as he pushes forward legislation that defies common business sense."

"You mean slavery," Leo jeered. "Your businesses are built by the work you force others to do without any recompense."

"Oh, the hilarity." Rowley laughed uproariously, the tinge of madness sending his mirth spiraling. "You of all people preaching to me about morality." He dusted tears of amusement from his eyes. "I'll not debate with you on a matter of logic that is beyond you. You need to be dealt with."

Ice scraped his spine. "Murder me," Leo stated. "You're referring to my murder." Of course, that end had been inevitable since he'd stumbled upon his superior's complicity.

"It didn't have to be this way." Rowley tacked that on, almost as an afterthought. "I didn't want to kill you," he admitted. "Oh, I gladly wished you dead and will be happy when you're, at last, in the ground, but I wouldn't have sullied my hands with your death."

"But you will now," Leo noted calmly. From the corner of his eye, he measured the distance between him and the gun on his desk.

"Pfft, please, I already told you. I don't plan on wasting the effort it would cost me to lift my hand and put that deserved bullet between your eyes. Why, I even threw my wife at you, but your uncle saved your post… once more."

"So that is why your wife was so bloody tenacious." Leo chuckled, biding his time, waiting. "To think that all along she truly was just a whore."

"Attempting to get a rise out of me?" Rowley arched an eyebrow. "I don't give a jot who she spreads her legs for." He paused. "Unlike you."

Leo's spine went ramrod straight. *Do not take that bait. He's trying to unsettle you.* "You foresee this meeting ending with my death, and yet, you don't intend to do it yourself?"

The viscount tossed his arms wide. "Don't be silly. You are going to see to the honors yourself." He waved four of his fingers at the instrument in question.

Leo glanced from the viscount to the gun and then back to the viscount. Mad. The man had gone utterly mad. "Just why would I do that?" he drawled.

"Because if you don't," Rowley all but purred, "then while I keep you company, I'll send a loyal servant on to deal with your wife. Her brother has surely deposited her by now."

Leo started.

"Didn't believe I knew you'd scuttled her off with Waverly as a companion?" He chortled. "I know… everything. And your lack of cooperation will result in her death."

Terror held him in its unrelenting grip at Rowley's gleeful threat. Every last fear he'd carried—the one that had kept him a bachelor and then had him send Chloe away—assailed him. On the heels of that came a belated, chilling realization…

Rowley had infiltrated the ranks of the Brethren. He was commanding agents within.

"You appear more amenable," Rowley noted.

"You expect me to put a bullet in my head?" he asked, searching for time. "To spare a woman?"

"Your staff talks. You have been unable to keep your hands off the pretty thing. And you sending the chit away speaks enough to how you feel about the lady."

Rowley had him.

Refusing to be bested by Rowley without the fight he craved, Leo yawned. "You're an even more shite agent than even I'd credited if you haven't given a consideration to how that shot would bring down my household, and with my staff knowing you were the last to meet me."

Rowley straightened. "Enter," he bellowed as he commandeered control of the exchange and Leo's office.

Leo shot his stare to the entrance of the room. All his muscles went taut as Holman entered.

Studiously avoiding Leo's gaze, the bespectacled gentleman hovered in the doorway. "You summoned, my lord?" he demurred, his head bowed.

"Close the door behind you, Holman. Though, everyone's been sent away, haven't they? Tomlinson's been taken care of. The maids and footmen dismissed for the evening."

Slowly unfurling to his full height, Leo growled. "I would expect such treachery from you, Rowley. But you, Holman?" What a bloody fool he'd been.

The younger man dropped his eyes to the floor.

"Do you truly believe Holman is content to be nothing more than a glorified clerk for you of all people?" Rowley drawled, removing another pistol from the waist of his trousers. "Is that what you craved when you were near his age? Or did you wish to be in the field?"

A thick curtain of rage descended briefly over his vision. "Holman?" Leo growled.

His assistant swallowed audibly, looking one sharp demand from Leo away from bursting into tears. "D-do you require my services?"

The slap of betrayal earned a bellicose laugh from the viscount.

Fueled by rage and a knowledge that the summons he'd sent would arrive too late, Leo barked at the man he'd taken under his wing. "Traitorous bastard," he hissed. He made a grab for the gun but Rowley leveled his pistol at Leo's head.

"Stop," Rowley warned.

Leo seethed; his fingers twitched with the need to grab the weapon so close at hand. There could be no doubting that his superior would fire. Dismissing him, he leveled his efforts on his apprentice. "You will never be anything within the Brethren or the Home Office, Holman."

"It is not about that," his clerk whispered.

Fury pulled the words from him. "What *is* it about?"

"Lord Rowley said you are a traitor. I—"

"Shut your mouth, Holman," the viscount snapped.

Sticking his chest out, the man Leo had hired and groomed faced Rowley. "You are not presenting the facts correctly," he said, his cheeks flushed. "You provided me evidence of his lordship's—"

With a tired sigh, Rowley fired at Holman. The loud report of the gun thundered around the office.

Holman's lips formed a small circle of surprise. And then, soundlessly, he pitched to the floor.

"Not another step, Tennyson," he barked, freezing Leo midstride. From the corner of his eye, he evaluated Holman's prone, awkwardly bent body, his face pitched to the floor. A small pool of blood had already begun forming. "One of us will be walking out of this office, and I intend for it to be me."

CHAPTER 32

CHLOE KNEW THE MOMENT SHE and Gabriel arrived that all was not right with her household.

There was no butler there to open the door.

Chloe lifted her gaze up at the townhouse she wanted to forever call home with Leo. The heavy cloud coverage briefly parted, the moon's white glow painting eerie shadows upon the structure.

She tried the handle, and it turned easily.

Holding a hand up, a frown affixed to his lips, Gabriel entered ahead of her.

As she joined him in the foyer, the unease in her belly grew. Henry sidled up to her, and she found a reassurance in his nearness. Silence surrounded them. Thick and deafening, the kind that rang in one's ears and buzzed loudly when all the house slept.

The mastiff's ears stood up, and he pointed his nose in the direction of Leo's office.

Danger.

She knew it, the same way she'd known her father's approach was near and that a beating was imminent. Heart pounding hard in her rib cage, Chloe patted her leg once and rushed forward. Henry matched her movements, neither passing nor falling back.

"Chloe," her brother whispered.

Glaring him into silence, Chloe continued on with Henry following in perfect step. The carpet muted the heavy fall of his paws and the click of his nails. Carefully dodging the floorboards she'd come to know were loose and staying close to the wall, Chloe didn't stop until she reached Leo's office.

Again, nothing but quiet greeted her.

And then she heard voices, low and muffled, by the door.

Her husband's was one.

Relief brought her eyes briefly closed. *He is all right.*

That relief was short-lived, dying at the smattering of words that reached through the panel and doused her in terror.

"I'm going to kill you gladly—"

"No," Gabriel rasped as Chloe reached for the handle and tossed it open. He grabbed her arm but she wrenched free.

It was harder to say who was more surprised, the unfamiliar mustached gentleman gaping at her… or her husband.

"Rowley?" her brother asked incredulously from behind her. He slipped into the room and moved slowly toward Chloe.

"Oh, bloody hell. This is unfortunate," the stranger muttered, pointing a pistol at Chloe's chest. Henry growled, baring his teeth. She immediately moved in front of the dog, blocking him from the gun.

Gabriel cursed and moved to put himself between Chloe and that gleaming weapon. "Not another step, Waverly. Your being here is deuced inconvenient. But it is certainly easier to explain that the angry brother did away with you, Tennyson, after you killed his sister."

Her stomach dropped. She wrenched her gaze away from those merciless eyes and looked to her husband.

Agony contorted his features. "I am so sorry," he whispered.

"I want to be with you." Chloe touched quivering fingers to her pounding heart. "I love you."

Lord Rowley cocked his pistol, still pointing it at Chloe. The sight of the gleaming weapon fixed on her stole stability from her legs. She damned the way they shook under her. She closed her eyes. "Touching," the gentleman drawled. "But I've really had quite—"

"No," Leo thundered, drowning out the remainder of that death sentence.

Life spun in a whir of noise and confusion as the sharp report of a gun pounded in her ears. Chloe's entire body recoiled, and she braced for the rush of pain… that did not come. Henry's furious barking thundered around the office, and her skirts fluttered as he raced out from around her.

Her eyes shot open.

Lord Rowley's mouth formed a small moue, and he touched the hole ripped in his shirt, before promptly falling over.

The prone gentleman on the floor, his spectacles eschew, lay with his arm outstretched and the unfired gun pointed at the man.

Henry snarled and barked at him.

A moment later, the stranger's eyes slid closed.

With a scream, Chloe raced over to Leo.

He met her in the middle of the room. Catching her in his arms, Leo pulled her to him. "Why did you return?" he wept into the crown of her hair. All the while, he searched his hands over her body for a wound he didn't find. "Why?" he pleaded.

Chloe clung to him, gripping him for all she was worth. "My place is with you, Leo," she managed to cry between her tears. She drew back slightly and looked to her silent, staring, and unharmed brother a moment. And then she returned all her focus to Leo. "And I am *not* letting you send me away." She gave his lapels a tug. "Is that clear?"

A shaky smile curved his lips. He cupped her cheek. "That is clear." Lowering his head, he claimed her mouth in a kiss that promised forever.

EPILOGUE

LEO WAS TERRIFIED.

More specifically, he was terrified out of his everlasting mind.

"You needn't be scared," his wife murmured, their arms looped as they strolled through Lord Waverly's—his brother-in-law's—household.

"Oh, no. Nothing to be worried about," he muttered. "It's merely the first gathering between my aunt and uncle… and your entire family, since you were nearly killed in my office." Any one of her male—and female—kin would be within their rights to off him for the peril he'd placed her in through their marriage. "What is there to be nervous over?"

"Precisely," Chloe beamed. "You will adore Alex. He, too, is a reformed rogue."

"I was a rake," he pointed out.

"Is there really a difference?"

"Oh, certainly. Rakes are far more scandalous and immoral." Had he truly lived that existence? In the two months since he'd been married, he couldn't imagine his life any other way than it was now… nights reading with his wife, discussing their plans to help children of the streets who'd suffered abuse and cruelty.

Chloe squeezed his arm. "But immoral is immoral. Different degrees of it do not different it make." They reached the next corridor, and laughter and rival discourses spilled from a nearby room. "We're here." She winked.

He wrinkled his brow. "You were distracting me."

Smoothing her palms over his lapels, she leaned up. "Did it work?"

"Undoubtedly." Leo slid his hands around her lower back, drawing her close. Chloe gave a small gasp. "I've been distracted by you since I stumbled upon you in Waterson's halls."

Her eyes softened. "Indeed?"

"Indeed," he purred, brushing a kiss along the corner of her mouth, lower, ever lower, until he found the sensitive skin at her neck. The flesh that, when attended, unfailingly drew forth her whispery sighs.

"N-now you are attempting to distract me," she challenged, breathless.

Leo husked his voice. "Is it working?" he asked, guiding her against the wall.

"U-undoubtedly."

He flicked her earlobe with the tip of his tongue.

"Even more so," she whispered.

Grinning, Leo moved to claim her mouth.

"Aunt Chloe is here!"

The child's voice doused his ardor. Oh, bloody damn. He winced.

A moment later, Violet was joined by her older sister.

"Eww. Were you *kissing*?" Faith balked and ducked her head inside the suddenly silent rooms behind her. "I believe Aunt Chloe was *kissing* Leo," she exclaimed on a horrified whisper. "She's all red and—"

Chloe snaked a hand around her niece's mouth, stifling her rambling.

"Mwhshaa," Faith muttered. "Yes, well, they've stopped, then," she announced with a flounce of her curls when Chloe released her. She skipped back into the room, her sister following along at her heels.

Chloe buried her face in his shoulder, her body shaking.

"I am so thrilled you find this to be of some amusement," he whispered against her temple.

Her eyes twinkling, Chloe took him by the hand and tugged him reluctantly into the crowded... and still silent room.

The first person Leo noted was the brother.

Not Waverly, who'd proven himself onerous in his own right. But rather, the spare, with ice in eyes slitted like razors, and all that seething ire was reserved for Leo.

A pretty, redheaded woman, cradling a babe in her arms, whispered something... that had little effect.

"Alex," Chloe cried, abandoning Leo as she bolted forward to greet her sibling. Tossing her arms about the other Edgerton male, she knocked him slightly off-balance.

He grunted, and all his attention shifted to his sister. Lord Alex folded Chloe in a protective hug and said something.

Chloe nodded and fired back with her own hushed words.

Through that discussion, Leo lingered at the entrance. His hands were clasped at his back. For a brief moment born of cowardice, he contemplated the door behind him.

Close-knit families and overprotective siblings were as unfamiliar to him as venturing off onto a new planet.

His uncle, where he stood with his wife and the dowager marchioness, taking entirely too much pleasure in Leo's misery, grinned.

"I'm not pleased," Lord Alex said, shifting his focus back to Leo.

"Of course you're not," Chloe said. Rushing back to Leo's side, she caught him by the hand and pulled him forward. "You've not yet had the pleasure of meeting my husband."

"We've met."

Both men said it simultaneously.

"Truly?" Chloe widened her eyes. "Perhaps one of you'd care to regale us with tales of your previous meetings."

Just like that, his wife managed to effectively silence her brother. Lord Alex stuck a hand out. "Tennyson," he greeted reluctantly.

"Lord Alex—"

His brother-in-law drew him close for a half hug. "If you hurt her," he whispered, "I'll kill you." He squeezed Leo's hand hard.

"And you may do so with my blessings," he promised.

As soon as the other man released him, all conversation resumed, with Chloe performing introductions to her sister-in-law Imogen and he performing the long-overdue ones to his aunt.

"So, you are the one who tamed Leo?" Aunt Elsie murmured, clasping Chloe's palms.

"Or rather, I'm the one who corrupted her," he drawled. He winced when Chloe delivered him a well-delivered pinch. "Ouch."

"Behave," she scolded.

"My apologies," he demurred, bowing his head.

"I always knew all you needed was the love of a good lady," the duchess said, affectionately adjusting his cravat.

Over the top of her dark curls, he winked at Chloe.

From across the room, Faith shot a hand up. "Come, Aunt Chloe. I want to hear how you saved Leo. Mama and Papa are refusing to tell us."

"Go," Leo encouraged, raising Chloe's fingertips to his lips for a lingering kiss. "Tell them all the ways in which you saved me. I'll be over shortly."

Chloe hesitated.

"I shall join you. I've still not managed to gather all the details from that day." Aunt Elsie sent a scolding look at Leo's uncle.

"I don't believe that," Leo said under his breath as the two ladies joined the girls.

"You'd be correct on that score," his uncle whispered. "There isn't a secret between us." His features formed a somber mask. "I trust she just sought to allow us some time alone."

Leo narrowed his eyes. "What is it?"

"Holman's expected to recover. He's suffered some paralysis, but has been quite... informative about the extent of Rowley's ring of lies and support."

Leo flattened his mouth. A large part of him chafed at the betrayal on the young man's part. But then... "Many of us have also made decisions we've come to regret." Leo had more regrets than every lord in London combined. "Holman was young, impressionable, and easily swayed." Leo had mistakenly seen only the devotion and not acknowledged the perils posed by that personality. "His injuries will always be a reminder for him," he said without inflection.

"Higgins wants me to convince you not to retire," his uncle said quietly.

Five weeks had passed since Leo had ended his tenure with the Brethren. This had been the first any talk of his decision or future with the agency had been broached by his uncle... or anyone.

"With Rowley dead," his uncle went on, "and you finding an internal rift within, Higgins wants to promote you to the late viscount's position. He wants me to convey how desperately the organization needs you."

There it was. What he'd always aspired to—respect within the ranks of the Brethren and a position that recognized his value to the Crown. He'd given almost thirteen years of his life to that service and had known nothing but the role he'd crafted.

Leo stared over at his wife. She squatted beside the camelback sofa, animated in the telling of her story. Chloe moved her hands and arms as she spoke. Her audience of three sat wholly enrapt.

But that was Chloe's power. She possessed an effervescent glow that commanded a person's attention and allowed one to see or hear only her.

Just then, she looked over. "I love you," she mouthed.

Faith tugged at her white puff sleeve, calling her focus away from Leo.

He contemplated his uncle's offer on behalf of the Brethren. Leo's had been a purposeful life, and yet... so empty, too. Chloe had slipped into his life and filled every void of emptiness that had made him the cynical, ruthless scoundrel he'd been. And selfishly, he didn't want to go back... not for the Crown, not for the king, and not for anything. He wanted only her. *Always.*

"I'm... honored," Leo finally said. "But the Brethren does not need me. Not truly. There will always be other good, honorable men to replace those who currently serve. I'm just a man."

His uncle slapped him on the back. "I knew the moment that girl caught you in Waterson's office that she was the one for you."

"I knew it, too," Leo acknowledged wistfully. His gaze was fixed on his wife. Deep down, in a part he could have never acknowledged nor accepted until now, with his heart opened to love, he knew Chloe had captivated him, mind, heart, soul, and body, from the very first.

His uncle squeezed his shoulder. "I am proud of you, Leo. If you'll excuse me, I'm off to join my duchess."

Leo remained at the hearth, observing the room filled with proper lords and ladies and leading societal matrons and small girls. At one time, he would have shuddered at the collection of guests assembled.

His wife sailed over. "Lord Tennyson," she murmured, sliding her arm through his.

"Lady Tennyson."

"Your discussion appeared… serious," she noted, no longer teasing.

"You miss nothing."

"What is it?" she pressed.

"They wish to promote me within the Home Office."

She wet her lips. "I see… and what did you say?" she asked haltingly.

How could she not know? How could she not know how much she meant to him? That she was all he would ever want.

"I said I am honored." Leo dusted his thumb over her lower lip, and that flesh trembled under the slight caress. "But I have a new life now. One with a wife I desperately love." Her lips curved in a tremulous smile. "And as you reminded me, there is so much for us to do—together. An establishment created by both of us to help those boys and girls who most need it." Several tears streaked down her cheeks, and he gently brushed them back. Leo held her gaze. "And one day, I hope, children brave and spirited just like their mama."

A small sob escaped her.

"Shh, love." He raised each of her hands to his mouth, kissing them. "Your brothers will have my head thinking I've hurt you."

"They can go hang," she rasped. Another crystalline drop rolled down her cheek. "I love you."

"I love you," he whispered.

This was his life.

He had that which he'd never known and had never so much as held the dream of—a family with Chloe… and the noisy, boisterous, devoted group gathered around them.

Leo smiled.

THE END

AUTHOR'S NOTE

ONE OF MY FAVORITE PARTS about writing *The Brethren* series has been that it's allowed me to really dig into some riveting moments in British history. The Cato Conspiracy or Cato Event which is a central part of the first two books in the series is based on the actual Cato Street Conspiracy—a plot carried out to murder all members of Prime Minister Lord Liverpool's cabinet.

It is uncertain just how deep the conspiracy run, which of course fueled questions in my own mind…and from there the series was born.

The Cato conspirators were known as Spencean Philanthropists and they were people motivated by the radical words of Thomas Spence. They sought to use the seeds of political unrest in the hopes of overthrowing the government. Most of their anger stemmed from a few events: the economic depression and political repression of the period, the Six Acts, and the Peterloo Massacre. All of which are mentioned in *The Lady Who Loved Him*.

The Brethren organization and the existence of a sub-plot involving Lord Rowley, however, are works of fiction.

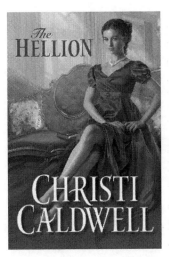

Coming Soon By Christi Caldwell
A Brand-New Series
The Wicked Wallflowers

COMING APRIL 3RD, 2018
USA Today bestselling author
Christi Caldwell's Wicked
Wallflowers series burns hot as
two rivals meet in the flesh and
feel the heat…

ADAIR THORNE HAS JUST WATCHED his gaming-hell dream disappear into a blaze of fire and ash, and he's certain that his competitors, the Killorans, are behind it. His fury and passion burn even hotter when he meets Cleopatra Killoran, a tart-mouthed vixen who mocks him at every turn. If she were anyone else but the enemy, she'd ignite a desire in him that would be impossible to control.

No one can make Cleopatra do anything. That said, she'll do whatever it takes to protect her siblings—even if that means being sponsored by their rivals for a season in order to land a noble husband. But she will not allow her head to be turned by the infuriating and darkly handsome Adair Thorne.

There's only one thing that threatens the rules of the game: Cleopatra's secret. It could unravel the families' tenuous truce and shatter the unpredictably sinful romance mounting between the hellion…and a scoundrel who could pass for the devil himself.

OTHER BOOKS BY CHRISTI CALDWELL

TO ENCHANT A WICKED DUKE
Book 13 in the "Heart of a Duke" Series by Christi Caldwell

A Devil in Disguise

Years ago, when Nick Tallings, the recent Duke of Huntly, watched his family destroyed at the hands of a merciless nobleman, he vowed revenge. But his efforts had been futile, as his enemy, Lord Rutland is without weakness.

Until now...

With his rival finally happily married, Nick is able to set his ruthless scheme into motion. His plot hinges upon Lord Rutland's innocent, empty-headed sister-in-law, Justina Barrett. Nick will ruin her, marry her, and then leave her brokenhearted.

A Lady Dreaming of Love

From the moment Justina Barrett makes her Come Out, she is labeled a Diamond. Even with her ruthless father determined to sell her off to the highest bidder, Justina never gives up on her hope for a good, honorable gentleman who values her wit more than her looks.

A Not-So-Chance Meeting

Nick's ploy to ensnare Justina falls neatly into place in the streets of London. With each carefully orchestrated encounter, he slips further and further inside the lady's heart, never anticipating that Justina, with her quick wit and strength, will break down his own defenses. As Nick's plans begins to unravel, he's left to determine which is more important—Justina's love or his vow for vengeance. But can Justina ever forgive the duke who deceived her?

ONE WINTER WITH A BARON
Book 12 in the "Heart of a Duke" Series by Christi Caldwell

A clever spinster:
Content with her spinster lifestyle, Miss Sybil Cunning wants to prove that a future as an unmarried woman is the only life for her. As a bluestocking who values hard, empirical data, Sybil needs help with her research. Nolan Pratt, Baron Webb, one of society's most scandalous rakes, is the perfect gentleman to help her. After all, he inspires fear in proper mothers and desire within their daughters.

A notorious rake:
Society may be aware of Nolan Pratt, Baron's Webb's wicked ways, but what he has carefully hidden is his miserable handling of his family's finances. When Sybil presents him the opportunity to earn much-needed funds, he can't refuse.

A winter to remember:
However, what begins as a business arrangement becomes something more and with every meeting, Sybil slips inside his heart. Can this clever woman look beneath the veneer of a coldhearted rake to see the man Nolan truly is?

TO REDEEM A RAKE
Book 11 in the "Heart of a Duke" Series by Christi Caldwell

He's spent years scandalizing society.
Now, this rake must change his ways.

Society's most infamous scoundrel, Daniel Winterbourne, the Earl of Montfort, has been promised a small fortune if he can relinquish his wayward, carousing lifestyle. And behaving means he must also help find a respectable companion for his youngest sister—someone who will guide her and whom she can emulate. However, Daniel knows no such woman. But when he encounters a childhood friend, Daniel believes she may just be the answer to all of his problems.

Having been secretly humiliated by an unscrupulous blackguard years earlier, Miss Daphne Smith dreams of finding work at Ladies of Hope, an institution that provides an education for disabled women. With her sordid past and a disfigured leg, few opportunities arise for a woman such as she. Knowing Daniel's history, she wishes to avoid him, but working for his sister is exactly the stepping stone she needs.

Their attraction intensifies as Daniel and Daphne grow closer, preparing his sister for the London Season. But Daniel must resist his desire for a woman tarnished by scandal while Daphne is reminded of the boy she once knew. Can society's most notorious rake redeem his reputation and become the man Daphne deserves?

To Woo a Widow
Book 10 in the "Heart of a Duke" Series by Christi Caldwell

They see a brokenhearted widow.
She's far from shattered.

Lady Philippa Winston is never marrying again. After her late husband's cruelty that she kept so well hidden, she has no desire to search for love.

Years ago, Miles Brookfield, the Marquess of Guilford, made a frivolous vow he never thought would come to fruition—he promised to marry his mother's goddaughter if he was unwed by the age of thirty. Now, to his dismay, he's faced with honoring that pledge. But when he encounters the beautiful and intriguing Lady Philippa, Miles knows his true path in life. It's up to him to break down every belief Philippa carries about gentlemen, proving that not only is love real, but that he is the man deserving of her sheltered heart.

Will Philippa let down her guard and allow Miles to woo a widow in desperate need of his love?

THE LURE OF A RAKE
Book 9 in the "Heart of a Duke" Series by Christi Caldwell

A Lady Dreaming of Love

Lady Genevieve Farendale has a scandalous past. Jilted at the altar years earlier and exiled by her family, she's now returned to London to prove she can be a proper lady. Even though she's not given up on the hope of marrying for love, she's wary of trusting again. Then she meets Cedric Falcot, the Marquess of St. Albans whose seductive ways set her heart aflutter. But with her sordid history, Genevieve knows a rake can also easily destroy her.

An Unlikely Pairing

What begins as a chance encounter between Cedric and Genevieve becomes something more. As they continue to meet, passions stir. But with Genevieve's hope for true love, she fears Cedric will be unable to give up his wayward lifestyle. After all, Cedric has spent years protecting his heart, and keeping everyone out. Slowly, she chips away at all the walls he's built, but when he falters, Genevieve can't offer him redemption. Now, it's up to Cedric to prove to Genevieve that the love of a man is far more powerful than the lure of a rake.

TO TRUST A ROGUE
Book 8 in the "Heart of a Duke" Series by Christi Caldwell

A rogue

Marcus, the Viscount Wessex has carefully crafted the image of rogue and charmer for Polite Society. Under that façade, however, dwells a man whose dreams were shattered almost eight years earlier by a young lady who captured his heart, pledged her love, and then left him, with nothing more than a curt note.

A widow

Eight years earlier, faced with no other choice, Mrs. Eleanor Collins, fled London and the only man she ever loved, Marcus, Viscount Wessex. She has now returned to serve as a companion for her elderly aunt with a daughter in tow. Even though they're next door neighbors, there is little reason for her to move in the same circles as Marcus, just in case, she vows to avoid him, for he reminds her of all she lost when she left.

Reunited

As their paths continue to cross, Marcus finds his desire for Eleanor just as strong, but he learned long ago she's not to be trusted. He will offer her a place in his bed, but not anything more. Only, Eleanor has no interest in this new, roguish man. The more time they spend together, the protective wall they've constructed to keep the other out, begin to break. With all the betrayals and secrets between them, Marcus has to open his heart again. And Eleanor must decide if it's ever safe to trust a rogue.

To Wed His Christmas Lady
Book 7 in the "Heart of a Duke" Series by Christi Caldwell

She's longing to be loved:

Lady Cara Falcot has only served one purpose to her loathsome father—to increase his power through a marriage to the future Duke of Billingsley. As such, she's built protective walls about her heart, and presents an icy facade to the world around her. Journeying home from her finishing school for the Christmas holidays, Cara's carriage is stranded during a winter storm. She's forced to tarry at a ramshackle inn, where she immediately antagonizes another patron—William.

He's avoiding his duty in favor of one last adventure:

William Hargrove, the Marquess of Grafton has wanted only one thing in life—to avoid the future match his parents would have him make to a cold, duke's daughter. He's returning home from a blissful eight years of traveling the world to see to his responsibilities. But when a winter storm interrupts his trip and lands him at a falling-down inn, he's forced to share company with a commanding Lady Cara who initially reminds him exactly of the woman he so desperately wants to avoid.

A Christmas snowstorm ushers in the spirit of the season:

At the holiday time, these two people who despise each other due to first perceptions are offered renewed beginnings and fresh starts. As this gruff stranger breaks down the walls she's built about herself, Cara has to determine whether she can truly open her heart to trusting that any man is capable of good and that she herself is capable of love. And William has to set aside all previous thoughts he's carried of the polished ladies like Cara, to be the man to show her that love.

THE HEART OF A SCOUNDREL
Book 6 in the "Heart of a Duke" Series by Christi Caldwell

Ruthless, wicked, and dark, the Marquess of Rutland rouses terror in the breast of ladies and nobleman alike. All Edmund wants in life is power. After he was publically humiliated by his one love Lady Margaret, he vowed vengeance, using Margaret's niece, as his pawn. Except, he's thwarted by another, more enticing target— Miss Phoebe Barrett.

Miss Phoebe Barrett knows precisely the shame she's been born to. Because her father is a shocking letch she's learned to form her own opinions on a person's worth. After a chance meeting with the Marquess of Rutland, she is captivated by the mysterious man. He, too, is a victim of society's scorn, but the more encounters she has with Edmund, the more she knows there is powerful depth and emotion to the jaded marquess.

The lady wreaks havoc on Edmund's plans for revenge and he finds he wants Phoebe, at all costs. As she's drawn into the darkness of his world, Phoebe risks being destroyed by Edmund's ruthlessness. And Phoebe who desires love at all costs, has to determine if she can ever truly trust the heart of a scoundrel.

To Love a Lord
Book 5 in the "Heart of a Duke" Series by Christi Caldwell

All she wants is security:

The last place finishing school instructor Mrs. Jane Munroe belongs, is in polite Society. Vowing to never wed, she's been scuttled around from post to post. Now she finds herself in the Marquess of Waverly's household. She's never met a nobleman she liked, and when she meets the pompous, arrogant marquess, she remembers why. But soon, she discovers Gabriel is unlike any gentleman she's ever known.

All he wants is a companion for his sister:

What Gabriel finds himself with instead, is a fiery spirited, bespectacled woman who entices him at every corner and challenges his age-old vow to never trust his heart to a woman. But… there is something suspicious about his sister's companion. And he is determined to find out just what it is.

All they need is each other:

As Gabriel and Jane confront the truth of their feelings, the lies and secrets between them begin to unravel. And Jane is left to decide whether or not it is ever truly safe to love a lord.

Loved By a Duke
Book 4 in the "Heart of a Duke" Series by Christi Caldwell

For ten years, Lady Daisy Meadows has been in love with Auric, the Duke of Crawford. Ever since his gallant rescue years earlier, Daisy knew she was destined to be his Duchess. Unfortunately, Auric sees her as his best friend's sister and nothing more. But perhaps, if she can manage to find the fabled heart of a duke pendant, she will win over the heart of her duke.

Auric, the Duke of Crawford enjoys Daisy's company. The last thing he is interested in however, is pursuing a romance with a woman he's known since she was in leading strings. This season, Daisy is turning up in the oddest places and he cannot help but notice that she is no longer a girl. But Auric wouldn't do something as foolhardy as to fall in love with Daisy. He couldn't. Not with the guilt he carries over his past sins… Not when he has no right to her heart…But perhaps, just perhaps, she can forgive the past and trust that he'd forever cherish her heart—but will she let him?

THE LOVE OF A ROGUE
Book 3 in the "Heart of a Duke" Series by Christi Caldwell

Lady Imogen Moore hasn't had an easy time of it since she made her Come Out. With her betrothed, a powerful duke breaking it off to wed her sister, she's become the *tons* favorite piece of gossip. Never again wanting to experience the pain of a broken heart, she's resolved to make a match with a polite, respectable gentleman. The last thing she wants is another reckless rogue.

Lord Alex Edgerton has a problem. His brother, tired of Alex's carousing has charged him with chaperoning their remaining, unwed sister about *ton* events. Shopping? No, thank you. Attending the theatre? He'd rather be at Forbidden Pleasures with a scantily clad beauty upon his lap. The task of *chaperone* becomes even more of a bother when his sister drags along her dearest friend, Lady Imogen to social functions. The last thing he wants in his life is a young, innocent English miss.

Except, as Alex and Imogen are thrown together, passions flare and Alex comes to find he not only wants Imogen in his bed, but also in his heart. Yet now he must convince Imogen to risk all, on the heart of a rogue.

MORE THAN A DUKE
Book 2 in the "Heart of a Duke" Series by Christi Caldwell

Polite Society doesn't take Lady Anne Adamson seriously. However, Anne isn't just another pretty young miss. When she discovers her father betrayed her mother's love and her family descended into poverty, Anne comes up with a plan to marry a respectable, powerful, and honorable gentleman—a man nothing like her philandering father.

Armed with the heart of a duke pendant, fabled to land the wearer a duke's heart, she decides to enlist the aid of the notorious Harry, 6th Earl of Stanhope. A scoundrel with a scandalous past, he is the last gentleman she'd ever wed…however, his reputation marks him the perfect man to school her in the art of seduction so she might ensnare the illustrious Duke of Crawford.

Harry, the Earl of Stanhope is a jaded, cynical rogue who lives for his own pleasures. Having been thrown over by the only woman he ever loved so she could wed a duke, he's not at all surprised when Lady Anne approaches him with her scheme to capture another duke's affection. He's come to appreciate that all women are in fact greedy, title-grasping, self-indulgent creatures. And with Anne's history of grating on his every last nerve, she is the last woman he'd ever agree to school in the art of seduction. Only his friendship with the lady's sister compels him to help.

What begins as a pretend courtship, born of lessons on seduction, becomes something more leaving Anne to decide if she can give her heart to a reckless rogue, and Harry must decide if he's willing to again trust in a lady's love.

FOR LOVE OF THE DUKE
First Full-Length Book in the "Heart of a Duke" Series
by Christi Caldwell

After the tragic death of his wife, Jasper, the 8th Duke of Bainbridge buried himself away in the dark cold walls of his home, Castle Blackwood. When he's coaxed out of his self-imposed exile to attend the amusements of the Frost Fair, his life is irrevocably changed by his fateful meeting with Lady Katherine Adamson.

With her tight brown ringlets and silly white-ruffled gowns, Lady Katherine Adamson has found her dance card empty for two Seasons. After her father's passing, Katherine learned the unreliability of men, and is determined to depend on no one, except herself. Until she meets Jasper…

In a desperate bid to avoid a match arranged by her family, Katherine makes the Duke of Bainbridge a shocking proposition—one that he accepts.

Only, as Katherine begins to love Jasper, she finds the arrangement agreed upon is not enough. And Jasper is left to decide if protecting his heart is more important than fighting for Katherine's love.

IN NEED OF A DUKE
A Prequel Novella to "The Heart of a Duke" Series
by Christi Caldwell

In Need of a Duke: (Author's Note: This is a prequel novella to "The Heart of a Duke" series by Christi Caldwell. It was originally available in "The Heart of a Duke" Collection and is now being published as an individual novella.

~★~

It features a new prologue and epilogue.

Years earlier, a gypsy woman passed to Lady Aldora Adamson and her friends a heart pendant that promised them each the heart of a duke.

Now, a young lady, with her family facing ruin and scandal, Lady Aldora doesn't have time for mythical stories about cheap baubles. She needs to save her sisters and brother by marrying a titled gentleman with wealth and power to his name. She sets her bespectacled sights upon the Marquess of St. James.

Turned out by his father after a tragic scandal, Lord Michael Knightly has grown into a powerful, but self-made man. With the whispers and stares that still follow him, he would rather be anywhere but London...

Until he meets Lady Aldora, a young woman who mistakes him for his brother, the Marquess of St. James. The connection between Aldora and Michael is immediate and as they come to know one another, Aldora's feelings for Michael war with her sisterly responsibilities. With her family's dire situation, a man of Michael's scandalous past will never do.

Ultimately, Aldora must choose between her responsibilities as a sister and her love for Michael.

Once a Wallflower, At Last His Love
Book 6 in the Scandalous Seasons Series

Responsible, practical Miss Hermione Rogers, has been crafting stories as the notorious Mr. Michael Michaelmas and selling them for a meager wage to support her siblings. The only real way to ensure her family's ruinous debts are paid, however, is to marry. Tall, thin, and plain, she has no expectation of success. In London for her first Season she seizes the chance to write the tale of a brooding duke. In her research, she finds Sebastian Fitzhugh, the 5th Duke of Mallen, who unfortunately is perfectly affable, charming, and so nicely... configured... he takes her breath away. He lacks all the character traits she needs for her story, but alas, any duke will have to do.

Sebastian Fitzhugh, the 5th Duke of Mallen has been deceived so many times during the high-stakes game of courtship, he's lost faith in Society women. Yet, after a chance encounter with Hermione, he finds himself intrigued. Not a woman he'd normally consider beautiful, the young lady's practical bent, her forthright nature and her tendency to turn up in the oddest places has his interests... roused. He'd like to trust her, he'd like to do a whole lot more with her too, but should he?

Book 5 in the Scandalous Seasons Series

Lady Patrina Tidemore gave up on the ridiculous notion of true love after having her heart shattered and her trust destroyed by a black-hearted cad. Used as a pawn in a game of revenge against her brother, Patrina returns to London from a failed elopement with a tattered reputation and little hope for a respectable match. The only peace she finds is in her solitude on the cold winter days at Hyde Park. And even that is yanked from her by two little hellions who just happen to have a devastatingly handsome, but coldly aloof father, the Marquess of Beaufort. Something about the lord stirs the dreams she'd once carried for an honorable gentleman's love.

Weston Aldridge, the 4th Marquess of Beaufort was deceived and betrayed by his late wife. In her faithlessness, he's come to view women as self-serving, indulgent creatures. Except, after a series of chance encounters with Patrina, he comes to appreciate how uniquely different she is than all women he's ever known.

At the Christmastide season, a time of hope and new beginnings, Patrina and Weston, unexpectedly learn true love in one another. However, as Patrina's scandalous past threatens their future and the happiness of his children, they are both left to determine if love is enough.

Always a Rogue, Forever Her Love
Book 4 in the Scandalous Seasons Series

Miss Juliet Marshville is spitting mad. With one guardian missing, and the other singularly uninterested in her fate, she is at the mercy of her wastrel brother who loses her beloved childhood home to a man known as Sin. Determined to reclaim control of Rosecliff Cottage and her own fate, Juliet arranges a meeting with the notorious rogue and demands the return of her property.

Jonathan Tidemore, 5th Earl of Sinclair, known to the *ton* as Sin, is exceptionally lucky in life and at the gaming tables. He has just one problem. Well…four, really. His incorrigible sisters have driven off yet another governess. This time, however, his mother demands he find an appropriate replacement.

When Miss Juliet Marshville boldly demands the return of her precious cottage, he takes advantage of his sudden good fortune and puts an offer to her; turn his sisters into proper English ladies, and he'll return Rosecliff Cottage to Juliet's possession.

Jonathan comes to appreciate Juliet's spirit, courage, and clever wit, and decides to claim the fiery beauty as his mistress. Juliet, however, will be mistress for no man. Nor could she ever love a man who callously stole her home in a game of cards. As Jonathan begins to see Juliet as more than a spirited beauty to warm his bed, he realizes she could be a lady he could love the rest of his life, if only he can convince the proud Juliet that he's worthy of her hand and heart.

Always Proper, Suddenly Scandalous
Book 3 in the Scandalous Seasons Series

Geoffrey Winters, Viscount Redbrooke was not always the hard, unrelenting lord driven by propriety. After a tragic mistake, he resolved to honor his responsibility to the Redbrooke line and live a life, free of scandal. Knowing his duty is to wed a proper, respectable English miss, he selects Lady Beatrice Dennington, daughter of the Duke of Somerset, the perfect woman for him. Until he meets Miss Abigail Stone…

To distance herself from a personal scandal, Abigail Stone flees America to visit her uncle, the Duke of Somerset. Determined to never trust a man again, she is helplessly intrigued by the hard, too-proper Geoffrey. With his strict appreciation for decorum and order, he is nothing like the man' she's always dreamed of.

Abigail is everything Geoffrey does not need. She upends his carefully ordered world at every encounter. As they begin to care for one another, Abigail carefully guards the secret that resulted in her journey to England.

Only, if Geoffrey learns the truth about Abigail, he must decide which he holds most dear: his place in Society or Abigail's place in his heart.

NEVER COURTED, SUDDENLY WED
Book 2 in the Scandalous Seasons Series

Christopher Ansley, Earl of Waxham, has constructed a perfect image for the *ton*—the ladies love him and his company is desired by all. Only two people know the truth about Waxham's secret. Unfortunately, one of them is Miss Sophie Winters.

Sophie Winters has known Christopher since she was in leading strings. As children, they delighted in tormenting each other. Now at two and twenty, she still has a tendency to find herself in scrapes, and her marital prospects are slim.

When his father threatens to expose his shame to the *ton*, unless he weds Sophie for her dowry, Christopher concocts a plan to remain a bachelor. What he didn't plan on was falling in love with the lively, impetuous Sophie. As secrets are exposed, will Christopher's love be enough when she discovers his role in his father's scheme?

Forever Betrothed, Never the Bride
Book 1 in the Scandalous Seasons Series

Hopeless romantic Lady Emmaline Fitzhugh is tired of sitting with the wallflowers, waiting for her betrothed to come to his senses and marry her. When Emmaline reads one too many reports of his scandalous liaisons in the gossip rags, she takes matters into her own hands.

War-torn veteran Lord Drake devotes himself to forgetting his days on the Peninsula through an endless round of meaningless associations. He no longer wants to feel anything, but Lady Emmaline is making it hard to maintain a state of numbness. With her zest for life, she awakens his passion and desire for love.

The one woman Drake has spent the better part of his life avoiding is now the only woman he needs, but he is no longer a man worthy of his Emmaline. It is up to her to show him the healing power of love.

A Season of Hope
A Danby Novella

Five years ago when her love, Marcus Wheatley, failed to return from fighting Napoleon's forces, Lady Olivia Foster buried her heart. Unable to betray Marcus's memory, Olivia has gone out of her way to run off prospective suitors. At three and twenty she considers herself firmly on the shelf. Her father, however, disagrees and accepts an offer for Olivia's hand in marriage. Yet it's Christmas, when anything can happen…

Olivia receives a well-timed summons from her grandfather, the Duke of Danby, and eagerly embraces the reprieve from her betrothal.

Only, when Olivia arrives at Danby Castle she realizes the Christmas season represents hope, second chances, and even miracles.

"WINNING A LADY'S HEART"
A Danby Novella

Author's Note: This is a novella that was originally available in A Summons From The Castle (The Regency Christmas Summons Collection). It is being published as an individual novella.

~★~

For Lady Alexandra, being the source of a cold, calculated wager is bad enough…but when it is waged by Nathaniel Michael Winters, 5th Earl of Pembroke, the man she's in love with, it results in a broken heart, the scandal of the season, and a summons from her grandfather – the Duke of Danby.

To escape Society's gossip, she hurries to her meeting with the duke, determined to put memories of the earl far behind. Except the duke has other plans for Alexandra…plans which include the 5th Earl of Pembroke!

TEMPTED BY A LADY'S SMILE
Book 4 in the "Lords of Honor" Series

Richard Jonas has loved but one woman—a woman who belongs to his brother. Refusing to suffer any longer, he evades his family in order to barricade his heart from unrequited love. While attending a friend's summer party, Richard's approach to love is changed after sharing a passionate and life-altering kiss with a vibrant and mysterious woman. Believing he was incapable of loving again, Richard finds himself tempted by a young lady determined to marry his best friend.

Gemma Reed has not been treated kindly by the *ton*. Often disregarded for her appearance and interests unlike those of a proper lady, Gemma heads to house party to win the heart of Lord Westfield, the man she's loved for years. But her plan is set off course by the tempting and intriguing, Richard Jonas.

A chance meeting creates a new path for Richard and Gemma to forage—but can two people, scorned and shunned by those they've loved from afar, let down their guards to find true happiness?

"RESCUED BY A LADY'S LOVE"
Book 3 in the "Lords of Honor" Series

Destitute and determined to finally be free of any man's shackles, Lily Benedict sets out to salvage her honor. With no choice but to commit a crime that will save her from her past, she enters the home of the recluse, Derek Winters, the new Duke of Blackthorne. But entering the "Beast of Blackthorne's" lair proves more threatening than she ever imagined.

With half a face and a mangled leg, Derek—once rugged and charming—only exists within the confines of his home. Shunned by society, Derek is leery of the hauntingly beautiful Lily Benedict. As time passes, she slips past his defenses, reminding him how to live again. But when Lily's sordid past comes back, threatening her life, it's up to Derek to find the strength to become the hero he once was. Can they overcome the darkness of their sins to find a life of love and redemption?

CAPTIVATED BY A LADY'S CHARM
Book 2 in the "Lords of Honor" Series

In need of a wife…

Christian Villiers, the Marquess of St. Cyr, despises the role he's been cast into as fortune hunter but requires the funds to keep his marquisate solvent. Yet, the sins of his past cloud his future, preventing him from seeing beyond his fateful actions at the Battle of Toulouse. For he knows inevitably it will catch up with him, and everyone will remember his actions on the battlefield that cost so many so much—particularly his best friend.

In want of a husband…

Lady Prudence Tidemore's life is plagued by familial scandals, which makes her own marital prospects rather grim. Surely there is one gentleman of the ton who can look past her family and see just her and all she has to offer?

When Prudence runs into Christian on a London street, the charming, roguish gentleman immediately captures her attention. But then a chance meeting becomes a waltz, and now…

A Perfect Match…

All she must do is convince Christian to forget the cold requirements he has for his future marchioness. But the demons in his past prevent him from turning himself over to love. One thing is certain—Prudence wants the marquess and is determined to have him in her life, now and forever. It's just a matter of convincing Christian he wants the same.

SEDUCED BY A LADY'S HEART
Book 1 in the "Lords of Honor" Series

You met Lieutenant Lucien Jones in "Forever Betrothed, Never the Bride" when he was a broken soldier returned from fighting Boney's forces. This is his story of triumph and happily-ever-after!

~*~

Lieutenant Lucien Jones, son of a viscount, returned from war, to find his wife and child dead. Blaming his father for the commission that sent him off to fight Boney's forces, he was content to languish at London Hospital… until offered employment on the Marquess of Drake's staff. Through his position, Lucien found purpose in life and is content to keep his past buried.

Lady Eloise Yardley has loved Lucien since they were children. Having long ago given up on the dream of him, she married another. Years later, she is a young, lonely widow who does not fit in with the ton. When Lucien's family enlists her aid to reunite father and son, she leaps at the opportunity to not only aid her former friend, but to also escape London.

Lucien doesn't know what scheme Eloise has concocted, but

knowing her as he does, when she pays a visit to his employer, he knows she's up to something. The last thing he wants is the temptation that this new, older, mature Eloise presents; a tantalizing reminder of happier times and peace.

Yet Eloise is determined to win Lucien's love once and for all… if only Lucien can set aside the pain of his past and risk all on a lady's heart.

Only For Their Love
Book 3 in the "The Theodosia Sword" Series

Miss Carol Cresswall bore witness to her parents' loveless union and is determined to avoid that same miserable fate. Her mother has altogether different plans—plans that include a match between Carol and Lord Gregory Renshaw. Despite his wealth and power, Carol has no interest in marrying a pompous man who goes out of his way to ignore her. Now, with their families coming together for the Christmastide season it's her mother's last-ditch effort to get them together. And Carol plans to avoid Gregory at all costs.

Lord Gregory Renshaw has no intentions of falling prey to his mother's schemes to marry him off to a proper debutante she's picked out. Over the years, he has carefully sidestepped all endeavors to be matched with any of the grasping ladies.

But a sudden Christmastide Scandal has the potential show Carol and Gregory that they've spent years running from the one thing they've always needed.

ONLY FOR HER HONOR
Book 2 in the "The Theodosia Sword" Series

A wounded soldier:

When Captain Lucas Rayne returned from fighting Boney's forces, he was a shell of a man. A recluse who doesn't leave his family's estate, he's content to shut himself away. Until he meets Eve...

A woman alone in the world:

Eve Ormond spent most of her life following the drum alongside her late father. When his shameful actions bring death and pain to English soldiers, Eve is forced back to England, an outcast. With no family or marital prospects she needs employment and finds it in Captain Lucas Rayne's home. A man whose life was ruined by her father, Eve has no place inside his household. With few options available, however, Eve takes the post. What she never anticipates is how with their every meeting, this honorable, hurting soldier slips inside her heart.

The Secrets Between Them:

The more time Lucas spends with Eve, he remembers what it is to be alive and he lets the walls protecting his heart down. When the secrets between them come to light will their love be enough? Or are they two destined for heartbreak?

ONLY FOR HIS LADY
Book 1 in the "The Theodosia Sword" Series

A curse. A sword. And the thief who stole her heart.

The Rayne family is trapped in a rut of bad luck. And now, it's up to Lady Theodosia Rayne to steal back the Theodosia sword, a gladius that was pilfered by the rival, loathed Renshaw family. Hopefully, recovering the stolen sword will break the cycle and reverse her family's fate.

Damian Renshaw, the Duke of Devlin, is feared by all—all, that is, except Lady Theodosia, the brazen spitfire who enters his home and wrestles an ancient relic from his wall. Intrigued by the vivacious woman, Devlin has no intentions of relinquishing the sword to her.

As Theodosia and Damian battle for ownership, passion ignites. Now, they are torn between their age-old feud and the fire that burns between them. Can two forbidden lovers find a way to make amends before their families' war tears them apart?

MY LADY OF DECEPTION
Book 1 in the "Brethren of the Lords" Series

This dark, sweeping Regency novel was previously only offered as part of the limited edition box sets: "From the Ballroom and Beyond", "Romancing the Rogue", and "Dark Deceptions". Now, available for the first time on its own, exclusively through Amazon is "My Lady of Deception".

~★~

Everybody has a secret. Some are more dangerous than others.

For Georgina Wilcox, only child of the notorious traitor known as "The Fox", there are too many secrets to count. However, after her interference results in great tragedy, she resolves to never help another... until she meets Adam Markham.

Lord Adam Markham is captured by The Fox. Imprisoned, Adam loses everything he holds dear. As his days in captivity grow, he finds himself fascinated by the young maid, Georgina, who cares for him.

When the carefully crafted lies she's built between them begin to crumble, Georgina realizes she will do anything to prove her love and loyalty to Adam—even it means at the expense of her own life.

NON-FICTION WORKS BY
CHRISTI CALDWELL

**Uninterrupted Joy: Memoir: My Journey through
Infertility, Pregnancy, and Special Needs**

The following journey was never intended for publication.
It was written from a mother, to her unborn child. The words
detailed her struggle through infertility and the joy of finally being
pregnant. A stunning revelation at her son's birth opened a world
of both fear and discovery. This is the story of one mother's love
and hope and…her quest for uninterrupted joy.

BIOGRAPHY

Christi Caldwell is the bestselling author of historical romance novels set in the Regency era. Christi blames Judith McNaught's "Whitney, My Love," for luring her into the world of historical romance. While sitting in her graduate school apartment at the University of Connecticut, Christi decided to set aside her notes and try her hand at writing romance. She believes the most perfect heroes and heroines have imperfections and rather enjoys tormenting them before crafting a well-deserved happily ever after!

When Christi isn't writing the stories of flawed heroes and heroines, she can be found in her Southern Connecticut home chasing around her eight-year-old son, and caring for twin princesses-in-training!

Visit *www.christicaldwellauthor.com* to learn more about what Christi is working on, or join her on Facebook at Christi Caldwell Author, and Twitter *@ChristiCaldwell*

Made in the USA
Middletown, DE
10 December 2018